Chicago Justice

A Macbeth Thriller

Dave Case

Genius
Book Publishing

Chicago Justice

Copyright © 2025 Dave Case

This is a work of fiction. Any resemblance to actual places, events, or persons living or dead is either coincidental or is used fictitiously.

Published by:
Genius Book Publishing
PO Box 250380
Milwaukee Wisconsin 53225 USA
GeniusBookPublishing.com

ISBN: 978-1-958727-75-1

250628 Trade

Contents

*This book is dedicated to my mom and dad, Peggy and Les Case.
I miss you.*

"Blood will have blood."
William Shakespeare, *Macbeth*, Act 2, Scene 2

The Day Before

The police radio erupted with static and the explosive sound of exerted breathing.

"Running north bound Sedgwick!" It was a man's voice, one that Macbeth didn't readily recognize.

"Unit with the emergency," the dispatcher said. *"Where are you?"*

"Male, black," the voice blurted. *"White shirt, blue jean shorSTOP!"*

"What're you chasing him for?" asked the dispatcher with the enthusiasm of someone waiting for her nails to dry.

Zito, who ate with his vest on, was already headed for the pub's door when he turned back to look at Macbeth. Zito stuck out his pierced tongue, exposing the stud, and snickered.

"Your turn to pay, Stace."

Zito was smaller than Macbeth, but wiry with receding sandy hair and a surprisingly light complexion despite his Italian heritage, while Macbeth was tall at six foot four and fair skinned with dark auburn hair. Both men were in their late twenties.

Macbeth stood and fished a couple of twenties from his pocket. He tossed them wistfully onto his plate, having taken only a single bite of his cheeseburger's charred perfection. He yanked his vest from the chair's back, lifted it over his head, and fastened the Velcro side as he rushed for the door.

"*GOT A GUN!*"

"*Units in the Eighteenth District,*" the dispatcher said with little change from her earlier monotone. "*Man with a gun north bound on Sedgwick. Where on Sedgwick unit?*"

"*STOP!*" the cop yelled; the rest of his broadcast came out with his exhalation. "*East bound… Evergreen… from Sedgwick!*"

"*East bound on Evergreen from Sedgwick. Just go units. Who's chasing?*"

"*He took the shirt off!*" The man's voice was labored. "*STOP POLICE! Still east bound!*"

Macbeth and Zito had left roll call and gone straight to the pub on Wells. Their sergeant, Ron Ryan, told them to eat fast and get into the projects, which was why they were in uniform instead of their usual plainclothes. It was a scorching afternoon in the summer and Cabrini Green was primed to ignite into a swath of violence that only pent-up frustration from poverty and gang conflict could create. It wasn't a question of "if" but "when" something would detonate the community into a turbulent maelstrom of blood and probable death.

As the two tactical cops ran from the pub, Macbeth knew full well they were close by the foot chase and could be sprinting headlong into that storm. The oppressive heat had been waiting just out of the bar, and when Macbeth emerged, he felt the grip of the heat radiating from everywhere, off the sidewalk as well as from the buildings, and the sun and the humidity permeated him inside and out.

"*Past North Park, still east bound!*" The running officer sounded out of breath.

Zito was unlocking the driver's door of their unmarked Crown Vic as Macbeth came up the stairs onto the sidewalk. He was staring north, expecting the male black to sprint from the intersection of Wells and Evergreen, which was down the street from where he stood.

Traffic was at a standstill in both directions, bumper-to-bumper from Division Street all the way to North Avenue. Rush hour lasted seemingly forever on the narrow streets of the Old Town neighborhood, despite it being adjacent to the Marshal Field Homes and its southern neighbor, Cabrini Green.

Zito looked at Macbeth. "Should we even try in this traffic?"

"Fuck it." Macbeth took off down the sidewalk and swerved through the parked cars onto the street at the first opening. He raced past the vehicles locked in their bumper-to-bumper dance as they crept along. He could hear the slap of Zito's feet behind him.

"*Almost to Wells,*" said the cop with a voice hoarse from screaming. "*STOP!*"

Macbeth flew past Goethe hitting his stride, despite the stifling air, when he saw the shirtless black man bolt off Evergreen turning north bound on Wells. The man had something small and dark in his right hand. It could have been a pistol.

The cop's voice crackled over the radio. "*North on Wells. Lost him.*"

Macbeth's short stemmed radio was in his vest pocket, but he didn't want to break his rhythm to get it.

Then Zito's voice broadcast loud over the radio. "*Male black. North bound Wells, crossing to the east side of street.*"

Macbeth knew there wasn't going to be any help coming soon with the gridlock all around them. He doubled down and willed himself to run faster, keeping his eyes on the man's right hand as he dodged parked cars to get back to the sidewalk.

The black man craned his head around on his skinny neck, his expression burst into one of surprise when he locked eyes with Macbeth.

Macbeth was gaining on the man, who had been running for a least three city blocks and was visibly tiring, while Macbeth was just hitting his pace, grateful for his hockey training regime.

The man passed whatever he was carrying to his left hand, then gripped a railing with his now empty right and spun up some steps into a building. The door cracked against the wall as the man rushed inside with Macbeth a couple of dozen strides behind him.

"*He went into…*" Zito's voice shouted from Macbeth's radio. "*Business on the east side of Wells, thirteen hundred block. Stand by.*" Then Zito was yelling at Macbeth directly. "Wait Stace! That fucker had a gun!"

Macbeth took the steps in a single vault, went through the door into the business, dodged left and stopped. He drew his Smith and Wesson 4586.

It was dim and his eyes needed to adjust, but even as they did, Macbeth knew something wasn't right. He could hear Zito yelling into his radio, something about a bookstore. Then it hit him.

He was standing in the Marquis de Sade adult bookstore. A glance to his left and he saw the store's counter, the curly top of a woman's head then a wide-opened brown eye peek over the countertop crowded with sexually orientated knickknacks, lubricants and one, very out of place, calculus textbook. She rose a fraction.

Macbeth forcefully whispered through labored breath, "Where'd he go?"

She nodded and her hand, with a single finger extended, tipped with a long, very sharp looking, very black nail, pointed toward the back of the store.

"What's back there?" He tried to control his breathing, though heavy it was manageable.

"The stockroom," she said in a wavering whisper.

"Anything else?"

"Booths."

Macbeth saw racks of lingerie in various colors, with black being the most prevalent, pedestals covered with vibrators and walls of more vibrators, dildos, and BDSM accoutrements. Up against a back wall were four press wood booths, maybe eight foot high, which looked less sturdy than a cheap armoire. Each booth had a door with a metallic address number nailed to its center, 1, 2, 3 and 4. There also was another door in the back wall farther to the right that evidently led to the back room.

"Is there an exit?" he asked.

She shook her head, then thought better of it.

"Yeah," she said, "but it's blocked."

"Did you see where he went?"

She shook her head.

"You hear anything?"

"A door slammed." Her voice wasn't much above a whisper.

Zito, panting, came through the door behind him, his Beretta in his hand. "Where is the fucker?"

"Back there." Macbeth used his .45 to point toward the back.

"What's back there?" Zito kept his Berretta at low ready and watched the back of the store.

Macbeth ignored his partner and looked at the woman. "Anyone else back there?"

Her head bobbed making her hair bounce.

"Are all the booths… occupied?" Macbeth asked.

"All but one," she said with a crooked smirk.

"Which one?"

She shrugged.

"Any customers other than those in the booths?" Macbeth asked not seeing anyone standing or on the floor.

She shrugged again. "Maybe, I was studying."

Zito kept his eyes toward the back but shuffled his feet like he was uneasy.

They had faced down any number of groups of gang bangers in Cabrini Green, but Macbeth couldn't remember seeing Zito this uncomfortable.

The front door ripped open behind them and the foot-chasing cop leaned in, his chest heaving as he wheezed for breath. "Are… you… kidding… me?"

Zito glanced back for a quick glimpse. "Go around back, cover the rear."

"Fuuuuuuck," the man said as if he'd been asked to jump out of an airplane, but he pulled back from the doorway and disappeared, the door slamming closed. Broken glass tinkled onto the floor.

"Mike," Macbeth said, "the back door is blocked, and he'd have to run a block just to get into the alley and then run back a block to cover the door that's blocked."

"Sounds like a problem for him," Zito said. "Let's do the back-room first."

"What," Macbeth said, "and leave those booths behind us? No way, booths first."

Zito shook his head. "Next guy can cover those 'til we're done."

"You just sent our back-up off on a wild goose chase," Macbeth said. "We're not seeing anyone anytime soon."

"Shit." Zito looked from the backroom door to the booths. "You know what those guys are doing in there, right?"

"C'mon, you cover the doors." Macbeth held his .45 caliber up against the bottom of his vest, his hand canted so the slide wouldn't hit the material should he have to fire. He moved forward and to his left in a crouch, to come up to the number one booth.

Zito stopped and squatted behind a display, his hands, holding his 9mm, rested on the ledge of the pedestal.

Macbeth looked at Zito, whose face was partially concealed behind a pair of foot long rocket-shaped vibrators. Trying to contain his amusement, he caught Zito's gaze and nodded, pointing to the booth doors, left to right.

Zito, whose head canted, was apparently confused by Macbeth's grin.

"You ready, rocketman?" Macbeth asked.

After Zito's nod of acknowledgement, Macbeth tried the knob on the first door. It was locked.

"You want the keys?" the girl from the front counter asked. "Please don't break the doors down."

Macbeth hurried back to the counter and took the set of keys she was holding out. She gripped the ring of maybe ten keys by two, one silver, and one gold.

"The silver one opens all the booths," she said. "And the gold the stockroom."

Macbeth took the keys and quickly returned to the leftmost door. He stopped, and not for the first time wondered what was inside—a desperate man with a gun, or an altogether different kind of desperate man gripping an altogether different kind of weapon?

"Hold on," Zito whispered, then with a raised voice. "This is the Chicago Police. You in the booths, come out with your hands first."

Nothing.

"Open the door and stick your hands out."

Nothing.

"We know you're in there. Come out."

Macbeth shook his head.

This was turning into a farce.

They didn't have any more time as it was, the muscles behind his neck were bunched, expecting to get shot any second. Macbeth slammed his open palm on door number one. All four of the booths shook.

The girl screeched from behind them. A quick glance showed Macbeth she'd only ducked back under the counter.

Macbeth was about to hit the door again when it opened. A pair of trembling hands emerged. They were white. Macbeth holstered his Smith and grabbed one of the wrists and pulled the man out of the booth. Macbeth twisted and pushed the man to the floor.

"Stay there."

The man nodded as if his head wasn't connected to his shoulders.

Macbeth pounded on the next door, number two.

Nothing.

"Hello," the voice was low and thready, and came from booth three, but didn't sound black.

"Stay put 'til I tell you," Macbeth said. He pounded on door two again. When his efforts were met with more silence, he tried the knob and it opened to show an empty closet-size space with a glass panel, behind which was a monitor. There was a roll of paper towels on a spindle and an overflowing plastic garbage can underneath. Some kind of movie advertisement blinked on the screen, naked breasts prominently displayed in the images.

Macbeth knocked on door three. "Hands first."

The door opened, but instead of one set of hands, two empty sets were extended from inside, one of which was black.

Two guys playing more than grab-ass.

Macbeth grabbed the black man's wrist and yanked him out. The fellow was lighter than Macbeth anticipated, and the man flew out. He was fully dressed and wasn't the man who was being chased. Macbeth pushed him to the ground and told him to be still and motioned for the white guy to get down next to him.

Macbeth pounded on door number four.

"Coming out," a voice said. The door cracked open and a pair of wrinkled, age spotted white hands emerged. Macbeth pulled the man out, less violently than the others. An older man stumbled out, his pants around his ankles, his tighty-whitey's pulled up to just under his nipples.

"Get on the ground with them others," Macbeth said.

The older man shuffled around and started to get on the floor. The other three men all scooched away from him.

Macbeth pulled his .45 and held it at low ready as he walked toward the stockroom door. Zito came around the pedestal and joined him. Then Zito elbowed Macbeth back.

"My turn to be in front."

They approached the door, Zito first, Macbeth just behind him, his gun pointed in a safe direction.

Zito reached out and tried the door.

It was locked. He put his hand out. Macbeth put the key ring in his palm, golden key separated from the others. Zito holstered his Beretta, then inserted the key. It was quiet, but there was some audible rattle of the mechanism. He glanced back at Macbeth, who nodded.

Zito rotated the key then turned the door handle and pushed.

The door wrenched inward and nearly pulled Zito off his feet.

The shirtless black man materialized in the doorway and swung something long and thick yet flexible into Zito's head with both hands. Whatever it was whacked Zito in the face with a distinct smack and sent him reeling in a semi-crouch.

Macbeth stepped around Zito and delivered a straight left jab into the man's nose with as much power as he could manage, being off balance and reaching around his partner.

The black man shook off the blow and swung the dark object toward Macbeth, who trapped the weirdly firm yet soft object under his arm. Then Macbeth brought his pistol in a devastating arc, slamming the flat of the weapon onto the side of the man's head.

The impact activated the magazine release, and the full mag dropped to the floor, rendering the firing mechanism of the Smith impotent. The magazine's butt plate failed, and eight hollow point rounds rolled onto the floor.

Zito erupted out of his crouch and shoved the dazed black man's sweaty chest, launching him back into the stockroom. Zito stepped to follow, and his boot came down on a couple of the bullets.

They rolled.

Zito fell hard, his breath exploding from his mouth. He twisted, his lungs laboring like a fish out of water.

Macbeth gripped his Smith with both hands, hoping the asshole didn't realize it was essentially empty. Smith and Wesson, having never had a military contract, wouldn't fire without a magazine even with a round in the chamber like the other army pistols were required to by spec.

When Macbeth stepped over Zito, whatever he'd trapped under his arm fell. Hitting his partner in the head with a thud.

"Fuck," Zito gasped, still trying to breathe. The long, more or less cylindrical object rested in the doorway.

"Hands in the air, asshole!"

The black man's eyes darted around the room, but apparently recognized he was caught. His hands raised into the air.

"Put 'em on your head," Macbeth said. "Turn around."

The man complied.

Macbeth holstered his .45 caliber "paperweight," pulled his handcuffs from his belt, and secured the prisoner. He glanced down and saw a small black starter pistol on the stockroom's floor, the kind used in track meets, but one that wouldn't be particularly effective in a gunfight.

No wonder he changed weapons, Macbeth thought.

"What the fuck he hit me with?" Zito asked.

The mousy voice of the counter girl chimed, "Oh no. It's not busted is it?"

"Is what busted?" Zito asked.

She rushed forward, all four-foot something of her, dressed in baggy black clothes over platform combat boots.

Instead of helping Zito to his feet, she bent over and picked up the roughly four-foot object from the floor. She examined it before hugging it to her chest in a protective gesture.

"What the fuck is that thing?" Zito stood and rubbed his face that had a large splotchy red mark where he'd been hit.

It seemed as if the girl reddened.

"It's our Secretariat model twenty-pound articulated horse cock dildo made by CTG Industries."

Zito's mouth gapped. "Horse cock?"

Macbeth's wide grin spread across his face, his uneaten cheeseburger all but forgotten. "CTG?"

The girl whirled and strode toward the counter. "Catherine the Great, of course." She set the object on the counter and began to examine it up close. "It's over seven hundred dollars."

"Sure, it is," Zito finally said.

"I wonder what weapon code would cover that on the case report?" Macbeth asked.

"You can shut the fuck up," Zito said. "This *never* happened, you got me?"

Macbeth laughed.

Zito shook his head and flipped off Macbeth. "You got one mean looking smile, fucking evil."

"Well, you were battered, Mike," Macbeth said. "This guy should be charged. Agg Batt to a police officer with a—what'd you call it?"

"An authentic Secretariat replica horse cock," the girl said as if proud.

Macbeth grinned.

"Fuck that guy," Zito said. "And fuck you too."

"Hey." The girl's shoulders hunched, and she leaned closer to the dildo, her fingers exploring the device's skin. "What's this?" She stood and threw her arm over her head. "Hold on! There's a tear in the membrane. Its ruined. Someone's gotta pay for it."

Zito flicked the back of the asshole's head with his hand. "Looks like you just bought yourself a replica horse cock, asshole."

"Man," the black man said, "I'm sorry officer, I didn't know what that thing was. Looked like some kind of a small baseball bat to me."

The girl approached Zito and handed him the dildo despite his reluctance to take it, her long black nail showing him the jagged tear.

The front door banged open, and two cops and Sergeant Ryan rushed in, their handguns out.

Zito and Macbeth looked up.

The foot-chase cop came in after them, his reddened face streaming with sweat.

Macbeth got on his short-stemmed radio and told the dispatcher to slow down any response to the store as the offender was in custody and the weapon was recovered. He noticed that Zito was blushing.

Ryan walked up, looked down at the hefty object in Zito's hand, and was about to say something when Zito held up his palm.

"Don't fucking ask," Zito said.

"What is that thing?" Ryan asked anyway.

"That there is a grade A replica of Secretariat's penis," Macbeth said, replacing his radio in his vest's pocket. "Resplendent with a little Mikey Zito saliva visible on the shaft right where that young lady is conveniently pointing."

"Man," Ryan said, a mischievous smile spreading across his face, "and I thought I was hung."

Zito glared at him. Ryan and the other cops laughed.

"*Units in the Eighteenth District,*" the dispatcher said. "*City Wide 1 is reporting shots fired at the police at 365 West Oak Street, called in by housing north units.*"

Shit, Macbeth thought. *Back to work.*

Chapter 1

Cabrini at Night

SUNDAY 2230 Hours

Macbeth pulled the bottom of his Kevlar vest away from his stomach and could feel the saturated uniform and undershirt stick to his flesh. Sweat ran freely down and pooled at his waistline, soaking his underwear, even his shins were clammy and his booted feet grew more damp by the minute. The squad car's air was on high, but he and his partner kept the windows open to listen for trouble.

The city felt like a powder keg. And in Cabrini, Macbeth knew the fuse was lit and burning. It was just a matter of finding out where. Hopefully before everything blew up.

Mike Zito drove. Zito pulled a cigarette from a pack of Kools, lit it, and blew smoke at the windshield. "How the hell." He took another drag, smoke billowing from his mouth as he spoke. "Did Timmy get the night off?"

"Ask Ryan." Macbeth missed working with Tim Hagen, his regular partner, but Macbeth and Zito were on a roll. And he really needed something positive right now. The turmoil surrounding his involvement in the death of a Cabrini gangbanger a couple of months ago continued to fester like an open wound.

Clusters of protesters gathered outside of the Eighteenth District with irritating regularity calling for Macbeth's termination and/or indictment. It didn't matter that he'd been cleared by IAD and the Cook County State's Attorney's Office. Nobody cared that the gang-banger had tried to knock his brains out with a two-by-four. It just didn't matter… cops were guilty until proven innocent in today's media.

Nothing mattered, Macbeth thought. Nobody, not the protestors, not the media, and not the politicians, was interested in facts. They only wanted to spin things to suit their own agendas. And everybody had one. Unfortunately, those factions coalesced at blaming the police.

The same could be said for Cabrini-Green. The huge high-rises stood like defiant, monolithic gateways to the lawless. Despite all the time, personnel, and money poured into them, they essentially remained a horizontal no-man's land where police and gangs struggled for control. The good people, with nowhere else to go, were caught in the middle. It was a war zone contained in a few city blocks.

The heat and humidity made things worse. The hot dome that had settled over the Midwest this summer had cranked the temperature and mugginess in Chicago to record highs. Even though the police leadership denied any correlation, every street cop knew that when the mercury rose, the bodies dropped. People were sticky miserable and on edge, and with the robust gang culture permeating the city's south and west sides, it turned into open season. The cops couldn't keep a lid on the chaos.

"*Eighteen Twenty-Two and cars on City Wide,*" the dispatcher droned on the police radio Macbeth had stuck in his vest cover's pocket. "*We got a man stabbed at Nine-Eleven Hudson.*"

"*Ten-four.*" The officer's voice was familiar. "*There an apartment number?*"

"*Fourth floor,*" the dispatcher said. "*Fire said they're not rolling.*"
"*Ten-four.*"

Zito cracked a U-turn and accelerated toward the call. "Fire must be busy, too."

"You think?" Macbeth rolled up his window.

Apparently Eighteen Twenty-Two had been close. "*Twenty-Two, can we get another car here?*" The officer's voice was calm; another voice in the background was anything but. "*No emergency, but our victim is drunk.*"

"*Do you need fire?*"

When the officer answered, the background voice had risen in volume, cursing. "*No, have the wagon stop by. It's bona fide, but he'll tear up an ambulance.*"

"*Eighteen Seventy-Two.*" The dispatcher sent the squadrol.

Zito parked behind Eighteen Twenty-Two on the street, and they half-jogged to the lobby of the 911 North Hudson building and took the stairs. They heard yelling when they passed the third-floor landing.

Macbeth glanced back at Zito as they approached the fourth floor. "Doesn't Lacey Bennet live on four?"

Zito shrugged. "He might, and wouldn't surprise me if somebody stabbed his ignorant ass."

The black cop from Eighteen Twenty-Two had pinned a black man, in his thirties, standing face against the wall. The man was shirtless, sagging jean shorts revealing red plaid boxers over hi-tops. Macbeth recognized Bennet as they made eye contact.

"Macbeth!" Spittle flew from the man's mouth, along with the heavy odor of beer as he spoke. "Tell this two-bit Uncle Tom motha-fucka I the one called the poh-leece!" Bennet's hands pressed against the brick wall like he was pushing back against the cop. "I been stabbed, goddammit! Take my ass to the hospital!"

"Calm down, Lacey." Macbeth shook his head. "We're going to get you there, just waiting on a wagon."

Zito ducked into the nearby open apartment door.

"Fuck all that!" Bennet's head turned quickly back and forth. "You ain't taking me to jail!"

"Ambulances are busy," Macbeth said. "The wagon'll take you to the hospital. Nobody's locking you up." Macbeth caught the eye of the cop holding Bennet on the wall. The cop shrugged as if saying he agreed. "But we need you to calm down."

"Don't you wanna know who stuck my ass?"

"Sure," Macbeth said. "But you got to calm down. We can't have you acting all crazy."

Bennet seemed to relax against the cop's pressure and eased forward against the wall. "I got you."

"Let me see." Macbeth gave a nod to the black cop, who took his arm down.

Bennet stepped away from the wall and turned to face Macbeth. There were multiple short-width puncture wounds crisscrossing Bennet's blood-covered torso. All of them oozed red, some worse than others.

Macbeth counted six holes. "They deep?"

Bennet held a thumb up, the other hand covering everything below its nail. Not overly deep, Macbeth thought, but still serious.

"Why ain't you asked me who cut me?"

"My partner is in the apartment with his partner." Macbeth pointed at the black cop. "Is whoever stabbed you inside?"

"Hell, no." Bennet shook his head vigorously. "That bitch ain't about to tell on her no-account son."

Macbeth took his notebook from his vest's other pocket and clicked a pen open. "Who stabbed you?"

"His name Damien Upton."

"How old?"

"He got to be eighteen, nineteen." Bennet fingered one of the cuts and blood started running out of it.

"You signing complaints?"

"Goddamned right I am," Bennet said. "Lock that fucker up, before I beat his ass to death."

Macbeth heard the other officer ask the ETA on the wagon for transport. The call of the dispatcher rose in crescendo as the wagon crew stepped from the elevator. They stopped a few feet from Macbeth.

The older wagon cop pointed at Bennet. "I don't see why he can't take an ambulance."

"He's calmed down a lot," Macbeth said, shooting the officer's partner a pleading glance. "It'll be easy, promise." Macbeth turned to

Bennet. "Lacey, you going peaceful with these guys to the hospital, right?"

Bennet stared at the wagon crew, then at Macbeth before blowing out a big breath. "Yeah, I guess."

The wagon cop spoke again. "Whose job?"

"Mine," the black cop said. "Be right behind you once I get my partner."

"Don't take all day, we want to grab a lunch." The wagon cop waved at Bennet. "C'mon." He prodded the bloody man toward the elevator.

"Man, I'm hungry, too," Bennet said.

"Shut up." The wagon cop pushed the down arrow.

After Bennet and the wagon crew were on the way down, Zito and the other half of Eighteen Twenty-Two emerged from the apartment, each sweating profusely. Zito cupped his cigarette with one hand and wiped his face with the other.

"Fucking blast furnace," Zito said.

"What'd she have to say?" the black cop asked of his female partner.

She had the new leather and fresh-pressed look of a PPO and referred to a small spiral notebook as she responded. "Said her boyfriend, this Lacey Bennet, was beating her son, Damien, for coming home late when the kid grabbed a knife and stabbed him a couple of times and ran."

"How old's the kid?" her partner asked.

"Fourteen. But she said he's big for his age."

"Beat him, like how bad?"

"She said he laid into him with 'lectric wire, whatever that is."

"Extension cord, more than likely," Macbeth said. "She say where he might've gone?"

"Had no idea," the PPO said.

Macbeth looked at the black cop. "We'll take a spin around, see if we can locate him. She say what he was wearing?"

"Cubs shirt, black shorts," the PPO said.

They were about to step off when something occurred to Macbeth. "Do you guys know this kid?"

"No," the black cop said. "The name doesn't ring a bell for me."

"Same here. Maybe he's a good kid. If we find him, we'll bring him to the hospital so we can figure it out."

The black cop nodded. "Thanks." He patted the PPO on the shoulder. "C'mon."

All four of them walked down the stairs. The wagon was gone by the time they left the lobby.

An hour later it was still well over eighty as Zito and Macbeth cruised through Cabrini-Green, with an eye out for Damien Upton. The streets were crowded. People were outside to escape the sweltering heat of the oven-like buildings.

Zito slowed the car by the basketball court at Hudson and Locust. Several teenage boys were playing a pickup game. There were no nets on the bent rims of the steel backboards, and a light at the top of a pole cast long, darting shadows across the court.

Zito nodded at the kids. "See that?"

"Yeah," Macbeth said. "Let's go."

Zito spun the wheel and guided the unmarked Chevy up over the curb. They crept to the basketball court and stopped. They got out, keeping their eyes on the game. The boys were shirtless and wore shorts of various lengths.

Zito whistled. The game halted suddenly and the ball bounced away until it was swallowed by the darkness. The players sauntered over to the cops. Seven boys stood apart from them, some breathing heavier than others. All of them were sweaty, their various skin hues glossy in the weak light.

"How old are you guys?" Curfew was ten p.m. on weeknights. Not that Macbeth cared, it just gave him probable cause. When no one spoke, he shined his flashlight, starting with the kid on the left.

The kid shrugged and said, "Sixteen."

Macbeth pointed at the next one. "Fifteen."

The third. "Fourteen."

"Fifteen."

"Fourteen."

"Thirteen."

"Fourteen."

The last kid, who stood a little farther from the others, was taller than the rest and thicker too. He was no less sweaty than the other boys, but he had drops of blood spattered on his sweat pant cut-off shorts and his legs were covered in long elliptical welts. Macbeth motioned for him to follow. The kid's eyes darted from Macbeth, to Zito, to their car that was still running and finally to the nearest project building, but it was over a hundred yards away.

"Bad idea," Macbeth said. "We're not in the running mood."

The kid shrugged and stepped over. Macbeth saw he had a swollen eye that was discolored and his lip was split and a dried trail of blood flacked under his nose.

"What happened to you?" Macbeth did a quick pat down.

"Got my ass kicked," the kid said.

"By who?" Zito asked.

"Momma's boyfriend."

"Before or after you stabbed him?" Macbeth asked.

"That's why I stuck his ass."

"Why'd he beat you up?" Zito asked.

"His drunk ass don't need no reason, just 'cause."

"You come in late?" Macbeth asked

"Know how hot it is up in that 'partment?" Damien wiped his nose. "Course I did. I didn't wanna listen to him and my momma… you know."

"I get it," Zito said. "How bad you hurt?"

"I'm a'ight," Damien said. "He ain't gonna die or nothing like that, right?"

"I don't think so," Macbeth said. "But we want to have a doctor look at you."

"That's okay." Damien stooped and lifted his blood-stained shirt from the grass.

"Wasn't a request, Damien." Zito lit another cigarette.

"Y'all gonna lock me up?"

"Don't think so." Macbeth turned for the car. "C'mon." He shepherded Damien to the car's back door, opened it, and had him take a seat.

"No cuffs?" Zito asked.

Macbeth shook his head, waving off his partner's concern like it was a fly.

It was after midnight when Macbeth and Zito pulled into the Eighteenth District lot, having been called in by their sergeant, Ron Ryan. They climbed the stairs in the back of the station to their office, where Macbeth found Ryan typing on one of the office's two computers. Ryan stopped and looked up at him.

"You could've called." The sergeant leaned back in his chair and folded his arms across his chest.

"Mike's taking a leak." Macbeth sat on the corner of the desk in front of Ryan. "What's up?"

"Just wanted to get a rundown on what you guys had. Heard you had someone in custody for aggravated battery."

Macbeth laughed. "It's complicated, but someone is getting locked up, just not the stabber. In this case, the stabbee, Lacey Bennet."

"Do tell," Ryan said.

"He beat his girlfriend's kid with an electric cord until he got stabbed."

"Injuries?"

"Bennet has a bunch of superficial cuts and the kid's got a bunch of ugly welts. They're both okay." Macbeth yawned. "Eighteen Twenty-Two is handling, we're just assisting."

The phone rang. "Eighteen Tac, Sergeant Ryan." He listened. "I'm looking at him. I'll send him right down." Ryan hung up. "Apparently, you have a visitor at the desk. Expecting anyone?"

"Not me." Macbeth stood. "Tell Mike I'll be downstairs."

The station was active, with a number of locals lining the small lobby vestibule since the city had declared a heat emergency, and all police stations were identified as cooling centers. Macbeth stepped up to the desk, but didn't see anyone he recognized. One of the officers behind the counter waved and then pointed. A middle-aged black woman was huddled by the front doors with two small children clutching her legs, and a teenage girl leaned against the wall next to her.

Macbeth walked to them. The kids weren't crying, but they seemed uncomfortable. A visit to the police station did that to people. The teenage girl had headphones in her ears and was staring at the street through the front doors. The woman was patting the kids' backs and making soothing sounds.

"Hi," Macbeth said quietly. "You're here to see me?"

The woman looked at him. "You Macbeth?"

"Yes," he said.

She looked around, suddenly apprehensive. "There someplace we can talk?"

"Sure."

She told the teen to watch the kids and then she followed Macbeth out the back of the station into the garage. It was empty, with two garage doors open to the parking lot. The overhead lights were on.

"You was always good to my daughter," the woman said.

"I'm sorry, but…"

"Latricia Gibbons."

"Oh." Macbeth instantly recognized the name. She'd been his informant that'd been killed a couple of months ago by a Mickey Cobra enforcer, who was her babies' daddy, after his release from prison.

"She always told me you was respectful and concerned for her and these kids a' hers."

Macbeth nodded. "What can I do for you?"

"Nothing," the woman said. "We leaving. But I thought, after all you done to try and help Latricia, I should warn you."

"Warn me, about what?"

"People be saying that monster getting out."

"Who, Huggins?" *That couldn't be true*, he thought. *Huggins had violated his parole and was awaiting trial on a felony gun possession case.*

"Him," she said with a venomous hiss. "Word in the building say he getting out. Some fancy lawyer getting him a new trial."

Stunned, Macbeth shook his head. "I don't see how."

"I got these two grand-chillren to raise and we leaving," she said. "But I thought you ought to know."

"I'll look into it," Macbeth said. "You want to give me a number to call when I find out what's really going on? Rumors being…"

"No," she said. "No need to tell me nothing. We're gone. Car's packed up outside. Watch your ass."

With that, the woman turned and walked out of the garage.

Zito passed her at the door. "Making friends and influencing people, I see." He smirked.

Macbeth shook his head. "That was Latricia's mom."

"Crispy critter Latricia?"

Macbeth nodded, pushing the image of Latricia's charred, rent flesh from his mind. "She said Huggins got a get-out-of-jail-free card."

"No fucking way." Zito waved, a dismissive gesture. "Don't believe that shit."

Macbeth took in a deep breath and slowly let it out. *Pure bullshit,* he thought. *It couldn't be true, could it?*

Chapter 2

Hear Ye, Hear Ye

MONDAY 0900 Hours

Lonnie Huggins awoke from the nightmare as the cop shot his mom who he'd had bent over the kitchen table. Huggins lifted his chin off his chest and rubbed his eyes. The holding cell was sandwiched between the courtroom and the jury room. He sat in the middle of the metal bench with his back against the cinder block wall, facing the cell's door. Only two others shared the cell. One was a shriveled old-timer with a grizzled beard, ash gray like his eyebrows and bushy Afro. The other was a skinny Puerto Rican hype who was looking pale and dope-sick shaky.

Huggins closed his eyes and waited.

"Hear ye, hear ye." The bailiff's voice was piped in from the courtroom over the speaker outside the holding cell. "Court is in session."

"Good morning, counselor," said the judge. "I understand you'd like to do a quick motion this morning?"

"Good morning, Your Honor. Actually, I'd like a short date." Huggins recognized the voice of his attorney, Sherman Gold. "We can mark it as a mutual request if that's all right with the state?"

"Let's see," the judge said. "State, are you ready on the Alonzo Huggins matter?"

Huggins heard papers being shuffled, then a voice he recognized from earlier conversations as the male Assistant State's Attorney. "Is that up today, Your Honor?"

"Didn't I just ask whether you were ready? Would I ask if you were ready if the matter wasn't up today?"

"Yes, sir, Your Honor, of course."

Silence followed, then someone spoke. This time it was a woman, maybe they thought the judge wouldn't be so harsh on her.

"Actually, no, Your Honor," she said. "We'd like a short date to bring in the officers."

"Okay," the judge said. "A day next week please, by agreement."

Huggins heard more pages being turned, and then the distant-sounding voice of the court clerk announced that next Wednesday was open.

"The Alonzo Huggins matter will be held over until next Wednesday. That okay with you, Sherman?"

"A moment, please. Nine?"

"Yes."

"Good, let me jot that down." There was a pause. "Then, keeping with Huggins, sir," Gold said. "I'd like to petition the court to release my client until we can have this hearing. I think we have cause to show that his arrest will be dismissed due to gross misconduct on the part of the arresting officer. And Mr. Huggins hasn't seen his children for quite a while."

"Excuse me," the woman said, breaking into Gold's speech. "That's quite irregular. Mr. Huggins is being held on a V.O.P., on his first full day of parole he was arrested in possession of two guns, Your Honor, and he was on parole for—"

The judge interrupted, "Does he have any bond forfeiture warrants?"

"Your Honor. His arrest record is quite extensive and more than a little violent—"

"Any bond forfeiture warrants?" The judge's voice had an edge.

"Well, no, but—"

"But nothing, counselor. Release Mr. Huggins to his attorney. If he hasn't run yet, he's not about to start now." The gavel banged hard and loud. Huggins felt his mouth widen in a grin. That was why he paid Sherman Gold so well. The guy was magic.

TEN MINUTES LATER, THE DOOR FROM THE COURTROOM OPENED and Gold walked in. His gray hair was pulled back into a ponytail and his silver suit shone brightly as his black Italian-cut loafers clicked against the tile floor. He shook Lonnie's hand. "We should have you out of here pretty soon, just have some paperwork to finish with the sheriff's office. Sit tight."

Huggins nodded, still grinning.

Gold paused. "Listen, though. I want you to stay out of Cabrini. I'll put you up in a hotel not far from there. After the press conference, you can go back, give me a couple of days. I know you're anxious. But this is important. We can't afford any police contact today or tonight. Okay?"

Huggins shrugged. "A'ight."

"Good." Gold patted his arm. "One of my associates will handle the paperwork and then take you to the hotel. Get you set up. You'll like it. We've got a lot to do for that press conference. After that, we'll be in the driver's seat." Gold lowered his voice. "We're going to get you out of here, get that cop off your back, and make a whole lot of money in the process."

Huggins nodded again in agreement. *Get me out of here, you Jew motherfucker*, he thought. *I'll take care of the rest, especially that fucking cop.*

Chapter 3

Presidential Event

MONDAY 1100 Hours

Alderwoman Mavis Stomps paused at the metal detector and placed her purse on the adjacent conveyer belt. This morning, she'd spent a lot of time in front of her mirror. She was black, and thirty-three. At five seven she had a starlet's figure that she worked very hard at maintaining; she was all about effort. She considered herself a renaissance woman, particularly in her community. She was considered by many to be the most powerful woman politician in the city. *They didn't know the half of it,* she thought. They didn't know about her and the Mickey Cobras, about her influence on the gang. They didn't know about Momma Stone.

She was amazed at what could be accomplished with federal funding. The school, in the heart of the Cabrini-Green Projects, had been scrubbed from roof to basement; fresh paint was applied anywhere it was needed, and probably a few places it wasn't. Power lines seemed to appear out of nowhere to run the different necessities, like the new metal detectors. The uniformed division of the Secret Service manned these detectors and they were certainly a step up from the usual security guards.

She showed her credentials; a couple of colored Secret Service-provided placards, each color denoting a greater level of access, and her City ID card, all strung together on a lanyard. She was waved through by the stoic officer. She collected her purse and hung the credentials around her neck, working the lanyard under her hair. She felt like giggling. Here she was, a girl from the projects, about to rub shoulders with the leader of the free world.

She had been looking forward to this event for some time now. This was the perfect place to plant some political seeds. She had a re-election campaign to run. But looking ahead, she wanted to make some moves that would put her in good standing for the mayoral race in two years. And her plans included using the current mayor's police superintendent against him. The mayor was vulnerable, as long as he stood behind Superintendent Plumb who was hated in the black community. She was going to make the most of that loyalty and see to it that it was covered by the media. In Chicago politics, racial issues always got preferential coverage.

The police department had been taking serious heat from some questionable shootings and would be getting more as soon as she could arrange it. These shootings were predominantly in black communities, and that just wasn't acceptable, particularly when she could steer media attention in that direction and bring pressure to bear on her future adversary. And these latest protests about the rogue cop, Macbeth, were working for her, too.

She milled around with the other collected officials, shaking hands and swapping small talk. It seemed that a charged current flowed through everyone. She'd heard the governor was here, she saw both of Illinois' Senators, a congressman, and a slew of elected statewide representatives and city politicians, along with local movers and shakers. It was quite unusual to see them all together. They mingled much better than the other power holders in Cabrini, namely the Mickey Cobras and the Gangster Disciples.

She followed the crowd into the gymnasium. A dais had been erected in the middle of the gym floor. The President and the mayor were having an animated conversation behind the podium, laughing and slapping each other's backs. She walked around the small crowd looking for Plumb.

Mavis worked the crowd until she found her assistant, Miles. He was a lot like her, young, hungry, and smart. His brains were more formally educated, where hers came from the street. Miles was short, always impeccably dressed, with round eyeglasses.

"Good morning, ma'am," Miles said.

"Yes, it is." She scanned the crowd. "Is fat ass here?"

"Superintendent Plumb?"

She nodded.

"I haven't seen him," Miles said.

"Just as well," she said. "Easier to plant my seeds without him hovering around."

"I have a line on the reverend running the protest you were asking about."

"Good," she said. "I'd like to talk to him, see if there's anything we can do to help out."

"They have some press coverage, perhaps we could arrange an interview on the picket lines."

"Yes, maybe also we could send some people over, make their community participation look better." She smiled. "Do you have the latest numbers?"

"Yes, ma'am." Miles removed a sheaf of paper from his inner suit coat pocket and handed it to her. "Broken down by wards and racial population."

She opened the paper and glanced at the totals. "This'll do nicely."

For the next little while, she watched the event and worked the reporters she could, knowing which were more likely to give voice to her point of view, namely, to look at the shootings. But she also directed their attention to the protest in the Eighteenth District. She smiled and hoped it didn't look as wolfish as it felt. Anything to keep His Honor and Plumb on the defense. Like she'd heard them all say, "If it bleeds, it leads." And this protest now had allegations of police misconduct and cover-up attached. And there would be a good deal more.

"Oh," her assistant said, bringing her back to the here and now.

"Attorney Sherman Gold called the office just as I was leaving. He said you'd be interested to know they'd been successful. Make any sense to you?"

Now she was sure her expression was one of guilty satisfaction, or maybe even of triumph. Some of her greatest accomplishments happened well out of sight, on events she'd started in motion through other means. Having Lonnie Huggins a free man in Cabrini would set a lot of things in motion. Not to mention return the Mickey Cobras' donations to her political coffers, and send their current leader, Cecil Jones, a clear signal to get off his ass. How different was she from POTUS, anyway?

What did he have on her, life and death decisions? Hell, she'd been making those regularly, ever since secretly teaming up with the Mickey Cobras. There wasn't much to it really, people did it every day in the projects.

Chapter 4

From The Inside Looking Out

MONDAY 1600 Hours

The waiter paused by their table on the patio at Tavern on Rush as Lauren Cahill swirled her finger over the two wine glasses. "Two more, please." She reflected on how great she felt and it wasn't even from the light buzz brought on by the wine. It was the class. She was in. Many had applied, but she was in. Her career was made if she played it right.

Lauren pulled her purse around into her lap and dug for her wallet. Once in hand, she flipped it open and pulled a fifty out. She had the class. A large smile spread across her face. She could feel it stretching her cheeks. She was so happy.

Rachel, Lauren's roommate seated across from her, leaned forward. "Well?"

"I'm in."

"That's so cool." They leaned together and Rachel wrapped her arm around Lauren's shoulders. "I knew it. You going to call your mom?"

Lauren shook her head, knowing that it was going to be another argument. Her mom and dad expected her to work at her dad's office at the Board of Trade this summer. "Let me enjoy it before I have to defend it." She drained the last of the merlot in her glass. It was warm, dry and smooth.

"What's their problem?"

"They think it's going to be dangerous, or something."

"Is it?" Rachel asked.

Lauren shook her head. "No."

"So, what're you gonna do?"

"It's our journalism school's independent study class. We work for the Program for the Wrongfully Convicted and do investigative research for one of their cases," Lauren said. "I can't wait to jump in and get my hands dirty. I'll do whatever's needed to prove the guy's innocent."

"You mean like defending murderers and rapists?"

Lauren frowned. "It's the Program for the Wrongfully Convicted." She stopped short of saying, "Duh."

"Sounds dangerous to me." Rachel pushed her glass away.

Lauren tapped a finger on the table. "I can't wait to get to the library and start my research."

"Why?"

"I got the name of the guy and want to see what I can dig up, you know."

"Anybody famous?"

"Just a guy from Cabrini-Green." Lauren sipped her water and made quotation marks with her fingers. "Supposedly a gang member. His name's Alonzo Huggins."

"Cabrini-Green?" Rachel grabbed her glass and drained the last of her wine. "Would it really be that bad being a runner for your dad?"

"I don't want to work for my dad." Lauren looked for the waiter. "I want to be a journalist."

"A reporter."

"Whatever." Lauren flicked her head to move a few strands of hair from her eye. "There's a girl in one of my classes last year, she got hired by the St. Louis Post-Dispatch with a recommendation from Rabinowicz."

"Who?"

"The professor who runs the classes," Lauren said. "He's famous."

"Yeah, how come I never heard of him?" Rachel laughed. "You want to live in St. Louis?"

"No, but a recommendation from him goes a long way." Lauren knew her roommate wouldn't understand. "It's just what I need to land a job and stay away from the Merc."

"The board doesn't sound that bad to me," Rachel said.

"You want a job? I got one for you."

Rachel laughed and leaned away as the waiter placed two more glasses of wine on their table. "I don't know," she said. "I don't think reporters make that much money."

"It's not always about the money." Lauren took a sip of the merlot. It was good and she could feel the effects in her cheeks. "My mom and dad have loads of it and they're not happy. For me, it's about getting to the truth."

"The truth?" Rachel laughed and picked up her wine glass, swirling it. "You think everything you read in the papers is true?"

"Yes, I do." Lauren set her glass down. "Most of it, anyway."

Rachel paused, her glass by her lips. "Roomie, you're kind of naïve for a girl who wants to be a reporter."

Chapter 5

Chicago Bound

MONDAY 2300 Hours

Jermaine Taylor leaned back against the headrest as the bus rumbled along the highway through Southern Illinois, having just crossed over from Missouri. He was wedged into the middle seat. On one side, his grandmother squeezed next to him. Snoring. On the other side was this real old dude, who kept taking his false teeth out, picking at shit wedged between them. And from the way the guy smelled, he probably had on diapers like Jermaine's grandma.

Jermaine and his grandmother had left their dirt road farming town in rural Mississippi sometime yesterday. The first leg of the trip, a jitney cab, Mississippi-style, to Jackson. Next, they were herded onto something like a Greyhound bus, but older and dirtier, for the all day and night trip.

Grandma coughed, bringing his attention back to her. She kept snoring. The doctors had been telling her to get herself tested for a sleep condition, but she was stubborn as she was heavy. Her head tilted and sagged his way further encroaching on his space.

As the green fields of corn and beans or whatever rolled by, he remembered all those times his momma yelled at and fought with his older brother. But now that Antwan was dead and buried, Momma couldn't live without Jermaine, Grandma either. He wondered what they really felt about *him*, Jermaine, the boy that's still alive. After all, his momma had kept Antwan and the twins by her in Cabrini and sent him off some eight hundred miles to live with a bunch of stinky-ass country people.

He could still remember Antwan's wake like he had just left, still could taste the sweltering radiator heat in that old-ass church in Cabrini, across the blacktop from where he'd grown up. The twins were four. He remembered Momma making them look at Antwan in the casket, all stiff and dead. The kids cried, being dragged down the worn-out carpet, past empty pews. She like to pull their arms out from their sockets. Grandma wailed in the background. The whole while he just sat, his butt hurting from the hard wood, not doing nothing, his hands folded in his lap, wanting to hit somebody, anybody.

Jermaine had finally gotten up and went to the casket. Antwan looked funny, something wasn't right. Some lady told his momma that the funeral home done good with his brother's make-up. That was it. He was made up like those old ladies in church. But it was all over his face, even on his neck, and Jermaine saw a smear on Antwan's shirt collar. His color was all wrong. Since the wake, anytime Jermaine thought of his brother, he saw him the wrong color, all because of that make-up job.

Some of Antwan's boys came by the wake to pay their respects. His momma, for all her fighting and shouting about it, didn't seem to notice, hanging on to the Reverend's arm. Grandma either, except she didn't hang on to nobody, by that time she'd wailed herself out.

Antwan's boys were hard and no older than he had been. Cobra Stones, with their red and black coats and blue ink homemade tattoos. His brother had a whole other life Jermaine didn't know about because he'd been sent away. Maybe Antwan would even be alive if Jermaine had been allowed to stay.

All these cats knew Antwan as Boo. He wondered what they'd call him if he was one of them? What would it be like to hang with guys like that? Guys who knew and did violence like it wasn't shit. He wanted that kind of respect, to belong to a crew that had each other's backs like that. He was going to be a Cobra. And he wanted to work for the best. Lonnie Huggins, Antwan said, was the deadliest man in Cabrini.

Grandma sagged toward him, her snoring growing louder. He jerked and pushed as best he could to get her to move. He was so uncomfortable and they had hours yet to go. When he didn't get a rise out of her, he used his free hand to reach around and poke her. Nothing.

"Get up off me, Grandma." He drove his fingers into her like a knife. He held back some, because he knew she was more slow than old, but she could swing a paddle like someone half her age.

She budged a little, enough that he could take a deep breath. His foot hit his book bag on the floor. The books in the bag were mostly kid books he'd taken from Grandma's. He'd packed a bunch and planned on giving them to the twins. But their real purpose was cover for Grandpa's old pistol he'd stolen. It was big and heavy, a black six-shooter with a short barrel, and looked like it worked. The grips were wooden, dark, and stained. He'd cleaned it best he could and oiled it too, with oil he found in the basement under the work bench. He even found some bullets. Not all of them fit, but enough did and he had a few left over. He kept the extras in the pocket of his bag, where he'd kept his pencils back when he was still in school. That cop was going to pay.

His brother, his big brother by a year, his best friend in the whole world, was planted in the earth. Dead. Thrown out a window by a cop, because of what? 'Cause he was a Cobra? It didn't make any damn sense then and it didn't still.

That cop had to pay. If Jermaine knew one thing—that cop had to pay.

Chapter 6

Motives

TUESDAY 1330 Hours

The door to the 27th Ward Alderman's office on Chicago Avenue opened, jangling the bells behind the glass. A black man in his early thirties stepped through from the street, dressed conservatively in a navy suit. Mavis Stomps watched from the back of the room under the switched-off overhead lights. She knew who he was but had only met him once since he'd come to his church as pastor. By all accounts, people seemed to believe he ran his church in Cabrini-Green for the glory of the Almighty and no personal agenda.

He was average height and weight and wore rimless glasses, and no jewelry. He had a smooth, caramel complexion and a close-cut beard matching a trimmed Afro. Everything about him was church conservative. As he stepped up to the receptionist's desk, she saw that he carried himself with confidence.

The girl working the front of the office looked up. Mavis snubbed out her cigarette on the window sill and blew the smoke toward the back of the hallway.

"May I help you?" the girl said in a nasally voice that just irked Mavis to no end.

"My name is Turner Galbreath. I'm here to see the alderman."

Mavis stepped from the shadows toward him. "Ah, Reverend Galbreath, thank you for coming." She extended her hand as she got close.

His manicured hand took hers, his grip strong and calloused.

"Let's go in back. We can talk." She gestured for him to follow.

Her office, paneled in dark wood, was Spartan, containing a worn desk and a couple of plastic chairs. The desk had come from another closed school, which had been another loss for her ward and her community. The plastic chairs were the white stackable variety. She led Galbreath in and shut the door before taking her seat behind the desk.

"I know you're a busy man. So I really appreciate your stopping by."

He settled into one of the chairs and looked around before nodding.

Given his silence, she continued, "I have been a bit slow getting together with my ministers."

His stare bore into her as if she had his undivided, borderline hostile attention. He must be an effective preacher with a look like that. "Your ministers?"

"You know, Reverend, the ministers in the ward is what I'm saying."

"I see. Please forgive my cautious nature, but I've been quite disappointed with public servants of late."

"Really?" She found herself wishing she'd taken the opportunity to slam a little more whiskey, but perhaps a clear mind was needed. The good reverend might prove a little challenging.

Elbows poised on the arms of the plastic chair, Galbreath steepled his fingers in front of him. "As assistant chairwoman of the police/fire committee, I'm sure you've heard about our picketing."

"As a matter of fact, that's why I wanted to see you."

He settled back into the chair and seemed to want her to continue, but finally went on when she didn't. "We've called and left quite a few messages with your office. We'd like to see you join us on the picket line."

"Perhaps." She weighed the option of a photo op. "But I prefer to work behind the scenes, where I can do more good as an elected official."

"That's all well and good," he said. "Your community would benefit by seeing you standing with us. Seeking those very same answers you say you're looking for." He made quote marks in the air. "Behind the scenes."

"My people know I'm at work."

"Do they?" he asked. "I can assure you that those members of our community who stand with me are skeptical."

Mavis felt her blood pressure begin to rise. "I promise you I do labor on behalf of the constituents of my ward and I don't appreciate anyone saying I don't." She crossed her legs under the desk and laid her hands in her lap, to keep them from betraying her rage. "I work tirelessly for my people."

"I didn't come to level allegations." Galbreath smiled. "Just telling you what some of 'your people,'"—he made the quotation gesture again —"have said in my presence. Though, I shouldn't think an alderman as powerful as yourself cares what a few picketers think or say."

"I do care, though." She clinched her hands in front of her face.

"Don't you see?" she said. "That's how this mayor works, dividing the people." She pointed at him. "First you're out there saying the poh-leece did this or the poh-leece did that, but then slowly you start saying, 'Where's Alderman Stomps?' Next thing you know, the poh-leece is all but forgotten and I'm on the hot seat."

Galbreath took a deep breath and slowly released it. "You seem a little defensive, Alderman."

"Damn right." She stood for effect. "Damn right I'm defensive." She quieted a little. "Wouldn't you be? Man I invite into my inner sanctum, accuses me of sitting on my hands, letting my people down, when he don't know jack about what I'm doing or why I asked him to stop by in the first place. But that's how this mayor likes to divide the people. I can't stand it and won't put up with it." She tried to look like she was calming herself down. "Sorry I cursed, Reverend, but I get riled up."

He watched her, like he was trying to decide to believe her or what to say, maybe both. "Okay. Why did you invite me?"

"You are leading the group picketing the poh-leece and I was wondering what is it you want to know?"

"It hasn't changed since we began. We're demanding answers about the circumstances surrounding the death of Antwan Simms."

"I know that part, IAD has reopened the investigation. But you know that, too. What else?"

"What else?" The man brought a certain majesty to the plastic chair in his lack of movement.

"Yes, what else are you looking for? You already know the cops have reopened the case. So that's not what you're protesting for. What else?"

"Nothing, other than Antwan's mother deserves to know how her son died, and the police should know already. That's it."

"C'mon, don't play me, Reverend. There's always some other reason, what's yours?"

"I don't know what you're driving at." His head moved very little. "You mean an ulterior motive?"

"Yeah, something like that. What is it?"

"I can assure you that we're seeking answers on behalf of Ms. Collins. She's a right to know the truth about her son's death. We know there's more to the story than we've been told, including allegations that Antwan might've been thrown from that building. There's supposedly a witness. If anyone has a right to know the truth, it's the boy's mother."

"Okay." Mavis settled back into her chair. The honest and righteous were pretty damned dangerous, but they could be useful. She smiled. "Good. I want to applaud what you're doing, Reverend. In fact, I asked you in here to encourage you to continue and protest more. Maybe escalate things a little, make the poh-leece and the media recognize that you're serious. What do you need?"

"Need?"

"Do you need more people? Signs? A loudspeaker? What do you need?"

"I think I've got all we need. We're looking for answers, not trouble."

"I bet you could use some more bodies. Everyone can use more bodies. I can provide you with those bodies. The media loves to see a crowd. I might be able to arrange a little more coverage, too. You've got to work with me is all."

"And you'll be working behind the scenes?" he asked.

"That's right. The more pressure you can bring to bear on the superintendent and the mayor, the easier it'll be for me to get your answers. And maybe even effect a little change in the process. And I will be there with you as well, tomorrow in fact."

"What are *your* ulterior motives, Alderman, if I may ask?"

"Sure. Sure, you can ask, Reverend." She sat forward and put her elbows on the table, leaning toward him like a co-conspirator. "We need to bring some change to the way the poh-leece do business in our community. If we lie down and take it, they'll just keep on kicking us in the teeth. I think it's going to remain open season on black people until that change comes about." *Not to mention*, she thought, *getting rid of that pompous ass white superintendent and getting a right-thinking man of color to replace him.* Someone she could exert some control over. "I need for there to be pressure on Plumb and the mayor, both media and community pressure. If we can stir up some interest, we'll be able to rally others to our cause and that'll add up to even more pressure from all fronts. That's the only thing these people respond to."

"Really? And what change is it that you hope to inspire?"

"That they treat us with the respect we deserve as a community and that our rights aren't trampled on like just some more garbage in the street. That a black man can leave his home and not be afraid of the poh-leece."

"I'm not afraid of the police," he said. "A lot more innocent people are gunned down by gang members than by police. My issue. Well, our issue, at least the issue we're trying to address, is about a particular incident, a particular officer, and perhaps a cover-up. I realize the police have their hands full, but on the whole, I have a lot fewer problems with them than those drug dealing, gun toting gangbangers."

"Reverend, you mean to tell me that when a poh-leece car drives by you with two white cops in it you don't get nervous? C'mon now?"

"I don't think I'm any more likely to be stopped by white officers than by black officers."

"You're wrong, sir."

"If anything, it's a power thing, or a covering for one of your own when something goes wrong thing, not just a black-white thing," Galbreath said.

"Reverend," Stomps said. "This is Chicago. Everything, and I mean *everything*, is black and white. You feel me?"

Chapter 7

What You Gonna Do

TUESDAY, 2200 Hours

Jermaine Taylor let himself out of his momma's Cabrini apartment and found the air close and humid, almost Mississippi thick, not that her crowded little apartment was any better. Five bodies in a small two bedroom heated up quick and stayed that way. Outside, he'd expected to feel a cooler breeze, something, but there was nothing but more humidity. He slid into the shadows of the stairwell and took the steps down. It was dark and stale and hot. Lights were out up and down the stairs. It stunk, too. He'd never gotten used to the smell of piss that hung in the air as if the walls were painted in the stuff. He avoided the trash and the puddles that he told himself were spilled pop.

He came out on the ground floor. A couple guys his age hovered at the mouth of the other stairwell. They were dressed in white T-shirts and shorts and looked at him for a second before going back to their conversation. Jermaine wanted to go up to them and ask how he could get into the Cobras but lost his nerve. He went out the lobby door to the parking lot instead.

Several groups of people, mostly men, were sitting on car hoods or trunks, on concrete pylons, or just standing around laughing and shooting the shit. Some were drinking beer, forty ouncers, usually in a brown paper bag, some were smoking. Just about everybody was laughing.

He didn't see anyone he knew. Like there was much chance of that. He put his hands in his shorts pockets and started walking. He didn't have a destination, but he had a purpose. He wanted to talk to some guys who knew his brother, some Cobras. But first he'd have to find the nerve to start that conversation.

It wasn't as easy as Jermaine had pictured it. He'd figured he'd just walk up to one of the kids working security and get introduced to whoever was running things. If Boo were alive it'd be simple, but then his ass would still be in Mississippi.

He imagined doing the cop who killed his brother. He pulled the trigger again, and again, and again, and again. The fucker fell dead at his feet in front of some Cobras who'd be impressed. The gun was hidden at his momma's, stuck up in his clean clothes pile. He didn't think the twins were likely to find it. He kicked a rock from the sidewalk into Division Street as cars shot past, no drivers eager to slow down by the projects.

Jermaine turned and looked at 1150 North Sedgwick. It was tall, sixteen floors of red brick. This side of the building was covered in windows, most of which were open, some with curtains hanging out. A couple of heads dotted the open frames, probably trying to get some fresh air. Jermaine figured there were lots of other eyes staring out too, some for the fun of it, some because they were bored. But some were Cobras, watching for cops or rip-offs.

"Watch yo'self!" a voice called from behind.

Jermaine turned as something hard plowed into him, knocking him to the ground. Something metal, a bike maybe, crashed nearby.

"Oof," a voice said.

Jermaine rolled up on his knees and took a breath, wheezing a little. Laughter erupted from down the street.

Boys. A group, all dressed in white T-shirts and shorts, were pointing, but not at him. Across the sidewalk, a kid was trying to untangle himself from a bike frame and handlebars.

Several boys, younger than him by years, laughed.

"Milk toast! Milk toast!" They ran around him and the fallen bicyclist toward the 1150 building, a couple lashing out at the kid as they passed by. "Bitch!"

Jermaine climbed to his feet and watched as the group flowed, like water through rocks, into the parking lot, then into the building. He looked back at the other kid, his age, maybe older. The kid was white. No… he was black but was colored white. He had funny sandy hair, still in an Afro, but nappy. His skin was really weird, a dirty milk color, like after you dunked cookies in it, almost grey. And his eyes were large and stuck out of his face like a frog's.

The kid wore a baggy T-shirt, white but ripped and streaked with grease, and long jean shorts. One knee was skinned, and blood leaked down his shin. The kid didn't wear any socks and his gym shoes, the red and black high-top basketball kind, weren't tied. He stood and shook like he was mad.

"Man! I said to watch out!"

Jermaine shrugged.

"You stepped right inta me, man. I had them beat." He turned and it looked like he was going to kick the bike. "Fuck it. Bitches, any damn way."

The kid tried to pick up the bike, but it was twisted-stuck. Jermaine stepped over and helped. He jerked one way and the kid another and it popped free from itself. The kid pulled the bike away, like he was afraid Jermaine was gonna take it. Jermaine stepped back hands raised.

"Just helping." He tried not to stare but couldn't. The kid was about the weirdest damned thing he'd ever seen.

The kid stopped and looked back for a minute. "Go ahead. Say it."

"Say what?" Jermaine asked.

"Say I look funny, go ahead. Everybody else do."

"You got something wrong with you?"

"Here's what I got wrong." He pushed the bike at Jermaine and took a swing. Jermaine stepped back. The kid stepped closer and punched again. Jermaine ducked and the kid's arm clipped the top of his head.

Jermaine pushed him, but the kid kept coming, kept swinging. Jermaine tackled him to the sidewalk where they rolled around, punching, but neither connecting.

After a few more seconds of shoving and clawing, Jermaine ended up on top, holding the kid's arms out, pressed against the concrete. "What's wrong with you?"

"Man, fuck you. You like all them other bitches."

"I don't want to kick your ass, but you gotta stop. Chill, man. I don't wanna fight."

The kid's efforts stopped, and he went limp. "Let my ass up then."

"All right, but chill." Jermaine shifted off him and stood. "You the one ran me over, remember?" The kid sat up and rubbed his wrists. Jermaine took a step back as the kid stood. "Why they do that?"

The kid picked up his bike off the ground a second time and looked at Jermaine. "They say I'm weak and I look different than them."

"You do look different. What's wrong?"

"Why it got to be something wrong with me? Why can't y'all have something wrong with you?"

"Just asking, man. But you the one look different than everyone else." Jermaine turned back toward his building.

"Hold up." The kid reached down and brushed off his leg and probed his scrape with dirty fingers. "Doctor says I got no melanin. That's why I look white."

"What's that?"

"Pigment." He shrugged. "Color, I guess. I'm albino. What's your name?"

"Jermaine. You?"

"Ronnell." He tried to push the kickstand down but couldn't. Finally, he squatted low and pulled it free with his hand. "But most people just call me White Boy."

"How about I call you Ronnell?"

"That's cool." Ronnell nodded his head like it was something of a first and he was trying it on for size. "Yeah, cool."

A few minutes later as they walked the bike toward 1150, Jermaine confided in Ronnell his plan to join the Cobras. Ronnell shook his head and stopped well short of the parking lot and the people.

"Man, they don't just take anybody," Ronnell said. "If they like you, they might give you a chance. But they gonna violate you in, you know."

"Violate?"

"Yeah, depends on how they do it. Sometimes it's everyone there or sometimes just a couple of the older guys kick your ass and see how you take it. If they like what they see, you're in."

"Who do I have to talk to?" Jermaine felt something thicken in his gut.

"You sure you wanna do this?"

"Damn straight." Jermaine cinched up his pants. "Let's go."

"Man, hold up a minute." Ronnell pushed his kickstand down. "You for sure?"

"Serious like a heart attack."

"Sounds pretty serious to me." Ronnell shrugged. "But remember. They gonna whoop your ass but good."

Chapter 8

Momma Stone

A shadow darkened the doorway of Mavis Stomps's community organizing office in a converted warehouse near Cabrini-Green.

"Anybody see you?" she asked from behind her desk, hands on her hips. She wore a T-shirt over shorts. It was late and hot, and this office didn't have air, just a fan that rotated. Her desk was tan scarred metal.

"Anybody see you?" She let a hint of impatience color her tone, and remained standing.

Cecil Jones gave one last shake of his umbrella before he propped it against the wall. Jones was dressed in a four-button charcoal gray suit and red silk tie.

"Come on," Jones said. His voice was deep. "I know better than to let anybody see me slip in your door." He loosened his tie and tugged at the lapels of his suit jacket. "Got something to drink? Something strong, hopefully, and cold."

She pointed to a wooden cabinet against the wall, on top of which perched a half-empty bottle of Crown Royal. "Help yourself unless you got your heart set on cold. What you all dolled-up for?"

Hefting the bottle, he found a plastic cup inside the cabinet and poured himself a couple of fingers. Mavis's cup was on her desk, empty, and he looked at her, lifting the bottle. She nodded. He stepped closer and poured her several inches of the amber fluid. The smell of the liquor set her mouth to watering. He handed her the cup and set the bottle on the desk, then took a sip.

"Ah, now that hits the spot." Jones took another hit of Crown Royal. "Momma Stone always got nothing but the best." He set his cup next to hers and stepped back. "These duds ain't nuttin'." He tugged on his lapels. "I took a ride out to Indiana and played some Texas Hold 'Em on the boat."

Mavis picked up her cup and gulped the whiskey without ceremony. She put the cup down and sat in her chair, shaking her head. "Get lucky?"

Jones spread his hands. "You know I always get lucky, Momma." It had taken her a while to get used to an older man calling her Momma.

"That's right. How could I forget?" She was at least ten years younger than him, maybe fifteen. He outweighed her by close to two hundred pounds at least, and she hadn't eaten much all day. Maybe she could out-drink him, but she didn't want to try. "You ain't one to go to the boats much, what gives?"

"Gold asked me to meet him there."

"What'd he want?" She sat forward. Sherman Gold was Lonnie Huggins's attorney and had already given her the good news through her assistant. But she'd set the process in motion.

Jones studied her face. "Mission accomplished."

"Really? How'd he manage that?" As if she didn't know. She poured herself another couple of fingers of Crown Royal and took a sip. She slowly swallowed; the burn felt delicious.

"He say that cop locked Lonnie up is a crazy poh-leece."

She sat back in her chair. Why had it taken so long for Jones to tell her Huggins was out? She'd learned on Monday before noon. What was his game? "The reverend's gonna do another protest tomorrow about that cop and I need you to round up some people to be at the church at nine to get on the bus. I'm gonna meet you there with some news people and I want a crowd in the background. Get some mothers and grannies this time, no gangbangers."

"Which church?" he asked.

"The Holy Rock or whatever, on Cleveland." She rose and poured Jones a little more. This guy wasn't going to be drinking up all her whiskey. She topped herself off and twisted the cap back on before putting the bottle back on the cabinet. She admired the whiskey a moment, and then pulled another mouthful. It burned just right. "When is Gold gonna know about a new trial?"

Jones shrugged. "Don't think he is." He sat back on the couch. The springs sagged and screeched. "Lonnie gonna go back to jail, new trial or no."

"Maybe." She took another drink and watched him. Sweat ran from his forehead along his eyes and down his cheek to disappear in his collar. Why was he sweating like that?

"You know," Stomps took another sip, knowing she had to slow down, "what these projects need is a good old-fashioned gang war."

"Don't say no crazy shit like that, Momma." Jones bolted forward fast for a guy his size. "Hell, we practically got one already. An' I got enough poh-leece attention as it is."

"I ain't talking about us." She set her glass down and pointed in the direction of the white buildings. "Those Gangster Disciples are trigger happy with all the shorties they got. Maybe they should start some-thing with the Vice Lords."

Jones sat back and smiled. "Oh, I see what you getting at. Keep the Cobras out of it."

"Might take some of the pressure off you." She emptied her glass and returned his smile. She hoped it was colder than his. Jones used to think for himself, but now he seemed to wait for her to tell him what to do, though he resisted anything assertive. "Those envelopes with my cut you giving me need to get back the way they supposed to be."

Jones looked at the floor and shook his head. He seemed to want to say something. She gave him some time, but his mouth stayed shut.

"You got something you want to say?" she asked him, finally.

"Naw, I been doing the best I can, but those slick boys just be messing with me like I'm the only game in the Greens."

"Spare me." She toyed with the thought of having another glass of whiskey but decided against it. "Here's what you're gonna do."

Jones looked up.

"Arrange for there to be some shooting between the GDs and Vice Lords. Let's get the action away from your front door."

"How you want me to do that?"

"That's your department. Just get it done. I'm going to see if I can't get these protesters to be a little more assertive and add some pressure that way."

Jones frowned until his bottom lip spilled over onto his chin. "A'ight. I see what you saying. Yeah, I could do that." He shook his head a little like he was afraid to shake it all the way. "Kind of was thinking, though, we'd lay low for a while and see what we can get popping."

"Come on, Cee." Mavis wondered about Jones. He was still confident. But something was going on, and she couldn't get a handle on it. Another reason she needed Huggins out. "Get the pack out of the lobby, bump it up a floor or two. You can't keep shutting down every time the poh-leece roll by. I need them greenbacks flowing in."

He closed his mouth and stared at the wall above her head. "You right. You right." After a moment, he looked at the floor. "Some of my boys is spooked 'cause of how much time the poh-leece be there."

"C'mon." Mavis settled back into her chair and flashed whitened teeth. This wasn't about them boys being spooked. This was about Jones being up to something. "Un-spook them and get them back to slinging rocks. No more shutting down just because the cops drive by. Can't expect me to run a campaign without nothing in the bank."

Jones shook his head, without much enthusiasm, and he'd been acting weird for a while now. He stood.

"You." She nodded at him. "Need to up production, too. I need that shit to be flying out of those buildings." She couldn't help but smile. "Got it?"

"Yeah, Momma."

"No, for real." Her smile melted off her face. She wanted him to fully understand what she was saying. "You hear what I'm saying to you?"

"Yeah, I hear." His gaze fell. Was he looking at the top of the desk or her breasts?

"No problem?" She had to get Huggins out to prop Jones up or figure out what his game was.

"I'm on it." He left without looking at her or taking his umbrella.

Mavis stood and stretched as the sound of Jones's footsteps receded down the hall. It was times like these she wished for a window. She wanted to see what Jones did or who he met when he left. She didn't trust him.

Maybe it was time for Momma Stone to arrange a leadership change in the Cobras, or maybe when Lonnie got out, Jones would straighten up. She hoped. A real change in leadership could get bloody and she didn't want the police attention on the Cobras that bloodshed would draw.

She swirled the whiskey left in her glass. She'd wiggled her way into the Cobras and even as Mavis Stomps, alderwoman of the 27th Ward, community activist and not-for profit organizer. She was Momma Stone and was all but running the gang from her alderman's office. Ever since she met Jones, she'd had his attention. Together they'd been good, but maybe it was time for a change.

It was time for a change in leadership in the police department too, time to get a black superintendent to look out for the welfare of her people. And it definitely was time for a leadership change in the city. She was the answer the people of Chicago were looking for, even if they didn't know it yet. They would soon enough, though. Soon enough, with the unwitting help of Officer Macbeth.

Chapter 9

So, You Wanna Be A Cobra

TUESDAY 2300 Hours

Jermaine and Ronnell followed Tea Bag through the lobby of the 1160. He acted and looked like a hard little fucker but was a couple years younger than Jermaine. The lobby was vacant of all but the uniformed guards lounging against the walls. Both were black guys in tired black polyester. None of them had the balls to mess with Cobras.

Ronnell seemed nervous, sweaty and wide-eyed. Jermaine was nervous too, but he figured he could weather whatever they was going to do. It wasn't like they were going to kill them or anything. He could take a beat down. He'd been fighting his whole life. He'd been disappointed to learn Lonnie Huggins was locked up.

Tea Bag hit the stairwell and started up, taking the steps two at a time despite his short legs. Jermaine kept up, but he knew he was out of shape. There weren't any stairs where he'd spent the last couple of years. Tea Bag seemed to float up one flight after another. Jermaine was breathing hard. Ronnell fell behind. Tea Bag glanced back and smirked.

"C'mon, Milk Toast." he said. "Can't be no Cobra if you can't run no stairs."

Jermaine couldn't make out Ronnell's response, but it sounded something like, "Shorty bitch." He had to give Ronnell some respect; he spoke his mind. And he didn't take no shit.

They reached the top. Jermaine felt the deep thumping of a stereo bass. He'd fallen a half flight behind Tea Bag when the young Cobra bolted out of the top of the stairwell at the sixteenth floor. Ronnell was further back but close enough that Jermaine could still hear his raspy breathing. Tea Bag was waiting, keeping a rhythm on his thigh with his thumbs, when Jermaine came through the open stairwell doorway.

"Arms out." Tea Bag nodded as Jermaine raised his arms. Tea Bag patted him down, finishing as Ronnell staggered from the stairwell. "Your turn, Milk Toast," Tea Bag said.

Ronnell leaned against the wall for support as Tea Bag slapped him up and down the body, searching more forcefully than he had with Jermaine. Jermaine wondered if Ronnell's complexion or his reputation was the cause for the rougher treatment. Maybe both.

Laughter erupted down the hallway along with the thrumming bass. Tea Bag walked toward the nearest apartment door. Behind him the chain link covering the porch bars was black from the lack of overheads. Tea Bag opened the door and disappeared inside. Jermaine followed, swallowing against the bass trying to break into his chest and hammer his heart. He guessed Ronnell was behind him but didn't chance a look.

Once through the door, Jermaine found himself in a cinder block kitchen that opened into a living room. He was surprised to find both rooms empty except for Tea Bag and the steady beat of the music. The naked windows showed the city lights, the lake was a dark stain somewhere on the horizon. Along one wall of the living room a large hole had been hammered through the white-painted cinder block into the next apartment. The throbbing rhythmic pulse and voices of men laughing and yelling came from the hole.

Tea Bag stepped through the hole and disappeared. Jermaine took a breath, ducked, and went next. Ronnell followed, his breath still coarse and loud. Before Jermaine could even straighten, he registered the smell of sweat and weed. He found himself in another empty room. A door stood open on the opposite wall, the noise of the party rolled through it. The low banging of the bass rushed over voices that were loud and bold, cackling and wild. Jermaine steeled himself, his stomach a painful knot, and walked through.

Tea Bag was in the living room. It was crowded with young black men in their early teens to late twenties. The room was growing hot and some of the men were shirtless. Their varied hues of skin were emblazoned with homemade tats that ran up and down arms, across shoulders and backs and stomachs and chests, and even spotted the occasional face and neck tats. Many in the room smoked cigarettes; a few had blunts, the smoke sharp and yet sweet. Empty beer cans and bottles littered the floor.

Tea Bag paused, scanning the crowd. Then he set off through the bodies like a bullet. Few moved without a shove or an elbow. Jermaine stayed close with Ronnell following behind. Ronnell's curses were louder, now, than his breathing. Jermaine could hear snickering as they pushed through the crowd and once or twice someone muttered, "Milk Toast" or "White Boy." Jermaine knew what membership in the Cobras meant to him, but he wondered why Ronnell would put up with the disrespect when there was so little chance that he'd get in.

Tea Bag stopped at a group of three older men gathered in the middle of the room. He tapped one of the men on the shoulder. Jermaine recognized Cecil Jones as he turned and grinned.

❦

Stacey Macbeth called his last informant. So far, he'd gotten nothing but static and fear. He put the phone to his ear.

"Wazzup," said the man who answered the call. His voice was strong and demanding.

"You cool?" Macbeth asked.

"Yeah." The man blew out like he was exhaling cigarette smoke. "For a minute."

"You hear anything about Huggins?"

"What else you wanna know?"

"Somebody told me Huggins was out. You seen or heard anything about that?"

"I ain't got shit to say 'bout that."

"What the fuc—" Macbeth spun on his heel, jamming the phone against his ear. "Man's locked up. He can't hurt you."

"Man, fuck all that." The informant inhaled long and steady. "If you axing 'bout Lonnie Huggins, you axing the wrong nigger." The line went dead.

§

JERMAINE STARED AT JONES. HE WAS TALL AND HAD TO WEIGH close to three hundred pounds. He wasn't fat, but he wasn't in shape either. He was dressed in a red shirt and black nylon gym pants. His black hair was razored close to his scalp on a big, fat head. His eyes were a deep brown and small, not the kind you wanted to look at for any length of time.

"White Boy." Jones raised his arms. The music stopped and the voices faded, then died altogether. "Boy, why ain't you a good for nothing rock head yet?" Laughter erupted all around them. Jones turned to Jermaine. "So, here's Boo's little brother." He stepped closer. "Why you think we should let you be a Cobra?"

Jermaine was shocked. How'd he know? He looked at Jones but couldn't see anything in the man's stare.

The crowd hooted, many raising their left hands, fingers clenched in a "C." It took a minute for the hollering to quiet down. Jermaine looked around before fixing Jones with what he hoped was his toughest glare. He swallowed. It was time he spoke, just like he practiced.

"My brother was a Cobra and died a Cobra. I want to be a Cobra like him." The crowd got loud again, many making baby sounds. Jermaine waited for the noise to dim and when it did, he went on. "I ain't but a year younger than Boo an' can take care of myself."

Jones held his big belly as he laughed. "But can you take your weight like your brother, may he rest in peace?" The crowd went up loud again. "Can you take care of your brother Cobras?" More yelling and chanting.

"Here's what we're fittin' to do." Jones raised his hands. The crowd quieted. "Here's what we're fittin' to do. Make the circle." Jones turned with his arms spread. The Cobras stepped back until it was only Jones, Jermaine, and Ronnell in the middle. "Where's Tea Bag?" Jones looked around. The kid stepped out. "You search 'em?"

Tea Bag nodded.

"Go ahead, Pac-Man." He waved at Jermaine and Ronnell. "Show them some more Cobra love."

A man taller than Jones stepped out of the circle. He was thin and had large ears that made him look even thinner. He was wearing a black Bulls basketball jersey and jean shorts, his arms covered in Cobra tats. He started with Jermaine. Pac-Man used his fists to search Jermaine up and down as if he was searching for weapons. Then he did Ronnell, his face split in a grin.

Pac-Man finished and stepped away, but quickly kicked Ronnell in the back, knocking him to the floor. Then Pac-Man spun and punched Jermaine's chest, throwing him back against Tea Bag, who shoved him. Pac-Man followed with an elbow catching Jermaine under the eye. He was driven to his knees as the tall Cobra bounced back to the circle, his eyes showing how much he liked it. Jermaine stood, ignoring the ringing in his ears.

Ronnell got up and stood, rubbing his back. "Okay." Jones stepped forward. "Back the fuck up! Make room!" He turned and stretched his arms out wide. "Back up. Give 'em more space." Once he was satisfied with the area, he turned to Jermaine and Ronnell. "These here brothers gonna fight it out, winner's in, and loser's, well… loser's a loser." He laughed.

"Now, brothers." Jones once again slowly turned. "If either of these two motherfuckers come within arm or foot's reach, tag 'em, but no shanks or guns. Teach 'em to keep they eyes open."

The crowd started hollering, like they'd love nothing better than to kill Jermaine and Ronnell both.

Man, Jermaine thought, *do I really want to do this* as he turned to Ronnell and caught a fist in the side of the head. Ronnell threw another punch, missing this time. Jermaine felt something glance off the back of his thigh. He'd stepped too close to the edge of the circle.

Jermaine launched himself at Ronnell and tackled him to the floor. They threw punches but were too close to really hurt one another. Jermaine tried to stay on top. Ronnell bucked wildly underneath. A boot caught Jermaine in the ribs. Then the only thing he seemed to be able to see were the bottoms of boots and shoes as the gang lashed out at the two of them.

Someone grabbed Jermaine by the shirt and wrenched him to his feet. He looked up into Pac-Man's eyes. The Cobra's teeth glistened with spit. "Don't fucking think so." Pac-Man punched him in the face.

Jermaine staggered and swung his fists all around him at once, trying to keep everyone away. But punch after punch after kick spun him so fast, he almost fell. It hurt to breathe, and he could feel blood dripping down his throat. He didn't know how much longer he could take it.

"Hold the fuck up!" Jones stepped into the middle of the circle. He grabbed Jermaine by the hair and yanked him back and down. Jones swung to his left and kicked Ronnell in the ass. "Enough." Jones grinned wide, showing his white teeth.

"We got one more test." Jones spun around, smiling at all in the room. "We fittin' to find out if one of these bitches is man enough to be a Cobra brotha!" The hollering started and got loud fast. Most of the Cobras in the room jumped around and high-fived one another like they'd scored a touchdown. Ronnell staggered as Jermaine got to his feet. They faced one another across the circle.

"Pac-Man," Jones said. "Ready the piece."

Pac-Man stepped out of the crowd and pulled a little black revolver from his pants. He flipped open the cylinder and dumped the bullets on the ground. The cheering got even louder as he retrieved the rounds off the floor. He slid one bullet into place and spun the cylinder like a cowboy before snapping it shut. He pocketed the rest of the bullets and handed the gun to Jones.

Jones held the gun up. "We gonna play a little Cobra roulette." The yelling started again, and Jones held his arms up. It got quiet.

"Somebody hold Baby Boo." Two big Cobras stepped out and took Jermaine by the arms, clutching him tight enough that he grimaced.

Jones stood in front of Ronnell. "Bet you didn't think we was gonna let you go first. Did you, White Boy?" Jermaine couldn't see until Jones stepped back. Ronnell stood holding the gun in front of him waist high, staring at it. Then he looked up at Jermaine. One of his eyes was purple and about swollen closed. "Go on, White Boy." Jones pointed at Jermaine. "There's your ticket in. Just put that barrel up to his head and pull the trigger. Nothing to it."

Ronnell stared at Jermaine. He couldn't seem to focus.

"Most likely nothing's going to happen." Jones pointed at Jermaine. "But one time in five, his brains get blowed out." Jones clapped his hands like he expected Ronnell to get on with it.

Jermaine couldn't believe this was happening. His body hurt so much, he just wanted it to end. "Do it," he said. The crowd screamed.

Ronnell stared at him; the gun shook. He stepped toward Jermaine. The gun hand dropped to his side as he took another step, slowly, like gravity had turned up a notch or two. Another step brought him close. Ronnell's hand came up, and the gun hovered in front of Jermaine's eyes. It wavered as if Ronnell's arm didn't have the strength to hold it that high. The barrel and cylinders were black with shadow. Ronnell's hand looked whiter. He moved a finger onto the trigger. The gun shook so much, Jermaine could hear the bullet rattle.

He forced himself to look at Ronnell instead of at the gaping hole of the revolver's barrel. Ronnell's face was screwed up tight. His lips were pulled back from teeth that were bloody.

"Do it!" Jermaine shouted. The gun shook more. Ronnell's hand dropped and he started sobbing, shaking his head like he knew he'd failed.

Jones reached down and snatched the revolver. "Hold onto him." The hands holding Jermaine let go and a different set of Cobras grabbed Ronnell, pulling him back a couple steps. Jones held the revolver in the air. "Should I spin the cylinder or let it stand?"

The crowd chanted, seemingly equal between the two. It went on for a minute before the crowd started to favor 'spin it.' Holding the gun over his head, Jones spun the cylinder like Pac-Man had and snapped it closed. He handed the gun to Jermaine. The grip was warm and a little small in his hand.

Ronnell struggled against the two holding him in place. He cried and slobbered. Jermaine hoped he wasn't about to kill this kid who'd given him his chance. He stepped forward and pressed the barrel against Ronnell's forehead. Ronnell's eyes tried to follow it and eventually crossed, then closed. His lips quivered and spit leaked from the corner of his mouth.

I gotta do this, Jermaine thought, *I got to do it*. A roar of laughter broke from the crowd and someone yelled, "He pissed hisself." Sure enough, when Jermaine looked down, a growing patch of darkness was spreading across the front of Ronnell's pants. Jermaine thought back to a second earlier when he had been waiting.

"Nothing personal," Jermaine muttered, hoping Ronnell heard. He put his finger on the trigger; it was cold compared to the rest of the gun. He pushed the barrel hard against Ronnell's head, then pulled the trigger back. It snapped, clicked, and nothing happened. Jermaine let out his breath and closed his eyes for a second.

The two Cobras holding Ronnell let go like he might have pissed on them. Someone from the crowd kicked Ronnell in the back and sent him sprawling. The closest Cobras commenced stomping on him again. Jones shouted for them to stop. He looked at Jermaine, then took the gun from his hand.

"Jermaine no more," Jones yelled. "You'll be Baby Boo from now on." Several Cobras cheered, but it seemed that most didn't really care now that the fun was over. "You got to live by Cobra Commandments from now on. You never, and I mean *never*, cooperate with the poh-leece. That's the first and most holy commandment. Number two, take your weight. If you get caught with something, just take it, don't rat nobody out."

Jermaine figured one and two were basically the same thing, but he kept his mouth shut.

"Three! Don't steal from your Cobra family. That includes skimming off any monies made dealing shit or taking the shit itself. Four! Do for your Cobra brothas what you can, we your family now." Jones gestured around the room. "Number five! Don't fuck a Cobra brothas woman 'less he say it okay." Jones paused. "Course, that don't exactly apply to all Cobras now, us higher-ups are afforded a little leniency in this regard."

Jones looked over to Pac-Man who was close by. "I miss anything, Pac-Man?"

The big-eared Cobra stared down at Jermaine like he still wanted to pound him to death. "No, Cee, that's about it. But I'll see if I can scare up a list so the little brother here can keep his shit straight." Pac-Man took the gun from Jones and reloaded it before slipping it back in his pants pocket. "We wouldn't want his skinny little ass to have to suffer any violations. That would just make my day."

Jones hooked a thumb at Pac-Man. "This here is our enforcer. And you really don't want him looking for your ass."

Jermaine surprised himself by speaking. "What about Lonnie Huggins?"

Jones's smile vanished and his stare darkened to something hard and cruel. "Never mind, you don't want either of those two cats to come calling on your ass if you fucked up. They both just plain mean."

Pac-Man smiled, looking Jermaine up and down like he was something to eat. "Yeah. I ain't killed nobody for a while."

Chapter 10

Looking For Lonnie

WEDNESDAY 2315 Hours

The two unmarked tactical cars sat side by side in the parking lot north of 1230 North Larrabee, their engines running, air conditioners on high, and windows open. Macbeth was in the passenger seat of his car. Hagen was driving and Zito was in the back seat. Macbeth's window was next to Teddy Ketchum's who was riding in the passenger seat of the other car. His partner, Frank Hampton, was behind the wheel.

"Let's go sit up in a vacant apartment and come down on them."

"C'mon, Stace." Ketchum tapped his unlit cigarette against the top of the door. "You know as soon as we show our faces they're going to shut down for the night. They may already be down."

"Lonnie's out," Macbeth said. "That shit's going to change for sure."

"We don't even know if he is or whether he's around." Ketchum lit the cigarette and blew the smoke up into the humid night air. "Let's make sure he's out and back before we think about fucking around over there."

"Fuck that, let's do it tonight," Macbeth said.

"Stace, you got to cool it with Huggins, man." Zito fished his cigarettes from his vest pocket.

"Macbeth," Ketchum took another drag and let the smoke slither out his nose, "you're in too big a hurry. See, there was these two bulls, father and son, sitting up on a hill overlooking a herd of cows. The son says to his dad, 'Let's run down and fuck us a cow.'" Ketchum took another drag and flicked the ashes on the ground while blowing the smoke through his teeth. "The daddy bull says, 'No, son. Let's *walk* down and fuck 'em all.'"

Ketchum laughed. Gray smoke trailed from his mouth. "Man, I been wanting to use that on one of you young bucks for the longest time." He flicked his cigarette over the hood of his car. "Seen that in a cop movie once."

"Yeah, yeah." *Didn't anyone understand,* Macbeth thought. *Huggins was a monster.* He'd killed Latricia. Burned her alive. If only Macbeth hadn't missed the dope in Huggins's car.

Ketchum took a deep breath. "Okay, for fuck's sake, let's go play hide and seek."

Chapter 11

Hide And Seek

WEDNESDAY 2330 Hours

Macbeth bailed out of his unmarked along with the cops from the other cars, running for the lobby of 1160 North Sedgwick. Before they'd even turned off the street into the parking lot several black teens ran ahead of them into the lobby. He heard shouts from inside of "Five-O! Five-O!" as he raced for the lobby with the other cops.

He ripped the metal door open and sprinted for the stairwell past the five people in the lobby, two of whom were security guards. One stood wide-eyed; the other barely raised his head from his newspaper. The three civilians were young, wearing the white T-shirts and shorts of gangbangers. Since they didn't run, they had to be distracters, there to keep the officers busy in the lobby while everyone else escaped.

Macbeth hit the stairwell and took the steps two at a time. Somewhere way up he heard a voice shout, "Slick boys!" The call reverberated in the cinder block stairwell.

A quick glance behind him showed Ketchum was on his heels, breathing hard. The man was a good fifteen years older than him, and smoked, too.

The noise ahead dissipated as they climbed. They kept going. Macbeth sucked in lungful after lungful of the rancid stairwell air, making sure not to touch the railings with his hands. The stink and humidity seemed to rob the narrow passageway of oxygen and his lungs burned. Behind him Ketchum labored.

They passed the tenth floor. Macbeth glanced back and caught Ketchum's eye. The man held up a hand, four fingers extended on it, for fourteen. Macbeth kept going but he could see Ketchum drop back to a fast walk. Macbeth made fourteen and did a quick peek into the breezeway. Empty. There were three boarded-up apartment doors down the hall.

Ketchum made the top of the flight and leaned against the graffiti-scarred cinder block. His face was covered with sweat as his hands dropped to his knees, his lungs working like a bellows. Macbeth sucked hard too, but he wasn't fighting back puke like Ketchum seemed to be doing. He raised a finger.

After another long minute, Ketchum straightened and they strode out onto the breezeway. Macbeth followed Ketchum to the farthest boarded-up apartment. A large sheet of heavy plywood had been screwed into the mortar, effectively closing the apartment off. Ketchum produced his Leatherman tool.

"We need a key to the roof. These little assholes can find us here."

"No shit." Macbeth glanced around as if he expected to be caught.

Ketchum pulled out the flathead screwdriver arm and began on a screw high up on the right side of the door. It came out easy, much quicker than it should have. He squatted and worked on the lower one. That came out quick, too. Ketchum pulled on the wood and it peeled away from the wall just enough for Macbeth to squeeze in. Ketchum followed, letting the board slam back into place.

The place smelled damp and moldy and was strewn with garbage and debris.

Macbeth breathed shallowly through his mouth. "Now we wait."

❧

Jermaine watched the cops run in. The lobby was suddenly filled with cops in street clothes, yelling, cursing, and pushing people around. He was forced to face the brick and told to grab some wall. Putting his hands up high, he stole a look behind him. Two cops ran up the stairs, one white and one black.

The other cops searched him twice, second time rougher than the first, not finding anything. Then the cops handcuffed him to the other two. Jermaine was in the middle, a kid on each arm. It didn't seem like these cops were going to run up the stairs after the other two. Weird. Why wouldn't they? Maybe nothing was going on up there.

A few minutes later, the handcuffs came off and the cops left, just like they arrived, quick and loud, but Jermaine was sure he didn't see the two cops that had run up the stairs again. They were still upstairs, why would the other cops leave? It didn't make sense.

A while later, Pac-Man came strolling into the lobby from the stairwell. *Should I tell him?* Jermaine wondered. But he didn't like Pac-Man, hated him. When they made eye contact, Pac-Man smirked. *Fuck him,* Jermaine thought. *I ain't telling him shit.* Pac-Man walked out of the lobby like he ruled the building or something. Once the door banged closed, Jermaine spat on the floor.

Chapter 12

Reassertion

WEDNESDAY 2330 Hours

Lonnie Huggins gripped a blanket to his chest, his knuckles sore from the effort. He'd had another dream. *Fuck that cop,* he thought. He was sweaty and cold. The room's air conditioner spewed a chilly breeze across his body. The light from the street streaked the hotel room through the open curtains. This wasn't that much better than prison if he couldn't go anywhere, though the pussy Keloid was bringing was certainly a step up.

He rolled out of bed and switched the air off. It was still too cold. The window was sealed, but he slid the patio door open and stepped onto the balcony. The hot, humid air outside eased his anxiety. He gripped the railing and stared down at the street.

Late-night traffic pulsed along Michigan Avenue's magnificent mile. There were too many buildings between him and the towering buildings of Cabrini. But he knew they were there. He could feel them. Waiting for him. *Soon,* he thought. *Soon. Fuck that, ain't no time like right fucking now.*

. . .

Lonnie Huggins waited for Keloid on the sidewalk in the thick night air. Heat still radiated from the concrete. His white T-shirt was damp by the time he slid into the passenger seat of the Oldsmobile Aurora. Keloid was riding with his seat reclined and one wrist on the top of the steering wheel. His large body still looked cramped, his knees high.

"What's up?" Huggins powered his window down and reached over to switch off the air that had been cranked up on max. He fingered the radio off before settling back in the seat. It felt good to be back in the city. Keloid pulled onto Michigan Avenue, merging into traffic before speaking.

"Man, Lonnie," Keloid said. "That hotel is bougie. You definitely moving up in the world."

"Fuck that, this ain't the fucking Jeffersons," Huggins said. "Fucking lawyers want me to play it cool for a while."

Keloid nodded. "Poh-leece came through a while ago and shut us down. Ain't back up yet. When I axed, they told me to mind my own fucking business."

"We'll see 'bout that. Who's running the spot?"

"Little nigger name a' Tea Bag." Keloid turned onto Chicago Avenue.

"We'll see 'bout that." They rode west in silence.

Some blocks later, Keloid turned onto Orleans. "I got some boys lined up if we need 'em."

"A'ight." Huggins watched as they skirted the western edge of Cabrini. The streets were dotted with people escaping the heat. The breeze from the open window was damp and heavy in his lungs like it didn't want to leave. Summer in the projects, Huggins thought. You even had to fight to breathe. He could feel violence in the air, too. He smiled. He was home.

Keloid pulled into the lot at 1150-60 Sedgwick and parked. People hung around, some sitting on hoods or trunks of cars. Others strolled slowly like they didn't have no other place to go. And they didn't. Here and there little puffs of cigarette smoke drifted up into the night sky, gray in the lights.

They got out. There were several groups of young men, Cobras mostly, all in white T-shirts and baggy blue jean shorts. Huggins felt out of touch. He didn't recognize any of them. But he'd been out of the sales end of things for quite a while. Time to get reacquainted, especially if he wanted to grow that bottom line.

Keloid led him to a group of shorties who were draped over an old box Chevy Caprice. One passed a 40 oz bottle of Old Milwaukee malt liquor to a high-yellow boy. The boy took a swig, put the bottle on the blacktop next to the car, and hopped up on the hood. Several of the teens greeted Huggins, but most glanced at Keloid, probably wishing they'd been nicer.

Huggins felt a little better as he took them in. He remembered their faces from around the building, even if he didn't know their names. He did recognize the anxiety in their eyes as he stood in front of them. They knew who he was and what he represented. "Where's Tea Bag?"

There was an awkward moment. One of the boys finally spoke up. "Upstairs with Pac-Man."

"Where?" Huggins asked. They glanced at each other. "I ain't gonna ask again."

"I don't rightly know, Lonnie." The high-yellow kid adjusted his legs on the hood like it was hot.

Huggins stepped over to the kid and lashed out with a backhand, connecting with the kid's cheekbone. The kid flew off the car. The malt liquor bottle spun across the parking lot, spraying amber liquor across the black asphalt. The kid thudded onto the ground, his sneakers pointed at the moon.

"I don't remember telling you it a'ight to call me by my government name." Huggins stared at those still standing, most open mouthed. He looked to see if anyone else wanted to get froggy.

The kid picked himself up and rubbed his jaw. "Didn't mean no disrespect." He was still shaky, but he started toward the lobby door. "I'll get 'em."

"Naw, take me to him."

Huggins followed the kid with Keloid trailing behind. They went up the walk ramp, through the heavy steel lobby door. Rows of fluorescent lights ran across the ceiling. A silent metal detector stood beside a pedestal fan running on high. It sounded like an airplane as it rotated back and forth. Out of habit, Huggins glanced at the floor. The metal detector was unplugged so the fan could have the juice, seemed like relief from the heat was more important than detecting weapons.

It didn't matter, Cobras ran the lobby, and wasn't any of them going through the machine if they were packing. The two guards leaned against a lobby wall. One was practically asleep. The other studied a newspaper.

A skinny youngster, maybe sixteen, faced into the fan, inches from the wire cage, as the fan whirred and rotated. He glanced at them when the door banged closed. "What's up?"

"Man wants to see you, Tea." The kid was still rubbing his jaw.

"What's up, Lonnie?" Tea Bag turned around with a big grin on his face. "What can I do for you, my brother?"

Huggins stepped close and drove his fist into Tea Bag's chest, then grabbed his T-shirt and drove him back and back and back, until he slammed into the stairwell door. It flew open. Tea Bag continued back until he crashed into the far wall. His head cracked against the cinder block.

"I ain't your brother, motherfucker. Has everybody lost their goddamned mind?" Huggins drove a knuckle into Tea Bag's sternum until the kid screeched. He pushed harder. "Don't be calling me by my name."

"A'ight." Tea Bag choked back a scream. "A'ight."

Huggins pressed harder, then eased back a little. "Why you shut down?"

"Poh-leece rolled through, man."

"Why you ain't re-upped?"

"'Cause that's what we been told."

"By Cee?" Huggins pulled back a little more.

"No, man." Tea Bag squinted. "Pac-Man, he been running it since you been gone."

"What else he been doing while I was locked up?" Huggins eased off altogether, but still held the shirt knotted in his fist and stayed close in Tea Bag's face.

"He been violating ma'fuckers too."

"Is that so?" Huggins said. "Where's the rest of the work?"

"What you mean?" Tea Bag squeezed his eyes closed.

"You shut down, should be something left. Where'd it go?"

"You mean the rocks?" Tea Bag scrunched up his face like he thought he was going to get hit.

"Yeah," Huggins said.

"Pac-Man got it." Tea Bag cracked an eye open. "He always take it."

"Where'd he go? Upstairs?"

"No." Tea Bag opened his eyes completely. "He split not long after, I think he take the work with him."

"Well, go get more." Huggins stepped back and let Tea Bag breathe.

"Work?" Tea Bag looked confused. "You want us to open up?"

"That's the idea." Huggins stepped up close again. "That a problem?"

"I don't know." Tea Bag grimaced. "Since Pac-Man been around, he been bringing the work with him and stuff. I don't know where to re-up 'cept from him."

"Call his black ass and get some more shit. We fittin' to open. Dig me?"

"He ain't gonna be happy."

"Then me and him can have a little talk 'bout that." Huggins grinned. He was starting to feel like he was back.

⚜

JERMAINE WATCHED MUNCHIE STEP OFF THE ELEVATOR, WEARING his wraparound sunglasses despite the darkness outside. His baby dreads bounced on top of his head. As Munchie circled the lobby, one of the Cobras who'd been in the lobby earlier with Jermaine asked, "Lonnie really back?"

"Yep," Munchie said. "And we fitting to re-up. So get your raggedy asses moving."

Munchie's eyes caught Jermaine's. "What's up, Baby Boo?"

"I don't think all the cops that ran in left out," Jermaine said.

"Really?"

"I was watching, and I seen a black cop and a white cop run up the stairs when they all came in. And they never left."

"You don't say."

&

Huggins listened to the kid and was impressed. This new Cobra had caught something the rest of them should've seen. Lucky for him.

Huggins thought he recognized the kid but couldn't place him. "Why they call you Baby Boo?"

"On account of my brother, Antwan."

"You Boo's little brother?" Huggins asked. "The one his momma sent to Mississippi?"

Jermaine shrugged. "Yeah."

Huggins saw it in the kid's face. The kid looked like his brother, had the same kind of round head, flat nose, and big eyes, almost buggy. He was dark, much more time in the sun than his brother. He was taller than Boo, looked stronger too, like he'd been worked hard on that farm in Mississippi. Antwan had had a mean streak that Huggins didn't see in this kid, but it was early. And with a little help, that could change. Huggins grinned.

"Your brother did right by me and I'm gonna do right by him." Huggins jerked a thumb at Keloid. "Boo was like Keloid there. He was my guy, you know, my main man. He did a lot of shit for me, spoke for me, and did what I told him." Huggins stood. "You think you can do that kinda shit?"

Jermaine's eyes opened like he was coming to life.

"Whoa." Huggins held out a hand. "I got to get another crew together. Get some Cobras I can trust, you feel me? Since you're Boo's baby brother, you gonna be one of 'em. Like them college fraternity brothers do. What do they call that shit?"

"Legacy," Keloid said.

"Yeah, that's it. We gonna start you slow and see how you do." Huggins adjusted his crotch with one hand. "I think he'd like that. We got to do something about that name, though. What's your real name?"

"Jermaine."

"A'ight, I'm gonna call you Maine. Yeah, I like that." Huggins looked at Keloid, who nodded back at him. "Okay, Maine, you got someone you trust? Someone who can work with you?"

Maine looked at the wall and seemed to be thinking on it.

Huggins laughed. "That a hard question?"

"Ain't but one person I even know around here since I got back, and I don't think he's Cobra material."

"Who's that?" Huggins asked.

"White Boy." Maine looked at the floor. "I got violated in with him, but he didn't pass."

"You mean that white lab-rat looking motherfucker?"

"Yeah."

Huggins laughed. "You think you can trust him? He seem kinda weak."

Maine looked up. "He want to be a Cobra so bad. He do about anything."

"Why didn't he pass?"

"'Cause they played Cobra roulette and he didn't want to put the gun to my head, that's why." Maine stood still like a soldier. "He'd do what I tell him. I know for sure he will."

"That good." Huggins stared down at him. *Every man needed his own bitch,* he thought.

Chapter 13

Hot Foot

Macbeth lay on his back at the foot of the Cabrini-Green Project building, gazing skyward propped on his elbows. Many of the building's windows had been opened to fight Chicago's outrageous heat. A hot breeze billowed curtains out as it pushed puffy white clouds across a vibrant blue sky. The sun was high. He could feel his skin burn as sweat gushed from his pores.

A black teenager stood next to him. Antwan Simms leaned over the iron railing brandishing a flashy straight razor. The blade descended. It was sharp but felt ice cold as it sunk deep into Macbeth's throat. Warm blood bubbled then erupted from the gash. Simms's face peered down at him, splashed with bright crimson. Simms grinned, his teeth splattered with gore as he straightened. Latricia's face, charred flesh rent with pink canyons, leered down at Macbeth.

"Wake up." Ketchum shook him gently.

Macbeth found himself on the floor in the front hallway of the boarded-up apartment, his back against the wall.

"We hit this fucker too early," Ketchum said. "Told you we should've waited until we knew for sure Huggins was back. You know they been shutting down for good every time we hit this motherfucker. We're wasting our time up here."

"Give it a little more."

Ketchum looked at his watch and shrugged. "I guess, we over an hour into it already. What're a few more minutes?"

MACBETH HEARD SOMETHING. HE SAT UP. SOMETHING OR someone was outside their hideaway. He peeked around the corner at the front door and the plywood. He got up onto his haunches, bringing his .45 to bear. Ketchum came around behind him. A dark liquid seeped under the door and spread toward the hallway.

"What the fuck?" Macbeth mouthed the words as the smell stung his nostrils. "Gas!"

"What?" Ketchum scrunched his face like he didn't understand.

A bright flash sparked as Macbeth drove Ketchum back. Heat seared the two cops with a poignant whoosh. Macbeth felt the oxygen sucked from his chest. He tried to yell but his voice was stolen.

Ketchum's eyes widened. A fireball blossomed over the pool of liquid and greasy black smoke curled up to the ceiling. Ketchum shifted his gaze to the windows in the living room.

"We got to get the fuck out!" Ketchum said in a croak.

Macbeth knew those windows overlooked the parking lot, but they were fourteen floors up. Every time he tried to breathe it was like his lungs were on fire. His eyes stung, and his nostrils burned.

Flames coiled under the plywood. Tongues of fire spread farther into the apartment, igniting the remnants of something hanging on the wall. The crackling of flames was unmistakable in the eerie quiet. Another whoosh. Someone was outside splashing more gasoline on the inferno.

Macbeth rushed over to the doorway, avoiding the flaming pool of gasoline. He felt heat emanate from the plywood. The panel was already loose. He looked back at Ketchum, who was tugging a window open. He holstered his gun and strode over to Teddy, yanking him back from the window.

"Forget it! We're fourteen floors up!" He coughed and dragged Ketchum toward the front door.

Macbeth turned his back to the plywood and mule-kicked the board as hard as he could, putting all his weight behind his boot. Of course it was the side whose screws weren't loose. The wood gave partially. Smoke leaked in at a faster rate. Macbeth could hardly breathe. He kicked through the flames again. The top screw came lose and the sheet yawed open, admitting roiling flames and clouds of turbulent black smoke.

Macbeth's lungs hurt, threatening to make him retch. He kicked again. The board fell awkwardly, bridging the flames. He could hardly keep his eyes open against the black boiling clouds. "Teddy!" His voice was a hoarse croak.

Macbeth felt Ketchum's hand on his shoulder. He drew his .45 again and charged across the warped, burning wood, keeping the pistol close to his body. He flashed through the flames and found himself in the breezeway. He turned left. Ketchum followed and went right. Ketchum yelled something he couldn't understand.

Macbeth turned and saw someone disappear into the stairwell.

Huggins?

Ketchum stood coughing and pointing, gripping his radio to his mouth. Macbeth pushed past his partner and raced after whoever it was. A dark form ran down the stairwell below him. He leapt down the stairs in pursuit. Two floors below, the man went into the breezeway. Macbeth followed, coughing up what he thought might be one of his lungs as he ran. When he made the breezeway, the running man was disappearing into the opposite stairwell. Macbeth ran faster, not taking the time to aim his handgun. He couldn't shoot, not yet.

The man was running up now and Macbeth hit the stairs, taking them two at a time, his lungs still on fire. It didn't feel as if he could draw in any oxygen. He retched and spat as he ran.

Was it Huggins? Maybe? But could he trust his own eyes? From below, Macbeth saw the man sprint into the sixteenth-floor breezeway, the top floor. Macbeth was still two floors behind, so he raced up to and out onto fifteen, sprinting for the other stairwell to cut his quarry off.

Just as he rounded into the stairwell, he ran headlong into a woman. They both fell. Macbeth's gun rattled down a couple of steps. She screamed at him. Ignoring her, Macbeth got up and grabbed his Smith and Wesson, then sprinted back to the other side. When he got there the man was already six or seven floors below, gaining with every step.

I'll never catch him now, Macbeth thought. He slowed, took two more steps, fell to his knees, and threw up.

After a few minutes, he made his way to the fourteenth floor. Ketchum had moved the burning sheet of plywood from the doorway. When Macbeth stopped and leaned against the fencing, Ketchum looked at him. The black officer's face was covered in soot, his cheeks streaked from tears. Blaring sirens could be heard from below.

Ketchum's Adam's apple bobbed as he swallowed. "Ain't no doubt about it, dude." His voice was a dry croak. "Lonnie's back."

Chapter 14

Too Close

THURSDAY 0010 Hours

Jermaine Taylor stood on Division, his chest still pumping hard from his run down the stairwell. He'd taken off as soon as the cop started kicking the wood. He expected the shooting to start at any second as he jumped down the stairs, half flight at a time. As he'd run off, he'd seen Huggins still pouring gas on the fire. Huggins was crazy mean, the look in his eyes insane. As Jermaine caught his breath, he watched cops run into the lobby and heard the sirens from the fire trucks down the street. He walked away but turned when he heard the lobby door burst open, banging against the wall. Huggins came out laughing.

Huggins stepped out of the lobby. He'd had to wait for the cops to run past the floor he was hiding on, and now he was out in the fresh air. He was thankful for the exercises he'd been doing in prison.

He needed to find Keloid and get the fuck out of there before more cops came. But he didn't see his big friend anywhere. He turned toward Division and started walking, hoping Keloid would pull up any second. He saw Maine walking along Division. Kid had some stones, stayed on fourteen until the cops started cooking. He smiled at the thought of those cops burning up. Fuck them. Now it was time to get down to business.

Huggins figured sales had to be way down with this Pac-Man closing shop every time the police came by. Why the fuck was Cee playing scared? It wasn't like he was afraid of the fucking cops. Hell, his ass wasn't slinging rocks. What'd he have to be scared about?

Huggins made Division and the traffic picked up. Where the fuck was Keloid? Plenty of people were driving through Cabrini. He could hear the sirens. Maybe he'd walk over to the orange doors and find a pay phone.

He waited for a gap in the traffic. He needed to put some distance between himself and cops.

Huggins crossed the street and was cutting across the back lot of the 534 Scott building when he heard a revving car engine. His first thought was the cops. He turned as tires squealed on the pavement. A four-door car swerved from the far lane into oncoming traffic, careening toward him. He crouched.

Huggins watched a hand stab out of the window. Bright orange flame pierced the dark. He saw the gun as the explosion reached his ears. He was already halfway to the cement when another shot exploded. He rolled and heard the car accelerate. Another shot rang in his ears. He couldn't tell much about the car other than it was big and dark with four doors.

Huggins got to his feet. He wasn't hit. He saw the car, a bubble Chevy, turn hard onto Clybourn and disappear. Across the street he saw Maine staring at him, mouth open, eyes saucer wide.

❧

JERMAINE PICKED HIMSELF UP OFF THE GROUND AND BRUSHED himself off. Lonnie Huggins was across the street doing the same thing, except that the gang enforcer was staring after the car with the shooter. Like he wasn't afraid of nothing, and he probably wasn't. Jermaine wished he could be like that, be like him. That's how Boo was going to be, never afraid; everybody scared of him, respecting him.

Jermaine had recognized the car and its driver, Pac-Man.

Chapter 15

Hedging Your Bet

THURSDAY 1030 Hours

Mavis Stomps dialed the number for the superintendent's office. The line was answered by a female. "Office of the Superintendent. How may I help you?"

"This is Alderman Stomps. I need to meet with the superintendent."

"Who is this?"

"Alderman Mavis Stomps, 27th Ward." She let some irritation creep into her voice. "Elected official. Assistant Chairman of the Police/Fire Committee."

"Of course, ma'am." The receiver was covered for a second then she was on hold, music playing in her ear. Another female voice came on: "Hello, ma'am? This is Peggy, I've got the superintendent's schedule in front of me. I understand that you'd like to come down and talk to him. I could fit you in first thing next week, would you be able to come by on—"

"I'll talk to him today." The irritation remained in her voice, with the promise of escalation.

"I'm sorry, ma'am, but he's not even in the state today. He's in

Washington, D.C. He should be back tomorrow, but he'll have a lot of catching up to do. I'm afraid I don't see a realistic opportunity until late this week at the earliest. If it's an emergency I could put you in touch with the First Deputy."

"That's unacceptable." Stomps took a dramatic deep breath. The woman started to say something, and Stomps cut her off. "I assume he has his portable phone with him, give me his number. I'll call him myself."

"I'm sorry, ma'am, I can't give that number out." The woman sounded a little annoyed or maybe a little on edge. "You could email him, though. He'll get that instantly and he's usually good about replying."

She didn't have any good response, so she hung up.

The computer on her desk wasn't on and hadn't been on in quite a while. She hated the thing, hated doing business through email, the phone was bad enough. She didn't like to leave any kind of trail. She hit the intercom button on her phone. "Email Plumb and have him call me right away."

"Yes, ma'am."

A few minutes later her secretary rang back. "He said he's in a meeting and will call as soon as he can."

That asshole. How long would she be made to wait?

TWO HOURS LATER, SHE WANTED TO PUNCH SOMETHING. SHE was close to giving in and having some whiskey when her phone finally rang. She snatched up the receiver. "Hello."

"Alderman Stomps. This is Superintendent Plumb. How can I help you?" The superintendent sounded jovial, but he usually did.

"I assume you're aware of the situation with this Officer Macbeth in the Eighteenth District?" She hoped she'd catch him by surprise and have an advantage over his pompous ass.

She thought she could hear voices in the background, maybe even dishes clattering. Was he eating?

"What is it you want to know?"

"I'd like to know when you're going to take that officer off the street, for starters. I understand there's evidence suggesting he's more culpable than originally thought."

"Really?" Plumb slurped something. "I'm sorry, but I'm not aware of anything of the sort."

"I can't believe you don't know about these new charges."

"Well, I can say there's an investigation into allegations involving this officer. I have the utmost confidence in IAD, but I don't ask them to inform me at every single turn of the investigation, just with solid conclusions substantiated by facts. I don't make snap decisions, nor do I make decisions based on partial findings. When the facts are all in, I'll make the right call."

"Sounds like a cover-up to me."

"I'm really disappointed that you feel that way."

"Then why hasn't the boy's mother been told the truth about how her son died?"

"You mean, ah… Ms. Collins, I believe? Ms. Donna Collins." A voice whispering in the background suggested that someone was feeding him information. "I believe we told her at the conclusion of the initial investigation how her son died. We're investigating these new allegations vigorously. Rest assured, if we uncover something that makes us suspect our original finding, we'll reopen the case. Until then, the original ruling stands."

"In the meantime, this poor woman has to sit there knowing some rogue cop killed her son. You think she doesn't know what the truth is? And the monster that murdered him is still out there on the street, free to kill some other mother's boy. That's pretty harsh."

"And pulling this officer off the street when, up to this point, our investigation indicates he did nothing wrong, that doesn't sound harsh?"

"The woman with the dead son clearly outweighs what one officer might suffer from being pulled off the street. You're a father. I can't believe we're even having this argument."

"Ma'am, we're obviously not going to agree and, quite frankly, I've got to go. If necessary, we'll have to continue this when I'm back."

"Really, I don't think I've said all that I wanted to."

"I'm really sorry, but I've got to get back to the committee meeting. Talk to Peggy. She'll schedule a time when we can continue this conversation. And maybe by then, there'll be more information available. So we can talk specifics and not supposition."

He disconnected before she could take the phone away from her ear. She could feel her face flush with anger. How dare he treat her with such disregard, like he didn't give a damn. He was going to find out how she felt. Asshole.

But Plumb's secretary had said something about the First Deputy Superintendent, the man who was second in charge of the department. And the man was better suited to her ability to persuade. She could make that work for her. Divide and conquer. Why hadn't she thought of calling him earlier?

Mavis looked up the number and tapped it into her desk phone.

"Chicago Police Department, Office of the First Deputy," said the woman who answered.

"This is Alderman Stomps. Is the First in?" She'd met James Parks on several occasions. He was responsible for day-to-day operations. Since he was black, it was surmised that he'd been given short shrift by Plumb. Parks had risen through the ranks of the department and was a staunch advocate for black issues. Maybe Plumb kept him out of the loop, so he and his cronies could continue to violate the rights of the black community. Even to her ears that sounded ludicrous, but the media would probably buy into it.

After a short half-a-minute hold, Parks came on the line.

"Alderman Stomps." His voice was low and syrupy. "What can I do for you?"

"Good afternoon, First Deputy." Stomps had discovered long ago that men loved being stroked, particularly those second in command. "I appreciate you taking my call."

"My pleasure."

Mavis heard Parks say something to someone else. She couldn't quite make out what, but it sounded like he was dismissing a subordinate. Then he said, "It's not every day that the assistant chairman of the police-fire committee calls, particularly one so young and attractive."

The other co-chair of the committee was a hag from the Southwest

Side. A lifetime of drinking and overeating had left her swollen, like an overstuffed sausage. This was going to be easier than Mavis had thought. Especially with Parks's reputation as a ladies' man.

"Flattery will get you whatever you want," she said. She tried to make her laugh sultry. Parks was old enough to be her daddy's play uncle. She had to admit, though, that the man dressed well and kept himself in shape.

"Will it, now," Parks said. She could practically feel his smile over the phone. "What would you have me do?"

"Are you familiar with Antwan Simms?"

"Not that I recall. Should I be?" he asked.

"He's the boy that was killed last winter by police in the Seventh District."

"Shot to death?"

"No, thrown from the second story of an abandoned house."

"Thrown by the police? Or fell?"

"Well, the official story is he fell, but there have been new allegations that the officer, a Stacey Macbeth, threw him out of a window," she said.

"A female officer?"

"No, male."

"And your concern about this is related to your position on the committee?"

"Actually, the boy was from my ward and I'm looking for some closure for his mother, who is one of my constituents. Some people here in Cabrini have started a protest at the Eighteenth District where the cop works. I'd like to get some answers without dragging the city, and the department, through the mud."

"I see. Have you spoken to Superintendent Plumb about this?"

"Yes, I have."

"And?"

"And nothing. He seems to be looking the other way. He says internal affairs is investigating."

"I would imagine they are. Plumb doesn't like to get ahead of an investigation."

"Meanwhile, Antwan's grieving mother's hearing all this, knowing the cop that killed her son is still on the street. That doesn't seem right."

"Well, I can see where you're coming from, but we do have procedure and policy to adhere to, contractual obligations as well."

"Oh, so you're going to parrot Plumb? Don't you have children?"

"That's not fair, ma'am."

"Please call me Mavis."

"Okay, Mavis, you can call me James. To answer your question, I do have kids. But I don't see that's an issue here."

"Sure it is, James. I don't have kids myself, but when I look at that woman, I can see the pain in her eyes. I don't see how any parent could let something like this drag on when it's in their power to assuage her grief."

"I assure you. If we find any wrongdoing on the part of Officer Macbeth, he will be held accountable."

"Do you think Ms. Collins will get any comfort from that?"

"Her kid was a gangbanger and there's no proof, yet, the cop did anything wrong."

"It's not wrong to throw gangbangers to their death?"

"We don't know that happened."

"Somebody does, and that's what I'm talking about. Shouldn't Macbeth be off the street or something until this thing is decided?"

"I'll tell you what. Let me make some calls and see what I can do. Give me a number where I can reach you, and I'll call you back by the end of the day."

Stomps chewed her lip a moment before answering. "I'm planning a little getaway tonight, staying downtown to relax. But here's the number of where I'll be staying, call me."

"Maybe I should reach out to you tomorrow so as not to spoil your getaway."

She paused, knowing she had him right where she needed him to be. "I'll be on my own, James, so please do call. I could use a little good news."

Chapter 16

Those Who Stare Into the Belly of the Beast

THURSDAY 1100 Hours

Lauren Cahill stayed in the air-conditioned apartment and watched for her ride through the beveled glass of the front door. It was way too hot. She wasn't looking forward to the summer since spring had been so godawful muggy. According to the papers, people were dropping dead from the heat all over the city.

She shifted her weight from one foot to the other. The private detective had told her to dress in a very particular way for their interview, but she couldn't bring herself to wear a tight shirt, a short skirt, and high heels, way too unprofessional.

She found the request insulting. *I'm no clueless bimbo*, she thought. She was really good and would be able to garner whatever information was needed through her ability to interview and investigate. She took herself seriously as a journalism masters student and knew, given the chance, the professor would too.

But when she'd talked to the private detective who was her contact, and essentially her professor's teaching assistant this semester, he made her feel slimy and totally cheap. They were going to be in the housing projects, and he expected her to be wearing high heels with a mini skirt. That was ludicrous.

When she'd spoken to Professor Rabinowicz earlier in the week, she'd found him to be driven, completely immersed in what they did for class, doing the legwork for the Program for the Wrongfully Convicted cases. He had said to listen to Jay Konrad, the detective, and while she might find his instructions unusual, she was to take them as if they'd come straight from the professor's mouth. He hadn't said anything about how to dress.

Konrad had told her when they'd talked on the phone to dress as if she were going clubbing. And Konrad had been insistent. "Show some leg," he'd said, "a great deal of leg, and boobs too." He'd claimed it "helped foster an enthusiasm to talk" in their subjects. She found Konrad creepy.

Finally, a dinged-up, robin's-egg blue, four door Japanese car crept down the street. She stuck her head out to get a better look. The guy she'd talked to said he was white, with curly dark hair. The driver matched the description, except his curly dark hair was all but totally receded.

She stepped out and double locked the deadbolt before making her way down the porch. When they made eye contact, Konrad waved. He wore a bright red Hawaiian shirt and plucked a cigarette from between his lips, then shook his head and scowled. He rolled his window down and flicked his cigarette out. Lauren slipped between two parked cars and opened the passenger door. Sliding her backpack on the floor, she hopped in.

She extended her hand and said, "Hi, I'm Lauren."

He looked her up and down. "Didn't you listen to what I told you?"

She didn't say anything.

"Go change," Konrad said.

"I don't really think—"

"If you ain't gonna listen, then you're out, doll. And I'll get a girl that can take direction."

"The professor never—"

Konrad grabbed a bag phone from between his feet and thumbed an icon. Lauren hadn't seen a phone like that before. He lit another cigarette while he waited for an answer.

"Hey, Professor. It's Jay." He blew smoke toward the open window. "Yeah, ah, Miz Cahill has a problem with the wardrobe." While he talked, the lit end of the cigarette bobbed up and down, the smoke curling in on itself. He held the phone out to her.

She took it and watched him as she brought the phone to her ear. "Hi."

"Miss Cahill." She recognized Professor Rabinowicz's voice, but he sounded preoccupied. "I thought I was perfectly clear that you needed to listen to what Mr. Konrad tells you."

"Yes, but he asked me to dress pretty inappropriately."

She heard him sigh. "Inappropriately?"

"Yes, sir. Real short skirt, tight shirt with cleavage—"

"A good journalist must be flexible," he said, interrupting. "Do you understand that?"

"Yes, but—"

"I'm not going to argue with you." Now it seemed she had his complete attention. "But if you're unwilling to follow instructions, I'll have no option but to replace you with someone who can. It's the '90s for god's sake."

"I see." Lauren felt tears collect in her eyes. She'd be damned if she'd let Konrad see them.

"What's it going to be, young lady?" She could hear the professor tapping his fingers on something hard, like his desk. "Are you with us or do I need to get my waiting list out?"

Lauren took a deep breath. "Can I go today as I am?"

"No. Certainly not. Do what Mr. Konrad told you."

She handed the phone back to Konrad and popped the door open. "I'll go change." She hoped he'd get a ticket while he waited.

WHEN SHE CAME DOWN FIFTEEN MINUTES LATER, DRESSED IN A tight-fitting top, a short skirt and her tall heels, she found Konrad still parked where she'd left him in the middle of the street. He'd put his flashers on, and she saw another car was having a hard time getting around Konrad's car. What an asshole. She got in, pressing her skirt's hem to her thigh so it wouldn't ride up, and closed the door. The car stunk of cigarettes and something else, stale fast food.

"That's more like it, honey." He extended a stubby hand toward her. "Now, you can call me Jay."

She took it. "Lauren." She glanced at the debris on the floor and back seat: newspapers, books, shirts, gloves and fast-food wrappers, mostly White Castle's.

Konrad whistled. "Man, the professor said you were a real looker." He eyed her breasts, then pulled away from where he was parked. "But even so, he didn't do you justice, not by a far stretch."

This guy made her feel slimy, but she was determined to not let him get to her. After all, they were tied together for at least this semester. "I'm sure you say that to all of the students." She put on the seatbelt, snugging it tight.

Konrad stopped at the end of her block. "I call them like I see them." He took a pack of cigarettes from on top of the dash and shook one out, pulling it from the pack with his lips. He tossed the pack on the dashboard. "Generally, the professor provides attractive girls for these cases, but you're a real cut above the rest." He pulled into traffic from her side street.

"Do you work with Professor Rabinowicz regularly?" Lauren said.

"Yeah." Konrad pulled a plastic lighter from his shirt pocket and flicked the flame on. He held it to the tip of his cigarette. He inhaled, then blew smoke toward his open window. "I do a lot of the legwork for him and the other attorneys in the program."

"This is my first outing, so I'm looking forward to the experience."

Konrad turned and took a long look. Longer than she was comfortable with, especially considering he was driving. He smiled, then looked back at the road. "You mean I got your cherry?"

"That's not the way I'd prefer you look at it." She stared at the road and settled back into the seat. "Doesn't the professor use any guys in his projects?"

"Not very often." Konrad pulled up to an intersection and looked down the cross street as if he was thinking about running the red light.

"Why not?" Now that she thought about it, she couldn't remember talking to any men who'd been involved in the classes.

"Well," the light changed and Konrad accelerated, "most of the people we're dealing with," he took a deep drag, holding the smoke in before speaking, "let's just say they react better to women."

"Considering how I'm being made to dress." Lauren shook her head. "I'd wager they like girls, and the more girl they see, the better."

"You got it," Konrad said.

This was starting to sound outrageous. She wasn't sure she wanted to go through with it. Still, the professor must have his reasons.

"What exactly am I expected to do?"

"Just sit there and look pretty," Konrad said. "First, we've got to interview the client. Then the real work begins when we track down the evidence he provides. I'll explain that phase of the operation to you when we get there. Hopefully today yet." He stared at her breasts again. "Do you have a push-up bra?"

"No."

"You might want to get one."

She folded her arms across her chest, hoping that would limit Konrad's view. "Is our guy's attorney going to there?"

"No." Konrad accelerated when the light turned green. "He's not even in the program anymore. Once upon a time he was, in fact, I think he might be one of the originals. But he got out before the program started making money hand over fist. Sherman Gold represents this asshole we're going to see today."

"Asshole?" She was taken aback. "Aren't we supposed to be on his side?"

He glanced at her. "Trust me when I tell you, this guy's a bad dude. I've seen his file."

"Really? Then why are we bothering?"

"Because that's what we do." He blew out more blue-gray smoke. "We do what the professor and lawyers say. I don't ask them lots of questions."

"So, what do we do then?"

"We run down leads, mostly, check the story this guy feeds us." He spat the cigarette out the window. "We talk to people. See what we can shake loose. You got that recorder the professor told you to get?"

"Yeah." She dug into her backpack and removed the digital voice recorder. She held it up for him to see. It was slim and chrome, with black buttons along one side.

"Oh, man." Konrad held out his hand. She gave it to him. "You splurged on a digital one. These puppies are expensive. Your mom and dad must be loaded." He looked at her, then to the road. "You got any pockets?"

"No."

"I don't suppose you want to stick it between your tits?"

She wanted to slap him. "What?"

"Okay, hold it under your notebook or something. It's important that you have it, has to do with discovery or lack thereof, actually. The professor says the prosecutors can't badger you students like they would us real investigators, but don't put that in your notes, definitely not in your paper."

He was referring to the summary she was expected to write following each outing, detailing what they'd done, who'd they'd talked to and what their subjects had to say. She assumed the recorder was to ensure she got everything right; they were, after all, going to release the information they gathered to the defense attorneys. The culmination of the class was to be a paper covering the entire quarter's efforts, written as if it were an investigative reporter's piece.

"Who are we going to see?" she asked, hoping to change the subject.

"File's on the back seat." Konrad pointed over his shoulder.

Lauren reached over and picked up the manila folder. She opened it and leafed through the pages, which comprised a criminal history printout for Alonzo Huggins. These sheets came directly from the prosecutor's office.

Huggins had twenty-seven arrests. Seventeen of them were felonies. He'd been caught carrying guns and taken in for murder twice. He'd only been convicted once, and the charge had been changed from murder to involuntary manslaughter and he'd only gotten three years. He'd been arrested for strong armed robbery and armed robbery. There were also drug cases. Battery to P.O. seemed to be added to just about every arrest, was that police officer or parole officer?

She finally leaned back in her seat and watched Greektown roll past. As Konrad drove, she recognized when he steered them onto the Miracle Mile, North Michigan Avenue. Cabrini-Green was close, but easily a mile west. Konrad glanced around like he was looking for a parking spot.

"I thought we were going to Cabrini-Green?" she said.

"Not initially." Konrad looked at her. "Gold has this guy stashed in a hotel on Michigan Avenue. Once we talk to him, we'll head over to the 'jets and see who we can find to talk to."

"Jets?"

"Short for pro-jects." He pronounced the second syllable as "jets." A few minutes later, Konrad fit his car into a tight spot on Erie, hopped out, and slid an orange parking ticket under his windshield wiper. He caught her staring. "What?" He shrugged his shoulders. "I can't afford these new meter rates, they're crazy." He started off down the street. "Not on what I'm getting paid."

"Aren't you afraid of your ticket fine increasing if you don't pay it right away?" She was practically running to keep up, wobbling in her heels.

He stopped and turned. "You think that's my ticket?" He laughed. "You got a lot to learn, honey. And don't record our client."

Huggins answered the door of his hotel room dressed in a fluffy white bathrobe that made his chocolate skin seem even darker. He wasn't huge, but he was lean and bulging with compact muscles that looked like they were made of wire. His hair was teased out in an Afro, making him seem taller than his six feet something. When his eyes locked on hers, it was as if he looked right into her soul.

Huggins asked, "Gold send you?" It wasn't a question as much as an accusation. His eyes looked like those of a python, flat and dark, devoid of any compassion.

"Yeah." Konrad wiped his forehead. "I'm Jay. This is Lauren." He gestured toward her. "She works for me." He offered his hand. "Nice to meet you."

Huggins smirked, stepping back from the doorway. "You a lawyer?"

Konrad cleared his throat and strode into the hotel room. "No, but I work directly for him."

"So, you his boy." A gleaming gold front tooth showed between Huggins's thick lips. "Shit, Sherman should be here." Huggins didn't speak loudly, but still made the point he was used to getting his way.

"He's pretty busy." Konrad took the file from Lauren and flipped it open. "This is a preliminary meeting and he's in court today." He looked up from the pages. "Besides, we're just here to take some notes so we can start running things down."

Lauren felt a bead of sweat trickle between her breasts despite the room's cold temperature. Konrad turned. Huggins closed the door, threw the bolt, and turned to face them. He folded his arms across his chest. What she could see of it below the robe's sleeves was covered with dark blue tattoos.

He stared right at her cleavage. Lauren was suddenly afraid the stress sweat under her arms would be visible, along with the flush beginning to creep up her chest and neck toward her cheeks. This guy scared her. Did that make her a racist? Who was she to make that kind of judgment against this man? He hadn't benefited from a comfortable upbringing like she had. Who knew what he'd been exposed to as a kid? Living in poverty and in the housing projects, probably none of this was his fault, really.

Huggins ran his tongue across his front teeth and turned his attention on Konrad. "You work for him, huh?"

"Yeah, I'm his investigator."

Lauren realized that Konrad had to get this guy to trust him to some extent or this was a wasted trip, and Professor Rabinowicz wouldn't like that. She could understand why a guy with Huggins's background would be distrustful of the system, especially one as broken as theirs.

Konrad pulled a yellow legal pad out of the file and took a pen from his shirt pocket.

Lauren tried to avoid looking at Huggins directly, but she felt his eyes on her. He seemed to be enjoying her discomfort.

Konrad continued, "Gold said you might have info relevant to the appeal he's putting together."

Huggins leaned back against the wall into a sliver of sunlight. Lauren could see the blue tattoos clearly, snakes and half-moons and five-pointed stars, and some names. She also noticed a deep blue teardrop tattoo under his left eye.

"My boy." Huggins smiled. "My lawyer boy, in prison with me, he say this be more like for a motion or some shit."

"Really?" Konrad said. "In the end, Gold will be the judge, but..."

Huggins frowned.

Konrad shrugged and wrote *motion* across the top of the blank page. "Okay, give me what you've got."

"That poh-leece, Macbeth. He the one keep locking me up. He don't like niggas much."

"Uh huh."

She noticed a slight tremor in Konrad's hand and wondered if his hand started shaking would he lose what credibility he had with this guy. Had he even established any yet? They hadn't covered how to establish credibility with this type of oppressed individual in grad school.

"Macbeth planted them guns on me."

"Okay." Konrad wrote on his pad. She couldn't see what he'd jotted down, but it looked like he was about to push the pen through the paper. "We're going to need more than that. What else? Got any witnesses?"

"Yep. That boy Boo, but they killed him."

"That's the kid who died on Sangamon, right? Ah." Konrad flipped through the file. "Antwan Simms."

"Yep. Like I said, that why Macbeth killed him. He knew the truth."

"Okay. What else?" Konrad didn't look up from his pad.

"Last couple times I been locked up, it's been Macbeth who done it. He been putting cases on me like he trying to keep me down. Locked up for shit I didn't do."

"Why would he do that?"

"Well, like I say, he don't like niggas. He a racist."

Konrad licked his lips and Lauren found herself trying to do the same. But her tongue was as dry as her lips.

"And?" Konrad said.

"Reason I found out was, he was banging my girl."

"By girl, you mean, ah, Latricia, right?" said Konrad.

Lauren couldn't help but look up. She found herself staring into eyes that could have been made of obsidian.

"Yeah," Huggins said.

"Latricia who?" Lauren asked, not recognizing the name.

"Latricia Gibbons. Macbeth kept locking my ass up so he could keep fucking her." Huggins's stare held Lauren's, but there was no feeling, just blankness.

"And how do you know this?"

"Latricia came to see me right before she—you know—passed. She told me that Macbeth was out to get me. She was warning me."

Lauren wished she'd read the file more thoroughly or had a copy as Konrad flipped through the pages for a minute. She didn't recognize the names or circumstances they were talking about.

"Passed?" Konrad took his pen from the pad. "You mean she was murdered, right? Someone put four or five bullets into her chest before they burnt her up." He paused and cleared his throat. He began tapping the page with his pen. "Police claim you had something to do with it. They think you ordered your boys to do it."

"Man." Huggins let out a breath. "That's some bullshit. I was in jail and my boys wouldn't touch her. She the momma of my babies." His voice rose.

"Sure, you don't have to convince me." Konrad wrote "*Macbeth + Latricia*" on his notepad and started to draw circles around it. "Hey, I thought you said he was a racist and didn't like black folk."

"That's people, man, people." The dark face twisted into a scowl. "Lots of racists fuck sisters. That don't mean shit."

Lauren was suddenly afraid Konrad was going to piss Huggins off.

"How do you know all of this?" Konrad asked.

"Like I said, she told me." Huggins shifted his stare to Konrad. "Ain't that like some kind of deathbed shit?"

"I'm afraid that would only carry weight in court if she knew she was dying when she said it. Unless you could tell me she knew she was about to die after saying it, I don't see how that could help us much. But it's something."

The band of Lauren's underwear suddenly felt tight and damp.

"Anyone else who can corroborate what she said?" Lauren asked.

"Yeah, that boy Dease." Huggins said. He stared at her breasts again.

"How'd you talk to Dease?" Konrad asked, shooting her a look that she thought was meant to keep her quiet.

"Bumped into him in county. He scared he gonna be next." Huggins sneered. "Like I said, Boo knew too much and that was why Macbeth killed him."

"Dease told you this?"

"Go ask him yourself." His voice rose again.

"Sure, Lonnie, I told you, you don't have to convince me."

"Macbeth probably killed her, too. Maybe she was kicking him to the curb, and he got homicidal like white people do." He paused and flashed his smile, but his eyes still looked hard and mean. The gold tooth glinted in the sunlight. "For all she was, the girl could fuck. I can see why Macbeth'd get crazy for that pussy."

Lauren felt herself flush.

"Anyone else?" Konrad asked.

Huggins was looking at her breasts again. His eyes drifted lower. "Yeah. Latricia's girlfriend, her name Liberty Collins. She was Boo's Auntie." He rattled off an apartment number. "Didn't Gold give you the list?"

"Okay. We'll get on it."

"Yeah, you do that." Huggins pushed off the wall. "Check Latricia's phone, I bet you find that cop's number on it. Check his, too. Talk to some of the people on her floor. I bet he made some of them special house calls, know what I mean."

"So, Latricia told you she was cheating?" Konrad asked.

"Shit, I was gone for a while. Bitch got needs too."

"Were you loyal to her?"

Lauren couldn't believe Konrad said it aloud.

"You mean while I was in prison?" Huggins said.

Konrad nodded and swallowed like he'd lost his courage.

Huggins turned, his eyes half closed and showing as much emotion as a shark before he takes your leg off at the hip. Slowly a big smile broke across his face. His gold tooth, with a star and moon cut out, shone bright.

Lauren couldn't help but think that was a "no." And that made her shudder.

Chapter 17

Killing The Day

THURSDAY 1130 Hours

Stacey Macbeth shoved the newspaper across the table. He couldn't read another word. The media had declared war on the police department: story after story about police officers "railroading" innocent men into confessing to crimes they "didn't commit," not to mention the coverage of the Cabrini demonstration against him. Some journalism program's professor's name kept cropping up linked with these stories. Was it really a fight for innocence or a money grab by the university? Most of the incidents didn't seem much different than his experience with Simms. It was so damn easy to second guess a decision an officer had a split second to make.

Macbeth picked up the TV remote and scrolled through the channels until something caught his eye. A picture of Cabrini was on the Chicagoland News Channel. He turned the volume up as the camera pulled back to cover a small crowd of people on the sidewalk in front of the Eighteenth District. A couple of the people in the background held signs. He couldn't read them, but he could easily guess what they said. A reporter extended a microphone to a pretty black woman who looked familiar. She said something, but it wasn't picked up.

The reporter fiddled with the mic. "Sorry, let me ask again. Alderman Stomps, you indicated earlier that you have some issues with the police department relative to their conduct within your ward, can you be more specific?"

Stomps, Macbeth thought, he'd heard of her.

"The police seem to treat the people of Cabrini like they're all criminals. I think it's past time we all get along and quit profiling African Americans as drug dealers."

"Is this something you've discussed with Superintendent Plumb?"

She laughed. "I can't even get that man to call me back to have a conversation, let alone to address an important matter for our minority community."

Macbeth snorted.

"Even given your status as co-chair of the Police/Fire Committee?"

"I think it's my status as a woman of color that keeps him from taking me seriously."

"Can you be specific as to a particular incident?"

"Take this young boy who was killed by the police just this past winter, Antwan Simms. We still can't get the police to tell us what really happened. And his killer's still working as a police officer right here in Cabrini-Green. I'm scared that he's going to victimize some other young black man."

Macbeth's jaw tightened.

"Didn't that happen in Englewood?"

"The boy was from here." She nodded vigorously. "And so was the cop. Tell me this, how does a cop from Cabrini go all the way out to Englewood to kill somebody and get away with it?"

Macbeth wanted to throw the remote against the wall, but just turned the TV off instead. No sense letting someone as out of touch as Alderman Stomps jerk his chain. God, it was hot. And apparently, it was going to get a good deal hotter for him.

He leaned the kitchen chair back to catch the faint breeze from the air conditioner. He had some time to kill. What was he going to do? He knew what he wanted to do! Go find Huggins and lock him up. But so far that hadn't come to pass.

He glanced at the clock, another ten minutes before he had to switch out his clothes from the washer. His landlord, a retired police sergeant, was always complaining if anyone left clothes to sit for more than a couple of minutes. Jack Camp was a pain in the ass. To hear him tell it, the old guy had been in some real tight spots when he'd been a cop. He loved to talk about them, always telling war stories every time Macbeth ran into him. Macbeth felt bad for the old guy, but still, he had better things to do.

He knew he should call his mom and dad. His sister would be at work and they'd be alone in the nursing home. But his mom couldn't talk since the stroke. She could hardly hold the phone, and his dad would give her the phone then forget. God, he hated calling, visits were depressing too. He stared at the phone but didn't move, feeling guilty for not being a bigger part of their lives. Was he an asshole? A bad son?

The phone rang. Caller ID said it was Hagen. He reluctantly answered. "What's up?"

"Going to the Sox game with Mike. Want to come?"

Macbeth considered his options. It beat sitting around feeling sorry for himself.

"What time?"

"One o'clock, I'll swing by and pick you up at twelve-thirty."

"Who's playing?" He wasn't that interested, but hearing Hagen's voice had brightened his spirits somewhat.

"Your Twinkies," Hagen said.

Macbeth chuckled, more to himself than to Hagen. Zito and Hagen both loved to bust his balls since he was from Minneapolis, even though he was a mostly converted White Sox fan.

"Beep when you hit the lot." Macbeth set the receiver in its cradle and stared at it. He knew he should pick it back up and call his parents, but he couldn't find the courage. *Maybe tomorrow*, he thought. *Maybe tomorrow.*

Macbeth brushed his teeth again and ran the shower, not letting it get very warm before he climbed in. He shaved under the jet of lukewarm water. He couldn't shake the thought of Huggins getting released. His gray T-shirt and olive-green cargo shorts were folded on top of his bed, a framed futon. As much as he'd been sleeping in the kitchen, a lot of clothes were left out atop the mattress, why put them away? Nothing seemed all that important anymore. Except putting that asshole Huggins back where he belonged.

A sharp beep sounded from the parking lot.

He grabbed his keys off the kitchen counter and pulled his White Sox hat on. He thought a second about grabbing his snub-nose off the top of the refrigerator. He hadn't carried it in a while. But characters like Huggins were out there. He picked it up and stuffed it into the back of his shorts.

He pushed out the door and locked it, then made his way down the three carpeted flights, thinking he should eat something before drinking. He opened the inner lobby door and abruptly stopped. His landlord was bent over in the foyer by the mailboxes, peeking outside. He wore an unbuttoned dress shirt and navy-blue uniform pants that were too short, white socks, and worn-out black loafers. One of Camp's arms extended behind him, fingers splayed, a signal to Macbeth to stop.

Camp had been a sergeant in Vice when he'd retired, and Macbeth had always managed a grudging respect for his time on the job. But the old guy was very opinionated and wasn't shy about broadcasting that opinion. Macbeth put up with it, knowing Camp was like an armed attack dog and was never without his little five-shot revolver.

The balconies of each apartment faced the other building and it was impossible not to stare into the apartment across the way. The end of each balcony featured decorative blocks made from concrete. More than one time, they'd saved Macbeth embarrassment as he'd climbed up and gotten into his own apartment via the sliding doors on the balcony. He always left them unlocked. The last thing he wanted was to buzz Camp and admit that he'd locked himself out.

For months, Camp had been complaining about someone's dog pooping on the little patch of grass that grew between the two apartment buildings. Before Macbeth could say anything, Camp ripped the door open and erupted from it surprisingly fast for someone of his age and condition.

"Can't deny it this time! I caught you red-handed."

Macbeth followed. His landlord confronted Lona Flores, the lady that lived on the second floor across the sidewalk from his apartment. She was in her fifties, wearing a sleeveless dress today. She clutched two leashes and a plastic baggie to her bosom, her two tiny dogs cowering behind her slender ankles. Macbeth tried to sneak around them and make for the parking lot.

Flores took a step back from Camp. She was sweet and spoiled her dogs like they were kids. Macbeth didn't know much about the pets other than they were small, hairy, and noisy. It was hard to tell, but Macbeth thought the things were trembling beneath their shaggy coats. He could hardly blame them. Camp could be intimidating. Macbeth slowed down to make sure the confrontation didn't get out of control.

"I been telling you for how long now not to let your mongrels defecate on my lawn?" It must have been a rhetorical question because Camp hardly paused for a breath. "Now I got evidence." He blocked her access to the two skinny samples on the lawn as if she was going to somehow destroy the steamy evidence.

Flores waved a plastic grocery bag at Camp. "I always clean up after my girls. I never leave any waste on the grass."

"Don't give me that shit." Camp put his hands on his hips. Macbeth was pretty sure the pun was unintended. "Still kills my grass, though, don't it. I don't care what you do, you're still gonna pay."

"It's not the feces that's bad, but the urine. And I don't let my—"

"Don't try and shift the blame after I caught you dirty."

Flores backed away a step. "You know, you're crazy." Her dogs had found some courage as they began to yap and hop around. "You're nuts."

Camp folded his arms across his chest as if he'd won. "I'm going to charge you to re-sod. That's what I'm going to do."

"What?!" Flores tightened her grip on the leashes. "That isn't enough grass even for one full piece of sod!" She shook her head. "Stay away from me." She looked around Camp at Macbeth. "You're my witness, you heard me warn him."

Camp laughed as Flores pulled something from one of the leashes. It was a black personal-use pepper spray canister.

"I'm warning you. I'll spray you if you get any closer!" She backed away and finally disappeared through her apartment building doorway, dragging the two dogs. As she made her escape, Macbeth did the same, ducking out to the parking lot to where Hagen was waiting in his car.

"What the fuck was that about?" Hagen asked as Macbeth climbed into the sporty Toyota.

Macbeth laughed. "You don't want to know."

Hagen cut through the alley, turning north on Austin. *Maybe this will take my mind off things*, Macbeth thought. He couldn't shake the memory of Huggins's smiling face, and the glint of his gold tooth. But he did find the jab of his five-shot into his kidney comforting.

Chapter 18

Once Upon A Time

THURSDAY 1230 Hours

Lauren Cahill's eyes tracked up the side of the Cabrini-Green Project building as Konrad pulled into the lot. The red brick monolith was huge. Collectively the buildings looked sizeable from several blocks away, but up close, they were absolutely gigantic and as wide as they were tall.

The afternoon sun glinted off row after row after row of window panes that made up the eastern face of the 1150-60 North Sedgwick building. Many of the windows were open, their curtains blowing in with the breeze from Lake Michigan. The air smelled clean and felt cool, but the heat was building and feeling heavy.

The car lurched and stopped. Konrad's cigarette dangled from his lips, threatening to spill ash as he threw the shift lever into park. They made eye contact, and he lifted his eyebrows.

"Grab your backpack." His cigarette jiggled as he talked, and the ash drifted like snow down the front of his red Hawaiian shirt. He adjusted a blue camouflage fishing type vest to cover the handgun holstered on his right hip. She figured the gun was legal.

They got out and she followed Konrad around to the trunk. He opened it and motioned with his head. "Throw your backpack in here." He hooked a thumb toward the project building. "You'll get us stuck up or killed. Just bring something to write on and write with, and the recorder."

She pulled out her reporter's notebook, digital recorder, and pen and dropped her bag down against the fender well. She stepped back, and he slammed the lid closed. He held his hand out, but she didn't understand.

He grabbed the notebook and recorder from her grasp. "Since you can't hide this nowhere on your person." He ran his eyes up and down her figure. She wanted to cover herself. "Hold it under the notebook like this." He demonstrated. She nodded and he gave them back. "Turn it on, sweet cheeks, and let's go."

He turned and walked up the wheelchair ramp toward the lobby door. Lauren followed. She shook her head, feeling ridiculous, wanting to hide. She accidently kicked an empty glass bottle and it skittered along the cement, making loud clinking sounds. The noise made her stomach cinch tighter and brought her attention back to where she was. This place was scary.

Konrad banged through the heavy steel lobby door. She trailed him and saw him step around both of the metal detectors set up just inside. A couple of black security guards stood farther within the lobby. The guards raised their hands for Konrad and Lauren to stop.

Konrad lifted his own arm, some kind of identification card in his palm. "It's all right, guys," he said. "I'm a detective." The guards exchanged glances. One of them shrugged, the other waved indifferently, and they resumed their conversation. Konrad and Lauren walked past them. Konrad knuckled the shiny elevator button as if he didn't want to touch it with his finger.

As they stepped into the elevator, the smell of urine assaulted her.

Konrad looked at Lauren over his shoulder. "Costume works every time." He jammed his ID in his vest pocket and spun to face the doors. "Can't expect too much for minimum wage." He reached over and pressed a button on the panel with his fist.

Lauren was too repulsed by the sticky tile of the elevator to see what floor he'd punched. The small, confined space was ripe with the stench of human waste. She wanted to hold her breath but realized it was much too late for that. Reflexively, she reached up and pinched her nose. Konrad laughed.

"Breathe through your mouth," he said. "But you might as well get used to it. Eau de Projects, available at your finest department stores." His laugh was amplified by the metal walls of the elevator. The floor rocked as the car stopped and the doors slowly rolled back with a clank, exposing a concrete hallway.

Konrad pushed past her and stopped in what served as an elevator lobby. He glanced at Lauren as she stepped off.

Stretching off to the right and left was a concrete path. On one side apartment doors were cut into the cinder block walls, on the other was heavy floor to ceiling chain-link fencing reinforcing a waist-height iron railing.

"The residents call this the porch." Konrad waved at the enclosed area in front of the apartments. "Once upon a time, like when the buildings were first built, the designers left one side of the buildings open; think of it as a communal balcony." He reached out and grabbed the top of the railing that still ran inside the fencing. "But the designers hadn't anticipated the nature of life in Chicago's housing projects. Soon, objects and the occasional person got pitched over the side, more times than not at the police." Konrad dug into his pants pocket. "As a result, the Chicago Housing Authority had to seal the balconies with thick fencing. It's still open as far as the sun, wind, and rain are concerned, not so much for the residents."

Lauren jumped a little when Konrad touched her shoulder. "Here." He thrust a wad of bills at her. She took the money. All twenties folded in half, hundreds of dollars.

"This shit don't go in your report either." His voice dropped to a whisper. "This is for the people we interview. They each get two hundred, but I can't give it to them. After we're done, tell them it's for lunch or something."

"Is that even legal?" This was not how she'd pictured this was going to be.

Konrad dipped his head toward her. "It is if you do it." He started down the hall. "Also, after you transcribe your tape when we're done, erase it."

She didn't have anywhere to put the money and finally slipped the bills into her bra and followed, promising herself she wouldn't let this asshole see her upset. "Professor Rabinowicz didn't say anything about money."

"Not everything is for publication, honey, which is why you're giving it to them and not me." Konrad stopped, pulled a list out of his pocket, and studied it, then glanced at her. "We're asking these people to take a chance out here. We can't expect them to come out of the woodwork just from the goodness of their hearts." He looked at his watch. "Is your recorder on?"

She nodded and checked the device that she was holding under her notebook to be sure. It was. She took a second to note the number on the apartment door.

Konrad knocked as he stuffed his list back in a vest pocket. While they waited, he pulled out his own notebook. The lock clicked and the door swung open.

A black woman stood in the doorway. She was about five ten and pushing two hundred pounds, and had on a tight orange sleeveless T-shirt. Equally tight yellow stretch pants showed the dimples in her thighs. Her feet sported lime green flip flops, her toenails were painted in alternating purple and gold to match her fingernails. She held an unlit cigarette between two fingers and looked from Konrad to Lauren as if she had been expecting two visitors.

Konrad motioned to Lauren. "I'm Detective Konrad. This is my associate, Ms. Cahill." The woman's eye slid from her to Konrad and back. Lauren half-waved. "Like I told you on the phone, Lonnie said we should have a conversation with you about Latricia Gibbons."

The woman opened the door completely and stepped back, allowing them in. Konrad entered. Lauren followed.

The room smelled clean and looked dust free despite the cigarette in the woman's hand. They were in the living room and there was a couch, a chair, and a child's playpen with a couple stuffed animals. Thin curtains hung in front of the windows and a TV atop a stand pushed up against one of the interior cinder block walls. The floor, white linoleum patterned with light blue-grey flecks, was covered by several throw rugs of various hues and patterns. The walls were painted white. Several brown and black replica paintings of native African girls hung on them. The kitchen opened around a corner. On the other side of the living room a hallway led deeper into the apartment to two doors that were both closed. Lauren figured a bedroom and a bath.

The woman shut the front door and locked it. "You want to know about Latricia fucking that cop."

"Yeah." Konrad flipped his notebook open. "Exactly." He twisted a pen and poised it over the notebook page before looking up at the woman. "But first," he said. "How do you spell your name again?"

"L-I-B-E-R-T-Y," she said. "That's my first name. C-O-L-L-I-N-S." Konrad scribbled in his notebook. Lauren wrote down the name, too.

"Okay." Konrad looked up at Collins. "You were saying that you were aware Latricia was having relations with a cop. Do you know his name?"

"Sure," she said. "Want me to spell it for you?"

"If you know how, you bet."

"M-A-C-B-E-T-H." Collins nodded with every letter. "I don't know his first name. But it's like Tracey or something."

"No need." Konrad was steadily writing. "We know who you're talking about."

"Right." Collins smiled.

"How is it that you know this?" Konrad asked.

"I was good friends with Latricia," Collins said. "She used to tell me all about it."

"Really," Konrad said. "Like what?"

"She told me that after the first time Macbeth locked up Lonnie, he came by and wanted to visit her." Collins removed a red disposable lighter from her bra. "He brought some beer and one thing led to another and the next thing she knew, he'd spent most of the night. After that, he come by all the time when Lonnie was locked up. He had the fever bad by then."

"Fever?" Lauren asked.

Collins laughed as she lit her cigarette. "Jungle fever, baby." She blew a stream of blue-gray smoke at Lauren. "Once you go black, you ain't never going back." She laughed, but her eyes hardened. Lauren wondered if she was waiting for an argument.

"Oh." Lauren felt intimidated by the woman's stare and caught a look from Konrad that he expected her to keep her mouth shut.

"What else?" Konrad asked Collins.

"After a while, I guess he started coming over while he was working. He got real comfortable." Collins took another drag on her cigarette. The smoke drifted down from her nostrils.

"What did his partner do?" Konrad asked.

"How I to know? Guess he stayed in the car. Or Macbeth came by hisself."

"What else?"

"She said he was always pumping her for information 'bout what Lonnie was up to. He was real concerned with Lonnie, like real hung up."

As Konrad and Collins continued to talk about the cop's visits, it occurred to Lauren that Collins didn't appear to have any verifiable information. Nothing exact, only rough time frames, like a week before she was killed or a month before Lonnie was released. And she could only confirm that Latricia said they were having sex and thought Macbeth might be putting cases on Lonnie to keep seeing her. It was all unsubstantiated hearsay and was nearly word for word what Huggins had said she would say.

Lauren walked to the window above the playpen and looked out. She could see several blocks before high-rises blocked the view of Lake Michigan she knew lay somewhere to the east. Looking down, she saw a pink teddy bear and a stuffed doggy with a pink collar in the playpen, a SpongeBob rattle, and a rubber teething ring. She turned back toward the others. They'd stopped talking and were watching her. She suddenly felt uncomfortable and wished she had something to say as a distraction.

"How old is your little girl?" Lauren asked.

"Huh?" Collins took the cigarette from her mouth.

Lauren stepped away from the playpen and motioned back at it with her notebook. "The baby. How old?"

"That for my nephew," Collins said. "I babysit him now and again."

Konrad cleared his throat. "We're finished here, partner." He looked at her and raised an eyebrow as he stuck his notebook and pen in his vest. "You ready?"

Lauren couldn't help feeling like an incompetent tag-along. Then she remembered the money in her bra. Oh God, the indignity of retrieving it from her bra in front of this woman. "Can I ask a couple of questions quick?"

Konrad looked at his watch. "I suppose, but don't take long." He shifted his weight, his foot bouncing up and down.

"Ms. Collins," Lauren said. "This is your apartment, right?"

Collins nodded and glanced at Konrad, her eyebrows raised. "Yeah, that's what I said, ain't it?"

"You said you were good friends with Latricia." Lauren looked at her notebook. "How often did you speak to her?"

"Eva'day." Collins said.

"Was that in person or on the phone?"

"Both," Collins said.

"Okay," Lauren said. "Was that usually in the morning, afternoon, or evening, or maybe all three?"

"Huh?"

"Time of day when you spoke to Latricia?" Lauren asked.

"I ain't no morning person." Collins puffed on her cigarette and eyed Konrad like she wanted some help. "Mostly like dinner time and in the night."

"Okay, thanks, Ms. Collins." Lauren wrote in her notebook. "When you called, did you use your apartment phone here? What's the number?" She nodded at a phone on the wall of the kitchen, its cord so stretched out that it lay on the floor.

"Huh?" Collins flicked her cigarette ashes on the tiles. "Yeah, I used my phone."

"Your apartment landline?" Lauren raised her eyes and watched Collins shift her gaze from her to Konrad. "What's that number?"

The detective cleared his throat. "Lauren, she said she talked to her in person and on the phone. I don't see the point of pinning down which was used more often than the other." Konrad tapped his watch. "We got a lot of places to visit yet and I want to be out of here before the building really starts to wake up, if you know what I mean." He made a rolling motion with his hand like he wanted her to move on.

"Oh, sorry." Lauren dug the money from her bra and counted out two hundred dollars. She handed it to Collins. The black woman took the bills and flipped through them like she didn't trust Lauren. Her cigarette dangled from her lips. Lauren added, "It's for lunch."

Collins didn't say anything. She flipped a twenty on the kitchen table and folded the rest, stuffing it into her bra. Lauren wondered what else she might have hidden in there.

"I sure could use some lunch, too." Collins took the cigarette out of her mouth. "I'm real hungry." She smiled at Konrad.

Lauren had the distinct feeling that she was the outsider here and they were sharing an inside joke at her expense. She asked, "Is there someone else you think we should talk to about this matter?"

Collins's brows scrunched together as she took a drag on her cigarette. Konrad waved dismissively. "I got plenty of people on my list," he said. "If we don't get started, we're going to have to come back tomorrow and that's not in my plans." He opened the door. "Let's go."

Lauren followed him outside and stopped. She heard, "Excuse me," from behind and had to get out of the way as Collins rushed out of the apartment and headed toward the stairwell, leaving the door to close on its own. Collins looked over her shoulder and grinned real big before stepping into the stairwell and disappearing.

Lauren's attention was brought back by Konrad. "Listen," he said, apparently not caring if anyone overheard. "Let's get something straight right now. I ask the questions. You take your notes and make your recording. You also give out the little paydays. And sometimes, when we got some difficult asshole, you get to display them pert little titties of yours, got it? Not so hard, right?"

She felt like he'd slapped her. *Titties*, what an asshole. "It just seems weird to me."

"What seems weird to you? What could possibly seem weird to you?"

"Everything." She tried to put her thoughts in words.

Konrad crossed his arms. "And what's that supposed to mean?"

"Too convenient," she said. "I thought it'd be harder."

"What would be harder?" Konrad leaned against the chain link fencing.

"That we'd have to dig more to find someone who corroborated Huggins's allegations."

"Why would you say that?" He laughed. "You watch too much television."

She shrugged. "Just seems to me that he's not the kind of guy who'd let everyone know his business."

"Well, Ms. Collins was Latricia's friend, close friend at that. And it wasn't as if Huggins had any say in this particular matter."

"All the more reason to keep it secret, this guy's a bad dude, right?" She held her hands out, palm up as if she was pleading. "But the first door we knock on?"

"I was provided a list of names and apartment numbers from Gold. He's Huggins's attorney, I might add." Konrad motioned with one arm at their surroundings. "I ain't going around Cabrini, this building in particular, cold knocking on doors. That could get you killed."

"C'mon." She thought he was being a little dramatic.

"You got any idea of where you're at?"

"Yeah."

Konrad shook his head. "I gotta talk to Rabinowicz. If I'm going to be expected to babysit naïve suburban girls, I gotta get paid more."

"Hey."

"No, you 'hey' for a minute!" He pointed at her, his bushy brows knitted together, his forehead crinkled, face reddening. "You do what I say, when I say, and keep your goddamned mouth shut. You got that?"

She stared at him. The hurt was changing to anger. Who did this creep think he was?

"You want to stay in this class?" This last sentence was sprayed at her as much as spoken.

She kept her eyes locked on his.

Konrad's voice dropped to a hoarse whisper. "We're standing in the worst building in this fucking complex. The Mickey Cobras run things, don't give two shits about anything but making money selling dope. And right now, we're their guests. So, we need to stay with the program. If we don't, you don't." His finger stabbed at her. "Then you might find yourself fucked in every hole by a bunch of these..."

His voice lowered even further. "Apes. I'd like to see what kind of term paper that'd generate." He put his hands on his hips, allowing his rant to sink in. "So, you will either listen to me or it's over. You're out." He spun toward the elevator but turned back to stare at her again. His voice rose as if he was no longer scared of being overheard. "I suggest you pull that pretty little head of yours outta your pretty little ass and let's go knock on the rest of these doors."

She nodded, feeling her face flush. This guy was a disgusting pig who really knew how to push her buttons. A total asshole. Apparently, he didn't remember that the digital recorder had been running for the entire conversation.

Chapter 19

Not Even Close

THURSDAY 1400 Hours

Stacey Macbeth squirmed in the plastic chair in right field, trying to find a comfortable position for his knees that were jammed into the seat in front of him and his five-shot that dug into his kidney. The game was close. Luckily for him, the Twins were ahead and that had kept Zito and Hagen relatively quiet. That and since they had to work tonight, no one was drinking. Macbeth stood.

"Where you think you're going?" asked Hagen.

"Men's room." Macbeth shuffled across the row. He made it to the aisle without spilling anyone's beer or sodas and started up the stairs. But he didn't need to use the bathroom. His knee was bothering him, and he wanted to stretch it out a bit.

He pushed through the crowd at the top of the aisle and walked onto the wide patio. He was deciding which way to turn when someone caught his attention. A large black guy, hair in corn rows, pushed into the men's room on the opposite side of the patio. Huggins?

It couldn't be, he thought. He took several steps, and then stopped.

No way, not at a White Sox game. But maybe he should take a leak anyway and then he could be absolutely sure.

The crowd suddenly felt like it was swelling in size and enthusiasm. He finally made it to the door and pushed it open. There was line after line for the urinals. Another black guy, in a billowing Sox jersey, was walking out already, shaking his hands. Macbeth kept skirting the edge of the waiting men, using his elbows more than once. He pushed out of the door and ran into a woman, almost knocking her down. She swore and juggled the two hot dogs she carried. He apologized and steadied her inattentively, his focus still on finding Huggins. Then the black guy turned. He had a large nose and perfect teeth, not to mention that he was fat and probably fifty. Not Huggins, not even close.

That fucker's becoming an obsession, he thought, *a Cabrini fever*. Macbeth felt a grin pull at his lips. Two ways to make this go away, put Huggins in prison or a pine box.

Chapter 20

Going South

THURSDAY 2030 Hours

Huggins walked slowly through the plush lobby of the ritzy Michigan Avenue hotel. He felt deliciously out of place and thoroughly enjoyed the way everyone looked at him out of the corners of their eyes. They were white. And they were scared, because they knew the King of the Jungle walked among them and there wasn't a goddamned thing they could do about it. He chuckled to himself. *Daddies better watch their wives and daughters*, he thought. He loved it. He was feeling good after his little antics in Cabrini last night. Lighting them cops up was the most fun he'd had in a long time, though he was going to have to hunt down the nigger who shot at him.

A gleaming black Lincoln Navigator was parked in the hotel's circular driveway. The setting sun reflected off the highly polished finish and tinted windows. This ride was his. It looked good. It was time to ride high and proud. Keloid leaned across the seat and popped the passenger door open.

Huggins jumped in and fist bumped his friend. Keloid crowded the space behind the wheel of the truck even with the seat gangstered way back. His round bald head shone deep chocolate brown in the dying sunlight, heavy rolls of skin curled up at the base of his skull as his shoulders sloped down to heavily muscled arms.

"What's up?" Huggins powered his window down and cut the air conditioner. He shut the radio off and settled back in the leather seat. It felt good to be back in the city. Keloid pulled onto Michigan Avenue.

"You got that cop's address?" Huggins asked.

Keloid shifted a toothpick in his mouth, his eyes glued on the street. "No, man. I ain't got it yet." Keloid turned west, into the setting sun. "What're we fitting to do?"

Huggins squinted. "Let's go see my mom."

"Cool," Keloid said.

"Later on, we going back to Cabrini to set things straight."

"Whatever you want, Lonnie."

"Maine said some cat called Pac-Man the one tried to take me out. Know him?" Huggins watched the city of the haves roll by, he never got tired of seeing how the white people lived.

"Tall, skinny nigger been hanging with Cee."

Huggins kept staring out the window. "Cee, what the fuck he pulling? Time to deal with his fat ass, too."

FORTY MINUTES LATER, THEY PULLED INTO THE NURSING HOME lot in Harvey. He wasn't impressed with what he saw. The three-story building was big and run down. Shingles were missing and the vinyl siding and windows were streaked with grime. Barren brown spots covered the lawn along with dead bushes.

He'd moved Mom out of Cabrini-Green to Country Club Hills a couple of years before, bought her a nice house, nice car. Now she was still recovering from a stroke she'd had while he was locked up. He'd hoped she'd been back home already. Though the suburbs were close to one another, Harvey wasn't Country Club Hills. Not even close.

Huggins had to wait for some African bitch, complete with head towel, to get off the fucking phone before he could find out what room his momma was in. The bitch was all wrapped up in colorful robes, with a hood over her head. The place stunk, smelled like shit, literally. Old people were on chairs, couches, in wheelchairs, mostly talking, but many were sleeping. A couple of old guys had a card game going next to an empty aquarium, but they spoke so loud, no one sat close by.

Huggins followed the woman's directions and got lost. He suspected the African bitch did that on purpose. He grabbed an orderly, who ended up being from fucking Africa, too. He made the guy walk him to his mom's room, one she shared with a roommate in the basement.

Huggins pushed the door open and immediately took a half step back. The odor was overwhelming. Hesitantly, he stepped into the room, the thick smell seemingly reluctant to part. The bed closest to the door was weighed down by some heavy woman propped up on pillows. Her eyes were closed. She snored deep and wet in her chest. She smelled like shit.

Huggins looked for his mom. She was laid up in the second bed. She too was propped up high but looked much smaller and thinner compared to the fat one. A small TV was mounted on the opposite wall. Her face brightened when she saw him. She reached out a narrow arm, her hand trembling.

"My boy," she said. "'Bout time you come visit your momma."

Huggins forced a smile despite the smell and walked to her. He took her gently into his arms, scared he might hurt her. Then, feeling her vitality in his grasp, he squeezed harder. He held her tight for a moment.

"I'd a' been here sooner, but you know how County is." He stepped back and finally gave in, waving a hand in front of his face. "Is it always this bad? What is it, backed up toilet?"

Mom looked away from his face, then down at herself. "That's me," she said. "And my roommate."

"C'mon." He shook his head. "Don't be fooling."

"I wish."

"How you mean?" He felt the skin on his scalp tighten and his heart beat a little faster.

She shook her head. "They don't change us regularly, sometimes not all day."

"What!" He squinted at her. "You mean—" He pointed at her hips. "You mean?"

She nodded her eyes downcast. "I get so sore."

Huggins's fists knotted. His breathing slowed as he felt his flesh heat up. "Don't they give you no bath or shower?"

"Sometimes," she said.

"They take you somewhere to eat?"

"Oh, we don't leave."

"No, I mean like to a cafeteria or something."

"They usually bring something here."

Huggins's jaw clenched until his teeth ground. He turned from his momma and strode from the room. The orderly wasn't in sight. He walked to the end of the hallway where he remembered seeing a nurses' station. He pushed through the door and found three people sitting in comfortable chairs watching a small TV on a counter. It was two women and the orderly who'd brought him to his mom's room.

"Which one a' you be taking care of Lainey Pitts in room 7B?" He didn't care whether it had been the tone of his voice or choice of words, but three sets of eyes popped wide. He stepped over to the TV and turned it off.

The three looked at each other but didn't say nothing.

"I ain't in the habit a' asking twice."

The man stood. "We all responsible for the patients down here."

"Well, why don't you take your responsible asses up to my mom's room and fix her up nice."

"She need something?" the man asked.

"Yeah, she do."

"Like what?" The man rubbed his hands together. "I can get whatever she need on my next round."

Huggins smirked. "You missing my meaning, brother."

The man looked confused standing in front of his chair. The two women looked at him rather than at Huggins. Huggins took a deep breath. He felt the energy rush through his chest into his arms. He stepped up to the man and took him by the throat, his grip tightening.

"I want you and these two bitches to get on up to my mom's room and take care a' her. Whatever she need." Huggins wanted to pop the guy's head from his shoulders, and he tried. The women stood and backed away. "Like a motherfucking shower. How 'bout helping her take a shit like a lady and not lay in it. Let's start with that, then we'll get to the harder stuff like clean sheets and that fat roommate she got."

He spun the guy around and forced him through the door. Huggins looked back at the women. "You coming?" They nodded and scurried out of the room.

"The king of the jungle's back." Huggins's face screwed up tight and hot. "And this

shit's gonna change, like right fucking now."

Chapter 21

Core Issues Arise

THURSDAY 2230 Hours

Lauren Cahill stopped typing on her laptop and stared at the screen. Frustrated with what she had written, she stabbed the delete button and watched the blinking cursor backtrack, eating the text line after line. She exhaled and lowered her face into her hands. No matter how she wrote it, it sounded like unadulterated bullshit. She had been there and couldn't make it sound legit. She blew a strand of hair out of her eyes and stood. She walked away from the kitchen table and her laptop.

Maybe what she needed was a glass of wine. She jerked the refrigerator open, knowing damn well what was bothering her. It was this story Huggins expected her and Konrad to buy. Everyone they'd talked to corroborated his allegations, no one strayed from the story even a little. And they all knew to expect money, too.

The bottle of pinot grigio was gone.

"Rachel!" Lauren stomped off to her roommate's bedroom. The door was closed. She knocked. There was no answer.

"I know you're in there." As she got ready to knock again, the door opened. Her roommate held a finger to her lips and a phone, cord stretched tight, pressed to her ear.

"Uh huh." Rachel rolled her eyes and waved Lauren in. Lauren saw the wine bottle on her nightstand, unopened next to an empty glass and a bottle opener. Lauren held up her own finger before returning to the kitchen for another glass.

By the time Rachel finally got off the phone, Lauren had refilled once. Rachel sat down heavily on the bed. "Don't you drink all my wine, bitch." She drained half of what Lauren had poured for her.

Lauren laughed. "Who was that?"

"My aunt."

"No," Lauren said in a raspy, theatrical voice of disbelief.

"Yeah." Rachel slugged the other half. She reached for the bottle. "You done with your homework?"

"No." Lauren held her glass out for more wine. "I'm kind of stuck."

"How so?"

Lauren chewed her lip a moment. "I was typing up my witness interviews and we're being fed a lot of bullshit. I just can't prove it."

"Does it matter?" Rachel sat the nearly empty bottle down on the table.

"What do you mean?"

"Just that," Rachel said. "Does it really matter? I mean, who cares? You know, you just want a good grade, right?"

"Don't say that," Lauren said. "I care."

"C'mon, not really." Rachel sloshed her wine around. "It's just a class."

"This is a special class, you know, with a real heavyweight professor. And we're working on real stuff that makes headlines. I'm not going to come off looking like an incompetent bimbo who'll fall for any insipid story. I'm better than that." Lauren swallowed a mouthful of wine. "I want to get a job out of this."

Rachel drank. "What're you going to do?"

"I don't know." Lauren did have an idea of trying to find out on her own, but she didn't want to contemplate going into Cabrini by herself until she was sure it was the only way. Perhaps she was wrong. They were going back tomorrow for more interviews. Maybe she could find some way to figure out the real story.

Chapter 22

Fishing In The Rows

THURSDAY 2300 Hours

The sun had long since gone down, and the air was still stifling hot and humid, making it an effort to move. Macbeth drove, his window open, and the air cranked on max, giving no relief. Hagen was next to him, his window open, too. Zito was stuffed in the back seat, sweltering. There were a lot of people out on the street in Cabrini. As hot as it was outside, it was cooler than being inside those brick project walls.

"Don't you have an interview at IAD in the morning, Stace?" Hagen asked. "It's eleven."

Macbeth glanced at him. "Yeah, don't remind me."

"It's about the thing with Simms again, right?" Zito asked from the back seat.

"They aren't letting it go," Macbeth said.

"Weren't you supposed to go home after roll call? Ryan said to get a good night's sleep," Hagen said.

"Fuck that," Macbeth said. "I'm gonna find Huggins tonight and lock his ass up."

"You think we can't find him?" Zito leaned forward.

"I'll find him."

"What if he ain't holding? What're you gonna do?" Zito asked. "Put something on him?"

Macbeth locked eyes with Zito in the rearview mirror.

"You know me better than that. He was the fucker that tried to burn us alive." He caught the look Hagen shot Zito. One that said Macbeth couldn't prove anything about the fire.

Macbeth gripped the steering wheel tightly. "I don't care, I saw him."

"You think you saw him," Zito said.

Macbeth turned down Cambridge, planning to go around the block to cruise the Cobra building again. He rolled slowly past the row houses toward Chicago Avenue. It was as crowded as if it were midafternoon. People walked the street, or were sitting on their front step smoking and drinking and passing the time as cool as they could. The streetlights were working, most of them, but shadows stretched down the narrow side streets branching east off Cambridge.

Macbeth eyed the people as they passed. He concentrated on the young men—age fifteen to their early thirties. They were the ones most likely to raise a pistol. Hagen covered his side of the street. It was like riding through Baghdad or Kabul, people hate-staring you everywhere you looked.

The radio was surprisingly quiet. Macbeth guessed people were just too spent with the heat to fight. But if the temperature didn't come down soon, the lid would blow, and it would rain blood.

"Hey." Zito swiveled to look at something they'd just passed. Macbeth's head snapped over. "What'd that guy drop?"

Macbeth stopped and shifted into reverse.

"What you got?" Hagen twisted around. "Which guy?"

"Young guy, dark shirt." Zito tapped the window. "Walking toward Iowa. He tossed something as we rolled by."

"Pistol?" Macbeth drew even with the guy as he turned east on Iowa.

"No. Dope. Weed, maybe." Zito grabbed the car door's handle and prepared to leap out.

The young man walked faster, his face turned straight as if his neck was a board, not daring a look at them. "He's gonna go," Macbeth said.

Zito popped the door and the guy bolted. Zito pried himself from the backseat and sprinted after him. "Police!"

Hagen dove out of the car and immediately started scouring the area. Zito had said the guy dropped something. Once the doors closed, Macbeth swung the car around and shot after Zito and the young man, who were bouncing in and out of the headlights.

He passed Zito, who looked a little winded. The bad guy was pulling away. Macbeth gassed the Chevy and kicked the driver's door open as he pulled alongside the teen. He screeched to a halt and sprinted out after the kid, who'd taken a hard left. Macbeth was right behind him and Zito was angling to cut him off.

"Motherfucker!" Zito gasped. "Stop or I'm gonna whoop your ass."

The kid somehow found a faster gear and took off. A wrought iron fence loomed ahead, and Macbeth knew the kid didn't have enough lead to get over it. He skidded to a halt and turned to face the cops.

"Who're you?" The kid looked scared and desperate. His eyes darted from side to side.

"Police, numb nuts." Zito's tongue stud clinked on his teeth as he bent over and rested his hands on his knees. Macbeth thought he might puke. "Why you running?" Zito gasped for breath.

"Man, you scared me." The kid's eyes never stopped shifting between the two cops.

"Give me a break." Macbeth took a step closer. "Put your hands on your head."

"For what?" The teen took a step back, into the fence. "I ain't done nothing."

"What did you throw by the car?" Zito stood straight.

"I ain't throw nothing." The kid turned, putting his hands on his head.

Macbeth stepped up and patted the kid down. He took his cuffs off his belt and snapped them on.

"Ain't this some shit." The kid shook his head.

"What's your name?" Macbeth took his arm and started for the car.

"Marlin." The teen hung his head. "Marlin Dempster." Marlin raised his head back up. "What you arresting me for?"

Zito pulled his radio from his vest pocket and twisted the channel selector to the car-to-car frequency. He raised it to his mouth. "Timmy, you find anything?"

After a moment Hagen responded, "Yeah, four bags of weed, I'm still looking."

"Come on, yo." Marlin threw his head back. "Don't do me like that, I didn't have no weed. Come on."

"What? You saying it was just laying there?" Zito said as Marlin shook his head. "You expect me to believe they just leave weed laying around on the street in Cabrini."

"Yo, poh-leece is always putting shit on us brothers."

Macbeth stopped him at the car and opened the back door. He eased Marlin in, watching his head so it didn't hit the roof. "How about this." Macbeth slid in behind the wheel. "You want out of this, let's talk."

"Talk about what? I don't know shit."

"Come on, we got your weed. I'm sure you don't want to go to jail. You gotta know something."

Zito climbed in the back seat next to Marlin.

"You ain't got my weed, yo."

"Stop with the *yo* shit, or—" Macbeth stopped himself. He didn't need any more trouble. "Give us something and maybe you could walk. Know anything about a Cobra named Lonnie Huggins?"

Marlin's eyes widened. "He the king of bad intentions, yo—sorry, no way I would snitch him out. But I don't know jack about him no ways."

Timmy Hagen walked up to the car, one hand filled with plastic baggies.

Marlin shook his head. "I don't know that cat. And I'm telling you that ain't none of my weed."

Hagen handed the little bags of marijuana through the open window to Zito, who stuffed them in his vest pocket.

"A'ight. Look." Marlin looked up. "I got up this morning and I was running late for school. And I accidentally put on somebody else's pants."

Macbeth couldn't help himself. He let out a laugh. Zito clapped Marlin on the side of the head, not hard, but enough to get his attention. Hagen opened the car door and plopped down next to Macbeth.

"Hey asshole." Zito leaned closer to Marlin. "That bullshit is weak."

Macbeth started the car and did a U-turn to head back west on Iowa.

Marlin swung his head from side to side and stomped his feet. "A'ight, look. That shit ain't mine. It's my momma's."

Macbeth jammed on the brake. The car skidded to a stop.

"She got cancer." Marlin's eyes were wide and wild. "She smoke it to feel better. It's some of that medical weed, right. I was just out getting her some and when I seen you, I panicked, you know."

Macbeth shook his head. "Just shut up. Exercise your right to remain silent."

Zito turned to the front and pulled his seatbelt on. "I wouldn't believe shit you had to say anyway. You're an asshole."

Marlin shook his head some more and looked out the window. "Why I gotta be all that?"

"Haven't you ever heard of taking your weight?" Zito asked.

Macbeth let off the brake and eased the car up to Cambridge. Pedestrians walked past. As they did, they watched the cops.

Pop! Pop! Pop, pop!

"Shit!" Marlin, still handcuffed, dove for the floor as shots sounded from somewhere close by. Pop! Pop, pop, pop!

Hagen pointed north up Cambridge. "That way!" He disconnected his seatbelt, then unsnapped his holster.

Macbeth turned off the headlights and swung the car onto Cambridge, going the wrong way toward Oak, accelerating past people ducking and diving for cover.

"Sounded like the other side of ten-seventeen," Hagen said, referring to the building located at 1015-17 North Larrabee. "Watch it!" Hagen pointed at a dark figure running across the street, oblivious to the police car flying past.

"Okay." Macbeth swerved and missed the man. He was coming from the wrong direction to be the shooter. "I'm going to Larrabee and see what's happening between Ten-Fifteen and Eleven-Twenty-One." As they approached Oak Street, he asked Hagen, "Your side clear?"

"Yes." Hagen braced himself against the dashboard. "No! Not..."

The air bag blew into Macbeth's face before he even registered the impact that took off their bumper. Macbeth's car spun up and over the sidewalk and crashed against a wrought iron fence post.

Macbeth couldn't see Hagen, Zito, or the prisoner. But he could see the marked police car through the haze of dust. The powder from the air bag and the overpowering smell of antifreeze made it hard to breathe. But he could hear the voices of Teddy Ketchum and Frank Hampton. They were on the radio, chasing a man with a gun.

Chapter 23

From Bad To Worse

FRIDAY 0945 Hours

Macbeth's back, shoulders, and neck were sore and stiff the next morning as he tried to stay awake for his interview at Internal Affairs. He'd foregone the pain meds, thinking they'd make him sleepy, but he still couldn't concentrate from the sharp stabs of pain and constant squirming in search of relief. His attorney, a short heavyset black woman named Flores-Perry, finally raised her hand holding her half-moon glasses. Police Agent Kaczynski interrupted his question and stared at her. The diminutive woman turned to glare at Macbeth, then turned back to Kaczynski, smiling.

"May I have a minute with my client, please?"

"Certainly." Kaczynski minimized his computer screen and rose from his chair. "Would either of you like something to drink?" They both shook their heads. He nodded and left the room, closing the door behind him.

"May I ask you something?" Flores-Perry didn't wait for Macbeth to answer. "Have you ever testified before?" She took a breath and kept going. "I'm serious, really. Have you? Do you have the first inkling about what the hell you're supposed to do?"

Macbeth lowered his head slightly. He was exhausted and Kaczynski's monotone wasn't helping. It had been a while since he'd been scolded. He had an ass chewing coming. Now that he thought about it, that wasn't entirely true. He'd been chewed out this morning after the accident, and the night in question late last winter. Both times, he'd been worked over by his sergeant, Ronnie Ryan, who had a much more liberal cursing policy. But Flores-Perry's scolding was altogether different, he knew he'd done wrong and deserved what he was getting. Worse yet, he knew she wasn't done.

"Yes or no, we talked about this before. Make him ask you yes or no questions. And when he *does* ask an open-ended question, keep your answers short."

Macbeth nodded again. Flores-Perry slipped her glasses on and looked down at the papers in front of her. Apparently, the scolding was finished.

After a few minutes of awkward silence, Kaczynski came back with a bottle of water.

"Ready?"

"Actually," Flores-Perry said. "Despite my instructions to the contrary, Officer Macbeth saw fit to go to work last night and was involved in a fairly substantial traffic accident. After observing his testimony this morning, I believe he's still suffering from the trauma to his head, and I can't in good conscience allow him to continue. I'm requesting a date for us to return, at your convenience, of course."

Kaczynski sat carefully, placing the bottle of water on the table. He seemed puzzled. "That's highly unusual," he said. "We should have discussed this earlier and should continue."

"It's my fault," Flores-Perry said. "I should have called you the second Officer Macbeth revealed the crash to me. He assured me he could proceed and to his credit, thinks he can continue now. But it's not the case; it just isn't in his best interest to carry on."

Kaczynski got up. "I'll have to speak to my supervisor. I'll be right back." He left the room again, closing the door behind him.

Macbeth glanced at the table.

His lawyer scrutinized him over the top of her glasses. "My job is to keep you employed and I happen to take *my* job seriously. If this isn't something you're going to approach with a degree of professionalism, don't expect me to."

Macbeth's gaze drifted to a department general order that had been taped to the wall. It explained that if you lied you could lose your job.

"Dammit," she said. "I work my tail off, at least listen to what I have to say. I hate to grovel. And that's what you got me doing here this morning. They don't have to grant us an interlude."

Kaczynski returned ten minutes later, this time with a paper in his hand. After he closed the door, he looked at Flores-Perry and held up the paper. "According to this, Officer Macbeth was indeed involved in a two-car accident late last night with another police car, responding to a man with a gun call." Kaczynski looked at Macbeth. "Next time, say something sooner. Before we call it quits, we have to finish up what we've covered so far."

Kaczynski sat at his computer and printed the interview as displayed on the screen. Then he put it on the table and asked Macbeth and Flores-Perry to read it. They were asked to make any necessary corrections and initial each page. When they were done, Flores-Perry asked Macbeth to wait for her in the lobby.

Macbeth was led there by another IAD officer, and he made for the couch and fell back into the overstuffed gray cushions.

The cop working the desk outside the Superintendent's office wouldn't even look at him. His statement had started bad and gotten worse in what had to be record time. He'd figured it would be like testifying at a trial, which he'd done hundreds of times on little or no sleep, but this was different. In reality, *he* was on trial. To be more accurate, his career was on trial and the standard wasn't "beyond a reasonable doubt," but a much easier burden to reach, "preponderance of the evidence." That wasn't much more than a hunch.

He closed his eyes and slouched back. Falling asleep would be so easy.

"You're snoring, Merlin." Startled, Macbeth opened his eyes. Sandra Flores-Perry stood in front of him supported by her walker.

Macbeth sat up.

"Look at me." Her expression broadcast her barely contained rage. "Are you planning on paying attention next time?"

He stood and nodded.

"Is that a yes or no?" she said.

"Yes." He thrust his hands into his pockets and felt like a school kid.

"Okay." She took a deep breath. "Go home. Get some sleep. Unless you hear different, be ready to go first thing Monday."

"We're done for the day?" He suddenly felt invigorated but knew that feeling wouldn't last the elevator ride down to the lobby.

"I think Kaczynski was happy to postpone." Pivoting her walker, Flores-Perry started for the door. "But it ain't over yet, and this fat lady hasn't even begun to warm up." She got to the door and when she wasn't immediately buzzed in, she banged on the glass with her walker to get the officer's attention.

"Get some sleep, Merlin."

MACBETH PARKED HIS JEEP IN THE SMALL PARKING LOT OFF THE alley of his apartment building and got out. He could barely keep his eyes open. God forbid if he encountered Jack Camp and his never-ending war stories. Inside the building, Macbeth bypassed his mailbox, worried that the sound of opening it would attract attention. All he cared about was dragging his ass up the three flights of stairs and lying down in his own place. Even the floor would feel good.

As he climbed the stairs a plane roared overhead, descending for a landing at Midway Airport. He opened his own door, went in, and shut and locked it behind him. He kicked off his shoes and walked through the front room of his one-bedroom apartment. It was very warm, with the windows exposed to constant sunlight. *From one sweat box to another*, he thought.

He longed for sleep. His body ached, but before he could lie down, he knew what he had to do. The pain did persuade him to swallow some Advil first. Give the medicine a few minutes to work as he made his call.

He sat in the kitchen and stared at the phone on the tabletop, the cup in his hand all but forgotten. The phone was coated with a fine layer of gray powder. When was the last time he'd dusted? He stopped himself. Was he about to let the need to dust derail calling his parents? What an asshole he'd become.

He stared at the phone some more. *It isn't going to dial itself,* he thought, and pushed up from the kitchen table. He picked up the receiver and referred to the paper taped to the wall, running a finger down the list to the number for his parents' nursing home. He dialed. His mom and dad's home phone number was burned into his cerebral cortex, but the new one was lost to him, even though they'd lived there for a couple of years already. Of course, if he called more often there might be a chance he'd remember it.

The phone rang. And rang. His confidence grew that he'd get away with leaving a message. That would be evidence he could use to keep his little sister off his back. She always had a crack about his absence, whether personal or telephonic. Though he had great respect for what she did day in and out for their parents, there was no way she could understand his predicament. It didn't help that he didn't either.

His dad's gravelly voice brought him back to the moment. "Hello."

"Hi, Dad." Macbeth squeezed the receiver, pressing it against his head. "It's me."

His dad's heavy breathing was all he got for a few seconds. "Who'd you say you were?"

"Stacey."

"Who? You're going to have to speak up."

"Stacey, Dad."

"Yeah..." His dad's voice was unsure, sounding confused. "I got a son named Stacey."

"No, it's me, Stacey." Macbeth shook his head.

"Why didn't you say so?"

"How are you and Mom doing?"

"Well." His dad paused. "Your mother ain't so good, she had a stroke, you know."

Macbeth closed his eyes and released a breath he'd discovered he'd been holding. His dad took his silence as a need to continue.

"Yeah, she can't talk much. Well, she don't really talk at all."

"I know—"

"Can't do nothing herself."

"Dad—"

"I got to feed her."

"I know—"

"I'm not strong enough to help her toilet, you know. They got these foreigners around here help her out."

"Dad, I know that." Macbeth squeezed his eyes shut. "The stroke happened a couple of years ago." He was grateful for the silence that followed for several heartbeats afterward.

"Oh, yeah." His father paused for a long breath as if he'd lost his train of thought. "I tell you about the foreigners they get around here, from Ethiopia and Egypt?"

"Dad, how are you?"

"Me?"

"Yeah, Dad, how are you?"

"Well, kind of lonely. My wife, she don't talk, you know."

Macbeth shook his head.

"You want to talk to her?"

Before Macbeth could answer, his dad's phone crackled as it was placed against his mother's face. In the background, he heard his dad say something, but he couldn't understand what. Then his mom's presence filled his ear. Her breathing was quite different from that of his father. Hers was quieter but had a dampness to it. A loud snap and crackle made him think his father had wedged the phone between his mom's head and shoulder.

"Hi, Mom!"

He heard a break in her breathing, and then a quiet sob. He talked through her crying, telling her he loved her and about the innocuous routine of his regular day, hoping she'd settle down. He didn't mention anything that might cause her any distress or anxiety. For a few moments her hushed weeping stopped or grew quieter.

Then his monologue started to repeat and her crying amped into a keen that gathered air and volume until he stopped talking altogether. Seconds later, there was a muffled crack and he heard the phone, on his mom's end, bounce off the floor. He could still hear her bawling as someone, presumably his dad, picked the receiver off the floor and rattled it back into its cradle. Then the dial tone.

Macbeth wiped a wrist across his damp eyes before hanging up.

Chapter 24

Waiting

Lauren slammed the phone's receiver back into its cradle on the kitchen wall. "That asshole!" She gave the phone the finger. *That was really mature*, she mused. Without looking at the wall clock she knew it was eleven o'clock. She'd been calling Konrad on the hour. He was more than two hours late with not even a courtesy call. *What a jerk*, she thought.

The phone rang. It was Konrad. "Get off the fucking line already, Jesus. I'm waiting for a call from Gold. I'll call you when I hear from him. And for God's sake, *stay* off the fucking phone."

It was an hour later when he finally called back. "Look, darling," he said, making her want to grind her teeth. She really didn't like the man. "I just got off the call with Gold. Apparently, Huggins is missing. We were supposed to pick him up at nine, but when I called to make sure he was up, I got no answer. I been calling, but still no answer, and finally I called Gold. He said to sit tight, see if Huggins comes back."

"Well, what're we doing?" Lauren let the anger show in her voice. "I have other things I wanted to do today. At least you're getting paid."

It wasn't entirely true, all she'd planned on doing was writing her first paper, but she wanted to finish it today.

"Don't know what to tell you, honey. Who knows when this nigger's gonna show."

"Can you refrain from the racist names?"

"Oh, sorry." He laughed. "Did I offend your precious north-shore ears?"

"C'mon, Jay. Act professional for once. I've heard the n-word more in this week than I did my whole life."

"So, y'all on the north shore don't call 'em niggers? What do you call them? Oh, I know. democrats. Wait, you can't use that, because that's what you liberal fucks are up there!" He laughed louder.

"For your information, I use 'asshole.' I find it covers a greater range of people, asshole!" She slammed the receiver into its cradle.

She sat down at the table and stared at her laptop. It occurred to her that she'd better use the free time to get something accomplished, but she still didn't know how she was going to conclude.

Maybe she could just start writing and hope the conclusion developed itself. She began to type. No longer did she feel stifled, but relieved. Even if the conclusion remained elusive, she'd get a good jump on the thing, there would be editing and rewriting regardless. Better to have it started than to not have it at all.

HUGGINS LAY BACK AND LET THE REEFER SMOKE SETTLE IN HIS lungs, let the weed worm its way into his blood. The girl was in the bathroom, cleaning up. He'd never forgotten how much he loved women. But in prison one had to make do with what was available. Most of the gumps in jail had shadow, were rough around the mouth, or had hairy assholes. The ones that had gone through hormone treatments and were smooth were usually taken out of general population. But this pussy was real. Shaved smooth, and sweet. He knew something else, too. He was never going back to prison. Never.

When the hotel's phone rang again, he looked at it. He vaguely remembered he was supposed to be doing something this morning.

Whatever it was, it could wait. Right now, the only thing he was going to do was smoke some reefer and fuck.

"Get in here, bitch."

She appeared in the doorway of the hotel bathroom. She was black, young, and thin. She didn't look much over sixteen, but he figured she was older. Earlier she'd done his hair into Afro puffs, little tufts banded together across his skull. He wasn't sure he liked it, but it had taken her an hour to do it. Her eye was swollen and her upper lip fat. Maybe now she'd be a little quicker to listen. He didn't think she'd say no again.

He smiled. She came to the bed and knelt on the mattress, crawling slowly toward him. It sure was good to be bedding a woman again.

❧

LAUREN HADN'T LOOKED AT THE TIME SINCE SHE'D BEGUN HER paper. When the phone finally rang, she glanced at the clock on the kitchen wall. It was nearly four-thirty in the afternoon.

"Hey, Lauren." Konrad had never called her by her name and she didn't know why he did so now. Had the professor got on his ass? "Be ready by five."

"I'm going to meet you there." She'd decided on that strategy earlier. She wasn't going to rely on Konrad for a ride home. "What time should I be there, since you can skip me?"

"Suit yourself, Peaches. Figure six-ish."

"I'm not wearing anything provocative, not at night."

"Wear something tight across your tits, at least. And stuff some toilet paper in there."

"Really, Jay."

He laughed.

"You're such an asshole."

"Don't be such a stick in the mud," he said. "We still got to get these bastards to talk."

"The last time we talked to these guys I don't think it made any difference how I was dressed. I don't see how my dressing like some kind of slut helps."

"Trust me, it makes everyone happy."

"You or the people we're interviewing?" She suspected she knew the answer already. "I hope whoever we talk to is more credible than the others we interviewed."

"Bite your tongue, girl. Better yet, let me bite it instead." He laughed again.

She hung up on him and swore at the wall.

Chapter 25

If At First You Don't Succeed...

FRIDAY 1830 Hours

Lauren sat in her Dodge Neon on Sedgwick just south of Division, waiting for Konrad to cruise by in his beater, not wanting to pull into the lot without him already there, parked and out of the car. Her car was still running, the air conditioner on low. She was splitting her time looking out the windows and checking her mirrors. She was tired from writing all afternoon but didn't dare fall asleep there.

A maroon unmarked police car drove by slowly. There were two guys inside. The car stopped at the entrance to the lot of 1150-60 North Sedgwick and spun a slow U-turn, coming back toward her. The passenger's window rolled down as the vehicle came to stop adjacent to her car. She rolled her own window down.

"What are you doing here, young lady?" the passenger cop said. He was white with sandy hair, bald on top.

She frowned and said, "Waiting for my colleague. Is something wrong?"

The cop shrugged. "Not necessarily, but this isn't the safest place in the world. What kind of work do you do?"

Now it was her turn to shrug. "Is that any of your business?"

He laughed. "Now, what kind of work do you do that you can't tell your friendly neighborhood police officer?"

She laughed back at him. "I've heard some of the cops around here are not very friendly."

"Not me," he said. "And my partner here, he's even nicer, just not as good looking." The driver elbowed him and said something she couldn't hear. The passenger shook his head and told him to hang on. "I don't suppose you're in any need of poh-leece assistance?"

"Afraid not."

"You wanna take my number down in case you need us?"

She laughed again. "Can't I just dial 9-1-1?"

"Sure." He fished out a pack of cigarettes. "If you want just any old cop. But if you want me and Stacey, I'll give you our office number."

Stacey? She froze. The cop that was driving had to be Macbeth, couldn't be too many men with that first name in CPD, let alone assigned to Cabrini. She didn't know what to say.

The passenger cop said something else she didn't hear. The maroon car started to roll away. His voice floated back to her: "If you change your mind, call 9-1-1 and ask for Zito and Macbeth." And they were gone, turning onto Division from Sedgwick.

❧

MACBETH CROSSED CLARK STREET TO THE UNMARKED CAR. He climbed in the driver's side, while Zito took the front passenger's seat. Hagen had back seat. Dinner was finished and he'd persuaded the team to hit the lobby of 1150 North Sedgwick afterward to see if they could find Huggins. They'd probably agreed only to shut him up, but what the hell. Worst case scenario, he'd argued, the Mickey Cobras would shut down their dope sales for the night after the cops' visit. Now he just hoped and prayed Huggins would be there. If he wasn't holding, Macbeth would run him in on the arson.

He let Ketchum and Hampton lead the way so as not to out-drive his back up. Petty and Barnhill would bring up the tail end.

❧

Since seven, Lauren and Konrad had talked to a dozen young men between the ages of fifteen and twenty-five. Huggins was their chaperone, and each and every one of those young men had lied from the moment they opened their mouths. She was convinced of it. Huggins's cavalier attitude reinforced her conviction. She was sure Huggins was high or drunk. His eyes were bloodshot and glassy, and her first guess was that he'd been smoking pot.

Her feet hurt and her legs felt rubbery from going up and down the stairs between floors of both the 1150 and 1160 sides of the tall building on Sedgwick. The only good thing was that she hadn't been threatened. One of the boys said something inappropriate, that she barely even heard, and he'd returned from a stairwell visit with Huggins with a puffy lip and a watery eye. Apparently, Huggins was caring for her safety personally, though that didn't make her feel the least bit comfortable. Earlier, Huggins had taken all of the money Konrad had given her. He said he'd distribute it later.

Finally, Konrad said they were through. On one hand, Lauren didn't have anything concrete to document, but on the other, she'd caught so many nods and looks passing between Huggins and the young men being interviewed that it would have been hilarious if this were a movie. But it wasn't, and there wasn't anything solid to point to. She looked forward to getting home and writing her paper, though she was still undecided as to how to conclude this first installment.

As they descended the stairs from three, a shout went out from both below and above, "Five-O! Five-O!"

❧

Macbeth jammed the car into park and ripped the keys from the ignition before jumping out and running for the lobby. The whole time, a mantra ran through his mind: "Be there, motherfucker, be there!"

❧

Lauren abruptly halted. Huggins moved to the side of the stairwell and jerked his head to indicate they should follow suit. No sooner had her butt contacted the cinder block wall when feet pounded up the stairs. A young black man, maybe eighteen, sprinted by, taking the stairs two at a time. His breathing was not the least bit labored. Another followed seconds later.

"Slick boys! Slick boys coming!" The shout descended from above.

"What's that mean?" She looked at Konrad, who shrugged.

Huggins glanced at her. "Cops in regular clothes, like Macbeth." She could hear doors slam shut above them, not far away. Once the way was clear, he started back down. Lauren felt a presence behind her and looked. Huggins's big friend had stepped out of the doorway into the stairwell from the second floor and was following them down, Keloid, she thought. She hadn't seen him all day. He had something dark in his hand, but she couldn't tell what.

As soon as Huggins hit the lobby, he saw the cops coming around the metal detector. The second they saw him, they yelled at him to grab some wall. He saw Ketchum right away, though he didn't think the black cop saw him. Fucking Macbeth was going to be there, too. Huggins had barely assumed the position with his hands against the brick when a hand snagged his hair puff just above his right ear, pulling his head back. Pain stabbed at his eyes and snaked into his brain. He squeezed his eyes shut, like that would make it sting less.

"Well, what have we here?" It was Macbeth. "If it isn't my arsonist friend."

"Macbeth, I ain't seen you since the last time you put a case on me." Huggins spoke through gritted teeth. The hair pull hurt, but Huggins wasn't about to show it.

"Go fuck yourself, Lonnie." Macbeth let go of his hair and his head snapped forward until it knocked hard against the wall.

Huggins felt more than heard the blunted clunk as his head hit the brick. A dull throbbing exploded up his forehead then down across his face. He smiled to himself and hoped Keloid had it on tape. "You gonna put another gun on me?"

"Don't have to put anything on you, Lonnie. You're always guilty of something." Macbeth searched him thoroughly, emptying his jeans pockets on the floor.

Huggins felt a grin tighten his lips. He knew he'd gotten into the cop's head. "That's what you want everybody to believe."

"That's the way it is." Macbeth pawed through his stuff.

"Says you. What you gonna lock me up for now?"

"I don't know. I'll figure something out."

"You get that, Keloid? He said he'd make something up."

MACBETH SNAPPED AROUND AND SAW A GIGANTIC BLACK MAN holding a video camera on his shoulder, obviously filming. Macbeth smiled outwardly but wanted to kick something, preferably Lonnie Huggins.

"I'm sure your cameraman over there got what I meant," Macbeth said. "That I'd figure it out, not make it up." He pulled a set of handcuffs off his belt and grabbed one of Huggins's hands, twisting it behind his back. He snapped on the cuff then brought Huggins's other hand around and ratcheted it secure.

"What's the charge?" This came from a dumpy white guy with a receding hairline who stepped from a small crowd that had gathered in the back of the lobby. He was wearing a Hawaiian shirt with huge sweat stains under the arms and carried a stenographer's notebook. Somebody else was behind him, partially concealed in the shadow of the stairwell.

"Who the hell are you?" Zito interceded as the man strode forward.

"Mr. Huggins is my client. That's who the fuck I am, and I want to know why he's being arrested."

"You his attorney?" Macbeth noticed the girl from the parking lot was standing in the stairwell doorway. What was she doing here?

"I'm not going to answer that." The man stopped out of arm's reach. "I want to know what he's being arrested for."

"If you aren't his attorney, you can go fuck yourself," Zito said. "We're taking him to the Eighteenth District for investigation."

"Investigation of what?" The man crossed his arms over his chest.

Macbeth pulled his second pair of handcuffs from their case and stepped toward the man.

"How about I lock you up for interference. Then you can see the investigation up close."

The man held up his hands in an "I surrender" fashion and stepped back.

"I didn't think so." Macbeth turned back to Huggins as he put the second set of cuffs away. "Come on, Lonnie, we got some talking to do." Macbeth took his prisoner by the arm and led him out of the lobby.

Once both cops were in the car with Huggins, they pulled away. Macbeth drove and Zito half turned in his seat to look back at their detainee. Hagen looked small next to him.

"I ain't got shit to say," Huggins said. "So, you do what you gotta do and tell me when I can call my lawyer."

Lauren stood motionless, hoping that none of the cops would notice her as they searched everyone in the lobby but the guards. Even those men had been questioned and reprimanded for their lax attitude. She was reminded of two aggressive football teams facing off. Konrad conferred with Keloid, who had been recording the incident as they walked toward the lobby door.

Lauren realized they were leaving her behind and followed them into the parking lot. She was hoping the kid with the watery eye and puffy lip wasn't anywhere near now that Huggins was gone.

Konrad went to his car and retrieved his bag phone. He set it on the hood of his car and made a call.

"Hi, Sherman. Sorry to bother you, but you'd said you wanted to know when Lonnie got locked up. And he just did." Konrad shuffled his feet and listened. Eventually, a grin spread across his face. "They wouldn't tell me... they threatened to lock me up too. Not even five minutes ago. Yeah, the Eighteenth District. You're going to love this part, none other than Stacey Macbeth. Yeah, can you believe it. Playing right into our hands. Keloid got it on camera. And Cahill was there too. Yeah, she was a way back, so I don't know if her recorder picked it up. I'll let you know. Okay, talk to you later. Bye."

Konrad tucked the phone back inside his vehicle and escorted Lauren to her car, away from everyone else. He'd told Keloid he'd be right back to get the tape from the camera. "Go back to your place and transcribe what you got. I'm especially interested in that encounter between the cops and Huggins. You know that was Macbeth, right?"

She shook her head. She'd thought the cops were a little rough, particularly the one who'd handled Huggins, but after what she'd seen of Huggins, she kind of understood. So that was Macbeth. Her whole perception of what she was working on was getting more and more distorted. She'd never seen cops act the way they had just now, the way Macbeth pulled Huggins's hair. But she'd just spent a couple of hours with the gangbanger enforcer and knew he'd probably done a lot worse. But they were officers of the law and were expected to be better, weren't they?

"What was he talking about arson for?"

"What?"

"When he first grabbed Huggins, he said something about being an arsonist. I don't remember anything about arson in Huggins's background."

"Who knows," Konrad said. "I must've missed that part."

Lauren couldn't help but wonder about that. She'd be willing to bet a lot of money that Konrad's recollection was selective at best, and subject to massive bouts of creativity at worst. This whole thing stunk, and she was beginning to suspect that there wasn't going to be an easy way out.

Chapter 26

Don't Think So

FRIDAY 2130 Hours

Macbeth slammed the phone down. He was glad he'd left the tactical office to call Bomb and Arson. He couldn't imagine giving Huggins the satisfaction of hearing him being turned down by the detective, who said Macbeth didn't have enough evidence to even warrant his coming to the Eighteenth District to seek charges against Huggins. He'd suggested Macbeth release the gang enforcer and try to dig up more evidence in the coming days. Released without charges. The absurdity of it all hit him like a gut punch. He kicked himself for not looking harder in the lobby for something illegal on the ground, or on one of the other gangbangers, anything he could hang on Huggins. But the big guy had been taping, so it wouldn't have looked good.

After a few minutes of staring at the walls, he picked up the phone again and dialed Area Three. "Is Toomer around?" He was put on hold.

Macbeth had called Area Three hoping Detective Toomer might be more willing to pursue felony charges where Bomb and Arson had refused. Macbeth knew Huggins set that fire the night before.

When Toomer picked up, Macbeth said, "Al, it's Stacey Macbeth in Eighteen…"

"I just got off the phone with your sergeant," Toomer said. "He told me the problem and gave me a rundown."

Toomer exhaled over the line. He was a notorious chain smoker. "Listen, Bomb and Arson's like anyplace else, they got their good guys and their not so good guys." He paused, then continued, "You know I'd do anything for you guys, all the help you give us. Unfortunately, this caper isn't going to cut it as it stands now. We need more."

"So, where's that leave me?" Macbeth asked. "Fucked?"

"I'd prefer to look at it as justice delayed," Toomer said.

"Great, what do I do with this asshole now? I don't want to just kick him loose."

"Your call."

Macbeth heard the ratchet of a lighter. Then Toomer breathed in. He must've been lighting up another cigarette. "Just be careful. You're not out of the woods on all that other shit yet."

"Yeah, yeah. Thanks." Macbeth hung up. He walked back through the hall to the tac office but met Ryan who was coming out.

"I gotta go see the watch commander," Ryan said. "Stand by." He walked off down the hall toward the stairs.

Five minutes later, Ryan beckoned Macbeth out of the tac office with his finger. The scowl on his face wasn't particularly heartening. Macbeth stepped into the hallway.

Ryan sneered and nodded toward the office. "His attorney is downstairs demanding his release. Finney wants to know what we're going to do."

Macbeth said nothing.

Ryan held up a hand. "I know you want this guy. But we got to *have* something to keep him, and we don't." Macbeth opened his mouth, but Ryan shook him off. "Hear me out. We go with some petty bullshit, it's going to look just like that, and then we got a problem later. We have a legitimate issue with the fire, but we jumped the gun."

Ryan put a knuckle to his chin. "We got good faith in our corner at the moment. But only if we release him now that we know we can't proceed. Finney will RWOC Huggins and let his attorney know it's because of Bomb and Arson, and not because of his bellyaching. We get to save a little face. You okay with that?"

Macbeth's mouth felt dry. He felt the skin under his collar growing hotter by the second, like his brain was going to burst into flames.

Ryan said, "We'll keep on this fire angle for as long as it takes, and hope this prick fucks up sooner than later."

Macbeth looked at his feet. He felt bad. He knew Huggins was behind the fire, but he couldn't prove it. Just like with Latricia's murder. He nodded.

"Yeah, go ahead. Tell Finney to do what he has to do and let me know when I have to walk him down."

HUGGINS KNEW IT WAS SHREDDING MACBETH'S GUTS TO BE letting him go. It was how he'd felt going out of the lobby earlier, in front of all his boys, without fighting. Macbeth released the handcuff from the wall-mounted iron ring. He yanked Huggins to his feet and pulled his other hand behind him, re-cuffing him.

"So that's how it gonna be, huh?" Huggins said.

"Damn right, Lonnie." Macbeth pushed him toward the office door. The other cop in the office suddenly found something to do instead of watching the two of them leave. Maybe they were embarrassed that Macbeth fucked up? He hoped so. That would make it all the sweeter.

At the top of the stairs, Macbeth stopped him. "I'm going to get you, it's only a matter of time."

Huggins laughed and shook his head. "You ain't got shit. You ain't gonna get shit. Dig?"

"See, Lonnie," Macbeth said. "The thing that bothers me most is, I'm becoming more like you. I'd give anything to see you take a header down these stairs." Macbeth pushed Lonnie forward. "It's taking all of my willpower not to throw your ass down them right now."

Huggins planted his feet. "Go ahead and try, motherfucker."

Then the moment was gone. The heat dissipated from the cop and he nudged Huggins ahead of him, turning toward the front desk where Gold stood talking to a lieutenant.

Macbeth released the handcuffs.

Huggins turned to face him, rubbing his wrists. He allowed himself a vicious grin. He was going to make this cop's life miserable.

Chapter 27

Warning

FRIDAY 2200 Hours

Mavis Stomps answered the direct line into her office when it rang. Not many people had this number. She held the receiver to her ear. "Yes?"

"Good evening. Sorry to bother you," Gold said.

"You're never a bother, Sherman." She couldn't help but think of his billing rate this late on a weekend night. "What can I do for you?"

"Just wanted to let you know that Mr. Huggins was arrested this evening and I got him released. They seem to think he had something to do with an arson fire yesterday in Cabrini."

"Really?" This didn't sound good.

"But there's some good news." The lawyer sounded jubilant. "Our old friend, Officer Macbeth, seems to be up to his old tricks."

"Oh?"

"And we've got recordings. I'll be seeing the judge first thing Monday."

She couldn't help but smile. "Sounds wonderful."

"Yes, indeed." Gold chuckled. "Yes, indeed."

Chapter 28

Nothing Comes Easy

FRIDAY 2345 Hours

Lauren stared at the computer screen and willed it to type on its own. Oh, how she wanted some way out of this mess. Why couldn't she have an epiphany and be shown the easy route around the tangle of snakes in front of her? Her head stung. Her eyes burned. The more she thought about this case, the less she wanted to have anything to do with it. Not with Konrad, not with Rabinowicz, and certainly not with Huggins.

She was convinced that everything she'd seen so far was orchestrated by Huggins. Anyone with half a brain could see it was all garbage. But she couldn't prove it. She couldn't discover a shred of evidence to the contrary, and she'd been looking for it all day. The way Konrad operated, making *her* hand out money, had to be against the law. He was covering his own ass and leaving hers exposed. Did Professor Rabinowicz know about the money? He had to. Konrad absolutely couldn't afford that kind of expenditure, not the way he lived. What good was purchased testimony anyway? Not that it would ever come out in any official way.

And now she was going to have to transcribe all these tapes, hours and hours of crap. What a great waste of time, her time. Obviously, Huggins was going to benefit from the proceedings. Anyone else? If there was a lawsuit, the attorneys would get a big cut, probably the school too. But what about the truth? What about justice? What about doing the right thing? They were dishing a lot of dirt on Officer Macbeth. Was he going to get into trouble?

Maybe. She got up and stretched. She needed coffee. She cinched her robe tighter, then cautiously went out into the hallway. She didn't want to surprise her roommate if Rachel's boyfriend was over.

The kitchen was dark. Lauren flicked the light on and stepped over to the coffee maker. She quickly filled the machine and added water. She found the coffee cups in the sink. A hissing sound came from the machine. It'd be ready in a minute.

There were no men's shoes sitting by the front door. No boyfriend. She listened at Rachel's door. Music was playing softly. She was probably studying. Lauren knocked.

"Yeah," Rachel said. "Come on in."

Lauren opened the door and leaned in. "I just put some coffee on, want any?"

"Coffee, what time is it?" Rachel looked up from the book she had been reading.

"Almost midnight," Lauren said. "I got a lot of writing to do yet tonight."

"Yikes," Rachel said. "Are you still having trouble with the stories being bogus?"

Lauren nodded. "Bogus as in fabricated, yeah."

Rachel used a stocking as a bookmark and put the book down on the bed. "I don't want any coffee, but maybe a glass of wine."

RACHEL PRODUCED A BOTTLE OF MERLOT AS LAUREN STIRRED creamer into her coffee. Once Rachel had a half full glass, they sat at the table.

"I don't see what you can do." Rachel raised her glass and her voice was muffled and reverberated as she went on. "It's not your fault they're full of shit." She took a sip.

"I need proof." Lauren blew on her coffee.

"How are you going to do that?"

"Go back." Lauren put her mug down. "Re-interview some people without that monster standing over my shoulder."

"Monster?"

"Lonnie Huggins." Lauren shuddered thinking about how scary he was.

"That sounds dangerous." Rachel scrunched her nose.

"Oh, I'll go at a safe time and I'll take someone with me."

"That detective?" Rachel tipped the glass up to her lips and drained it.

"God, no. He's an asshole." Lauren watched Rachel finish her wine. "Besides, he's in on it."

Rachel shrugged. "Who, then?"

"I'm looking at her." Lauren laughed as Rachel's eyes shot open.

Chapter 29

Shades Of Trouble

SATURDAY 0230 Hours

Before Macbeth even opened the door to his apartment building foyer, he could hear the pounding and hollering. Camp. Great, just what he needed to cap the evening. He checked his mailbox, hoping that within those twenty seconds something would bring a resolution to whatever his landlord was beefing about at the girl who lived on the second floor. But no mail awaited, and Camp still railed on the stairway.

As Macbeth rounded the first flight and came into view of the second-floor landing, it occurred to him he could've gone through the back and avoided this altogether. Shit.

His landlord was on the landing in all his glory, wearing only his wife-beater and undershorts. A red, wormy-looking scar jutted from the top of his shirt, which left the bottom quadrant of belly exposed above his cotton boxers. His bony legs ended in white socks and black, slip-on dress shoes. One of his toothpick legs was decorated with a zipper scar from a vein extraction surgery a few years earlier. His face was dark and ruddy.

Macbeth shook his head as he glimpsed the plastic grip of the man's five-shot revolver hooked to his boxers. He hoped they'd stay up. He sympathized with the girl. She'd never given him any trouble. He thought she might be Polish because of her accent. She was maybe twenty-five and thankfully didn't have any kids.

Macbeth breathed deep and said a little prayer as he threw himself into the breach. "Hi, Mr. Camp. I appreciate you staying up for me." He was about to make a smartass comment about the boxers but thought better of it at the last second. "What's up?"

"Up!" Camp glared at the apartment door as if it had committed some kind of trespass. "Up!" He planted his knuckles on his hips and turned to Macbeth.

"I'm *up*, for one." Camp thrust a finger at the door. "She's up too, I can tell you that. And whoever else's in there with her." His shrill voice carried in the cramped stairway.

"Really?" Macbeth shrugged. He didn't hear anything. "Seems quiet now."

"You think so?" The way Camp said it made it obvious that he didn't agree. "This ain't the first time I been out here." He crossed his arms. He didn't look as if he planned on moving out of Macbeth's way anytime soon.

"God dammit," Camp growled. "After the first time, I left and they were right back at it. Second time too, and I can tell you I'm right tired of this shit."

"She have the music up too loud or something?"

Camp glared at him. "Fucking too loud."

"Seems like she turned it off. I'm sure she's in bed now. Probably too embarrassed to come to the door."

"You ain't listening to me," Camp grunted. "They're in bed, all right. They're fucking too loud. Fucking. You know. Having sex."

"Oh." What could he say to that?

"Sounds like she's spent the better part of an hour banging her skull off the headboard, wall, and anything else he could run her into."

"She okay?"

"Sure sounds like it to me and every-fucking-body else. It ain't like she's telling him to stop or anything like that. What the hell's wrong with people these days? Ain't anybody got any decency left?" This coming from an armed guy wearing a dago-T that was way too small and boxer shorts. Macbeth kept his mouth shut, but he wasn't able to suppress a grin.

"I'm bushed, Mr. Camp." Macbeth didn't want to push past him, particularly considering his manner of dress. "Tell you what. I bet she's got the message, but if they start up again, I'll come down and take a crack at it. Save you the trouble."

Camp looked at him suspiciously, then started down the stairs. He waved at the apartment door and in a loud voice said, "She's got to come out sometime. He might get away, but I'll get the last word, I can assure you that."

"I'm sure you will. No one gets past you." *Including me*, Macbeth thought, making room as Camp stomped by him.

"Don't patronize me." Camp turned and pointed at him. "I thought it was you banging her head off the wall." Camp reached the bottom of the stairs and opened his apartment door. Shaking his head, he said, "What's fucking wrong with the youth these days?"

"Goodnight."

"Goodnight, my ass."

Macbeth pushed his apartment door open and trudged in. His shoulders ached as if his head weighed a hundred pounds. He kicked off his shoes and closed the door behind him, locking it. It was muggy in the apartment. He walked through his front room, around the couch that was bathed in shadow, and threw open the balcony drapes. The streetlight glow from the parking lot spilled in through the sliding door. He pulled the door open and stepped out onto the balcony. He could hear the hiss of tires as cars drove along Sixty-Third Street.

The building immediately north of his was a mirror image. Where his balcony and foyer doors faced north, theirs faced south. Standing on his balcony, he could stare into a young woman's apartment, a nurse he rarely saw. Her balcony blinds were closed, and the apartment was dark.

Macbeth took hold of the iron railing and leaned forward, trying to get the kink out of his back.

It was too hot. He stepped back inside and closed the door. Skirting the computer desk, he dropped his keys on the kitchen table, undid his belt buckle, and placed his holstered Smith and Wesson on top of the refrigerator along with his snub-nosed revolver.

There were a half dozen Leinenkugels in the fridge. He grabbed one and twisted the cap off, tossing it in the direction of the garbage can. The cap made a tinkling sound as it skittered across the floor. He'd missed, just like he did with Huggins tonight.

The first mouthful didn't stay long enough to register a taste, nor did the second or third. When he stopped swallowing to breathe, he finally could taste the beer. He took one more pull and sat the empty on the counter. Being a cop in the summer took its toll, with the vest, a car with air conditioning issues, and a frustrated, miserable, overheated populace. He felt dry. Nothing a couple more beers wouldn't solve.

He pulled the fridge open again and grabbed another two bottles. He popped their caps off and dropped the caps in the garbage, along with the one on the floor. Taking the two bottles in one hand, he went back to the front room and sat on the couch and drank. The beer tasted good, cold and wet.

The sun would be up in a couple of hours. He had a gazillion things to do, not the least of which was to figure out another angle on taking Huggins down. He needed to get to bed so he could get an early start, nothing pressing, just all the little things that came with living.

He felt a dark specter hovering on the edge of his mood, and it seemed like he was approaching a profound moment in his life. Keep fighting or move on, give up. It would be so much easier to surrender, and that seemed so much more appealing at the moment.

But surrender wasn't something he was willing to consider, never had been. What he *was* going to do was down these two beers and go to bed. For starters, he was going to get a good night's sleep. That's what he needed most.

Hopefully, he'd wake up with a fresh take on everything. And if not, he'd at least be thinking clearer and that would be a good start. Like his mom used to say, "Things won't look so bad in the morning." Then again, in her condition, one day would be as shitty as the next, but he could only guess at that, because she couldn't tell him.

He closed his eyes and could hear Camp's voice in the back of his mind. When Macbeth had first moved in, Camp caught him by the washing machine, his laundry basket full of his academy gym clothes. The old guy said, "When you take this job, kid, you put one foot in the grave and the other in the penitentiary. You spend the rest of your career tight-roping between the two." Macbeth raised his bottle in a toast. He hated to admit it, but the old man had a point.

He took a deep swallow, not to quench his thirst, but to extinguish the smoldering embers of frustration.

Chapter 30

What Goes Up

SATURDAY 0245 Hours

Jermaine stood on the fifteenth-floor breezeway of 1119 North Cleveland. It was the next Cobra building west of 1150 North Sedgwick. The Cleveland building's top floors were vacant and abandoned. There was only one empty doorway on the entire floor. All the other openings had been boarded up with sheets of plywood. But inside, holes had been smashed through many of the cinder block walls, so you could go from one apartment to the next by stepping through the wall.

Jermaine hadn't seen a soul as he walked up the stairwell. The building was quiet above the tenth floor. That was the last one where people lived. He stood next to the elevators and the stairwell opening, looking through the chain link at the ground below. If he thought his stomach was upset before, it was on fire now.

He didn't have grandpa's gun and felt naked even though he'd only carried it once up from Mississippi. He was scared and something inside him kept saying to pray. But he didn't think he was entitled to pray anymore. He looked down and saw someone approach the building on foot. There was no doubt in his mind who it was. Game on.

Jermaine swallowed. His mouth was bone dry. His stomach tightened, and he was sorry he'd eaten earlier. It would be over soon enough, one way or the other. Violence wasn't pretty up close and when it was by your own hand, it took on a whole different feel. It wasn't good.

Finally, after what seemed like forever, he heard footsteps coming up the stairs. Pac-Man walked out of the darkened stairwell. His head swiveled from one side to the other, then he looked at Jermaine.

"Thanks for the call, little man. Where he at?" Pac-Man whispered, lifting his shirt. He had a gun stuck in his waistband.

Jermaine swallowed. It was time, no turning back. "He in that last apartment with a girl." He pointed to the last door on the floor with plywood hammered across its opening.

"Why he take her here and not someplace else?" Pac-Man fingered the handle of his gun and looked around the breezeway. Pac-Man was sweating, but whether from climbing the stairs or being scared, Jermaine couldn't tell.

"She young," Jermaine said. "Real young."

"How I get in?"

Jermaine pointed at the shadowy doorway. "Go in there, then through the wall to the next one over. There's a mattress in the back bedroom."

"How long he been in there?"

"A while, but he say he was gonna be a long time." Jermaine was glad his voice didn't break or crack like he felt his heart was about to do.

Pac-Man tugged his gun out, a big black revolver. "I want to cap him before he nut. Don't want him to leave this life on a good note. Let him die with a stiff dick and blue balls. C'mon."

Jermaine turned and followed Pac-Man toward the open doorway. Pac-Man reached out and took his elbow.

"I go first." He started toward the door. "I don't want you fucking up."

Jermaine swallowed down bile as they walked into the apartment.

The air was stale and filled with floating spots of dust in the light coming from the windows. It smelled like broken cement, dirty and dusty. In one corner a pile of matted fur was all that remained of a cat, the white of its skull winking from beneath the black hair. In the back bedroom, they came to a pass-through that had been hammered through the cinder block.

Pac-Man stopped and tilted his head as if that would let him hear better. The hole was small, and waist high, not nearly big enough to step through. They were going to have to crawl. Pac-Man bent down and peered through the opening. Then he stuck his head in for a better look.

After a couple seconds, Pac-Man pulled his head back from the other apartment and stared at Jermaine. Jermaine swallowed for like the hundredth time and looked away. Pac-Man shoved the revolver in his waistband, then pushed his head and shoulders through the tight opening. He wiggled and kicked, scraping his belly over the cinder block. Then he stopped.

Jermaine could hear a voice on the other side, then the sound of other people coming into the bedroom behind him. Huggins stepped up next to the hole and grabbed the back of Pac-Man's pants with one hand, while the other reached under him and grabbed the revolver. He pulled it out and handed it to Jermaine.

Huggins yanked hard and Pac-Man was back in the living room. His head banged the cinder block on the way out. Huggins pushed him down on the floor.

"Howdy, motherfucker." Huggins pushed a fist into Pac-Man's chest. "Remember me?"

Pac-Man lay on his back on the tile and stared. He had to know he was fucked. Huggins twisted Pac-Man's shirt in one fist while the other hand searched him again. After Huggins finished checking Pac-Man's ankles, Huggins punched him in the balls, making the enforcer curl up as much as he could under Huggins's pressure.

"You must be one crazy nigger thinking you can shoot at me." Huggins slapped Pac-Man's face several times. Then he lifted the taller man off the floor and stood him up as if he was a child. "You got his gun?" he asked Jermaine.

Jermaine nodded. "Yeah, sure do."

"That the motherfucker he used to shoot at me?"

"Maybe, I don't know."

Huggins looked over his shoulder. "Keloid."

"Yeah." The big man's voice came from close by. In the hallway?

"You got the key?"

"Yes."

"Let's go." Huggins ripped Pac-Man toward the door. "We got a little something for you, my brother."

Tea Bag crawled out of the hole and stood. He had an automatic in his waistband.

Pac-Man didn't beg, or cry, and Jermaine respected that at least. Pac-Man seemed to accept the fact that he was done. Huggins pushed him backward through the hallway, out the apartment door, and toward the elevator. Ronnell waited outside.

Ronnell was pasty white, almost as damp as if he'd just stepped out of a shower. Jermaine recognized the look in Ronnell's eyes and hoped he didn't look as scared. Keloid stood next to the elevator, a crooked hanger in one hand.

Pac-Man's head snapped around when he spotted White Boy. Huggins shoved him along, then spun him face first against the elevator door.

"Put your hands behind your back."

Pac-Man didn't move, so Keloid stepped over and pulled his elbows back. Ronnell tucked the gun in his waistband. He walked over and slid plastic ties over Pac-Man's wrists, cinching them together. Hands locked behind his back, Pac-Man was pinned against the metal doors. Huggins smashed the back of Pac-Man's head with an elbow, bouncing his face off the doors. The enforcer's knees almost buckled, but he stayed upright, wobbling from side to side.

Huggins took one of Pac-Man's earlobes and dragged him a couple of feet back, then pulled and twisted his ear hard. Keloid stepped up to one side of the elevator doorway. He slipped the crooked hanger into the small hole high up on the door close to the frame and rotated it. Keloid's tongue came out as he concentrated. The hanger caught on something, followed by a clank. He spun the metal a little more and pulled. The elevator doors parted a little.

"White Boy," Keloid said.

Ronnell jerked as if he'd been somewhere else, and stepped up to the crack between the doors. He pushed against the doors with his whole weight and finally got them to move. He kept pushing, slowly spreading them apart. Keloid took the hanger out of the hole and helped. Once the doors were open, Keloid wedged a block of wood at the base of one door, keeping it open. Ronnell did the same on his side.

Huggins yanked Pac-Man close to the gap. The elevator car hung above it, stopped on the sixteenth floor. It was a fifteen-story drop down the elevator shaft. Jermaine thought he could feel a breeze rolling out of the opening that stunk like an overflowed dumpster.

"Long way down, ain't it?" Huggins said. Pac-Man stayed quiet. "Cee behind you shooting at me?" Pac-Man didn't speak. "You and Cee keeping money for yourselves? You working with anybody else?" There was a long silence, then Huggins shook his head. "Gotta give you credit, lots other niggers woulda squealed already." Huggins motioned to Ronnell, then pointed at Jermaine. "Give White Boy your piece."

Jermaine looked down at Pac-Man's gun and handed it over to Ronnell.

"I don't like it," Huggins told Pac-Man. "But I gotta respect you not saying nothing. Now I gotta know some things." He twisted Pac-Man's ear upward, forcing him to stand on his toes. "White Boy, this motherfucker make life hard on you?"

Ronnell didn't say anything.

Huggins glared at him. "Well, did he, boy?"

"Yeah, I guess."

"Stick that pea-shooter up against the back of his knee."

Pac-Man struggled against Huggins's hold, but couldn't get free. "Knock it off." Huggins pressed Pac-Man toward the opening. "Or I'll just throw your ass down." As Huggins held him, Ronnell stuck the gun up behind Pac-Man's right knee.

"It gonna hurt." Huggins's voice was clipped and gravelly. "All you got to do is tell me what I wanna know. Cee behind you shooting at me?" Huggins's arm trembled with the pressure he was putting on Pac-Man's ear. When the enforcer didn't say anything, Huggins looked down at Ronnell. "Do it!"

Ronnell's hands shook.

"What you waiting for?" Huggins said. "Do it, you little pussy."

Jermaine stepped up and saw that Ronnell's eyes were filled with tears. Jermaine looked at Huggins. "Let me."

Huggins looked away. "Somebody gotta do it!"

Jermaine took the revolver from Ronnell and pushed it deep behind Pac-Man's knee. He squeezed. There was a loud bang and the gun jerked back in his hand. Pac-Man screamed. He would've fallen if Huggins had let go. Blood spurted from a ragged hole below Pac-Man's knee. Then more blood oozed out of the hole and ran down his leg, over his shoe, and onto the cement. Pac-Man ground his teeth together, his lips open and twisted.

"Now," Huggins said. "Cee behind you shooting at me?"

Pac-Man shook his head.

"That's more like it. You decide that on your own, did you?"

Pac-Man mumbled something that sounded like, "Yeah," and nodded the best he could with his ear in the vise of Huggins's grip.

"Cee know what you was fittin' to do?"

Pac-Man didn't do or say anything for a couple of seconds. Huggins gave his ear a tug. "C'mon, don't stop now."

A shudder ran through Pac-Man's body. He nodded slightly and tried to say something, but drool spilled from his mouth. Huggins sighed and shook his head.

"You both been skimming, right?"

Pac-Man nodded again. Jermaine thought he saw something on Pac-Man's cheek. He stepped closer. It was a tear, but just one. Jermaine had to admit that Pac-Man was tougher than he would have thought.

"What'd you do with the rest of the work once you shut down?"

Pac-Man shuddered. "Sold it—West Side."

"Cee working with anyone else?" Huggins tugged harder on the ear. "Who's this Momma Stone I been hearing about?"

Pac-Man's head shook a little as if he was trying to answer.

"Momma Stone," Huggins said again.

Pac-Man looked back at him blankly.

"Okay," Huggins said. "That the way it gonna be."

Pac-Man looked at Huggins out of the corner of his eye.

"I don't think he know," Keloid said.

"Good." Huggins reached his free hand behind him, toward Keloid. The big man took a folding knife out of his pocket and unfolded the blade. He stepped forward and laid the handle on Huggins's outstretched hand. The knife was big, and its blade was black. Huggins's hand closed over the handle.

"Since you been acting like a man, I'm gonna spare you some misery." Huggins brought the knife up and sliced down hard against the side of Pac-Man's head. "But I need this here."

The knife made a *swfft* sound as it sliced through his flesh, separating his ear from his skull with such force that the blade cut into his shoulder. The enforcer's body crumpled toward the edge of the shaft as he let out a screech that degraded into a howl.

Huggins lashed out and kicked Pac-Man into the elevator shaft. A second later his scream came to an abrupt, crunching halt with a thump of soft tissue meeting steel and concrete.

Jermaine moved up and peeked over the edge. The reek of trash was almost overwhelming. He couldn't see anything but the blackness that stretched down and down and down into forever where Pac-Man's broken body lay.

Chapter 31

Cabrini Justice

SATURDAY 0400 Hours

Jermaine leaned against the brick outside of Cecil Jones's apartment high up in the 1150 North Sedgwick building. Ronnell was further back on the breezeway holding the tools, with Keloid and Huggins up by the apartment door with the whore. She'd knocked and knocked again. She was skinny and looked dope-sick shaky. Finally, Jermaine could hear a deep voice mumble something from inside the apartment. *Show time*, he thought. But the door didn't open. Huggins prodded the whore.

"C'mon, Cee." Her voice was high, whiny. "Just wanna party like old times, baby girl make you feel real good." Jermaine couldn't make out the response, but the door still didn't open. Huggins whispered something in her ear.

"C'mon, baby." Her voice was unsteady, and she leaned against the apartment door as if her balance wasn't any better. "Your boy Pac-Man sent me over, said we had some celebrating to do." She drummed her long red nails on the door.

After some seconds dragged past, Jermaine heard the bolt rattle and the door cracked open. Huggins ripped the whore back. She fell against the chain link and landed hard on the concrete. Keloid swung around and kicked the door. It exploded inward. Keloid and Huggins rushed through the opening. A heavy crash came from inside. Jermaine stepped over the whore and went in too, with Ronnell following.

"Now, Cee." Huggins stood over the gang boss. "We gonna have ourselves a little talk."

CECIL JONES'S FACE WAS BLOODY FROM WHERE THE DOOR HAD caught him. His nose was busted crooked and he'd lost a couple of front teeth. One of his eyes was swelling shut, but Jermaine wasn't sure whether that was from the door or the beating that had followed.

Now Jones sat on a kitchen chair and leaned across the table, his arm fastened to the tabletop by two large steel C clamps. Huggins leaned against the kitchen counter, his eyes hard, but relaxed, like it was no big deal.

Jermaine's job was to turn the music up when Jones's gurgling screams threatened to get too loud. So far, he'd had to turn the volume up three times. Each time had coincided with one of Jones's fingers being pulled back until it snapped, then twisted around a little for effect. Jermaine's stomach was upset, even worse than it had been for Pac-Man's killing.

"Okay," Huggins told Jones. "You see, I know most of the answers already. I told you. Save yourself the pain. Pac-Man did."

Jones nodded vigorously.

"Where's my money?"

When Jones didn't say anything, Huggins nodded at Keloid. The big man stepped up and grabbed the next finger and started to pull it back. Jermaine had to look away as Jones's screaming started. He upped the volume.

Ronnell stepped out of the bedroom holding a zippered athletic bag. His mouth was open as he presented the contents toward Huggins. It was filled with bundles of cash.

"Well, look what we got here." Huggins took the bag from White Boy. He sat it on the counter and poked inside it. "There's a lot here,

Cee." He looked back to White Boy. "Keep looking, there's gotta be more." Ronnell nodded and disappeared back into the bedroom.

Jermaine saw that Jones was staring at the bathroom doorway, his mouth open, teeth broken. His eyes vacant, like nobody was inside. Maybe he'd given up.

Huggins stepped up to the table and looked in the direction of Jones's empty stare. Then he looked at Keloid and nodded toward the bathroom. The big man pushed away from the counter and headed that way, then stepped inside. Seconds later, Jermaine heard a metallic bang, followed by a grating sound, then a crash.

Huggins banged on Jones's head to get his attention. Jones's eyes, purple and swollen, leaking blood, tore away from the bathroom door and settled on Huggins.

Huggins was right above him, staring down. "Who else was involved, Cee?"

Jones shook his head slowly. His lips moved, spittle drooling from the corner of his mouth. No sound that Jermaine could hear. Huggins squatted and turned his ear toward his former boss.

"Say again," Huggins said.

Jones spurted.

Huggins nodded and stood. "Okay."

"Got some more," Ronnell shouted from the bedroom.

Huggins smiled, his gold tooth bright in his dark face. He patted Jones's head, then grabbed a handful of the man's nappy Afro and jerked his head back. He stared into Jones's face. "You think you can steal from me, from my mom?"

Jones didn't say nothing, just stared blankly up. Huggins let go of his head and squatted again. "Who's Momma Stone?"

Jones's eyes rolled back into his head. Huggins held a hand out to Jermaine, who left his post by the stereo, went to the sink, and filled a glass with cold water. He handed it to Huggins, who tossed it in Jones's face. "Stay with me now, Cee." Jones's head rolled and his eyes fluttered, then kind of focused on Huggins.

"Who's Momma Stone?"

Jones mumbled and Huggins leaned closer.

"She little Mavis Stomps? I know who that is."

Blood and saliva spilled from Jones's mouth.

Huggins straightened. He grabbed a small personal phone book off the table and leafed through it, then finally stopped. He looked back at Jones and held the book so the former gang frontman could see it. "This her?"

Jones nodded and closed his eyes.

"You steal from her too?"

Jones nodded. A fresh trail of blood trickled from his nose into his mouth.

Huggins stood. "You and Pac-Man fucked up." He stepped back by Jones's chair. The gang leader didn't try to follow Huggins with his eyes. "Ain't nobody gonna steal from me." Huggins banged a fist off his own chest. "And you ain't gonna steal from my mom."

He kicked the chair out from under Jones, who lurched and fell, his shoulder yanking against his secured arm. Something popped loud, the kind of sound Jermaine remembered hearing when his mom took a chicken apart. Jermaine turned the music up. Jones's body hung weird from the table. Something was horribly wrong with his shoulder. Jones tried to scramble to his knees, but something about his shoulder prevented him.

"Don't nobody fuck with my mom." Huggins circled around Jones, looking down at him. "Dig."

Jones squirmed and screamed. His face twisted in agony. Jermaine kept his hand on the volume knob.

"Then, you going to let this two-bit wannabe take a shot at me and not tell me about it. After all we been through? Did Momma Stone know about that? Tell me, Cee." Huggins drew back a leg and kicked Jones in the chest. The blow lifted the injured man off the floor and slammed him back down.

Jones blubbered—incoherently, as far as Jermaine could tell. Huggins squatted and looked at Jones hard. Huggins cocked his head to one side and spit on Jones before he stood. Then Huggins kicked Jones again and again, in the chest and stomach. Jermaine half expected his arm to rip off with the powerful strikes.

Keloid walked out of Jones's bathroom, a gym bag in hand. Jermaine craned his neck to see through the open bathroom door.

The medicine cabinet was gone and there was a gaping hole in the wall.

"How much?" Huggins said.

"A whole bunch and there's more bags down in the wall where this one came from."

Huggins grinned. "Nice." He looked at White Boy, who'd come out of the bedroom. "Open the window."

White Boy went over, pulled on the lip of the frame, and drew the window up. A warm breeze snaked in, bringing with it a stench like body odor. The smell came from the nearby meat processing plant; the wind was blowing just right.

Huggins looked at Keloid. "Take his arm."

Keloid yanked Jones's free arm back and held him firmly in place.

Huggins had a hard time loosening the C clamps. When one clamp did come off, Jones's injured arm shifted, and he screamed. Huggins quickly undid the other clamp and tugged Jones's arm free. Jones's scream melted into a hoarse groan. He puked. Jermaine felt the taste rise in his mouth, thinking he might puke, too, at any moment. This was beyond crazy, he thought. How'd Antwan hang?

"Got some Cabrini justice for you, Cee." Huggins lifted the Mickey Cobra leader.

They dragged Jones over to the open window and then heaved him up and through the screen. But only his head and torso made it outside. Huggins shifted his grip to Jones's legs and lifted him, pushing out. With a final scream Jones fell, a shoe kicked off to land on the floor next to Huggins's feet.

Keloid stooped to pick it up.

"Leave it." Huggins slid a chair by the window. "It'll be more real-istic." He scanned the room. "White Boy, get the clamps. Maine, wipe down everything you touched. An' let's go."

Keloid stepped up next to him. "You really think the cops'll buy he killed hisself?"

"I don't think they're going to care. If they think they can make it a suicide, maybe they'll stop looking too hard."

"Maybe."

"Fact is, I don't care neither. Let them think whatever. They ain't going to be able to put it on me."

"I dig that."

Huggins looked at Keloid and slapped his back. "We just tying up loose ends, Brother. Just tying up loose ends is all."

Jermaine wiped down everything he could, what wasn't coming with them. No way did he want anyone knowing he was in on this. No way. All he wanted was to kill that cop, avenge Antwan, but this— man, this was raw.

Chapter 32

New Leadership

SATURDAY 1200 Hours

Mavis heard the intercom beep and shifted her attention away from First Deputy Parks. "Hang on a sec, James." She put him on hold and punched the intercom. "Yes?"

"There's a guy on the line that won't take 'no' for an answer. He keeps asking for Momma Stone. I told him he had the wrong number, but then he asked for you."

"Okay," Mavis said. There was only one light blinking besides the one Parks was on. "Tell him I'll be right with him."

When she broke back into the line with Parks, he was still yakking as if she'd never left. She should've been elated. Parks was accomplishing what she wanted; she was playing him perfectly. Gold had pulled off the legal hocus pocus and now she had the pieces in play to get around Superintendent Plumb.

"James, sorry to interrupt. I got another call. Call me later, I want to know how he reacts. But I got to go." She disconnected and pushed the remaining blinking line. "Hello."

"Momma Stone?" The voice wasn't Cecil's.

"Speaking."

"You know who this is?"

"I don't know," she said. "You're not who I expected. Where's Cee?"

A bubbly laugh hissed over the phone. "Cee retired, I'm the new Cobra leader." The voice was confident and deep.

"Really?" She knew it had to be Huggins. "Lonnie?"

"We need to talk."

"I suspect we do." She smiled.

"Yeah," he said. "Now."

"I'm a little busy."

"Make time." His tone was commanding.

"Meet me at my office on Chicago Avenue," she said.

"I don't think so."

"What did you have in mind then?"

"Something private. You don't want to be seen talking to me."

"Don't suppose I do," she said. "But I don't know you and I don't feel *comfortable* being with you in private."

"We all on the same side. I don't see what you got to fear."

"Who said anything about fear? This is about trust. I don't trust people I don't know." She paused and listened, but didn't hear anything, not even breathing.

"Me and you been getting ripped off," he finally said. "I'm gonna tell you by who and what I done about it. I think you gonna be very 'preciative, especially when I lay some green on you I recovered."

"Now you have my attention." She opened her desk drawer and looked at the little automatic lying on top of the papers. It was small, but she'd been told it was adequate when used up close.

"Thought you might find that interesting."

"You know where the community center is on Clybourn?" she asked.

"That don't sound private."

"I'll leave the second-floor landing door off the alley open for you, there won't be anyone around. I'll be inside." She lifted the gun. For such a small thing it was deceptively heavy.

"How long?"

"Give me a half hour. And don't bring any trouble with you. I'll have protection."

Huggins climbed the stairs two at a time. He had a good feeling about this. He adjusted the strap of the gym bag on his shoulder. It contained a very small percentage of the money they'd ripped out of Jones's place. He had no idea how much Stomps was getting from Jones, but he was about to find out. If she thought she was going to keep getting paid, she was going to have to convince him she deserved it. And, of course, the amount was going to have to be renegotiated. He smiled and felt the first pulse in his dick. He reached down and grabbed himself, tugging downward. Maybe he was going to get lucky in more than one way.

Mavis heard footsteps coming up the stairs. She had to be careful. Even though she'd never met Huggins, he didn't seem like the kind of man who would like to take orders, much less from a woman. His propensity for violence was well known. He was one of those brothers destined to succeed in whatever he chose to do; he'd just chosen a life of crime.

She set the gun on the desk blotter. It was important he know she could handle herself and that she wasn't afraid of him. Well, not too much, at least. A figure stepped through her open office door. He was large but not huge, dark, with his hair done in Afro puffs. He smiled and a gold tooth glinted warmly. He placed a gym bag on her couch and sat on its arm.

She smiled. "You don't look like the Cobra leader I know."

"Like I told you. Been a change," he said.

"Do I want to know what happened to the other guy?"

The figure shrugged.

She nodded at the door. "Why don't you close that so we can talk."

He looked over his shoulder, and then rose. He closed the door.

Turning around, he pointed at the gun on the desk. "You fittin' to shoot me with that?"

She shrugged. "Not unless you make me."

Laughing, he said, "You gonna need something a whole lot bigger."

"Do you know who I am?" she asked with her elbows on the desk, then steepled her fingers over the gun.

"You the one called Momma Stone." He sat on the couch next to the gym bag. "You the alderman from around here." He spread his arms out wide.

"Besides you and Cecil, does anyone else know of my involvement with the Cobras?"

"Not on account of me they don't."

"I'd like to keep it that way," she said.

"Bet you would." Huggins crossed his legs and sank deeper into the couch as if he didn't have a care in the world. "What's your deal with the Cobras?"

"I helped Cecil think through some things," she said. "I did what I could from city hall to help around here."

"And he paid you for that?"

"Yes, he did, though he'd been holding back for the last couple of months."

"That's two of us." Huggins took the gym bag and tossed it on the desk next to the gun.

"What's this?" She didn't move to open the bag.

"Maybe some of what you lost," he said. "Found it at Cee's place."

"Where was Cecil at?"

"He'd dropped out."

"I see." She kept watching Huggins as she unzipped the bag. When she pulled the flaps apart, she saw bundles of rubber-banded money. "How much is here?"

"I don't rightly know, but we found a couple bags and I figured some of it was yours. So here we are." He was so confident and at ease that she couldn't help but admire him.

"Yes, here we are." She let go of the bag and settled back in her seat. "So, what's your plans?"

He grinned big. "Plans for what?"

"The Cobras. Me?" She was feeling less threatened but kept her hands on the desk near the gun. He wasn't giving off any violent vibes, but instead, she felt drawn to him, to his power. "What do I get out of it? For my advice, my help?"

"You wanna get paid for that?"

"Of course, don't we all." She smiled back. "Running political campaigns is expensive. Don't you want a friend in the City Council?"

"I ain't never had a friend at city hall before," he said.

"You have and just didn't know it," she said. "After all, it was me getting the ball rolling on your new trial."

"If you work at city hall, you can get me a cop's address."

"Who, Macbeth?"

Huggins smiled and nodded.

"Don't worry about him. I've got something planned that'll keep him away from you."

"I got something planned, too," he said. "And mine gonna be so much more satisfying."

She had to play this carefully. The last thing she needed was some rash move against the cop. Not until she'd ridden the controversy to re-election and then the mayor's office. "Do you think the heat that'll bring will be worth it?"

"Don't care."

"Why don't you let me take care of that problem for you?" She bit her lower lip.

He smiled. "How 'bout you do what you want to, and I'll do what I got to, and see which one is more permanent."

She stood and came around the desk, stopping in front of him. She could feel the heat emanate from the man.

"Is that the kind of advice you gave Cee?" he said. "Don't cause too much trouble, shit like that? That why he shutting down all the time?"

"Not at all." She stared down at him and felt a magnetic attraction to him. He had charisma that had come from a lifetime of proving himself on the street. And she found that exciting. Where Jones had been intelligent, Huggins was street smart. Both men were strong, but

Huggins's strength was so much more vibrant, so alive. Sexuality pulsed off him like an odor.

"Sometimes I advocate violence." She ran her hands down her thighs, as if her palms were wet. "Just the other day, I told him that we'd be better off with a war between the Vice Lords and the GDs."

"What'd he say?" Huggins sat up on the couch. His face wasn't two feet from her waist.

"He was scared." She licked her lips. "He was scared of his damn shadow, always thought the police were onto him."

❧

Lonnie Huggins stood. Stomps was close, well within arm's reach. She was hot, coming on to him. He grinned and stepped toward her. She backed up against the desk. He reached around her, took the gym bag off the desk top, and tossed it to the floor.

"You think the GDs should be killing Vice Lords?" He leaned into her and sniffed her throat as she nodded. She smelled like damp woman and that was all good. "And Vice Lords should kill GDs?"

"Uh huh," she said.

He pushed his face into her neck until his lips contacted her flesh. He ran his mouth up to her ear and bit down. She gasped. He grabbed her ass with both hands and lifted her onto the desk, pushing himself between her thighs, spreading her legs apart. He pulled at her dress's hem and yanked her panties down. They were damp and he couldn't contain his grin. She wanted him.

He unbuckled his belt and dropped his pants. His gun fell to the carpeted floor with a loud thump. He pulled his shorts aside and grabbed himself. Pushing her down on the desk, he crushed her with his weight and pinned her.

She pushed as hard as she could against his chest. "Wait. Stop."

His body didn't budge as he worked his himself against her. "Ain't no stopping."

"But I need you to wear a condom." She struggled hopelessly against his weight. "I have one in my purse."

"Fuck that shit." He pushed himself inside her.

She moaned and pushed against his chest as they fucked. With each thrust, the desk scooched across the floor with a grating screech. He grabbed a handful of her hair and pulled hard, banging her head against the desk. She gasped and pushed against him. He crushed her mouth with his, their teeth clanking together forcefully. He could taste blood.

She mumbled something he couldn't hear and didn't care. He felt his control slipping and with a cry from her, it was over.

MAVIS, TEARS STREAMING DOWN HER CHEEKS, ROLLED OFF THE desk as Huggins stomped down the stairs. The impression of her gun felt like it would be permanently embedded into her spine, not to mention how he'd used his forehead to bang her face. She sat on the office floor for a minute and gathered her thoughts.

Everything hurt, her face, especially her nose, her neck, the back of her head, her breasts, bite marks still visible with bruising starting to darken beneath her skin. She hadn't thought their meeting would be anything like this. At some level, she'd wanted it, but she didn't think that had mattered to him. She was glad she was on the pill, but was he clean? He'd been in prison for a while.

What was scarier was that she could feel the hum of the violence under his skin. Never had she encountered a man so barely under control. How the hell had she thought she'd be able to control him? Maybe not, probably not, who did she think she was kidding? She wiped her hand across her mouth, and it came away smeared with blood. She'd been a fool.

He was going after the cop next, stirring up more trouble, derailing her carefully laid plans. She'd opened the gate and let out a primal beast and now recognized that monster was out of control.

Chapter 33

Back Into The Jaws

SATURDAY 1750 Hours

Lauren, wearing a dark blue polo shirt and jeans, pulled into the lot at 1150-60 North Sedgwick a little before six in the evening. The sun was still high in a cloudless sky. The cars in the parking lot were ablaze in sunlight sparkling off windshields and paint. Rachel leaned over the dashboard of Lauren's Dodge Neon and looked up at the building.

"Holy shit," Rachel said. "How tall is it?"

"Sixteen floors," Lauren said. "I think ten apartments on each floor."

"Holy shit," Rachel said again. It had taken a lot of convincing before she'd finally agreed to come along. Lauren was thankful that she had and didn't quite know how she was going to make it up to her.

As Lauren parked, she found her confidence evaporating. The lot was filled with cars and there were several groups—mostly teenage boys—hanging out, sitting on the hoods and trunks of parked cars. Many of them were dressed in white T-shirts or muscle shirts and jeans or shorts. They were talking; smoking, laughing. Music blared from car radios. Lauren saw at least one bottle passed around, wrapped in brown paper.

She pulled her key out of the ignition. "Be sure to lock your door," she said. But Rachel was already out of the car. Lauren reached over and threw the lock herself. Her shirt had *Trevians* embroidered on the left breast in green. She hoped she could convince the guards that the word stood for a social agency or advocacy group, instead of her high school mascot. She grabbed her reporter's notebook, stashed a pen in the wire spiral, and got out. She slipped the digital recorder into her jeans pocket and locked her door. She checked her notes for the apartments they had to visit and stuffed the notebook in with her recorder.

Rachel was wearing a tight gray T-shirt with *Pink* written across her breasts, and jeans with gym shoes. She stood next to Lauren's car surveying the parking lot as if it were a firing squad. She looked back at Lauren, fear dancing behind her eyes.

Lauren played it off, feeling the same fear gnaw at her own gut. But she wasn't going to let Rachel know how she felt. Lauren tried to ignore that the conversations and laughter had come to a stop. Only the throbbing beat of the radios was left. Obviously two white girls were not a common sight around there.

"Come on, Rach," Lauren said. She waited for her roommate to acknowledge her before she started for the lobby door. Inside, Lauren fished out her notebook and told the guards that they were headed to the first apartment number on the thirteenth floor. When the guards didn't stop the two of them, she wanted to think her plan had worked. But she was pretty sure Rachel's boobs had really got them in.

They rode the elevator up with a teenage girl who had bright maroon extensions woven into her hair. She was chewing gum, cracking it to the beat leaking from her headphones. The girl was braless, with a cropped purple spandex top and black spandex leggings with a white thong showing over the waistband. She also wore luminescent yellow house slippers. Lauren was thankful for the distraction. As soon as the girl got off the elevator, the smell invaded Lauren's nostrils and she could practically taste the foul gunk that was all over the floor. Rachel didn't seem to notice, though she made a face and giggled after the girl left.

Before the elevator even opened on the thirteenth floor, Lauren could hear the deep thrum of the bass and the cackle of voices. *Oh, my God*, she thought, *a party. Already?* She closed her eyes and wished the doors of the elevator would stay shut. The doors shuddered and pulled back. The pulsing music flooded the elevator as Lauren fingered the Close Door button. The ding of the elevator's arrival was practically lost in the beat. Rachel peeked out and quickly pulled her head back in. A lurid whiff of pot rolled in after her.

The doors stayed open despite Lauren's repeated efforts on the close button. They could skip the apartment on thirteen, Lauren thought. She just wanted the elevator door to close before someone noticed them. Rachel reached over and pressed eleven. The ding was faint again in the torrent of sound emitted from the hallway. The doors shook and slid closed, but before the car began its descent another ding announced it was opening yet again. Lauren punched the Close Door button, over and over. The elevator shook and the doors popped back.

Two teenage boys stepped toward the elevator but stopped abruptly. The closest one was dark complected, his hair in short dreadlocks. He was shirtless. White boxers hung low on his hips, black baggy jean shorts hung even lower. He had on white tube socks, the right one pulled up to his knee, the left down around his ankle. A cigarette hung from his mouth like it had been forgotten.

The other boy was lighter skinned, also bare chested, his hair buzzed close to his scalp. His mocha skin was graffitied with home-made tattoos in blue of five-pointed stars, pyramids, crescent moons, the initials M.C., snakes, and a black panther. Plaid underwear showed above his shorts. He thumped a beat on his stomach with his fingers and thumbs.

Lauren prayed and pushed the button desperately for eleven. The boys stood still and stared, their eyes glassy and red, lids half closed. The brown boy turned to look at his darker friend. The first boy's cigarette fell to the concrete as the doors began to close. Lauren realized she was holding her breath. She exhaled as the doors nearly shut. But dark fingers thrust between them and the doors reversed themselves yet again.

When the door opened wider the boys were grinning. The darker kid entered; his friend followed. Lauren quickly punched eleven again. The two teenagers looked first at Rachel, or at her breasts, then at Lauren, and back to Rachel. The doors finally closed, and the elevator shook as it started to descend.

The elevator went to eleven and stopped. The doors slid open. Lauren let Rachel go out first. As Rachel passed the door's threshold, the lighter-skinned kid slapped Rachel's ass. It sounded hard enough to leave an imprint. Lauren shut her eyes and prayed that was all. The doors started to close with the two teenagers inside. She said, "Thank you," under her breath and ran into Rachel's back.

Her friend had come to a dead stop.

"What y'all want?"

Lauren stepped around Rachel and found their path blocked by a black girl, almost six feet tall, who had to weigh two hundred pounds. But she wasn't fat. She was a living, breathing example of big boned. Her bright green T-shirt had to be huge, because it hung on her like a tent. Her shorts, what could be seen under the shirt, were tight. A black panther crawled up one thigh. Her legs were long, and her feet were in flip flops, her toes painted a matching green.

Two more young women flanked the girl, completely blocking the way. The tallest, easily six foot, but rail thin, looked older than the others. Her hair was yanked into a severe topknot on her head that added another five inches to her height. She had on wraparound sunglasses and a white spaghetti strapped T-shirt, an orange bra underneath. Her long legs were encased in orange leggings with sequin stripes, and white stiletto pumps accounted for at least four inches of her height.

The third girl was shorter than the others, and probably weighed as much as the two put together. Her hair was in an Afro and she had on an oversized T-shirt with the Cookie Monster on the front.

Rachel stood still, like if she didn't move, they couldn't see her.

"What y'all white bitches doing here?"

Lauren held up her notebook. "Working. Now if you'll excuse us." She stepped in front of Rachel and, as she kept moving, the girls made a narrow path for them. Lauren glanced back to make sure Rachel was behind her. She referred to her notebook, then looked at the nearest door. They were on eleven. She certainly wasn't going back to thirteen, which meant the next apartment they needed to visit would be on nine, two floors down.

She grabbed Rachel's arm and pulled. They went to the stairwell. It was dark and it stank. The lights were out, and litter was scattered on the steps. Graffiti covered the cinder block walls in paint, and marker, the symbols she'd seen on the light-skinned teenager, symbols and snakes—gang stuff. Lauren gripped the railing and started down.

Rachel groaned.

"What?" Lauren looked back at her friend, who was still by the stairwell door.

"Those two boys just got off the elevator."

"Come on." Lauren picked up speed. The wall adjacent to the next landing was labeled ten. "Just one more." She could hear footfalls on the stairs above her. "Shit." Then she heard the click, click of the stilettos, too.

Lauren peeked out on the ninth floor. It was clear. She stepped out of the stairwell and turned to grab Rachel. The two girls hugged the wall and side-stepped away from the door as footsteps kept going down. As Rachel kept watch, Lauren checked her notebook for the apartment number. She didn't remember this floor, but it was on her page. With the red brick and doors, every floor looked the same.

Lauren took a deep breath and walked down to the apartment without looking to see if Rachel was with her. She tapped on the door. She closed her eyes for a second, praying that the people in the stairwell hadn't heard her knock. She felt Rachel bump into her, smelled her perfume. Lauren knocked again. Nothing.

There were two apartments on eight. She waved for Rachel to follow and made her way to the stairwell at the other end of the floor. She listened and heard distant noises, music and voices.

No one was home at the first apartment on the eighth floor. Lauren was at the second door when Rachel, who was waiting by the stairwell, shrieked and raised her hands on either side of her face. "They're coming back up."

Lauren pounded hard on the door as Rachel scooted down to the opposite end of the floor and the other stairwell. Lauren knocked again, then gave up, joining Rachel at the top of the stairs as Rachel stepped down. Lauren grabbed her arm and pointed up. They shot up the stairs as voices shouted from outside the stairwell.

A female voice said, "See if them bitches is in the stairs!"

Rachel stopped on nine and Lauren gave her a little shove to keep her going up. On ten they ran over to the elevator and pressed the down button.

A loud crash and the tinkle of glass shards on concrete burst from the stairwell as the elevator doors shuddered open. Lauren and Rachel found it was empty and hopped on. Lauren slapped the lobby button. Rachel looked at her, eyes brimming with tears.

"This place is awful," Rachel said. "Don't invite me to come with you again."

Lauren nodded. The doors slowly closed. The elevator shook and descended but stopped at seven. Lauren stared at the indicator. She wanted to cry. She looked at Rachel.

"We got to get off," Lauren said. Rachel nodded meekly. "We don't want to get trapped in this elevator. So, when that door opens, get off, okay?"

The door slid open. Rachel and Lauren got out. An old woman stood watching them. She was dressed in a housecoat. Lauren took her notebook out and made for the one seventh floor apartment on her list. Maybe someone would be home and they could get out of sight for a few minutes. She pounded on the door.

Voices drifted in from above and below, but Lauren couldn't tell what was being said. She pounded on the door again. Rachel sniffed and wiped her eyes with the hem of her T-shirt.

Lauren wanted to give up, but she knew she wasn't coming back, and so far, she hadn't found out anything. Was that because Konrad's information as to when to go calling was that good? There was one apartment left to try and that should've been the first stop. She knew they had to get out, and she certainly owed Rachel some relief, but this was her last shot.

"One more, Rach." Lauren watched her friend as she said it. The girl's eyes were wide and wet. "Just one more." Before Rachel could argue, Lauren headed for the stairwell and the sixth floor. That's where she would find Liberty Collins's apartment.

As Lauren knocked, she could smell frying meat. The door swung open. A woman in her mid-twenties stood in the doorway, holding an infant dressed in nothing but a diaper and a pink plastic hair clip in her curly black hair.

"Hi," Lauren said. "Is Ms. Collins here?"

The woman tilted her head. "Who?"

"Liberty Collins." Lauren opened her notebook and verified the apartment number.

"I don't know who that is." A chorus of loud voices came from the closest stairwell, and the sound of more glass breaking. Lauren didn't want to look but when she did, she saw Rachel staring at the dark opening.

"Here pussy, pussy, pussy," a voice called from the stairwell. "Where is you?"

"Get in here." The woman had stepped back and held the door open. She reached out and grabbed Rachel's arm, dragging her inside, too. The woman closed the door and shook her head.

Lauren's insides were quivering. She took a deep breath and slowly blew it out. She looked at her notebook again. She had to blink several times to bring it into focus. The notebook was shaking. "Thank you."

"What on Earth are you two girls doing here?" The woman shifted her baby from one hip to the other. "You know you could get hurt out there."

"Yeah." Rachel ran her hand across her eyes, wiping tears away. "Can I use your bathroom?"

The woman nodded and pointed down a hall with her free hand.

"Look," Lauren said after Rachel was gone. "I'm sorry to bother you, but I was here yesterday a little after noon. I talked to a woman who said she lived here, and said her name was Liberty Collins."

"Not in my house you didn't."

"I'm not here to cause you any trouble, but I'm not making this up, either." Lauren felt she was recovering and tried to sound professional.

"You gotta be mistaken." The woman nodded. "I don't know any Liberty Collins."

"Okay." Lauren squeezed her pen in frustration. Then she pointed over the woman's shoulder, at the playpen. "You've got a pink teddy bear and a stuffed doggy in there, and a teething ring, too. Or at least you did yesterday."

The woman stared at her a moment. "I don't know what you're talking about."

"I'm not going to make any trouble. I haven't even asked your name. I'm not going to tell CHA or anyone else that I talked to you, I promise." Lauren tapped her notebook with her pen, then reached into her back pocket and switched off the digital recorder. "But I got to know the truth, please."

"You with the police?"

Lauren shook her head and would've laughed if she wasn't so close to crying. "No."

"Why do you care who lives here?"

"Like I said, I was here, but something wasn't right, you know." Lauren waved in the direction of the bathroom. "I was with someone else."

"You're not making sense." The woman held the kid to her chest. The little girl grabbed a handful of the woman's shirt and held tight, playfully yanking it back and forth. But the woman's gaze was locked on Lauren's.

Lauren tapped her note page. "We're working for the defense of a guy who lives around here, and we were interviewing possible witnesses. We were told someone in this apartment could help him out. Help us get him out of jail. Then we came by and talked to this Liberty Collins who said she lived here."

"You said all that already. I asked why you care about all this?"

Lauren sighed. "I care about the truth. But somebody is trying to sell me a bunch of crap."

The woman laughed, and it wasn't a pretty laugh. It belonged to someone a hundred years older. "Who are you trying to help?"

"Lonnie Huggins."

The woman looked over her shoulder at the front door. She looked back at Lauren and leaned closer, whispering. "I don't need nothing coming back on me."

"I won't reveal who said anything." Lauren held her notebook to her chest. She could reference an anonymous source who was too scared to come forward and still make her argument. The woman stared at her. The baby played with her shirt and cooed. The woman blinked hard and let out a breath.

"This can't come back to me." She held Lauren's stare. "They paid me to let them use my apartment for a couple hours." She bounced the baby higher in her arms. "I was going to work, you know. I need the money." As she straightened, the woman's gaze dropped to the floor.

Lauren reached out and grasped her forearm. She saw fear in the woman's face. "Thank you, nobody'll ever know we talked." Lauren tapped her own chest and made a zippering motion across her own lips.

When Rachel returned, her eyes were red and her face wet. She looked at the door. "How are we going to get out of here?" Her hands fiddled with her jeans pockets, maybe to keep them from shaking.

Lauren swallowed. "We'll be okay."

"But those boys—"

The woman put her hand up. "They was after you?"

Lauren nodded.

"Shoot." The woman shifted the kid to the other hip. She eased past Lauren and went into the kitchen. She moved the baby again and took the phone from its cradle on the wall.

She dialed and held the receiver to her ear.

"Yeah, I live at Eleven-Fifty Sedgwick on the sixth floor. There's a bunch a' boys fixin' to fight and I heard one of them say he got a gun. You got that? I ain't telling who I am." She hung up.

"The police will be here in a few minutes. When they come, y'all get the hell out and don't come back."

Lauren and Rachel followed a line of cops down the stairwell to the first floor. She and Rachel walked out of the lobby with three uniformed officers and one in jeans and a T-shirt. The plainclothes officer was white and had a receding hairline. He wasn't too tall, definitely not Macbeth, but Lauren recognized him from the lobby as being with Macbeth the last time she was here. There were several blue and white police cars in the parking lot. Lauren had never been so happy to see her dinged-up little Neon. Her car was blocked by a dark gray car with headlights winking on and off.

She and Rachel walked to the Neon and leaned on the trunk to wait for the police to pull out. The cop in plainclothes walked to the gray car and lit a cigarette. He took a deep drag and blew the smoke into the air above him before stepping over to their car.

"What brings you two ladies to Cabrini?"

Rachel pointed at Lauren. "I'm with her."

"Okay," he said. "You don't look like professionals, so I've got to assume it's personal business."

"What do you mean by professionals?" Lauren tried to see if this guy recognized her as well. Apparently, he didn't, and she found herself grateful she'd stayed in the background when she was there before. "You mean like hookers?"

He laughed and coughed, waving at the air in front of him. Another plainclothes cop banged out of the lobby and strolled toward them. Lauren recognized him instantly. It was Macbeth.

"If you are *those* kinds of pros, I'm the starting center for the Bulls," the shorter cop said.

"Are you trying to say that we couldn't be hookers? That we're not pretty enough or something?" She felt silly arguing, but her brain was stuck in neutral and she couldn't come up with anything better to say.

"Shit, Stacey." The smaller cop took a short puff on his cigarette. "Check this little spitfire out. First, she's pissed thinking I called her a whore, and then she gets even madder when I say she couldn't be one. Can't win, that's what I get for being nice."

"You've had that effect on women since I've known you." Macbeth opened the passenger door of the unmarked car and seemed about to get in. Then he stopped. "What *are* you two doing around here?"

"What's that supposed to mean?" Lauren said.

"Ouch, Mike, what'd you do to her?" Macbeth sat as his partner walked around the front of the gray car.

"That's what I'm saying. Ain't you listening?" He flicked his cigarette onto the pavement.

Macbeth squinted at Lauren and leaned across the front seat as if to get a better look. "Weren't you with that white guy yesterday in the lobby of Eleven-Fifty?"

Lauren didn't say anything. She didn't know what to say. He had seen her after all.

"The guy who said he was Lonnie Huggins's lawyer?"

The shorter cop's face tightened. His stare pierced her.

"I'm working on his defense team," she said.

"Then I'd be careful if I were you." Macbeth closed his door. "You're working for a monster."

The other cop got in and started the car. The tires squealed as he backed up, then he shifted into gear and sped out of the lot.

"Holy shit." Rachel looked at Lauren with wide eyes.

Lauren waved for Rachel to get in as she sat behind the steering wheel of the Neon. She took a deep breath. "Shit."

"What?" Rachel asked.

"I didn't think he saw me yesterday."

"Don't worry about it." Rachel fastened her seatbelt. "I thought they were kind of cute."

Chapter 34

Urban Economics

SATURDAY 1800 Hours

Huggins patted his trump card as the Escalade bounced into a lot off Sixty-Fifth Street in the rain. Tea Bag, who was driving, stopped away from a knot of pickup trucks parked by the old brick warehouse that had been converted into a gym. It was part of an industrial park outside of Chicago, in the village of Bedford Park. Jet airplanes took off and landed close by at Midway Airport, and their exhaust lingered in the air with the other chemical fumes from the nearby factories. It stank.

Huggins watched the lot before he finally stepped out of the black Navigator. Rain pounded his newly twisted braids. The Cobra enforcer walked to the door of the gym, the water cascading down his face. He felt uneasy being away from his home turf, going into another man's jungle. But he couldn't let it show. To exhibit weakness was death. Just like being inside.

Keloid followed, leaving Tea Bag alone in the Lincoln. The parking lot was secluded, cut off from easy surveillance by other buildings. A tricked-out purple bubble Chevy bumped into the lot and stopped behind the Caddy. Three more Cobras got out and joined them.

As Huggins got close, the door to the gym swung open. Standing in the doorway was a tall, bald white man in his twenties. He was shirtless with blue jailhouse tattoos crawling up his arms, spilling onto his chest, and stretching across his chiseled gut. There was a gun stuck in his waistband, but his hands stayed well clear. The man stepped aside to let Huggins and his crew in.

Coming through the door felt like he'd walked into a sauna. The heat and humidity were like a wet glove. Sweat popped from Huggins's flesh to mingle with the cool rain.

It was dark except for a light that shone above a boxing ring raised off the concrete floor. Shadows swallowed everything outside of the lone bulb burning over the canvas and thick ropes. A figure leaned on the far side of the ring. His features were obscured by the edge of the shadow. Huggins felt doubt cloud his mind. He was taking a chance, but he wanted this *very* bad.

Keloid climbed up and held the ropes apart. Huggins followed and stepped through into the ring. The shadowed figure, a white man, moved into the light.

Russell Paramore was the leader of the Almighty Popes, whose reputation for violence was almost as infamous as the Cobras'. The Popes' leader was a good six feet of steroid fueled muscles straining to burst through skin decorated with brightly colored tattoos. They were twisted religious symbols, dominated by the cross, and there was nothing cheap or jailhouse about them. These were professional and represented thousands of dollars.

Paramore smiled. "What's up?"

Huggins returned the smile with his own, knowing his gold tooth would show. "I'd like to conduct a little business." Keloid stayed by the ropes, but the other Cobras had stayed back from the ring, only their shoes visible in the light.

Paramore's smile widened.

"See." Huggins let his arms rest at his sides; this was it. No turning back. "A cop been giving me fits and I'm told you might be able to tell me where he live. Maybe where his family at." Huggins ran his tongue along his front teeth, feeling the gold-plated front tooth.

"I come across addresses now and again." Paramore flexed his arms, making his tattoos dance and wiggle. "What you figure it's worth to you?"

"Depends."

"Depends?" Paramore asked. His eyebrows crunched together over his nose as he squinted at Huggins. "What's that mean?"

Moisture ran down Huggins's scalp. He didn't know whether it was rain or sweat. "I could track the bitch down my own self for free, but I'm in a hurry and I figure you could save me time."

Paramore shrugged. "Being in a hurry can make things complicated. What're you willing to pay for the info?"

"How much you asking?"

Paramore stared at him. "How important is it to you?"

"C'mon, quit playing, give me a price."

Paramore wiped sweat from his face. "Listen, man, you must want this prick bad if you're willing to talk to me. So why shouldn't I get paid all I can?"

"You got a point." Huggins found himself wishing for something to chew. "It's like this. I don't usually play that Folks and People bullshit. Yeah, I'm a Cobra and my boys is like family, but if you ain't in my shit, I give a fuck, know what I'm saying. Fuck all that shortie gangbanging bullshit, far as I'm concerned. But we both People, feel me?"

"Okay." Paramore waited.

"How much?" It was Huggins's turn to shrug. "Just don't fuck me. You fuck me, I gotta decide what I'm gonna do 'bout that."

"By 'decide what to do about it,'" Paramore crossed his arms, his stance more defensive, "you mean like come back on me or something?"

"Could be." Huggins shrugged again. He had to turn this around. "If you play me for a bitch, then I got to make some kind of play for the disrespect. But why it got to be like all that? Way I see it; we could help each other out, you know? Maybe some time you need something done that white boys can't do, then I can have my niggas do it. Simple urban economics."

"Urban economics?" Paramore laughed. "You've been thinking real hard."

Huggins laughed, too. "Man, I got me a lawyer cook up that intellectual shit."

Paramore scratched his head. "All that aside, man. I'm gonna need some big-time Franklins."

This was exactly what Huggins wanted, it wasn't "no," but how much. Time to bring in his ace in the hole. "Remember that nigger stuck your little brother while he was in Stateville?"

Paramore nodded, frowning.

Huggins dug in his jeans pocket, pulled out something wrapped in paper. He tossed it onto the canvas. The paper opened and a small dark thing bounced out. "I figured you might consider this a show of goodwill."

Paramore stared at the ear as if he couldn't figure out what it was. He moved closer and stopped. His mouth split in a grin, showing large white teeth. "That what I think it is?"

Huggins nodded. "I didn't have time to cut out ol' boy's heart, 'fraid his ear gonna have to do." The pressure in Huggins's gut melted away. "Rest assured, he ain't still breathing."

Paramore laughed. "I like your style, Lonnie. Shit I heard about you don't do you justice. When you bring it like that, how could I say no? Who is this cop got you so pissed off?"

Huggins lifted his shirt, shifted his pistol to the side, and pulled out a torn paperback book cover. "This old dude wrote a book about some motherfucker long time ago had the same name." He handed it to Paramore. The cover read *Macbeth*. Huggins had written his number on the back.

"I'll put my people on it." Paramore waited a second or two like he was expecting more. "I'll call you when we got something."

"Cool." Huggins turned and ducked through the ropes Keloid held for him and hopped down. Keloid followed.

They left the gym as they'd come in, quiet and smooth. In the parking lot, the crew split and loaded up just like they'd come, except the rain had stopped. Keloid motioned for Huggins before they climbed in the Navigator.

"Lonnie." Keloid shook his head. "Man, how'd you know Pac-Man stabbed this motherfucker's little brother?"

Huggins grinned and licked his gold-plated tooth. "Pac-Man didn't stab that boy."

"Then how'd you know they didn't already take care of the nigger done it?"

Huggins laughed and leaned toward Keloid, speaking softly. "'Cause I'm the nigger that cut that cracker's heart out."

Chapter 35

Put Up Or Shut Up

SATURDAY 2000 Hours

Lauren set her wine glass in the sink and dropped the empty bottle of red wine in the trash. At this rate, they were going to have to restock. Her stomach was still woozy from the close call earlier. Rachel's reaction was even more profound than her own. They were both half drunk and seemed content to achieve full drunkenness before the night was over.

"Come on, Lauren, since when did you become a chicken?" Rachel, chiding her.

"You're going to call me that after tonight?" Lauren said. "I'm not going to call a cop at—" She squinted at the clock on the wall. "Seems like it should be later. We don't even know their number." The real reason she was reluctant was that she knew Macbeth had associated her with Huggins. That made her uncomfortable. But Rachel didn't want to hear about it.

"We're just calling the police station, for Christ's sake," Rachel whined.

"I don't think that's a good idea."

"Get off it, girlfriend. I'll call." Rachel reached for the notebook on the table and spun it toward her.

"No, you won't." Lauren turned from the sink and dove for the notebook. Too late. Rachel scooped it up and pressed it against her chest.

"What could it hurt?" Rachel's bottom lip curled into a pout. "You're just a college student. Please?"

"I don't have a penis for a brain." Lauren rested her hands on her hips. "And don't you have a boyfriend?"

Rachel's expression drooped. "That hurts me, deep down." She held a hand over her heart. "I didn't say let's go fuck these guys, just go out for a drink or two. What could that hurt? Hell, it might help you, even."

Lauren sighed. "You think they might go out after work?"

"Who knows, cops are heavy drinkers, aren't they?"

"Really?"

"Everybody knows that." Rachel held the notebook out to Lauren, who recoiled as if it were a spider.

"You said you'd call," Lauren said.

"See. You *are* chicken!"

"Bitch." Lauren laughed. "No, really, you call."

They huddled around the phone as Rachel dialed the number. It rang several times before someone answered. Even from a foot away, Lauren could hear voices in the background.

"Hello?" Rachel rolled her eyes as if she was on hold. "Hi," she said after another minute. "May I speak with Officer Macbeth?"

Rachel listened a moment, then covered the mouthpiece. "What's tac?" Lauren shook her head, confused. Rachel took her hand away from the phone. "Yeah, I guess."

Lauren covered her mouth and giggled. The uneasiness in her stomach was gone for the moment and she felt like a teenager. Maybe she should slow down on the wine?

Rachel said, "Oh," and then, "Hang on, let me write this down." She shook her hand to hurry up as Lauren flipped the notebook to an empty page. Lauren slid both across the counter to her roommate. Rachel scratched out a number and hung up.

"This is his pager." She started pressing the numbers. "Maybe they'll meet us for a bite to eat."

"Fat chance." Lauren found herself hoping they would. She wanted a closer look at Macbeth.

❧

MAVIS STOMPS STARED AT HER REFLECTION IN THE BATHROOM mirror. Her face looked swollen and she hurt all over. The bastard hadn't been gentle at all. She was still spotting blood and remembered how it had felt—his heat driving into her, his whiskers penetrating her skin. Everything about Huggins was about confrontation and domination. *What a fool she'd been,* she thought, *getting him out of prison, bringing him back.* With Cecil she'd been in control, but Huggins was a force. She needed to decide whether to try and ride it or get out of the way.

He'd told her last night he'd get things rolling between the Vice Lords and the GDs. So, she'd have the gang war she wanted. Now she just had to maximize it and grab some press to lay into the police for being ineffective. She'd figure out what to do about Huggins afterward.

❧

MACBETH HAD STARTED ON HIS SECOND DIET COKE WHEN HE saw the two girls they'd met earlier in the day come through the front door of Pequod's Pizza on Clybourn. Zito waved at them from their table past the bar under a large flat screen TV. Macbeth stood as the two women approached. They introduced themselves and shook hands before sitting at the table. It felt like a business meeting.

The girl who'd said her name was Lauren looked around the restaurant. "I've never heard of this place."

Macbeth watched her closely. She was good looking, but she was still working for Huggins or his attorney. That made her the enemy. But damn, she was pretty, and he didn't figure he could get into any trouble for having pizza with her.

"Best pizza in Chicago," Zito said. "And take it from me, I'm Italian."

"Yeah, he's got every Dean Martin CD ever produced." Macbeth nodded and watched the short brunette, whose name was Rachel.

The waitress stopped by with a tray holding several beers. The glasses were full, topped off with foam and covered with ice chips and condensation. *It would be cold and taste so good,* he thought, *but they were still on duty.* Lauren and Rachel both ordered a glass of wine and Macbeth felt his throat constrict, wishing he could have a beer.

"Pizza's ordered," Zito said. "Should be out pretty soon."

Zito and Rachel began a conversation, talking about the weather, the Cubs, and Macbeth's so-called preference for the White Sox and his being a "Twinkies" fan. But Lauren was quiet. Her eyes seemed to wander everywhere but to his. He wondered if he made her uncomfortable, but then why was she here? Maybe Rachel was interested in Zito? Macbeth's partner was opening his mouth, displaying his tongue stud.

The waitress dropped off the wine and confirmed Zito's earlier assessment that the pizza would be out shortly. Finally, Macbeth made eye contact with Lauren. She smiled somewhat uncomfortably. "Stacey's an unusual name for a guy."

"Yeah." He'd had this conversation many times before. "Actually, it's my middle name, but I get that a lot."

"What's your first name?" Lauren asked.

He laughed. "Trust me, Stacey is better."

The waitress appeared with a steaming deep-dish pizza. The aroma was intoxicating, promising hot cheese and mouthfuls of flavor. Macbeth loved their caramelized crust and found himself wanting that beer more than ever.

As the waitress spatula'd the pizza onto plates, handing them to Zito to distribute, Macbeth decided to surprise Lauren with a question of his own.

"What do you do for Huggins's defense team?"

Lauren met his gaze for a moment, then looked at the pizza slice on the plate slid in front of her. She sighed deeply. "I'm a journalism grad student. Ever hear of the Wrongfully Convicted Program?"

"*Eighteen Twenty-Two.*" The dispatcher's droll voice tore Macbeth's attention away from Lauren. "*And units in Eighteen, I've got shots fired at Division and Clybourn.*"

Macbeth glanced at Zito, who'd turned to stare at him.

"C'mon, Stace," Zito whined. "Can't we let it go? We're a long way off."

"*Units, we're getting multiple calls of a man shot. CFD says they're not rolling.*"

Macbeth threw his napkin on the table and stood. He wanted to get away before he said something stupid. He found himself liking Lauren after only a couple of minutes, even if she worked for Huggins.

"You stay, Mike. I'll just look and be right back." Macbeth pulled his wallet from his jeans pocket and dropped a twenty on the table as the girls' eyes bounced from Zito to him and back to Zito. Macbeth extended a hand for the car keys.

Zito threw his napkin on the table. "Yeah, right. Fire department ain't even going, they're not running away from dinner like me." Zito looked at Rachel and then Lauren. "Sorry." He threw a twenty on top of Macbeth's.

"Me too," Macbeth said. "Eat and take home whatever's left if we don't make it back."

"I'll call you later," Zito said to Rachel, and they walked quickly out of the restaurant.

They jumped into the unmarked and pulled a tight U-turn that had traffic in both directions stopped. Zito stomped on the gas and rocketed down Clybourn. "God dammit, I just start making time with a girl with really great tits and you go dragging me to a fucking shooting."

Macbeth smiled. "Life's a bitch sometimes." But he found himself thinking about how pretty Lauren was.

The crime scene lay a couple of miles down the road, through a bunch of lights and busy intersections. Macbeth hoped they'd arrive to find Huggins lying in a pool of blood. It was only a block from 1150 North Sedgwick.

Some copper got on the radio. "*It's bona fide, better get fire over here.*"

After a minute of zigzagging around cars and through intersections, his lights and siren on, Zito pulled up behind a blue and white. Its blue lights strobed the scene. A slowdown was being barked over the radio by a sergeant, and several squad cars blocked off a part of the wide intersection of Clybourn and Division. The nearby sidewalks were full of people gathering and milling around, trying to see past the police cars. They were jostling for position to get a look at what was unfolding, their faces curious, alternating with the blue lights and the shadows.

A uniformed female officer had already started to work the crowd, but she was getting shrugged off. No one here wanted to get involved. A small knot of uniformed officers surrounded a man writhing on the ground. Blood from his head splattered their feet. Down the street, an ambulance nosed out of the firehouse. Its siren activated as it pulled onto the street and slowly made its way to the scene.

Macbeth and Zito floated around the knot of officers but kept facing the crowd, looking for anyone familiar, or someone with an aggressive expression, or perhaps someone who looked content, like he'd gotten his man.

"He got anything to say?" Macbeth asked as he eyed the crowd eyeing him.

"No," said one of the older cops. "Just that it hurts."

Macbeth stepped up next to the man on the ground. Not Huggins. Macbeth squatted and tried to catch the guy's attention, but his eyes were screwed shut with the pain and his hands covered his face and head. "Who shot you, man?" Macbeth realized he didn't recognize the guy. Maybe Ketchum would.

The man didn't say anything, just moved his head around like Ray Charles, except his was bleeding heavily. His hands were clamped tight, blood covering his fingers.

"You a Cobra?" Macbeth asked.

"Fuck you," the injured man cried. "Get me to a doctor."

"Who shot you?" Macbeth leaned closer. "Lonnie Huggins have anything to do with it?"

"Fuck you, get me to the hospital."

"See." The older cop shrugged and dug a pack of cigarettes from his vest pocket. "Today's victim, tomorrow's offender. Or is it the other way around?"

"Does it matter?" Zito held out his hand for a cigarette and offered his lighter to the officer in exchange.

The CFD ambulance stopped nearby. Its red lights blinked brightly as its siren wound down. The paramedics clambered out of the cab and went to the back to get a stretcher and backpack. As they walked over, one of them fashioned the stretcher into a chair. The cops parted and gave them access, keeping the growing crowd at bay.

"What's wrong, my man?" The paramedic was skinny and had deep acne scars on his cheeks. He put the backpack down next to him and squatted across from Macbeth.

"Nigger shot me." The man still wouldn't open his eyes, like he was afraid they might pop out.

"No shit?" The paramedic tugged a zipper open on the backpack and pulled out latex gloves. He put them on and let out a deep sigh as if this was his hundredth run of the night. "Okay. Where are you shot?"

"In my brains man, they got me in my brains!"

The paramedic looked at Macbeth and raised his eyebrows; a grin cracked his face. "I sincerely doubt that," he said. "But you're gonna have to let me take a look." The paramedic reached into a pocket on his trousers and brought out a small steel flashlight. He snapped it on. "Hands down, my man."

"Fuck you." The man rolled away. "Take my ass to the hospital."

The paramedic waited as if he had all night. Finally, the man's hands lowered. The paramedic upped his light and started examining the wound. There was a neat hole in the man's forehead, a little right and above the center. The paramedic probed with his fingertips. The man screeched and tried to knock his hand away.

Macbeth reached out and grabbed the victim's arms, telling him, "Relax."

The paramedic clicked his light off and put it away. He looked up at the cops. "Bullet just glanced off his coconut, didn't have the energy to penetrate the skull. It's either still under the skin or popped out somewhere in the back of his head, might still be in his hair." He ripped a package of gauze open. "I'll let the doctors figure it out. But I'm confident he'll live long enough to get shot again." He applied the gauze to the wound. The man screamed as the paramedic pressed it down.

By the time Macbeth had washed the man's blood off his hands and they motored back to Pequod's, the girls had gone. The waitress said they'd just left in a taxi. Zito said he'd call Rachel later and make plans for the next night.

Zito clapped his hands together. "Well, what do you think?"

"About what?" Macbeth grinned.

"About my chances of getting that babe in the sack tomorrow night?" Zito sighed. "I think she digs me. Don't you think?"

"Yeah, right," Macbeth said.

"Seemed the other girl liked you," Zito said. "Might do you some good to get laid and quit thinking about Huggins."

Right, Macbeth thought. *If only I could.*

Chapter 36

False Flagging

SUNDAY 0100 Hours

Huggins pointed and the driver curbed the dark green Buick Deuce and a Quarter on Oak Street. They were just west of the 500 West Oak building, the only building held by the Cabrini faction of the Traveling Vice Lords.

Quantrell McKnight, known as Q, shifted into park and then turned in his seat. "This where you want me, right?"

Huggins flipped up the passenger seat's vanity mirror and decided his new cornrows made him look different enough he didn't need a hat. "Yeah, this is cool."

He lifted the bottom of his black T-shirt and shifted the large automatic over so it would quit pinching his stomach. He dropped the shirt and ran a hand over the stenciled message on it, *Don't ask me for shit.* He turned to stare at Q. "You know where you're going once we back in?"

Q rolled his eyes. "We gonna go left up there." He pointed at Larrabee, a hundred feet in front of them. "Then we gonna go down across Chicago and make the first turn."

"Left or right?" Huggins didn't want to waste a second. Their getaway was at stake. Paying attention to these kinds of details helped keep him out of trouble. And according to what Gold and Momma Stone had said, he couldn't afford any.

Q hesitated. "Left."

"Then what?"

"I stop by the truck and let you guys out." Q looked at him and smiled. "Then I go to the Ryan and head south."

"You got it." Huggins nodded. "What you got to do when we in the lobby?"

"When I hear shooting, I light these." Q held up a long string of firecrackers.

"Maine, what you got to do?" Huggins turned to the back seat. Maine was pressed against one door, his head up against the glass. He was sweaty and Huggins found that amusing. White Boy was scrunched up against the street side door. Keloid rode the hump between them, legs spread out and relaxed.

Maine tried to shift but couldn't. "I do what you tell me to, no sweat."

Huggins wanted to say, "No sweat, my ass. Just look at your face," but he decided to give the kid a break. Instead, he asked, "Where your piece?"

Maine tugged a rusty revolver out of his waistband, turned it in his hand. Huggins reached back and pointed the muzzle away from him. Maine carefully tucked it back in his pants. Huggins turned to the other kid.

"How 'bout you, White Boy?"

White Boy's watery eyes, somewhere between brown and blue, shifted from the street to him. The kid looked fucking weird.

"I'm doing whatever Keloid say."

If the kid was any paler, he'd be bone white. Huggins nodded. "Keloid, you know what you're doing?"

"We cool." Keloid nodded and patted his side. "I'm strapped." The picture on his T-shirt was a rapper silhouette giving the finger, the message in bold letters was *Fuck You!*

"C'mon, man," Keloid said. "Let's go kill us some hooks."

Huggins slid his gun around to his back, making sure his T-shirt covered the grip. It was time for Momma Stone's gang war to start.

&

JERMAINE FOLLOWED CLOSE BEHIND HUGGINS AS THEY WALKED away from the car. His heart beat so hard he thought it was going to come out of his mouth. Ronnell was next to him, his lips thin and tight. Keloid moved behind them like a big shadow. They rounded the corner of 500 West Oak and kept walking toward the ramp leading to the lobby door. Jermaine kept his head down like Huggins had told him.

Huggins opened the door and walked through. Jermaine, Ronnell, and Keloid followed. At the top of a few concrete stairs, a wooden desk blocked their progress. A uniformed black woman guard was asleep, resting her head on the desktop.

When Huggins got near the desk, he squeezed past. The woman never raised her head. Jermaine figured she was awake. The only thing going on this time of night wasn't something she wanted a part of.

"Gimme one," Huggins called across the lobby. A voice responded from the stairwell, but Jermaine couldn't make it out. He watched the guard. Her eyes fluttered but didn't open. She knew to keep out of it. Not so different from the guards at 1150.

Huggins strode down the lobby toward the elevators and stairwells in the back. Jermaine skipped up next to him. Huggins said, "I need one, my brother."

There were five guys hanging in the shadows in the back of the lobby, but it was dark and hard to tell if they had guns. Jermaine flexed his fingers. The weight of the gun was heavy in his waistband, the steel cold pressed into his skin.

Huggins reached around his back like he might be getting his money but came out with the gun. Jermaine ripped his own revolver out of his waistband and stepped away from Huggins. Flame leapt from Huggins's pistol as it jerked up. Jermaine pushed his gun out and pulled the trigger. The gun tried to flip out of his hand. Orange fire shot toward the Vice Lords. Real bullets made the thing in his hand violent and hard to hang on to.

Bodies dived in front of them. Two men tried for the stairwell. One man backed away with his hands up as if to stop the bullets. The other two dove for the floor. Huggins shot again, so did Jermaine. His mouth felt like he was sucking on a handful of pennies. The lobby was murky from billowing clouds of smoke.

The two hooks on the floor jumped up and ran into the stairwell as screams rolled down from floors above. Word was out. Huggins shot again. A kid not much older than Jermaine in a black and gold basketball jersey, Vice Lord colors, sank to his knees clutching his stomach, his mouth open, spittle streaming down the front of his shirt before falling on his side.

Huggins stepped up and kicked the kid. Then he hopped over to the stairway and ducked his head in and out quick. A loud bang followed. Huggins shoved his gun hand in the stairwell and blasted up the stairs. He pulled it back and nodded his chin at Jermaine.

"Check him."

Jermaine looked at the kid on the floor. The boy's eyes were white slits, showing no pupil. Blood wet his lips as he clutched his gut. Blood leaked out around his fingers.

"What?" Jermaine said.

"Get his money, get his work, c'mon!"

Jermaine knelt next to the kid and rolled him on his back. The boy groaned and shuddered, his hands still grasping his middle. Blood pooled under him and Jermaine was careful not to lean into it. He checked the kid's pockets. Nothing. He felt around the boy's waist and found a little automatic. He pulled it out and stuck it in his pocket.

Huggins shouted at Ronnell and pointed to the kid on the floor. Jermaine stood and stepped back. He wondered where Keloid was. He looked around and saw the big man writing on the wall with a fat blue marker. False flagging explained what Huggins had said earlier, they were going to make it look like the GDs had paid a visit.

"C'mon, White Boy." Huggins pointed his gun at the man on the floor. "Jermaine shot him. I shot him. It's your turn."

Ronnell took a half step and hefted Keloid's big black semi-auto.

The gun shook in his hand. Ronnell brought his other hand around and held the gun tight. It still shook, but the trigger yanked back. BLAM!

Jermaine braced himself as the gun bucked. The boy's shirt ticked up on his chest and he tried to roll over, but Huggins's booted foot stepped down hard on his shoulder.

Huggins looked from Ronnell to Jermaine. "You all passed." He tucked his gun back into his waistband and held a palm out to Ronnell. The kid hesitated, and then laid the gun in his hand. "You all mine now, work for me." Huggins took the big black semi-auto and held it up for them to see. "Watch close."

Huggins bent over the kid they'd shot and looked back at them over his shoulder. "This is what's gonna happen if you even think of fucking me."

He took the gun and jammed it through the kid's lips and teeth, forcing it deep in his mouth. Huggins snaked his finger onto the trigger, and with half the barrel wedged down the kid's throat, yanked the trigger back, blowing the back of the kid's head across the lobby floor and wall.

Chapter 37

Getting Ready

SUNDAY 2200 Hours

Lauren looked at herself in the full-length mirror on the back of her closet door. She was going casual, white T-shirt and jeans. The T-shirt did have a V-neck that offered up some cleavage. If her boobs were bigger there'd be more to see, but she was happy, despite Konrad's comments. What an asshole.

She figured the cops, Mike and Stacey, weren't going to a club after they got off work. They'd probably chosen something with more of a neighborhood tavern feel, where club clothes were likely to stand out, though they wouldn't stand out as much as they had in Cabrini.

She inspected her outfit and decided she looked good, cute even. It occurred to her that she didn't know what she was hoping to get out of this. She was, after all, actively involved in an ongoing investigation into allegations of misconduct on the part of the cop she was about to meet, at a bar, no less. Somehow it didn't strike her as the smartest thing she could be doing, but that could be said about so much of her life recently, and certainly many of her latest decisions. Besides, who would ever know?

She pulled her hair out of the ponytail holder and shook her head more vigorously, combed her fingers through her hair. She was going to leave it down, even with the heat. Her hair was long, full and dark brown. Natural highlights ran through the length, and in the summer, they got more pronounced. She'd have preferred straighter hair that was easier to manage. She shrugged. The human condition, right? Wanting what you didn't have. She slid the holder into her pocket in case she needed it later.

Rachel opened the bedroom door and walked in barefoot. She wore a black bra and panty set. Where Lauren was tall, Rachel was short.

"What're you… oh, is that what you're wearing?" Rachel asked.

"Sure is."

"Oh."

"What?" Lauren asked.

"Nothing, I just thought we were gonna, I don't know, dress up more."

"Rach, these guys are getting off work and going to a bar. Yesterday, they were wearing jeans and T-shirts. I don't think we're going somewhere fancy. But wear what you like. I'm sure you'll be fine."

Rachel put a finger to her lips and considered that. Lauren took a last look at her hair and turned away from the mirror.

"Rach."

Rachel came out of her trance and looked at her.

Lauren asked, "Is this stupid?"

"What? You look cute, you know, collegiate."

"No, dummy, meeting Stacey?"

"Why?"

"I've only been investigating him for false imprisonment of this guy and sleeping with the guy's girlfriend while the dude's in jail."

"But you have doubts about all that."

"Yeah."

"So, what's the big deal?" Rachel brushed off her concern.

"I don't know, just seems like so much could go wrong, a hell of a lot more than could go right."

"It's not like you're fucking this guy or anything, right? Relax, don't be so damn uptight." Rachel winked at Lauren. "I'm going and I've got a boyfriend, but I don't hear you telling me I'm doing something wrong. So relax. Have fun."

Rachel spun on her heel and walked toward the door, calling over her shoulder. "I'll just be a minute, I know what I'm going to wear. We can have a beer or something, then we'll grab something to eat. I know a great place close to that bar."

⁂

MACBETH WATCHED SERGEANT RYAN SQUARE OFF WITH FINNEY in front of the district's desk. "Lieu, I'm sending my guys home if that's all right with you. They've been running all week and I want them to wind down a bit." Macbeth was eager to get to the bar and talk to this girl. Maybe he could learn something useful.

Finney glanced around, his gaze sticking to Macbeth and Zito for a second longer than anyone else. He turned to Ryan.

"Yeah, Ronnie, go ahead. You guys did good work this week. Enjoy."

MACBETH PULLED INTO AN OPEN SPOT CLOSE TO THE BOSS BAR'S door. He parked and ran his fingers through his hair. He didn't see any of the guys' cars on the street, so he must be the first to arrive. He decided to leave the top down and jumped out.

He used the revolving door and found the bar crowded, at least for a Sunday night. The interior was dominated by the long, thin rectangular bar in the middle of the floor, leaving hardly any room for tables except for at the front and back of the establishment. The front wall of the place was two large glass paneled garage doors that were now open, keeping the place from getting stuffy when it was crowded. In the back, along with tables, were a pool table and the restrooms.

Monica was working the bar. She was a hot blonde dressed in a tight T-shirt that displayed her surgically enhanced breasts. The shirt was cut off too, showing off her flat, tanned stomach and pierced belly button. Monica was nice to look at, but you had to watch her. She was known for having sticky fingers and deducting too much from the kitty. But she was supposedly the owner's girlfriend and kept her job despite any complaints.

All the bartenders at the Boss were women and every one of them was gorgeous. None of them was an accomplished bartender, but no one complained. It didn't take too much skill to pull a tap or pop a cap. Their popularity was derived from being strikingly beautiful with a desire to flaunt their beauty and assets.

Macbeth punched in some music selections on the jukebox, mostly Stevie Ray Vaughan and Green Day. Then he grabbed a stool across from the front door to keep watch. He hadn't seen Rachel or Lauren when he'd looked around the bar, but it was crowded. Monica came over, and he dropped a twenty on the bar and ordered a Guinness. As he checked out Monica, making sure she took only what was necessary, he wondered what Lauren would be wearing.

Chapter 38

Meetings

SUNDAY 2300 Hours

Huggins stared at the flat screen TV. He couldn't get enough of this shit. He could care less that it was the war on terror. He'd been in enough stores in the ghetto to know the Arab owners needed to have their asses kicked for jacking up prices. But he also had a grudging respect for how they'd carried out their terror plan, always blowing something up, killing cops and civilians by the busloads. He was fascinated by suicide bombers and knew they had to have handlers behind the scenes. He kept wondering how he could do the same here. In some ways, it was similar to gang banging and dope dealing. The Cobras were not only in it for the brotherhood, but for the money, too.

"Lonnie?" Tea Bag said. "Some lady here to see you."

Huggins punched the mute on the remote and turned his attention to the short, dark Cobra. "Who?"

"She say her name's Collins."

"Get me a beer and bring her in."

Tea Bag sent White Boy to get the beer, then he brought in a black woman. Huggins looked her up and down. Probably forty, straightened hair, a little off her shoulder. She wore a T-shirt, jeans, and sandals. She was proud, probably someone's mom. She was too old to be one of his hoes.

"Who are you?" Huggins asked.

The woman stared at him, but not in the eyes, maybe trying for defiant, but looking more afraid. "Donna Collins."

"What you want, Ms. Donna Collins?" Huggins asked.

"Is my son here?"

"I don't—"

"Jermaine Taylor."

"Who?" Huggins said.

"Jermaine Taylor. He just moved back here from Mississippi."

Huggins's deep laugh rattled his throat. "That so."

"I heard that he's been staying here." She looked at his face but didn't make eye contact.

Huggins shrugged.

She looked at the floor. "Someone told me to come up here and see you."

"Who told you that?"

"I don't know their name." She lifted her eyes.

"I bet you don't."

White Boy came in with his beer. Huggins took it from him and turned to look at an older Cobra in a red shirt. "Go get Maine."

The Cobra left. Huggins took a swig of beer. "So, what you want, mama?"

"My first son was a friend of yours and he's dead now." She looked at the floor again. "I don't want that for Jermaine. Please." She raised her eyes and finally met his stare.

"Your first son?"

"Antwan."

Huggins took a deep pull off the beer and swallowed. "Don't you put Boo's death on me, poh-leece killed that boy."

Her eyes darkened. "He was working for you."

"I was locked up."

"Yeah, and you called my apartment every day to talk to him and give him orders."

"Bitch." Huggins stood and glared at her. "You in my fucking house, better watch your tongue."

"I just want my boy. I want him to be with our family, to grow up with his little brother and sister." Her voice grew steady. "Please."

Huggins looked around the room. He pointed at White Boy. "Search this bitch, see if she wired up."

White Boy stepped up to her and tentatively patted her along the waist and down the outside of her pants, gripping one ankle, then the other. He stepped back.

"Motherfucker, that was weak." Huggins pointed at her chest. "Check her tits." White Boy hesitated. "God damn, boy. Step the fuck up and search her right."

The woman looked at White Boy. She took her shirt off over her head, handing it to the albino. Then she reached back and unfastened her bra and pulled it off, keeping one arm across the front of her breasts. She handed the bra to White Boy too. She lifted her breasts so that Huggins could see their underside. She took her bra back from White Boy and put it on. Then she unsnapped her pants and pulled them down and off. She pulled her panties up tight to show that nothing was hidden within. She spun on the ball of her foot so that Huggins could see her backside was likewise empty. His dick stirred in his pants.

Lauren came out of the Boss Bar's girls' room and joined Rachel at the pool table. Upon their arrival, the bar was practically empty, so they took the pool table and racked up a game. They'd been playing ever since, not that they were any good, but it kept them from drinking too much. Or so she hoped. They were having a lot of fun too.

Rachel was keeping Lauren's mind off everything. After a couple of games, the place had gotten crowded. And a steady stream of guys had been circling the table, checking them out.

As she bent down to line up a shot Lauren caught the eye of a guy at the bar. Macbeth. And he was looking down her shirt. She shanked the shot and stood, waving at him nervously.

He smiled or smirked; it was hard to tell in the dim lighting. He took a sip of his dark beer, maybe trying to hide his embarrassment at being busted. He put the beer down and waved back. There was something… intimidating about his grin, like a cat contemplating a canary.

He stood. He wore a black White Sox T-shirt and jeans with holes in the knees. She was glad she'd gone casual. Rachel was wearing a T-shirt and jeans too. And Lauren had talked her into wearing her spiked heels, said it made her ass look even more irresistible.

Rachel said something that was mostly drowned out by the jukebox. When Lauren didn't respond, Rachel jabbed her in the backside with a pool cue. "You still playing?"

"Stacey's here."

Rachel spun around beside her. "How about his partner?"

"Not that I see," Lauren said. "He was looking down my shirt."

"Nice," Rachel said. "Here he comes."

MACBETH KNEW SHE'D CAUGHT HIM looking at her boobs and wanted to crawl under the bar. *She's working on Huggins's defense team. He must be nuts.* He took a long sip of his beer even though the head hadn't receded. He figured he had to go over now, so he set the Guinness down on top of his change and walked over to the pool table.

"Hi."

Lauren put out her hand to shake. Her hand was warm and soft. "Hi." She rested the pool cue on the floor. "Where's Mike?"

Macbeth took Rachel's hand. It was warm too.

"He should be here any moment," Macbeth said.

A commotion at the front of the bar caught their attention. They turned. Zito and Hagen made their way through the crowd along the bar, arguing. They came up, and Macbeth introduced Rachel and Lauren to Timmy. Zito and Hagen vied for Rachel's attention as Lauren and Macbeth stepped to the side. Ketchum, Petty, and Barnhill came up to the bar and threw their twenties into the kitty Macbeth had started.

Everyone settled in, talking and jockeying for comfortable positions as someone pumped more money into the jukebox. The noise level rose to where it got difficult to hear without shouting. Macbeth wanted to talk to Lauren but didn't want to have to yell. He grabbed her hand and pulled her toward the door. Outside, they discovered a couple having a cigarette and they just settled for small talk while waiting for the couple to finish. Finally, the couple went inside, and he broached the subject he was really interested in.

"So, Lauren, I got to ask. You work for the defense team, why'd you want to meet me?"

She stopped smiling. "I'm curious."

"Curious about what? Curious about what kind of crooked cop I am? Or how a killer like Huggins gets released from an airtight case and has a high-priced legal team traipsing around Cabrini on his behalf."

She waved her hands in front of her. "Listen, I'm not here officially at all. In fact, if they knew I was here I'd be in a lot of trouble."

"So why risk it?"

"Well, for one thing, I don't think you're going to run over and tell them. And, quite frankly, I think they're full of shit."

"Join the club," he said.

"But, it's my master's program, you know. I guess I just wanted to meet you and feel for myself whether you're the bad guy they'd have me believe."

"Bad guy? Me?" He laughed. "What's your assessment?"

"Hard-nosed cop, maybe."

"It's not against the law to be hard-nosed."

"True. Actually, I'd just as soon see Huggins stay in jail. He's scary."

Macbeth nodded. "So what are you going to do?"

"About what?"

"Being caught in this bullshit," he said.

"Don't know yet, still trying to figure it out."

"You going to let the bullshit go unchallenged?"

"A lot of what I feel is unsubstantiated, I don't have any proof. It's a lot of he said, she said."

"Great." He looked at the ground. "So, let me guess. They're going Johnny Cochran on me."

"Something like that."

&a.

THE WOMAN REACHED FOR HER CLOTHES AND HUGGINS SHOOK his head. A nearby Cobra put his hand on the folded shirt and pants. She stopped and looked to him. "Please."

Huggins stared at her in her bra and panties. For a momma of four kids, she was sexy. Two of those children were almost to their twenties, too. He grabbed himself through his jeans. Maybe he'd have to see how bad she wanted Maine back.

"I'm begging you." A line of moisture cut down her cheek, from her eye to her quivering chin. "Let me have my child back. He's got a little brother and a sister who adore him. I can't lose another boy."

Huggins squeezed himself again. "How bad you want your boy?"

"What do I have to do?"

Huggins grinned, pointing to his dick.

She lifted her chin and her back straightened.

He snorted. "Then march your proud black ass out of here."

The trembling started in her shoulders and grew, swelling until her whole body shook. She lowered her face into her hands and cried.

Huggins stole a glance at the muted TV. Foreign soldiers patrolled a dusty street in some desert with their assault rifles slung in front of them, helmets on their heads, single file after some bomb had gone off.

"What..." Her voice caught somewhere in her throat. "What do you want me to do?"

Huggins looked at White Boy, Munchie, and Tea Bag. His eyes settled on Tea Bag who was thumping his thigh to an unheard tune. He was about Maine's age. "Suck his dick."

Her eyes followed his to Tea Bag. She stared at the kid and swallowed. "You'll let Jermaine go?"

"It ain't like I'm holding him hostage." Huggins folded his arms across his chest. Why didn't people understand? These kids wanted to be Cobras, fought to be Cobras, to belong to the family, their brotherhood. "Here's what I'll do, you suck my boy Tea Bag and if Maine wants out, I'll let him go without violating him."

Her nostrils flared as she raked in breath after breath. She tried to hold his stare but couldn't, breaking it to look back at Tea Bag. His face showed something between panic and excitement.

"And if I don't?"

"If he wants out?" Huggins spread his arms wide. "We violate him like any other nigger want to turn his back on his brothers."

"Violate?" She choked back a sob. "What's that mean?"

"We stomp his ass 'til we wanna stop or he dead."

For a minute she didn't move. Then she walked over to Tea Bag. "Where can we go?"

"We gonna watch," Huggins said.

Her chin raised a fraction and something like anger flashed across her eyes. "Leave me a little dignity."

Huggins thumbed toward the hallway. "Use the bathroom." As soon as he heard the bathroom door close, he took the TV off mute. The apartment door opened, and the older Cobra walked in with Maine.

Maine looked confused, as he stared around at the other Cobras, all of whom took to looking at the floor.

LAUREN LOOKED AT MACBETH. THEY WERE ALONE ON THE sidewalk. She much preferred the quiet outside to the inside where the jukebox drowned out anything but shouts. Lauren felt herself attracted to Macbeth, realized she had been since she'd first seen him. In fact, she wished that he'd stop asking questions and kiss her. Good thing she was outside without her wine, how much had she had?

He was her type, tall, good-looking, athletic. She was sure, from the way he looked back at her, he was interested as well. Unfortunately, most of the time she attracted guys that she despised. Konrad was an example. He was such an asshole.

Lauren looked around. "You want to go for a drive?"

"Now?" Macbeth asked.

"Why not?"

When a grin split his face, she knew she'd been dead on, and quite frankly, it felt good. His misgivings about her involvement with Huggins's legal team must have been put aside. Her anxiety was gone, replaced by a desire to get closer. Who knew where a drive could lead? Any adventure that didn't involve Cabrini-Green was welcome.

JERMAINE COULDN'T UNDERSTAND WHAT WAS GOING ON, WHY Lonnie had called for him. He still had the work in his pocket. He wondered if Huggins knew. He took out his work bag filled with pieces of rock knotted in smaller bags and held it in his palm for Huggins to see.

Huggins looked at Munchie and raised his eyebrows. Munchie took the pack out of Jermaine's hand and left the apartment. Jermaine looked around, then he noticed the little pile of clothes by the couch. His stomach sank and his head wanted to explode as he recognized his mom's sandals.

Jermaine pointed at the pile.

Huggins's lips twisted, and then parted so he could run his tongue across the front of his teeth, lingering on the gold-plated front tooth.

"Yeah." Huggins nodded. "She here."

"Why are her clothes on the floor?"

"She wants you out of the Cobras?"

"What's that got to do with anything?"

"Well, she came to get you out. She offered to blow each and every Cobra to do that." He picked up his beer and took a drink, shrugging. "She doing Tea Bag now and he the last."

"But I don't want out."

"I tried to tell her that, but she didn't seem to care much." Huggins's laugh was shallow and spiteful. "Maybe she just wanted to suck some dick."

For a second Jermaine was afraid he was going to puke. Why

would she do this to him? How could she do this to him? She'd showed him she didn't care when she sent him to Mississippi. *That's bullshit.* Jermaine pictured his mom, on her knees, in front of Tea Bag. His heart tightened, but more than getting smaller it got hard, like brick, so it couldn't be hurt. The muscles in his face felt like they were turning to stone. His eyes hardened into cold black marbles.

The bathroom door opened, and his mom came out, followed by Tea Bag. She jerked to as stop when she saw Jermaine. Tears rolled out of her eyes, her head tilted, and she sobbed.

"Baby, baby, baby." She rushed to him. "I did it for you, don't you see?"

When she reached toward him, Jermaine slapped her hand away.

"Don't touch me." He turned aside.

She stared at him, her throat working up and down like she was swallowing her words. Fresh tears leaked from her eyes and trailed down her face. Her nod to him was almost imperceptible.

"Here's what we fitting to do." Huggins clapped his hands. "Maine, you got to choose between Cobra life or this." He gestured to Ms. Collins. His grin was wide and filled with malignancy. "Momma, give your boy a little kiss."

She sobbed and stood there for several seconds as if in cement. He could hear her breathing, loud, and ragged. Then she grabbed her clothes and ran out of the apartment.

"Don't never forget, boy," Huggins laughed quietly, "they're all just a bunch of whores."

Chapter 39

Let's Go For A Ride

SUNDAY 2345 Hours

Macbeth steered his Jeep past the yellow tubular gate that had been pulled closed and locked on Solidarity Drive on the Museum Campus, which included the Field Museum, the Shedd Aquarium, the Adler Planetarium, Soldier Field, and Meigs Field. The First District was responsible for the area and locked it down against people doing exactly what Macbeth intended to do—an after-hours visit.

The tree-lined boulevard, surrounded on three sides by Lake Michigan, stretched east a quarter mile and ended at the Adler Planetarium. At the end of the street, Macbeth used the bus turnaround to head back west. He pulled over at the first meter and shut off the engine. Lauren stared at the city's skyline extending north. It was breathtaking. The tall buildings along Michigan Avenue were lit up, and the rest of the Loop provided the backdrop.

"It's stunning," she said.

"I think so." Macbeth didn't want to break the spell, so he didn't say anything more. He let the cityscape speak for itself and allowed Lauren to drink in the splendor. The tick of the engine blended with the chirp of insects to provide background music. He could sit here for hours. In northern Minnesota, where he'd grown up, he'd had several spots where he'd go to sit and absorb nature. He'd always felt those locations helped him relax; ultimately, they made him think of how insignificant he was.

Here in the city, it was different. He found that this particular vista wound him tight. He was awed by what civilization had become. What the city meant to different people, and he was part of it. But he also knew what his part entailed. He protected those people, naïve people who were no more than sheep among the wolves. He didn't aspire to be a shepherd; there was no guidance in him, only protection. Others had described cops as sheepdogs, but Macbeth saw himself as a predator of predators. Though, at times, it was hard not to feel that the stupid deserved exactly what they got.

Lauren was mesmerized by the scenery. Even the blossoming trees and flowers contributed to her intoxication. And all the while, Stacey just sat next to her, comfortably quiet and patient. She had to force herself to turn toward him.

"Thanks."

"For what?" he asked.

"For sharing this place with me."

He smiled. "You're welcome."

She didn't really want to change the subject, but she had to before they jumped each other. She certainly was feeling the desire and imagined that he was, too. She sighed out loud. "They're going to ask for fifteen mil."

"No shit?" He didn't sound surprised.

"Yeah."

He shook his head and looked up into the sky.

"Huggins is making all these wild allegations," Lauren said. "Says you were sexually involved with his girlfriend and kept him in jail so you could get together with her."

He laughed. "Nice."

"He even suggested you killed her."

"That'll go nowhere," he said. "He did it, or had it done."

"Maybe, but there're a lot of people corroborating what he's saying."

"But you said it was he-said-she-said, so there's no evidence to back it up."

"If he sues in civil court," she said. "The standard of proof is only preponderance of evidence, not beyond a reasonable doubt."

"Let's forget for a second that Latricia was my informant and that I have a solid alibi and witnesses to where I was when she was killed," he said. "Did you see the police and autopsy reports?"

"No."

"She was taped up, stuffed in an abandoned car in front of Eleven-Fifty Sedgwick. The car doors were chained and handcuffed shut. Latricia was shot, four to six times, I forget which. And then the gas tank was set on fire." He stopped. "Do you really think I'd do that?"

"Oh, my God."

"Yeah. Something like that'll make you question whether there is a God."

She looked away and tried to recapture some of the magic of the skyline, but it seemed to have dimmed. "I take it you've been sued before?"

"It comes with the job."

"Doesn't it bother you?" she asked.

"Only when the bad guys win," he said.

"Is it that simple?"

He was silent for a time.

"No, not really." His voice dropped an octave and grew far away. "I remember when I was working tac in the Seventh District; guys on the team had a car chase. A hot car. It was early on a Sunday morning. No traffic on the street, no people in the way. These guys did everything they were supposed to do. They had their lights on, siren going. They even had one of those blue dashboard lights that they'd bought themselves."

He stopped and looked at her.

"A seventy-year-old woman going to church was stopped at a red light that morning. This kid tried to make the corner and lost control. He T-boned her. Killed her instantly. Her family sued and they apologized to the cops who had arrested the kid. Said they didn't have the money to bury their mom and needed it to cover loans they'd taken out for the funeral. They only asked for fifteen thousand."

Macbeth continued. "The kid's family sued, too. Said the injuries he suffered were from a beating at the hands of the police, and not the accident. They asked for five hundred thousand." Macbeth paused. She thought he would keep going, but he didn't. He looked away.

"Well, what happened?" she finally asked.

"The woman's family settled for eight grand."

"And the kid's? Please tell me they didn't get anything."

"They settled for ninety-nine thousand."

"What?" She couldn't believe that.

"That was the most they could get without City Council approval. The city always settles out of court, still do."

Huggins sat back against the seat as Keloid steered the Navigator along the Stevenson Expressway toward the address provided by the Pope's informant. Luckily, Keloid knew the neighborhood and had already driven by. Keloid signaled and got off at Central. Huggins reached up and throttled the stereo down, no need to attract any unwarranted police attention. If they got stopped out here it would raise some eyebrows.

The Lincoln climbed the exit ramp and came to a stop at a red light. At the top of the ramp, an old, ragged white man dressed in dirty camouflage fatigues shook a plastic White Sox cup and held up a cardboard sign that said he was a veteran. The man approached Huggins's side of the SUV and shook his cup.

"I don't fucking think so, Pops," Huggins said, even as he thought of the young soldiers in the TV news clips. There was something to be said for going out young, in a blaze of glory, for not getting old and decrepit like this guy. Even though Huggins figured this guy was full of shit, probably never been in the army, let alone seen combat. Huggins half turned in his seat and caught Maine looking at him from the back. He nodded at the younger man, smiling.

"What?" Maine asked.

"You and me," Huggins said. "We got a common enemy."

"Yeah?"

"Yeah." Huggins turned back to look out the windshield as the light changed and Keloid drove south. In a few minutes, they were going to pass the airport. Then they'd be close. "And I been thinking about what we're gonna do about that."

❧

Lauren shifted, putting her back against the full metal door of the Wrangler. Macbeth had his back to his door as well and was looking her way, though she couldn't tell for sure if he was watching her because his eyes were hidden in shadow. He'd grown quiet after their talk. She hadn't known what to say.

"So," she said, "have you ever been disciplined before, like for excessive force or anything like that?"

"No." He waited before elaborating. "Working cops get accused routinely, and I certainly have had my share of beefs, but I've never taken any time—been found guilty, I guess you'd call it."

"Really, I hadn't thought of it like that."

"Dope dealers and gangbangers beef regularly, trying to slow us down," he said.

"Does it work?"

"No." He adjusted his leg up toward the gear shift. "I did take a day once when I was a recruit."

"Took a day?" she asked.

"Day off without pay."

"For what?"

"Being too aggressive."

She stared into the shadows where his eyes lurked but couldn't see what was hidden there.

"What happened?"

"My partner and I on-viewed this guy shooting by a park at Fifty-Ninth and Damen."

"Was he shooting at you?"

"Don't know," he said. "But we saw the muzzle flashes by the field house and rode over to see."

"Okay."

"He must've seen us because he ran, still holding the gun. He went up to a car stopped at a red light, yanked the woman who was driving it out, and drove off."

"He didn't shoot her?" she asked.

"No." He chuckled. "He yanked her out by the hair, only her hair extensions came out in his hand."

"Ow!"

"Yeah, then he grabbed her by the face," he said.

"Why didn't she just bite him?"

"She was so surprised—it happened so fast—and so scared, I don't think it occurred to her. Or maybe she saw the gun and didn't want to get shot. Anyway, he threw her down and drove off."

"Did one of you help that poor woman?" she asked.

"Well," he said sheepishly. "Not exactly."

"Not exactly?"

"We radioed in her location and kept going."

Lauren folded her arms across her chest.

"Save it," he said.

"Fine, then what?" She had to smile at the comfort level they had developed. It had happened quickly, to have a conversation like this.

"We chased him for a while, and I might've nudged him with the car."

"Nudged his car, you mean you made him wreck?"

"And he kind of hit a firehouse," he said.

"If he was injured, they could've given him first aid right away."

"If he hadn't run."

"Then what?" she asked.

"Well, we chased him in the car and took him into custody."

"How's that being too aggressive?"

"Thank you. That's what I said."

"There isn't any more to the story than that?"

"Well." He grinned. The shadows gave his face a menacing appearance.

"What?"

"I might've drove up and kicked my door into him as we were about to pass him by."

"Okay, so?" she asked.

"It knocked him down."

"This is like pulling teeth." She couldn't help but smile. "What?"

"When he fell, I kind of drove over one of his legs."

"Now we're getting somewhere."

"He isn't going to be running from the police anymore."

She stared at his face. An expression she read as satisfaction set into his jawline and the angle of his eyebrows. But she was still attracted to him, even after his tale. She had no doubt he was capable of violence, but he wasn't evil, like Huggins. Everything she saw in Macbeth told her he was a hero. He bent toward her, his face suddenly visible in the streetlight. His eyes were soft, and his lips parted ever so slightly.

She met him halfway. Their mouths pressed together. He gently licked her. She parted her lips. Her tongue rose to touch his. He slid his hand behind her head. His fingers worked into her hair.

Chapter 40

Put It On The Board, Yes!

MONDAY 0100 Hours

Huggins had Keloid back into a tight spot in the alley. It was a perfect place to watch the parking lot of the apartment building Macbeth supposedly lived in. It was dark and they would be hard to see. The bad part was they couldn't get out of the truck. It was *that* tight. There was an old Oldsmobile Ninety-Eight already in the lot and a small two door, plus a bunch of empty spaces and a dumpster.

"What we waiting for?" Maine asked from the rear.

"Just sit back and watch, little brother. You'll see soon enough."

Huggins reached for the stereo knob and throttled the sound down even more. He didn't want anyone calling the cops. He nodded at Keloid, who stopped the engine. Now they just had to wait.

MACBETH COULDN'T BELIEVE HOW WARM LAUREN'S LIPS WERE, and soft. He could kiss her all night. He was surprised that he trusted her so easily. He didn't think she would betray that trust, though he hadn't said anything damaging. It was all the truth and he didn't have anything to hide. But were the feelings growing in his chest and lower parts any more than sexual attraction? Was this fair to Lauren? Was this fair to him? Did he care?

As if reading his mind, Lauren broke away from their embrace. She looked up at him, her eyes twinkling in the light from the streetlamp.

"Is something wrong?" she said.

"No. You're beautiful and I really like the way you kiss. I've got to admit, I never thought we'd be doing this, right now."

"Me either." She looked down.

He suddenly felt that he'd missed something. "What's wrong?"

She didn't respond, nor did she look back at him. He reached over and nudged her chin up so he could see her eyes.

"What?" he said.

"Let's go back to your place."

Huggins perked up when he saw a pair of headlights swing into the alley from Sixty-third Place. It was a blue Jeep Wrangler that had the top down and two people in it. It spun quickly into an open parking spot. Once it stopped, the people got out. Huggins could see Macbeth had been driving, but he couldn't make out the passenger, except that it was a girl.

Macbeth went to the back of the Jeep and wrestled with the folded-down top. The girl stepped back and helped. She stayed in the shadow and Huggins couldn't get a better look. It took a couple of minutes before they had the top secured. Huggins was sure Macbeth could have done it himself, probably as fast, but he was obviously enjoying the company. The motherfucker was laughing and talking, but Huggins couldn't hear what was being said.

Macbeth and the girl met in front of the Jeep where Huggins could barely see them for the dumpster. They were standing close. They were kissing.

Suddenly Macbeth stepped away and went to the corner of the first-floor balcony. He peeped through the slits in the concrete sides, then waved at the girl. She joined him. He took her hand, and they walked together under the porch light into one of the building's doors.

Huggins sat back, suddenly holding his breath. "Shit."

Keloid, still behind the wheel, turned toward him. "That who I think it was?"

Huggins didn't answer at first. "Get me to a phone."

There were two pay phones outside of a 7-Eleven a block away. He dialed.

A groggy voice said, "Yeah."

"Wake up, motherfucker. You want to tell me why your little bitch assistant is fucking Macbeth?"

Lauren followed Macbeth up the stairs to his apartment. She was glad his landlord hadn't been out on his balcony. The man sounded awful, though compared to Konrad or Huggins maybe not so bad. The building wasn't old and seemed clean.

Macbeth said the guy was on top of things, he just had his share of flaws.

Don't we all, she thought, though she suspected Macbeth was understating his landlord's. As she followed him, she wondered what *his* flaws might be.

On the third-floor landing there was just one door. Macbeth unlocked the deadbolt and the doorknob, then opened the door and held it for her. She stepped into the dark apartment and immediately felt the humidity. Somewhere she heard an air conditioner, but it was failing miserably. She stepped aside and let him follow her in. He flipped a light switch and a standing lamp came to life in the corner.

She found herself in a small living room complete with an old TV on a table covered in a thin layer of dust. A couch in brown and white marbled fabric was across from the TV. A well-worn leather armchair was adjacent to the couch. Together, couch and chair created a divide from the rest of the living room, where a drawing table held a computer monitor. The PC on the floor sat next to a tall swivel seat on rollers. Bookshelves lined the back wall of the office area. The shelves were filled with books—hardcover, paperback, three-ring binders, and texts. Lauren wanted to peruse the titles on the bookshelf but would have to wait until they'd finished what they had started on the lakefront.

"Come on in." He stepped over to his balcony doors and pulled the curtains closed. Lauren walked around the chair and glanced out the narrow gap still left. She saw a sliver of the apartment across from his. There was no light on in it, but she thought the curtains were open.

She followed Macbeth into the kitchen, and he turned on the overhead light. The kitchen table was an old model with metal legs and a Formica top. Four matching chairs surrounded it. Their upholstery was shiny black and looked new, but the chair legs were scratched like those of the table.

When she looked away, she saw Macbeth had taken his holstered gun off his belt. He slid it on top of his refrigerator. There was something else up there too. He caught her looking.

"How many of those things do you have?" she asked.

"Guns?"

She nodded and folded her arms across her chest.

He shrugged. "Two."

Then she noticed the wallpaper. It was green and white paisley on silver foil that vibrated in her vision. It was absolutely hideous. "Oh, my God."

"By the look on your face I can tell you like my wallpaper. It's a John Camp special. When I saw it, I knew I had to live here." He laughed. "Can I get you something to drink?"

She shook her head and hid her eyes with a hand, then laughed. "How long have you lived here with that… that wallpaper?"

"Eight years," he said. "I don't turn on the kitchen lights much. I'm going to hop in the shower quick. I must smell as bad as this wallpaper looks."

"You'd have to have been dead for a week."

He smiled at her joke. "Make yourself at home. You sure I can't get you something? I got beer, pop, water even."

"No thanks," she said. "I'm going to look around. I want to look at your books."

"Knock yourself out. I'll only be a minute."

❧

While Huggins waited for Konrad to get his shit together, Keloid asked, "We got time to get something to eat?"

Huggins settled his hard stare on the man. How could Keloid be thinking of his gut right now? But even as Huggins had that thought, his own stomach growled. He realized he didn't know when he'd eaten last. He nodded and covered the receiver.

"Cool," Keloid said. "You want something?"

"Get me some Flamin' Hots."

Huggins had a lot on his mind. He knew where the cop lived. And now he knew a girl from his defense team was getting busy at this very moment with the man he hated more than anything.

Finally, he heard Konrad pick up the phone.

"Lonnie." Konrad's voice had lost its earlier grogginess. "You know, she's been asking a lot of questions."

"She your assistant. Isn't that what she supposed to be doing?"

"No, this is different," Konrad said.

"Like what?"

"She was saying how convenient everything seemed to tie in with your story. As if she had doubts about what your witnesses were saying. Her questions make me think she wasn't buying it."

"What'd you do about it?"

"Told her to shut her mouth, that you were paying the bills and we were in your house, shit like that."

"Did that take care of it?"

"Don't know," Konrad said quietly.

Huggins snorted. "You expect me to bet my freedom on, 'Don't know'?"

"She doesn't know anything anyways."

"That supposed to make me feel better?"

"Come on, Lonnie." Konrad's voice took on a whiny tone. "What could I do about it?"

"Would you take that kind of chance with your freedom?"

"It's not like that. I can control her. And if I can't, I'll call the professor and have her kicked out."

"Right now, the last man on earth who should be laying pipe to that bitch is hip deep in that pussy. And you want me to believe you can take care of it? You can't control shit. Where she live at?"

"Lonnie—"

"Shut the fuck up and gimme the address."

There was silence. Then a sigh followed by an exhale. "I'll call the professor—"

"You gonna make me say it again?" Huggins put an edge to his voice to make sure Konrad knew he was serious. "Maybe I got to come pay you a visit first."

Silence, then, "You know where Little Italy is?"

"No."

"UIC?"

"What the fuck is that?"

"How about the Abla Homes?"

"Now you're talking my language."

MACBETH LET LUKEWARM WATER SPLASH DOWN HIS FACE AND cascade down his body in waves. He'd elected to go with something-a-good-deal-less-than-hot in case things didn't go as he hoped. But he'd stopped short of all-out cold. It hadn't had the least effect on his... Had it been that long?

There was something about Lauren that got him cranked. He couldn't put it into words but thought it was probably different things. She was cute-gorgeous, a regular girl-next-door type who had a hint of something dirty below the surface. She was obviously smart and had the good sense not to believe everything someone tried to feed her.

At the same time, his rational mind was saying he should stay the fuck away from her. He shouldn't be talking to her, shouldn't have anything to do with her, technically she was the enemy. But that didn't matter to his less than rational self, or his penis.

Macbeth felt a draft and froze. Someone stepped into the shower behind him. Arms slid around his body. Hot flesh pressed against his back.

"Oooh, that's cold," Lauren said. "Make it warmer."

He shut his eyes and told his rational self to fuck off, while twisting the faucet's lever to hot. "I didn't know if—"

Her hands ran up his stomach to his chest. "That's better," she said as the water grew from warm to hot. She kissed his back and licked him. "You taste clean." She stood on tiptoes and sniffed where his neck rose out of his shoulder. "Umm. You smell clean too."

He turned. She stood in the mist created by the spray on his back. Her eyes were brown and large like a doe's. Her expression was soft, eyes half closed, lips parted. Her hands moved slowly up and down his sides. He wanted to speak, but whatever he said would probably come out wrong.

He brought his lips to hers. The kiss started soft but grew more frantic as their tongues traced one another. He caressed her. His hands moved from her back to her front. He traced her neck with his tongue, ending at her ear. He breathed hard and whispered hoarsely, "We can wait."

Her breath hot on his neck, she whispered, "Like hell we can."

She turned him and pushed him onto the edge of the tub. The shower curtain caught under his butt and his weight pulled the bar down. The curtain fell onto the bathroom floor; the spray splattered the bathroom as she lowered herself down.

LAUREN ALLOWED MACBETH TO HELP HER OUT OF THE TUB since her legs shook so badly. He dried her off a bit and left the towel across her shoulders. Water was everywhere. They each grabbed a towel and dried the other off as thoroughly as they could manage. She was thankful for the heavy warm air as they walked out into the dark hall-way. Thank God she'd turned off the lights and pulled the blinds.

They sat at the kitchen table. She leaned over and rested her head on his shoulder. Her hair was wet and cold, but he didn't seem to mind.

"Wow," he said. "That was incredible."

"Yeah," she said. "I can barely walk."

His phone rang until his answering machine kicked in. "If you need to, answer it."

"No thanks." He draped his arms across her shoulders. They were warm and thick and heavy with muscle. "No call this time of night is good."

"It might be important."

"Oh, I guarantee it's important to somebody."

"Aren't you curious?"

"I'd rather sit here and hold you." The phone went silent. He said, "Here's the real test."

"What?" she said.

The phone went off a second time and his head dropped. "If it's really important, they call twice."

Chapter 41

Exertions

MONDAY 0200 Hours

Huggins opened the door of the Navigator and sat in the passenger seat. His stomach full.

"We fittin' to go home?" Keloid asked.

Huggins stretched back in the seat. "No. Drive by the cop's one more time."

"What you got in mind?"

"Don't know. Do Jeep columns peel?"

"I think," Keloid said.

Huggins nodded. "Maybe burn it."

"A'ight."

Maine climbed in the rear seat and closed the door. The kid didn't say nothing as Keloid pulled out into the night.

❧

MACBETH JAMMED THE PEDAL TO THE FLOOR AS HE FLEW DOWN the onramp onto the Stevenson. Ryan had recalled the team but hadn't said why. Technically, they were supposed to be still at work. Something must've happened. What could be that important, to recall the team?

‰

LAUREN RE-HUNG THE CURTAIN AND TOOK ANOTHER SHOWER. Then she mopped the floor with a bath towel. The walls were splattered too, and the mirror. She'd been pretty distracted, but thought she'd turned the shower head in time to prevent this kind of mess.

Macbeth had been called back to work. He'd offered to drive her home on his way but had said that he'd prefer her to stay and wait for him. He seemed thrilled when she agreed, and told her he wouldn't be too long.

She was surprised she didn't feel guilty or dirty for having sex with Stacey after knowing him for so short a time, but it felt so… right. She usually approached the physical aspect of a relationship slowly. There were plenty of old boyfriends she'd never slept with. In fact, she'd had a relatively small number of lovers compared to her friends. But she didn't feel she'd missed out. And this had just happened. Maybe it was because of what they were involved in, the stress and stuff. Well, she'd ride it out and see where it brought her. She laughed at her own pun.

As soon as she was done in the bathroom, she was going to his closet to find a shirt to wear. She'd always wanted to do that. Then she'd have a go at his bookshelf, find something good to read. After that she planned on getting comfortable, maybe have one of those beers he'd offered and wait for him to get home.

She giggled. What would Professor Rabinowicz say?

‰

HUGGINS NODDED AS THE LINCOLN PULLED THROUGH THE ALLEY and past the parking lot of Macbeth's building. The blue Jeep was nowhere to be seen. Huggins grinned.

"Go 'round the block." Huggins twisted around and laid his arm across the back of the front seat. He stared at Maine. "When we come back 'round, you going to get out and break into that cop's crib, dig?"

Maine nodded.

"Climb up the side of them porches. Let's see if ol' boy keep his balcony locked. You be in quick. Get in there and steal something."

"You think he's dropping off the chick?" Keloid said.

"Maybe. Who cares, he gone."

Jermaine got out of the Navigator and walked to the side of the building, looking hard at the balconies, but trying not to look up at the third floor as he got closer. He felt a lump in his stomach. It wasn't as bad now that he was out of the truck. Even though he didn't think there were many black people around here, he'd been nervous with Huggins over his shoulder telling him what to do.

Jermaine didn't have the nerve to say how scared he was. Now that he was out of the truck, he could breathe; it didn't seem as if the walls were closing in on him anymore.

The building rose three stories and the sides of the porches were made of decorative blocks that allowed for hand and foot holds. This was going to be easier than he thought. As he got close, he saw that the other side of the balconies had the same design but were more hidden by shadow. The side closest to the alley was lit up by the big lamp and parking lights. Jermaine crossed to the dark side of the ground level porch and climbed.

When he got to the second-floor balcony, he used the iron railing on the front of it to stand on. He tried to be quiet, figuring it wouldn't do to be caught in the act. It must have taken him a minute to climb the two floors; it was a lot easier than he expected. He slipped silently over the third-floor railing and felt vulnerable in the glow from the streetlight.

The curtains were drawn, so he couldn't see inside. Glancing back at the street, he worried that the cop might be home. Parked around the corner or something. But Lonnie said it was okay. Jermaine reached for the balcony door's handle. He didn't realize he was holding his breath until he'd tugged, and the door slid back an inch.

He let out his breath and pulled it further open, pushing the curtains aside as he slipped in. The place was dark, but the streetlights filtered in from the windows. An air conditioner was running in the window by the kitchen table. It was loud, and he thought it was on high. But the place felt hotter and muggier than it should have been. Maybe the cop expected to be back quick. Maybe the girl didn't live that far away.

Jermaine looked around. The TV wasn't something he could get down by himself. He spotted the computer. The monitor was old, so the PC was probably just as old. He crept in further and could see into the kitchen. The floor squeaked under his foot. He wasn't worried, since there wasn't nobody home. A glint from something on top of the refrigerator caught his eye. He stepped over and reached up, patting the dusty top of the machine. The second his fingers touched the metal, he knew what it was. He pulled the gun down and smiled. Lonnie was going to like this.

Lauren heard the noise. Was Stacey home already? It had to be, didn't it? Maybe his job got canceled. She hadn't even finished cleaning the bathroom yet. She reached for a clean, dry towel, but stopped and smiled as a thought occurred to her. Surprising him naked might have its advantages. She opened the door and stepped into the short hallway between the bedroom and the kitchen. Standing next to the refrigerator, stuffing something in his pocket, was a black teenager.

Lauren froze. A flashback to Cabrini shot through her mind, and her first thought was to cover up. She crouched and grabbed her shoulders with her hands, hiding her breasts. She jumped back into the bathroom and slammed the door, screaming as loud as she could.

The naked woman's screech hit Jermaine like a bitch slap. He stumbled backward but managed to keep his feet under him. The tightness in his chest made him think maybe his heart had stopped. Maybe the cop *was* home.

He ran for the apartment's front door, unlocked it and bolted out into the stairwell as another scream split the air. He scrambled down the stairs as fast as he could and yanked the inner door open, then the outer door, and sprinted into the parking lot. Looking around, he saw the Lincoln down the alley. As he ran toward it the back door popped open. Jermaine dove in and slammed it shut behind him, and the truck took off.

"What the fuck," Huggins said. "What's the matter with you?"

"Fucking girl's still there! And she's naked."

"Get the fuck out," Keloid said, yanking the wheel to the right at the first street.

"The bitch was naked?" Huggins asked.

"And screaming her ass off." Jermaine nodded between deep breaths.

Huggins laughed. "Man, you should've fucked her or something."

Jermaine sat up in the back seat, desperately gulping air into his lungs. His chest was on fire, his side ached, and he still felt like he was going to shit his pants. He could feel sweat pop out of his skin and trickle down his body. Finally, he calmed enough to dig into his pocket. He brought the pistol out and handed it to Huggins.

"Hey, I got this."

Huggins held it up in the streetlights as they rolled west. "Now that's what I'm talking about."

Lauren screamed for a while until she realized the man had probably run. No one was kicking the bathroom door in to get her, so she peeked out. Nothing. She opened it and snuck into the hallway, heading for Macbeth's bedroom. A light switch just inside the door turned on an overhead. She grabbed a collared shirt from the closet and had only fastened a couple of buttons with her shaking hands when someone called out from the front door.

"Hello?" The voice was tentative and shaky and sounded like a woman. "Are you okay?" Lauren recognized an accent.

"In here." Her own voice was shaky and uneven, her throat raw and sore. "I'm okay."

"God damn!" A voice bellowed from somewhere below as heavy footsteps clomped up the stairs. "What the fuck's going on up there?"

Lauren looked down at her bare legs and figured the shirt hid all that truly needed hiding. She'd have felt better with pants on, panties even, but she stepped out of the bedroom nonetheless. The apartment was still dark, except for spill from the streetlights, and she couldn't see anyone through the short hallway into the kitchen.

"I'm back here." She stepped into the kitchen and looked for a light switch, couldn't find one. A light came on in the living room. She saw her fingers were still trembling.

"I'm a cop," a man's voice said. "Make sure your hands are empty and come on out."

"I'm a guest of Stacey's." Lauren held her hands up. She walked slowly toward the kitchen. "Here I am."

She could see the front doorway now. A woman was peering in, next to a squat, heavyset man, who stood breathing hard. His belly hung over striped pajama bottoms. He had one hand on the doorjamb, the other down by his side. He shifted a little and she could see he held a small gun.

"What the hell's going on?" he said.

"Someone broke in," Lauren said. "I saw him by the fridge. He ran away when I screamed."

"What'd he look like?"

"Black kid."

"How old? What was he wearing?"

"I don't know," she said, trying to breathe. "Maybe fifteen, sixteen, kind of tall, wearing a white T-shirt and shorts."

"Was he dark or light complected?"

"I don't know, it was dark."

"You sure he was black, not Mexican or something."

"No," she said. "He was black."

ZITO WAS WAITING IN THE DISTRICT'S PARKING LOT.

"Dude," said Zito. "I just got off the phone with that chick we met, Lauren."

"What?" Macbeth felt his throat seize. His tongue felt dry as if it was covered in dust.

"Yeah. She called the office. Some shithead just broke into your apartment. She's got your landlord and a neighbor with her and the police are on the way. You need to get your ass back there, post-haste."

"She okay?"

"Yeah, but hightail it back. Ryan knows."

"Thanks." Macbeth hung up, then swung his Jeep out of the lot and stomped on the gas. Once he got on the entrance ramp his accelerator needle climbed fast.

LAUREN SAT AT THE KITCHEN TABLE AND WATCHED FOR MACBETH through the window above the air conditioner. The cop from the local district was at the table too. He had a notebook and was asking questions. She didn't understand why he was badgering her. She'd told him all she knew, and he'd been staring at her and he gave her the creeps. He made her feel so uncomfortable that she'd buttoned up all but the top button on Macbeth's shirt.

Macbeth's landlord, Camp, had hung around too. He was somewhere close by. She'd heard him talking to the cop when he first arrived. The cop wanted her to go down to his car to make out the report. But Camp insisted she stay in the apartment. She found herself liking the old guy. He wasn't so bad. She certainly didn't want to go into any squad car with this cop. She was thankful she'd put on her panties and jeans before the cops arrived.

She heard tires squeal and Macbeth's Jeep roared around the corner, skidding to a stop at an angle in the parking lot. He jumped out and ran. She smiled when she heard him pound up the stairs. It hadn't been that long since she'd called his partner, but it seemed like forever.

She heard Macbeth say something to Camp in the hallway. She

stood as Macbeth barreled through the door. As she came around the table, he stepped over and hugged her tight.

"You all right?"

She nodded and whispered, "Yes." Despite her best effort not to, she started crying. Lowering her face onto his shoulder, the tears came unbidden. His squeeze tightened and he rocked her gently. His hand pressed her head against him. "It's okay. I'm here now."

The cop stood and cleared his throat. "Officer Macbeth?"

Macbeth turned toward him. "Yes?"

"The young lady didn't see him take anything, so if you find that something's missing, call Area One. I've left you the victim's notice with the RD number on it."

"You got an ET rolling?"

"Sure do, but they're crazy busy and probably won't be here until the morning. Said they'd call first."

"Thanks."

"Don't mention it." The cop stepped around them and walked toward the door. "I'll let myself out."

Lauren continued to rest her head on Macbeth's broad shoulder. It felt so good. She felt safe, like nothing or nobody could harm her now.

Chapter 42

A New Day

MONDAY 0900 Hours

Huggins yawned and sucked breath deep into his chest. He was uncomfortable, dressed in a suit provided by his attorney. They were standing around a small high-top table in a corner of the snack bar on the first floor of the courthouse at Twenty-sixth and California, waiting for his attorney, Sherman Gold. Keloid, Maine, and White Boy were there too, but White Boy was off taking a piss.

The cafeteria was packed well beyond its capacity, filled with defendants and a few attorneys and even fewer victims. Most were men, the majority black, but there were some Mexicans and Puerto Ricans and whites, too. Conversations were loud, and some people talked fast in Spanish. The room smelled like sweat, but not from exercise, from the nerves of men whose freedom was at stake.

Huggins checked his watch. It was a quarter after nine. Keloid shifted his feet, and Maine glanced around, probably looking for White Boy. Huggins was getting pissed his attorney was late.

"What's happening today?" Maine asked.

Huggins peered at the two doors at each end of the cafeteria. "A hearing. Gold said it wouldn't take long."

"Then what?" Keloid asked.

"I got a couple ideas." Huggins nodded at the big man. "I want to make some plans, but I got to figure things first." He was glad he and Stomps had worked out. Killing her would've brought serious heat. Maybe she could be his regular punch. Now that he had the goods on Macbeth, that cat was about to pay for all the shit he'd done. The assistant girl posed a serious problem. But she was also the easiest to deal with.

Huggins saw Konrad's head, with its curly receding hair, as the man strolled into the room. Huggins nodded at Keloid. "Be cool. I'll be back." He left the table and met the private detective at the door.

Konrad stepped back into the hallway. A few seconds later, Huggins followed. Konrad had his hands stuck in his pockets. Huggins snickered, thinking he had the bastard so scared he didn't trust his own hands not to shake.

"Where the fuck's Gold?" Huggins asked.

"Upstairs, waiting for you." Konrad turned toward the elevator lobby. "Come on."

Huggins followed, staring at the back of Konrad's head. His hair was dark and curly, but not Afro kinky. On top, his pasty white skin showed through and was spotted with freckles plus a couple larger red spots. His skin hadn't seen much sun. When they made the lobby, they joined the crowd of people waiting to push into the dozen or so elevators as they dinged open. Eventually, he and Konrad squeezed into an elevator. Konrad pushed a button and stood away from him. The smell in the elevator was much the same as the cafeteria, only more powerful.

Upstairs, Gold stood in a large open hallway with ceilings thirty feet high, outside tall wooden doors. The Jew motherfucker smiled, but with no warmth. He was tanned and wore an expensive, perfectly tailored suit, several gold rings, and a Rolex. He seemed to sweat money, and Huggins couldn't help but think that the Cobras had probably paid for most of his shit. That pissed him off. But the man was good. He delivered. That couldn't be argued.

"Lonnie." Gold held his hand out, and they shook. "This shouldn't take long, and it will be painless. I promise."

"That's what I'm paying you for," Huggins said.

"Listen to this guy," Gold said to Konrad, who still had his hands in his pockets. The detective only nodded, looking uncomfortable. "The judge is waiting. Shall we?"

Gold pulled one of the double doors open. It didn't make a sound as it swung out. In the courtroom, pews on either side flanked a center aisle. The seats were crowded with people.

The judge's bench stood against the far wall with a witness stand next to it. A microphone stuck out from one of the wooden railings and hung in front of the chair like a long, skinny, crooked dick.

A podium stood twenty feet in front of the witness box. Off to its side were two long wooden tables, one each for the defense and prose-cuting attorneys. A crowd of lawyers surrounded the defense table. A small woman in a dress sat on the prosecutor's side. The jury box was on the left with fourteen chairs, all of them empty.

Huggins followed Gold to the defense table. Several attorneys with their suit coats off milled around, talking quietly. The judge was reading something, his eyeglasses pushed up on his forehead. He was white and old, real old, like maybe a hundred years. His name plate at the top of the bench had his name stenciled on it, but it was long, had to have twenty fucking letters. Huggins didn't even try to read it, let alone pronounce it.

The judge's clerk, a little Mexican in a yellow smock, sat on a lower seat. The clerk waved at Gold and started to shuffle through files in front of him. He pulled one out and put it in front of the judge. The judge dropped his glasses onto his nose and pulled papers out of the file. He shuffled through them and finally looked down at Gold. He tucked the papers back in the file, leaving one out.

"Sherman," the judge said. "C'mon up."

Gold put his briefcase on the table and popped the clasps simulta-neously. He withdrew a file of his own and stepped around the other attorneys. He walked to the bench, his arms spread.

"Good morning, Your Honor," Gold said. "Thanks for seeing me on such short notice. This matter does have some urgency to it."

"Well, we'll see."

Gold spun around and waved Huggins forward. He turned back to the judge. "You wouldn't mind if I have my client step up too, would you?"

"No. C'mon, Mr. Huggins."

The judge held a piece of paper in his hand and read it carefully. At one point, he glanced at Huggins for a second, then went back to reading. He stopped, lifted his glasses to rub his eyes, and lowered the glasses back down to read some more. Finally, he said, "Mr. Gold, this is a bit unusual, isn't it?"

"Perhaps, but very appropriate in this instance."

"And you can substantiate these allegations?"

"Most certainly, Your Honor." Gold removed pages from his file and held them up. "Right here in black and white."

"May I see?" The judge reached over the front edge of the bench and took the papers from Gold. He shuffled through the pages slowly, scanning each one. "Everything seems to be in order. You've described the actions, I think, well enough, though I must say this is highly irregular."

"If I may, sir," Gold said. "I think it's the behavior of this police officer that's highly irregular and pushing this action to the extreme. I'm aware that it's a bit radical, but I've the welfare of my client at stake. I think I've more than made a case for the concern we have for his safety and freedom. You'll find the video Mr. Huggins's associate took to be particularly convincing."

The judge stared at Huggins. "Is what's written here truthful and accurate?"

"Yes." Huggins fought to keep a straight face.

"Thank you, Mr. Huggins." The judge waved toward the back of the room. "Ms. Prosecutor?"

The woman at the prosecutor's table stood and walked to the bench. The judge handed her the paperwork Gold had given him, and she read it quickly, making several comments under her breath.

Huggins took this chance to check her out. He couldn't tell about her figure in the sack she wore for a dress, but her legs, what he could see of them, looked good in the stockings. But she was too old, even at thirty.

"Mr. Huggins," the judge said. "Step back to the defense table."

Huggins nodded and walked away.

The judge placed his hand atop something in front of him, a microphone maybe. He and Gold and the prosecutor had a conversation in low tones. A couple of times, the prosecutor gestured toward the table where Huggins stood. Her voice rose somewhat, but he couldn't make out what she said.

Finally, the judge lifted his gavel and banged the bench's top. He uncovered whatever he'd had his hand on and said, "I'm signing this order. But Mr. Gold, I'm only giving you thirty days. If you need to extend it, you'll have to appear in front of me and convince me that's necessary." He took the papers from the woman and signed several times before handing them to his clerk. "Make copies of these and give them to the State so they can notify the parties involved. Give Mr. Gold a copy as well."

OUTSIDE THE COURTROOM, GOLD HANDED THE PAPERS TO Konrad. "Make copies of these and deliver one to CPD immediately. In fact, ask to see First Deputy Parks. I'll make sure he's expecting it."

Konrad nodded and went off. Gold turned to Huggins. "Be careful, Lonnie, and don't fuck up."

Huggins nodded and felt a smile tighten the muscles around his mouth. Oh, he'd be careful all right.

LAUREN GLANCED AT HER WATCH. IT WAS ALMOST TEN AND SHE knew she had to get back to her apartment. She had so much to do. But it had been so—hard to say relaxing, because she and Stacey hadn't done much relaxing, but being together had been fun. It felt comfortable, too. And he was hot, exquisitely hot. Right now, he was in the shower. She'd promised not to distract him again, though she was tempted to go back on her word.

Macbeth's apartment phone rang. She got up and stuck her head into the hallway. The bathroom door was still shut.

"Your phone's ringing," she said, loud enough that he should be able to hear. He said something but she couldn't make it out. She stepped up and pushed the bathroom door open. "Your phone's ringing?"

"Let the machine get it."

She shut the door and walked back into the kitchen. Macbeth had an old-style answering machine. When the ringing stopped, it clicked on. The volume was turned up and she heard Macbeth's voice ask the caller to leave a message after the beep. She felt peculiar, like she shouldn't be listening.

"Stace, this is Ryan." The voice belonged to one of the other cops, she didn't remember if she'd met him, but thought it might be Macbeth's sergeant. Lauren felt dirty, like she was snooping. "Call me when you get up."

Lauren heard the water stop. She felt a stirring to go back on her word again. He'd be naked. But she had a paper to write when she got home, and didn't she have to hit the grocery store first? She was out of coffee and a few other essentials, like wine. Maybe she'd invite him over for a home-cooked dinner once she had the time to make one.

"Who was it?" Macbeth came out of the bathroom in baggy shorts. He was toweling off. His body was nice, bordering on exceptional. She liked how muscular he was. Big and strong. When she saw the scratches on his chest extending up over his shoulders, she felt a blush creep up her neck. Maybe she had been a little too… assertive earlier.

"Ryan, said to call once you were up," she said.

He kept drying his hair. "He say what about?"

"Nope." She tried to ignore his physique. "You should call him."

"Spare me." He threw the towel at her. "I'll call him later."

Lauren caught the towel and heaved it back at him. "Okay." He grabbed the towel as it left her hand and used it to wrap around her shoulders and draw her into his chest. "Hey, you're wet," she said.

"But are you?"

She pushed him away. "Is that as romantic as you can get on the

South Side?" She twirled away as he grabbed for her. "Am I wet? Give me a break. You brute."

"That's excessive foreplay in some parts of the South Side." He stopped and turned back to the bedroom. "I better get dressed."

"Yeah, you do that." She picked up the towel and threw it after him. "Dry off too, Romeo."

A LITTLE OVER AN HOUR LATER, MACBETH PULLED AROUND THE corner, and his gaze followed Lauren's outstretched arm toward her building. "Parking's a bitch when school's in, but exams were last week so it shouldn't be too bad for the next week or two."

He found a spot a little past the gray stone three-flat and pulled to the curb. She turned to him. "Thanks."

"For what?"

"Everything." She kissed him quickly on the lips. "I had a blast, but if I don't get out, we'll be here all day."

He laughed, feeling awkward, and grabbed her shoulder as she tried to slide out of the Jeep. "Hey, when can I see you?"

"Let me get that paper written and I'll call. You're off tomorrow, right?"

"Tomorrow and the day after."

"Cool," she said. "I'm a fast typist when I'm motivated."

MACBETH WASN'T TWO BLOCKS FROM LAUREN'S PLACE WHEN HIS pager went off. It was Ryan and he'd attached a 9-1-1. Macbeth shook his head and started to look for a pay phone.

He found one at a White Hen down the street.

"Sorry, Ronnie, I forgot to call you back," he said when his sergeant answered. "What'd I do now?"

"Hell if I know, but this is really starting to piss me off." Ryan's voice was a low growl.

"I'd be happy to change places."

"No doubt." Ryan's voice lost none of its edge. "Seems you're wanted in the Office of the First Deputy."

"Why?"

"Good fucking question. Call me when you know."

"Can't I just call in?" Macbeth asked.

"Nope, they were adamant, in person."

"Am I picking up a subpoena or something like that?"

"I don't know, Stace, go find out. Call me afterward or I'll just see you at roll call."

"Fine."

They disconnected, and Macbeth replaced the receiver on its cradle and stared at the graffiti-laden phone. Maybe all this bullshit about the IAD investigation was about to come to an end. Perhaps the First Deputy was going to tell him it was over—that he was cleared.

He hoped so. He was due for some good luck.

Chapter 43

Easy Come, Easy Go

MONDAY 1100 Hours

Jermaine listened as Huggins laid out the plans to the four of them: Jermaine, White Boy, Tea Bag, and Munchie. The latter being in charge. After Huggins was done talking, he looked at them one at a time.

"We clear on what's fittin' to happen?" Huggins asked.

Munchie and Tea Bag nodded. White Boy muttered, "Yes." Jermaine just stared. Huggins caught his eye, arching an eyebrow.

"Well," he said. "Maine, there a problem?"

Jermaine shook his head. "No." He hoped he sounded more confident than he felt.

Huggins continued. "Keloid's cousin got a van we going to use."

Tea Bag's face scrunched like he was confused.

"Listen," Huggins said. "You four are going to drive over and do the thing, while Keloid and I establish our alibi."

"What's that?" White Boy said.

"I'm going to be the first one the poh-leece look at, but me and Keloid going somewhere and make sure people remember us. Dig?"

White Boy nodded and said, "Oh, I get it."

МАСВЕТН WAS ESCORTED BY A UNIFORMED FEMALE POLICE officer into the inner office of the First Deputy. As soon as Macbeth walked through the door, Parks turned in his seat. He looked tall and trim in a way that showed he exercised regularly. He had a dark complexion, made even darker by his starched white uniform shirt and a gold stud in one ear. His head was smooth and shiny. His uniform had been pressed and starched until the creases could cut bread.

Parks grabbed his phone from its cradle. "Edna, would you call Agent Kaczynski and let him know we're here." He hung up. "Sit," he told Macbeth.

Macbeth took a seat and rested his hands on his thighs. He met the First Deputy's stare. Parks turned away and looked out the window. The office faced west and had a view over the parking lot, past State Street and the expressway. The horizon was dominated by the fluttering flags and superstructure of the White Sox baseball stadium, U.S. Cellular Field.

Macbeth's gaze shifted, and he looked around at the office itself. The walls had been painted robin-egg blue, and the one directly across from the door was covered in plaques, framed letters, and pictures of Parks with various people, politicians and reverends and celebrities. The wall behind Macbeth was lined with bookshelves, many of which contained knick-knacks. A silver bar stuck out from the end of the last bookshelf and the First Deputy's dress uniform blouse hung from it, encased in a cleaner's bag. His uniform hat was on a shelf, also in plastic.

Parks leaned back in his seat behind his large desk, his fingers making a steeple, elbows on the arms of his chair, and stared at Macbeth again. There was a white envelope on the desk blotter, but no other paperwork.

"Officer Macbeth, do you have any idea what's going on?"

"No, sir."

"You don't?" Parks studied him from behind his fingers, his forehead furrowed. "That surprises me."

Macbeth shrugged, not knowing what else to say. He'd planned on staying quiet and keeping his answers short—less chance of getting into more trouble. His attorney, Flores-Perry, would be proud of him.

Macbeth's pager chirped.

Parks scowled. "Turn that goddamned thing off."

Macbeth pulled the pager and saw Lauren's number on the display. He turned it off and returned it to his belt.

Parks picked up the envelope and opened it. He slipped a tri-folded paper out, unfolded and spread it on the blotter. He smoothed out the folds and looked at Macbeth.

"In all my years on this department," he said. "I've only heard of something like this, never actually seen it." Parks pressed hard on the paper, like he wanted to push it through the blotter. "It's embarrassing for our organization, like we don't know how to police our own. Do you know what I'm saying?"

"Not really, sir."

"No, I don't suppose you would. The more reason to take action since you're apparently unaware of your transgressions."

Macbeth shrugged. Parks looked at the paper, picked it up. "Are you aware of what a restraining order is?"

"Yes, sir."

"What is it?" Parks asked.

"A court order stating that a person isn't supposed to go near another person or place."

"What's the penalty if you violate such an order?"

"You get locked up." Macbeth stared at the First Deputy.

"Right. You go to jail." Parks put the paper down. "Seems a judge over at Twenty-sixth Street was convinced by some lawyer to grant a restraining order to an Alonzo Huggins. Do you know him, Officer Macbeth?"

"Yes, sir."

"So." Parks stared at Macbeth. "We've established that you know what a restraining order is, and its consequences, and that you know Mr. Huggins. Do you want to guess what comes next?"

"No, sir." Macbeth fought the urge to make fists. He willed his hands to lie still on his thighs, not a twitch. This couldn't be happening.

"By order of the court," Parks said. "You are not to go near Alonzo Huggins. You will not place him under arrest. You will not search him. You will not go to his abode. You do know what an abode is, right?"

"Yes, sir."

"Very good." Parks held the paper out to him. "This is your copy of the order of protection against you. Read it, know it. Violate it and you will find yourself hauled off to Twenty-sixth Street to see the judge."

POLICE AGENT KACZYNSKI LED MACBETH TO THE IAD OFFICE on the other side of the fifth floor. At first, they didn't speak, but when they were well away from the offices of the First Deputy, Kaczynski finally spoke up. "Sorry, this isn't how this sort of thing should be done, but it's out of our hands."

"What sort of thing?" Macbeth asked.

"I got to take you to Sergeant Easter."

"Yeah, and?"

Kaczynski walked for several strides without speaking as if deciding whether he could say or not. "They're placing you on restricted duty."

ONCE IN A CONFERENCE ROOM IN THE INTERNAL AFFAIRS offices, Macbeth was ordered to sit next to a black sergeant in a green and gray pantsuit. Her hair was short. She had on eyeshadow, but no earrings and her nails, cut short, were painted a light blue. Her department ID was clipped to her jacket lapel. Kaczynski took a seat across from him.

"My name is Belinda Easter. I'm a sergeant in Internal Affairs." She held out a hand to Macbeth, and they shook. "Sorry to meet you under these conditions."

She turned back to her paperwork and peeled off the topmost form. She slid it over between them and said, "I have to read this to you and you're going to have to read along and initial where I indicate." She pointed to the top of the form where the lines for his initials began. "By the order of the Superintendent." She put her hand on the form and stopped. "And here, what it should really read is by the order of the First Deputy Superintendent." She made a notation on the form and initialed it.

"You are being stripped of your police powers pursuant to the above order in relation to the following complaint register investigation." She used her pen to point at the specific investigation number in the corner.

Stripped—professionally neutered. He wanted to, what? Hit something? He could feel the emotion start to gather in his belly, and his jaw set. He'd be damned if he let anyone see him react.

Ten minutes later she'd taken his star and identification card, and he'd been made to sign a form acknowledging his police powers had been revoked. Sergeant Easter put his star and ID card in a bag. Then she and Kaczynski escorted him to Graphic Arts on the second floor where his picture was taken, and he was issued a new ID card. This one was red and had the word *Restricted* stamped across it.

They returned to IAD and he was eventually instructed to report to Records Division the next morning. That was where he was going to work until this was settled. In under an hour, he technically wasn't the police anymore, and he'd been reassigned to clerical work. Just that quick and easy. He'd been told he couldn't carry a gun, though he could maintain the one on his hip until he got home. It was his, after all. He wasn't allowed to make arrests, couldn't testify in court, wear a uniform, or drive a department vehicle. Kaczynski led him to the elevator lobby on the fifth floor. He asked Macbeth if he was all right but didn't really seem that interested. Or maybe he was but was at a loss as to what to say. Either way, Kaczynski left him alone.

Macbeth stood there staring at the buttons. His face had to be red from the anger rising from his belly. This was such bullshit. He hadn't done anything wrong, yet he'd had no say in the matter. Guilty until proven innocent. They hadn't even told him what the charges were, how could that be possible? Didn't he have rights?

He was about to punch the down button when he heard someone clear their throat behind him. He turned and for the first time noticed Sergeant Ryan and his attorney, Flores-Perry, seated on the gray couches. They stood, though Flores-Perry had some difficulty rising.

. . .

THEY WENT TO THE CAFETERIA ON THE SECOND FLOOR. WHILE Ryan went to the vending machines to get them drinks, Flores-Perry sat across from Macbeth at a table by the windows overlooking Michigan Avenue.

"I've done a little investigating since your sergeant called me with the news," she said. "The City of Chicago instills police powers and feels they can take them away at any time for any reason."

Macbeth heard her talking but the words didn't really resonate in his head. He just wanted to get out of the building.

"I've got a call in to Kaczynski," she said. "I'll find out what's going on. I assure you."

She stood, using her walker for support. "As soon as I get anything, I'll call." She patted his shoulder. "This is nothing, my boy. Don't let it get you down." She hobbled off as Ryan set a soda on the table.

A SHORT TIME LATER, HE RODE THE ELEVATOR TO THE LOBBY with Ryan. They walked out of the building in silence, ignoring the passersby. The wind was warm, working on hot, the sun relentless and bright, promising a very hot afternoon. Ryan stopped and turned to Macbeth.

"You all right?"

"Yeah." Macbeth shrugged. "Pissed off more than anything."

"No doubt." Ryan folded his arms across his chest. "I can't believe this."

"Me neither."

"Have they completed their investigation?"

"No, this is over something new, I think."

"What?" Ryan's expression was one of disbelief. "Don't they have to do some kind of investigation before they strip you?"

"Apparently not. They didn't even give me any allegations."

Macbeth didn't want to talk to anyone and was afraid he was going to run into more people he knew. Ryan talked him into lunch at an out-of-the-way restaurant that wasn't frequented by cops.

Macbeth walked to his Jeep. He got in and started it and turned the air up. What the hell had just happened? He wasn't a cop anymore, just like that. And he couldn't even say why. He had no idea who'd complained. What the charges were. Nothing. Guilty until proven innocent. He looked for Ryan and saw him idling down the street, waiting for him.

Macbeth pulled into traffic and then remembered his pager. *That can wait*, he thought as he fell in behind Ryan.

JERMAINE KNEW HE'D NEVER BEEN IN THIS PART OF THE CITY before. But it wasn't all that different from Lincoln Park and other areas close to Cabrini. Brick and stone buildings lined the streets. It was nice. Munchie said they were close, and he was going to park.

A SMILE CREPT ACROSS LAUREN'S FACE AS SHE REMEMBERED Macbeth's awkwardness when she'd gotten out of his Jeep. She thought it was cute. The apartment phone rang. She stopped typing and answered.

"Hi."

"Hi, sweetie," her mom said. "How are you?"

The syrupy sound in her mother's voice brought another smile to Lauren's lips. Funny what a little snuggle with a cute man could do to change the anxiety surrounding her parents.

"I'm good." Though happy for the call, Lauren wondered what her mom wanted. She supposed Mom would get around to it sooner than later. "Aren't you and Daddy out on the boat?"

"Yes, your dad's gassing it up, and I thought I'd call. What're you doing?"

"Trying to finish my paper, then grocery shopping."

"Really? I thought you and Rachel usually did that later."

"Typically, we do, but I need a couple things desperately."

"Oh."

"So, what's up?" Lauren asked.

"Nothing." Her mom breathed out as if she was blowing her hair out of her eyes. "I just wanted to call and make sure you're okay. I know we've been pushing this summer job thing."

"Yeah." Lauren laughed. "But I haven't been paying it much attention."

"Thought as much, just wanted to be sure."

"So, you're okay with it?" Lauren asked.

"Hmmm." Her mom paused. Lauren could picture her looking around to make sure Dad wasn't within earshot.

"I want you to be happy, safe and happy, and part of me agrees with your father," she said. "He's made a very good living and I don't see any harm in encouraging you to follow suit."

"And the other part?"

"Well, on the other hand," her mom paused as if choosing her words carefully, "I know you're a smart, self-assured young woman."

Lauren recognized "self-assured" as code for stubborn.

"As a mother, your mother, I'm always going to worry about my little girl. And this thing you're doing just sounds so dangerous."

"Mom, please," Lauren said. "We've gone over this a bunch of times. I'm not on my own. I have a partner, a private detective with lots of experience. He's armed, for Christ's sake." Better to not mention what a racist, sexist asshole he was, she thought. "Besides, we're deep into it already."

"I know, honey," her mom said. "I know you've mentioned it, it just all sounds so, awful."

"Mom." Lauren struggled to keep the smile on her face. "I'm glad you called. I was going to call you, in fact. I wanted to talk to you about something else."

"What's that, honey?"

"I've met a boy." Lauren's grin split her face. "He's a cop."

AFTER GETTING OFF THE PHONE WITH HER MOTHER, SHE PAGED Stacey without luck, and finally called his machine and left a dorky message. "Miss you."

How lame. She saved her work and shut down the computer. Time for a break. They needed to go shopping, but she didn't have time and was going to stick to the "must haves." As she got ready, she wished Stacey would call, but no luck.

She grabbed her car keys and stepped outside. The weight of the heat and humidity settled on her shoulders, her hair was just going to be frizzy this summer. She locked the deadbolt and turned. Where had she parked? It seemed she only remembered when her car was off the block, around the corner.

As she looked for her car, she saw a dark van at the intersection, parked across the crosswalk. There were two guys in the front seats, and she sensed they were staring at her. She couldn't make them out too well, but she could see they were black. She'd never been very observant before, but her recent experiences in Cabrini had made an impression. Still, it made her feel dirty to think, just because they were black, she should be afraid, like she was a racist.

Something about the van or the guys bothered her, though. She turned and went back into the apartment. She marched to Rachel's room and knocked.

JERMAINE WAS IN THE GANGWAY OF THE HOUSE NEXT DOOR. They'd watched her come out of the apartment but turn around and go in again like she forgot something. Munchie had sent him and Tea Bag out, while Munchie drove around the block to get in position. She had to be back out soon. This had to be quick. Tea Bag wanted to wait until she got to her car, but Munchie pointed out they didn't know where that was, or she could be walking.

Chapter 44

Snake Bit

Lauren knocked again. Rachel finally responded softly. "Yeah."

"Get up, sleepy head." Lauren opened the door. Rachel was in her bed, covers thrown off, with an oscillating fan blowing on her from the desk.

"Seriously, it's after twelve," Lauren said. "Want to go to the grocery store with me?"

"Later." Rachel threw an arm over her eyes.

Lauren went into the kitchen. She felt stupid, but still called Stacey and started to leave a message on his machine about the van. When the machine gave her the option to erase the message, she did. She was being paranoid. She palmed her pepper spray and left. Even though it was the middle of the day, better to have it in hand than the other way around.

When she stepped out, the van was nowhere to be seen. Relieved, she turned to lock the deadbolt.

As she pushed her key into the lock, someone shoved her from behind, smashing her face into the door, cutting off her scream. Arms wrapped around her, crushing the air from her lungs. Her vision was blurry. Her thumb was impeded by the protective block on the pepper spray. She fought and kicked and finally got her thumb under the plastic top. She screamed again and waved the canister as she depressed the button.

JERMAINE WAS A HALF-STEP BEHIND TEA BAG WHEN THE GANG banger chucked the girl hard into the door and then threw his arms around her. The girl fought and kicked. Tea Bag growled as he tried to control her.

Jermaine waited to stuff the cloth in her mouth. Tea Bag struggled as Jermaine reached to ram the rag between her teeth. She sprayed him with pepper spray. His eyes snapped closed and he grunted. So did Tea Bag, and Jermaine wondered if the bitch had just sprayed them all.

THE CANISTER WAS SLAPPED FROM LAUREN'S HAND AS SHE screamed again and kicked. Her eyes burned and she was forced to close them against the pain. Somebody punched her, then dragged her legs from under her.

JERMAINE SQUINTED AGAINST THE AGONY IN HIS EYES AND helped drag the girl to the van by a leg. He punched her again, trying to take some of the fight out of the bitch. But she kept squirming and kicking and trying to scream. Jermaine had ropes of snot running out of his nose.

ROUGH HANDS DRAGGED LAUREN DOWN THE STAIRS AND punched her. Black hands grasped at her and punched as they carried her. They stumbled across the sidewalk and crashed into a parked car, smashing her face into the metal.

She screamed, "No! Stop!" But something was thrust into her mouth. She tried to spit it out, and bite at the fingers that sought to shove it deeper. An engine gunned. A big dark shadow screeched to a stop.

She craned her neck and saw the van waiting in the street. Someone opened the side door as they hauled her between the parked cars. She was punched again, and then shoved through the open door. Hands grabbed her and threw her down onto a seat. Someone pinned her arms behind her as others punched her in the head and body.

Someone shouted. The rag was stuffed farther into her mouth until she gagged. The door rolled closed with a bang and the van leapt forward, tires squealing.

Oh, my God, this can't be happening.

JERMAINE THREW HIMSELF IN THE VAN AS MUNCHIE FLOORED IT. Tea Bag kicked the girl while Jermaine pinned her arms behind her. White Boy dove on her legs and tried to pin them down, but he couldn't. Tea Bag finally stopped hitting the girl and reached for the tape.

THE VAN MOVED. TIRES SCREECHED AS IT SPED OFF. SOMETHING made a loud ripping noise then sticky tape wound around Lauren's legs. She fought against the hands that pinned her. But they were too strong. Tape caught in her hair, over her eyes. Still, she fought through the burning of the pepper spray. Tape encircled her head, her eyes, her mouth.

Jermaine took over wrapping her with tape. The bitch was a fighter, that was sure, but she wasn't project-strong or mean. White Boy tried again to hold her down but failed. Tea Bag grabbed a wrench and hit her in the head. That knocked the fight out of her, and she lay still.

Macbeth turned his pager back on when he stopped behind Ryan across the street from a Thai place on State Street. He heard the rattle and knew he had messages. He was expecting one, at least, from Lauren. He found himself needing to hear her voice.

Inside, Ryan grabbed a table, while Macbeth went to a pay phone by the bathroom. He dialed her apartment and waited.

"HELP!"

Macbeth's heart stopped at the sheer panic in the voice on the other end of the line. "Lauren?"

"HELP HER!"

Macbeth plugged his open ear with a finger. "Who's this?"

The girl on the other end of the line sobbed. He didn't think it was Lauren. "Rachel?"

"They took her!"

"What?" he asked.

"Someone," Rachel sounded like she was hyperventilating, "just grabbed Lauren from the porch and took off in a dark blue van."

"A dark blue van?"

"Yes!" Rachel seemed to be getting it together. "They went toward Loomis!"

"Who took her?"

"Black guys," Rachel said. "Three, no, four black guys. Hold on, one might've been white."

"What happened?"

"I heard her leave for the grocery. She went out the front door." Rachel took a breath. "Then I heard a bang and she started screaming. By the time I ran to the door, I saw them throw her into a van and take off."

"A gunshot bang? Did they shoot her?"

"No." Rachel's voice was ragged. "Like they were fighting and hit the door."

"Hang up and dial 9-1-1."

Macbeth disconnected and ran from the restaurant. He hadn't even opened his Jeep's door when Ryan rushed over.

"What the fuck you doing, Stace?" Ryan's tone was meant for a crazy person.

"They took Lauren!"

"What?"

"Three or four black guys just snatched her from over by UIC." He ripped his door open and jumped in.

"Hang on, I'm going with you." Ryan ran for his car.

Macbeth started his Jeep and pulled up by Ryan. His sergeant grabbed a black bag from the floor of the back seat and ran for Macbeth's passenger side. Once he was in the Jeep, Ryan pulled a phone from the bag and powered it up. As Macbeth drove toward Lauren's, Ryan called the dispatcher and had an emergency flash message sent to every radio frequency in the city.

Jermaine watched out of the back of the van as they crawled along the Eisenhower Expressway. There was a traffic jam and they were caught in a sea of cars and trucks, they just crept a foot here, another there. Jermaine couldn't tell whether it was construction or an accident. What if the cops had set up a roadblock? That seemed unlikely.

The girl was quiet, lying on the floor all taped up. She wasn't bleeding from where she got clunked but she didn't look too good, either. Her color was wrong, kind of pasty white where she'd had color before.

"See any cops?" Tea Bag said from the front seat. Munchie was still driving, his eyes darting from the street to the different mirrors and back to the street. Everybody seemed out of sorts, except Munchie. He was cool. White Boy looked freaked, his eyes wide and all jittery.

"No," Jermaine said.

Tea Bag caught Jermaine's eyes in the mirror. "Maybe we should just shoot the bitch now and dump her out west?"

Munchie shook his head. "Can't do that, Lonnie'd have our heads, man. Just relax, we cool. Ain't shit wrong."

LAUREN LAY ON THE FLOOR, ON HER BACK, AND CONCENTRATED on breathing. Her head and eyes were on fire and she thought she was going to throw up. But her mouth was taped with the rag inside, throwing up would kill her. She tried to think what she could do. Her feet were fixed together tight, but she could move her legs at the knees and hips. Her hands were secured, but not done nearly as well as her feet. *I'd be better off not moving until I have a plan*, she thought.

They were talking about killing her. Oh, my God. It was so surreal, but this was actually happening. She was on her own. She doubted anyone had called the police, there hadn't been enough time. She prayed and fought to stay awake. The darkness was there, waiting. Even though her eyes hurt like they'd been stung by bees, she tried to open them. She could barely crack them enough to see.

MACBETH HARDLY USED THE BRAKE. RYAN HAD HIS SEATBELT fastened tight. When he'd been on the phone, he'd not reacted to what was happening outside the Jeep. But once he disconnected, he clutched the roll bar and dashboard like his life depended on it.

"Fuck!" Ryan yelled. He pointed at a sign above the windshield. It read *Top not designed to keep the occupants inside the vehicle in the event of a crash.*

JERMAINE WAS SUPPOSED TO BE WATCHING OUT THE BACK, BUT there wasn't anything to see but a shitload of cars. Traffic was funneling into the southbound Dan Ryan Expressway. The six lanes of the Eisenhower were squeezing down to two, then one going south. They couldn't see the reason for the gridlock. They inched along. The girl was quiet. White Boy watched her.

This was getting too damn crazy. He'd joined the Cobras to get revenge for Antwan, to kill that cop, not to kill some girl. What had Huggins gotten him into?

❧

THE ONLY PERSON LAUREN COULD SEE WAS A KID NEXT TO HER. He was different looking, an albino, and he was crying. *Maybe if I can talk to him,* she thought. *Maybe he'll see me as a person and let me go.* She tried to talk but it only came out as a moan around the rag.

The kid looked at her. "Shhh."

❧

MACBETH DROVE WILDLY, SWERVING INTO ONCOMING TRAFFIC, honking his horn, jerking the wheel left, then back right, punching the gas pedal.

"God dammit, Stace! We can't help if we're in a fucking body bag!"

Macbeth didn't know what else to do, so his whole focus was to get to Lauren's place. It had to be Huggins. Why, though? Maybe Huggins knew she was having issues with his story. Or he found out somehow that she was going to derail his hearing. Certainly, the gangbanger couldn't know they'd hooked up. Or did he? The black kid breaking into his place last night?

Okay, if Huggins took her, where would they go? Cabrini? Unlikely. It would be too hard to smuggle a white girl in there. Out in the Seventh District? That was Boo's play, but it didn't seem right either. Where? Where the fuck were they going?

❧

Jermaine saw the red and blue flashing lights up ahead. A couple of state cops were sitting on the side of the road in front of the big yellow Minuteman trucks. Every car that got close to the state cops hit their brakes, like they were going too fast, even though they were crawling. A car in front of the police was smashed up. An accident. Once the cars rolled past it, they picked up speed. All they had to do was get by these cops.

Lauren heard them say something about cops being up ahead. She gathered her courage to try something. What, she didn't know. To scream she'd have to dislodge the rag. Could she even do that with the tape? She had to try.

Jermaine watched the girl as they approached the cops. Her legs moved, and he thought she was looking at something, maybe White Boy. What the fuck was she doing?

Lauren tried to spit the cloth out of her mouth and breathe deep. Then something heavy hit her back, ejecting the air from her lungs. Someone had jumped on her. She couldn't roll. She sucked in what breath she could and looked up at the albino kid. He stared out the back window, sweating.

Macbeth gunned his Jeep through the intersection at Roosevelt Road. He could see the blue lights of squad cars as soon as he turned onto Lauren's block. The cops were at the opposite corner, several houses away from her graystone. He skidded to a stop and jumped out of the Jeep. One of the squads rolled toward them.

Macbeth pointed at the open door of Lauren's apartment. "That's where she lives."

❧

JERMAINE'S HEART QUICKENED WHEN WHITE BOY SAID ONE OF the state cops had pulled into the road. Even though he was way back, that didn't make Jermaine feel any better. There was panic in White Boy's whiny voice.

Jermaine pushed himself off the girl. "Relax," he said, more to himself than to his friend.

Munchie looked at the rearview. "Cool out. They done with they report is all. Just chill, don't sweat it."

❧

AS THE KID GOT OFF OF HER, LAUREN COULD FINALLY BREATHE. Her lips moved in prayer under the tape as she desperately tried to think of a way out.

❧

JERMAINE FELT THE VAN DRIFT TO THE RIGHT. HE LOOKED OUT through the windshield. A large green sign read *I-55 South, St. Louis.* The van hugged the curving entrance ramp to the Stevenson and headed west. As they descended onto the expressway Jermaine saw the state police car follow.

❧

STACEY MACBETH RECOGNIZED THE TWELFTH DISTRICT sergeant who emerged from the nearby marked car. Joe Avila. Avila went to the back of his car and opened the trunk. He pulled out a roll of crime scene tape. As he walked over to Macbeth and Ryan, he tilted his head to his shoulder mic, the twisted cord bouncing with his purposeful steps. When he got closer, Macbeth could hear the dispatcher talking, but couldn't make out what was said.

Avila held out his hand and shook Ryan's, and then he hugged Macbeth, patting his back with his free hand. "Don't worry, brother. We'll get her back."

"Thanks."

"State police think they have them on the Stevenson."

"What?" Macbeth said. Why the hell would they be on the Stevenson?

"Yeah, just heard it on the zone, man. They're following behind, waiting for backup."

Macbeth ran for his Jeep, with Ryan right behind him.

JERMAINE BRACED HIMSELF AGAINST THE ROOF WITH HIS HAND. Nobody was saying nothing about being calm anymore. The cop back there was tailing them, making every lane change Munchie made. Now that he was speeding up, the cop was too. It didn't look like he was going to be dropping back anytime soon.

Munchie looked around. "What's the next exit?"

"Damen." Tea Bag's voice sounded tense.

"I'll do the next one," Munchie said. "I'll get off, let's see what Five-O do."

"K," Tea Bag said.

LAUREN SAW THAT THE ALBINO KID WAS MORE CONCERNED about the police following them than with what she was doing. She hoped that was true for the other kid, too. She drew her legs back under her, painfully slowly so as not to get caught. She wanted to be ready to kick.

Macbeth raced back east on Roosevelt Road toward the entrance ramp to the southbound Ryan just past Halsted. He pounded his horn and swerved into the oncoming lane, practically pushing the pedal through the floorboard.

"You're hell bent on getting us killed." Ryan gripped the handle in front of him. "If you don't kill me first, remind me to puke all over your car."

Macbeth glanced to the right, out the window more than at his sergeant. But he did see Ryan white-knuckling the handle and shook his head. He jerked the Jeep hard left. "Hang on." They hit the curb and bounced over a section of grass before jumping the next curb onto the ramp. Finally, on the shoulder, he accelerated hard.

Jermaine called out, "They still there."

The state cop wasn't far behind. Their attempt to throw him off at Kedzie had been wasted. He followed and got even closer.

Then Jermaine saw lights coming up fast from behind, blue and red, another state police. "Shit, here come more."

"Punch it!" Tea Bag crawled into the back of the van. The van lurched forward. Tea Bag fell and caught himself on Jermaine. Something metal banged Jermaine's knee. He looked down and saw the automatic pistol. Tea Bag pointed at one of the back windows and looked at White Boy.

"Break that bitch out."

White Boy picked a wrench up from the floor and scooted to the window. He swung the wrench. It bounced back, the window intact. White Boy swung again, harder, with the same result.

"Fuck it." Tea Bag pulled White Boy to the floor and pointed the gun at the window. BOOM!

The noise was so loud that Jermaine thought his eardrums had burst. Stinky smoke filled the van. Jermaine saw a small hole in the window. Cracks ran from the hole toward the outside edges of the glass. Jermaine snatched the wrench from White Boy's hand and cracked the glass hard. It exploded, pieces falling inside and out onto the road. Jermaine rattled the wrench all around the window to knock the rest of the glass out. Then he fell back, making room for Tea Bag.

Tea Bag stuck his hand out the opening and fired again. Jermaine didn't know whether it was his ears or the fact the gun was outside, maybe both, but this time he didn't hear anything.

When Jermaine looked back out, he saw the cop car swerving back and forth. Tea Bag tracked it and fired. Jermaine couldn't tell whether he'd hit anything. Tea Bag shot again.

Then Tea Bag turned to Jermaine and shouted. Jermaine couldn't understand. Tea Bag yanked him closer by his shirt. "Tell Munchie get off at the next exit." His voice sounded funny. Distorted.

Jermaine pulled himself up next to Munchie, who was diddling his ear with a finger. He shouted as loud as he could and was happy that he could hear his own voice inside his head. Munchie cranked the wheel to the right and the van veered hard. Jermaine tried to grab hold of something but fell into White Boy. They went down and rolled onto the girl.

Lauren couldn't see what was going on, but the gunshot clued her in. Her ears ached and she couldn't hear. Then she was plastered by bodies falling on her. She found herself eyeball to eyeball with the albino kid. His eyes were wide; she didn't think she'd *ever* seen anyone so scared. She wondered what he saw in *her* eyes.

The albino lifted from her, onto all fours. He looked around as if he was checking out what everyone else was doing. Another explosion ripped through the van. The kid flinched. He brought a finger to his lips and then tore the tape away from her wrists.

She flexed her fingers, found that she could move them. Her hands were free. She rolled on her side and her eyes filled with tears.

Traffic was stopped. Macbeth rode the shoulder of the Stevenson, blowing past cars so fast they were a blur. He heard Ryan identify himself to the person on the other end of the phone, probably a dispatcher. Macbeth saw Kedzie looming ahead. He got ready in the event some car pulled out in front of them.

Ryan stopped talking and listened, then shouted, "Shots fired out of the van."

Shit, Macbeth thought. It was them, all right. *Please, God, just let her be okay.*

Jermaine watched Munchie as their van accelerated up the ramp onto Pulaski Road. The intersection was crowded, and he thought Munchie was going to get them boxed in. Munchie steered right at the top of the ramp. He jammed on the brakes and slowed, approaching behind the car in the furthest right lane. Then he corrected the wheel and yelled, "Hold on!"

Twenty feet more and he tromped on the gas. The van lurched and crashed into the car, which spun into the intersection. A northbound pickup collided with the car and both vehicles skidded and spun further down the overpass. The van careened through the intersection as Munchie steered hard left. Luckily there was no other cross traffic. The wrecks and debris littered the northbound lanes. Munchie swung over to the southbound lanes and punched it again.

Tea Bag got back up to the rear window and hung his arm out. He fired again and again. As they sped down the overpass, Jermaine saw the state cop pull over. He had a couple holes in his windshield and a crinkled fender.

"Fucking good shooting!" Jermaine wondered if Tea Bag could even hear him.

Macbeth sped past the Kedzie exit and flew down the shoulder. Ryan pointed forward.

"Off at Pulaski." Ryan fingered his windshield. "They're off at Pulaski, southbound."

Macbeth felt a bulge in his throat. He knew where they'd been heading. How did Huggins know? He glanced at Ryan, made eye contact.

"They were headed to my house, Ronnie. There isn't any other reason for these fuckers to be headed out on the Stevenson. They were going to dump her on my doorstep."

LAUREN HAD BOTH HANDS FREE WHEN THE VAN SWERVED. SHE could feel the impact of the crash more than hear it. She rolled and banged into someone. Her ears rang. She rolled on her stomach and curled up, trying to rip some of the tape and rag away from her face. She blinked; one eye was free. Hair came away with the tape, but she finally got a full breath into her lungs.

TEA BAG BROUGHT HIS GUN ARM IN. JERMAINE REALIZED THE slide was locked back, out of bullets. Tea Bag threw it down and cursed.

Jermaine kept watching, expecting Tea Bag to pull another gun out and get back to shooting. Instead, he looked up at Jermaine and shook his head.

Munchie took another hard right. Jermaine, Tea Bag, and White Boy fell. Another hard right had him on his back staring at the ceiling of the van. There was a hard bounce, and then Jermaine saw dust rise behind the van. Where the fuck were they? A hard left rolled them to the other side of the vehicle.

Tea Bag fought to get to his knees. He looked out the back of the van and motioned for Jermaine to get up. Jermaine did, and held onto the empty window frame for balance. A dirt road stretched out behind them. BAM! They hit a dip in the road. Off to the right was the canal, its dark waters reflecting the sun off its oily surface. Tall weeds reached up on either side of the road. BAM! Jermaine's head jammed into the ceiling. The van fishtailed. State cop cars and maybe Chicago's swung onto the dirt road; their lights flashed in the rising dust.

Tea Bag pointed at the handle of the back door. Jermaine grabbed it. Tea Bag held up a hand, signaling to wait. He grabbed the girl by the hair and pulled her up on her knees.

"I'm fitting to kill her now," he yelled. "Gimme that fucking tire iron or something to stab her with."

LAUREN CLAWED AT THE MAN'S CHEEKS. SHE FELT HER NAILS SINK deep into his flesh as she dug with all her strength. He flung her down and punched her in the face, once, twice, three times. Her head banged hard against the floor of the van, and he punched her again.

Her mouth was suddenly grimy with filth. Her head was wrenched up and she grabbed at the hands in her hair. She felt more hands on her body, grabbing at her breasts and arms. Then she was thrown out and for a split second she was in a free fall. A second later the ground materialized in front of her as she hit hard, bouncing and rolling, bouncing and rolling.

Oh, God, it hurts, she thought as her world went black.

THE VAN HIT A HOLE AND JERMAINE NEARLY WENT OUT OF THE door himself. Jermaine and Tea Bag looked at her rolling. One second they were fighting, the next she was gone, lost in the cloud of dust. He saw Tea Bag scoop up the gun.

Tea Bag played with the weapon and the slide slammed home. He scooted forward and yelled at Munchie. There was another hard turn, a dip, and the van went airborne. Then they were in the parking lot of a warehouse. Tea Bag pointed at a delivery truck that was pulling out onto the service road. Munchie nodded and drove toward the truck as Tea Bag threw the side door open.

Jermaine gripped Tea Bag's shoulder and pointed at the gun. "That's empty."

Tea Bag smiled. "That motherfucker don't know that."

Jermaine's stomach was in knots again and he felt like he was going to shit his pants. This wasn't what he wanted, wasn't what he'd signed up for. This was fucking crazy.

Chapter 45

Cut And Run

Macbeth jammed his Jeep halfway into the weeds alongside the dirt road and jumped out. Ryan hadn't moved. He was still in the passenger seat, his phone pressed to his ear. Macbeth ran past a long line of police cars. The fifteen or twenty at the end were from Chicago. The three at the front were Illinois State Police cars.

The third trooper car was jammed into the weeds. It looked like the driver had swerved to avoid the second car. The second car was stopped in the middle of the dirt road, but was cocked like the driver had stomped on the brakes, too. Suddenly. Unexpectedly. The driver's side was torn up, like it had sideswiped a guardrail. The first car was stopped dead in the middle. The front bumper and fender were crunched and a couple of star-shaped impacts in the windshield marked where bullets had hit.

In front of the squad cars was a large white CFD ALS ambulance, but facing toward them like it came from the other direction. The doors were open. The paramedics, assisted by a couple troopers, were wrestling a gurney to the back of the emergency vehicle. Someone was strapped to the gurney and Macbeth saw enough hair on one end to know it was Lauren.

He skidded to a stop. He wouldn't make their job—carrying her over the pock-marked ground—any more difficult than it was. An arm encircled his shoulders. It was a trooper.

"Let them work on her. We'll get you in before they go," she said.

Macbeth opened the ambulance door and was about to get in when Ryan called his name.

"What hospital?" Ryan said.

Macbeth turned to the paramedic driving. "Where we headed?"

"St. Anthony's closest."

"Is that the best?"

The paramedic shrugged. "There's better."

"Go there, then."

The paramedic looked at him. "You police, right?"

"Yeah, take her to wherever you'd take your wife or kid."

"With her injuries, County. Tell your buddy we're headed to County."

Macbeth turned to Ryan, who had the keys to his Jeep. "County!" He jumped into the ambulance.

Ryan gave him a thumbs-up and jogged toward the Jeep.

Jermaine listened as Munchie explained over the phone to Huggins what'd happened. He repeated, "But we ran out of bullets," and, "They were on the expressway already and started following us."

Jermaine was glad it was Munchie on the cell and not him. He wondered if his brother Boo had to make phone calls like that. Jermaine didn't think Huggins handled disappointment well. The delivery driver was at Jermaine's feet in the back of the van. He'd been taped up too, Tea Bag had been right, the gun had taken the fight out of the guy.

MACBETH JUMPED OUT OF THE AMBULANCE AS IT BACKED INTO the bay at County's ER. The backup beep drowned out the driver's protests about his exit. The paramedic had done a fine job of arriving quickly despite the traffic. The other paramedic in back must've been busy; hospital staff was awaiting them in the dock.

That worried Macbeth, since it was unusual for hospital staff to be outside. Lauren must be bad. No one had given him any idea as to her condition. She was unconscious and looked like she'd been dragged along the dirt road. Abrasions covered most of her exposed skin and he hoped she hadn't been hit by a car. He remembered one of the troopers saying that he'd avoided hitting her, though he'd been shocked to see her sail out of the van.

Macbeth had watched from the front of the ambulance as the paramedic in back did his thing. He'd gently examined her body, feeling her with his palms. Macbeth figured he was looking for bullet wounds and/or broken bones. He'd kept an eye on her vitals.

By the time Macbeth got around to the back of the ambulance, the doors were open. The gurney was rolled out, its undercarriage dropping automatically to the ground when it cleared the ambulance deck. A nurse on each side steered the gurney through the double doors into the ER. Macbeth followed at the back of the crowd.

They wheeled Lauren into a trauma room, just up the hall from the doors. Macbeth stopped so a woman in scrubs driving a mobile X-ray unit could get past. He tried to get in, but a young intern kept him out. The intern's eyes were red and blurry, like he hadn't slept in days.

"Someone will be out in a moment to get some info but let us get started." The intern shut the door.

Macbeth fell back against the nearest wall. He wanted to know something. He wanted to know something right now, but he knew they didn't know anything, yet. And he knew this was the best place for Lauren to be. They'd taken care of millions of people, and if anyone could help her, they could.

He felt a hand on his shoulder and turned to look into a pair of green eyes. A nurse, dressed in colorful scrubs, looked at him. "Are you okay?"

"Yeah, I came in with the girl on the ambulance."

"Are you injured?" she asked.

"No, I just want to be with her."

"Are you family?"

"No, but—"

"Don't worry, those guys are good. Someone will be out to talk to you as soon as they assess her condition. Probably somebody from registration, too. You should get a hold of her family. They need to be here."

He leaned back. How the hell was he going to do that? She might've told him her last name, but he didn't remember it, let alone a date of birth. He realized he knew very little about her, no last name, birthday, address, or parent's names. Fat lot of good he would be. *Her roommate, Rachel*, he thought.

He found the police room and called the apartment. No answer. Zito, maybe his partner was with her? He paged Zito.

Zito called back within a minute and listened to Macbeth. When he finished talking, Zito said, "Holy shit, I'll go find Rachel."

Chapter 46

Seize The Day

MONDAY 1430 Hours

Macbeth slumped in the chair in the ER waiting room. The adrenalin high was long gone; he was fading fast and had already worked through a bout of the shakes. Zito and Rachel were en route. Rachel had reached Lauren's parents, who were also on their way. They'd been in Milwaukee on their boat, so it was going to take a while. Apparently, they'd been in touch with the hospital to give whatever authority they needed for treatment. He'd given the registration woman the information he had, essentially Lauren's name; he couldn't provide an address. She didn't have an ID on her, and he didn't even know how old she was. He felt useless.

He mulled his next move, wishing he could do something positive. How had they gotten her address? It didn't seem reasonable that she'd hand it out, especially to Huggins's crew. Was it even his crew? It had to be. Stuff like this didn't happen randomly in Chicago. Macbeth couldn't remember the last time he'd heard of a woman getting snatched off the street by a pack of thugs, certainly not a white girl being abducted by black guys from the University of Illinois at

Chicago area. That shit happened on TV, and in the movies, not real life. Another part of his brain wondered where Ryan was with his Jeep.

The waiting room was hot and crowded. The chairs were filled with people, clustered in groups of family or friends. It was quiet, though. The flat screen TVs accounted for the majority of what noise there was. The murmur of conversation was broken occasionally by a fit of coughing or crying.

§

HUGGINS FIGURED THAT DETECTIVE HAD TO BE AT THE HOSPITAL by now. He was amused that it was the TV news that told him where she'd been taken. He was expecting an update about the girl's condition. Bitch didn't have no business being alive after getting pitched out of a moving van. He sat back and spread his arms along the back of the couch.

The day hadn't gone as planned, not even close. Did she recognize any of the Cobras he'd sent? The TV showed the hospital, but it also gave him the answer to Macbeth. It had been in front of him all this time. Them fucking Arabs had been showing him what to do for weeks. He just hadn't seen it until now.

He grinned and grabbed the phone, and made a call.

"Listen up," Huggins said. "Gather the crew and gun up. We going for a ride."

§

JERMAINE WAS IN THE BACK SEAT AS THE NAVIGATOR CRUISED along the Stevenson Expressway the same way they'd taken in the van, seemed weird at night. He was tucked between Tea Bag, who was drumming with his thumbs, and Munchie with his dreadlocks and a swollen eye. Lonnie had violated him for their fucking up. Huggins was in the front seat and Keloid drove.

Huggins's eyes reflected spill from the streetlights as he looked at Jermaine. "This your chance, homie, you want that cop that killed your brother, right?"

Jermaine had been dreaming of this moment for weeks, and now here it was. He nodded, then realized Lonnie couldn't see him.

"Damn straight." He sounded braver than he felt.

"Good." Huggins pointed out the windshield toward the city beyond. "We gonna lay up and when we see that cop's Jeep turn, we gonna let you out. You stroll across the street, then through them two buildings and catch him going to that ground floor door. Then you gun him down. You keep going to the parking lot, and we'll scoop you up. Dig?"

Jermaine nodded again before he caught himself. "Yeah." He gripped the rusted revolver tucked into his waistband. The one he'd brought from Mississippi. He'd loaded it and unloaded it a half dozen times. The handle was slippery with sweat and he was afraid that if he took it out it might shake. He told himself that was because he was so excited to get the chance to kill the cop. But he knew in the pit of his gut, he was scared. He was ready, or at least as ready as he was ever going to be. It might as well be tonight.

MAVIS WAS DRYING HERSELF OFF AND THINKING THAT THE HOUR spent soaking in the hot tub had made her feel slightly better. Huggins. Why hadn't he stopped for a fucking condom? She'd have to visit the clinic soon. If that asshole gave her something or worse... But she didn't even want to think about that.

The television news was broadcasting the latest about a gang-related shootout in Cabrini. At least that fucking Huggins had done his part to stir up trouble between the Vice Lords and the Gangster Disciples. That would give Plumb a few headaches to deal with and allow her some more camera time as she spoke for her outraged constituents.

As she looked in the mirror to reassess the bruises, her phone rang, and she picked it up.

"Hello, James," she said, putting just enough chocolate velvet into her tone to keep the fish on the line.

"Hi." Parks's voice was deep. "Hope I'm not disturbing you."

"Not at all. To what do I owe the pleasure?"

He sighed. "Well, I just wanted to give you a heads-up. There's been some trouble in Cabrini."

"I saw it on the news."

"There's more. One of the gang leaders was found dead."

She frowned. How far had Huggins gone?

"It was a man named Cecil Jones," Parks said. "Leader of the Mickey Cobras. Did you know him?"

"Know him?" She had to be careful. "I might've met him a few times. Why?"

"Well—" Parks's voice trailed off, like he was searching for the right words. "We're investigating his death as an apparent homicide. Looks like someone threw him out of his fifteenth-floor window."

"Oh, my God." Huggins was anything but subtle.

"There's something else." His voice was hesitant. "We found some papers of a sensitive nature in his apartment."

"Papers?" She felt her heart speed up. This could be bad. "What kind of papers?"

He waited a few seconds before saying, "They appear to be intelligence reports from the department. Highly classified material. That's why I was notified."

"Goodness." Mavis felt the sweat flooding her armpits and neck. She'd told that fucking idiot to destroy any correspondence so it wouldn't lead back to her. And he'd assured her that he had. Was the motherfucker just lazy or was he keeping something on her just in case? "How did he come in possession of them?"

"That's the question we have to figure out."

"How will you do that?"

"The papers are old, but we sent them to the lab. They'll be able to pull up any fingerprints. We've got other ways to backtrack them, too. It'll take time, but we'll trace them back." He laughed. "We'll know more after we subpoena his phone records."

She felt weak in her knees. This couldn't be happening. It was only a matter of time till they traced things back to her. Or maybe to her office?

"So." His tone deepened even further. "I was wondering if I could stop by. Maybe take you to dinner, or eat in."

That was the last thing she needed. "Oh, James, it's so sweet of you to ask, but this is a really bad day."

"Oh?"

"My cycle started early." That would bring him to a screeching halt. "I hope you understand."

"Of course," he said. "Perhaps later this week."

"Sure," she said, and after a quick goodbye she hung up.

Momma Stone's going down, she thought, unless she figured something out quick. And Momma Stone would take Alderwoman Mavis Stomps, front runner to be the first black female mayor of Chicago, with her.

All because of that motherfucker, Huggins. That fucking monster was like a runaway train and she was caught on the tracks with nowhere to go.

Chapter 47

Get A Grip

MONDAY 1600 Hours

Macbeth's eye was caught by a white guy who'd just come into the waiting room. He was medium height and had receding hair. The man asked the charge nurse about Lauren Cahill. Macbeth recognized him immediately. This was the guy who'd been in the lobby of 1150 North Sedgwick. He was part of the defense team.

Macbeth stood and approached the man as he leaned over the registration clerk. The woman was talking to an elderly lady about her companion who'd been wheeled into the ER a few minutes earlier. As he got closer, Macbeth could hear the woman telling him he'd have to wait his turn and to take a number like everyone else.

"But I'm just trying to confirm she's still alive." He fished his wallet from his pants pocket. Macbeth grabbed his arm.

"You hear the lady?" Macbeth tugged the man back. "She said you had to wait."

The man tried to pull his arm from Macbeth's grasp. "Get your hands off me."

"I'm the police," Macbeth said. "Relax."

"I know who the fuck you are, and I said get your hands off me." The man's face reddened, and his nostrils flared as he tried to break the hold on his arm. "What have you done to my assistant? Nurse, nurse," he said, not looking at the woman at the registration desk. "You're my witness. This officer's assaulting me."

"Actually," Macbeth said. "It's battery once someone puts their hands on you." He cranked up the pressure. He knew it would leave a mark on someone as fair-skinned and out of shape as this guy, but he was way past caring. "We need to talk."

Macbeth half lifted the guy and spun him away from the desk, steering him toward doors leading into a nearby hallway.

"Get away from me," the man said. "Let go of me. You're hurting me."

"Listen." Macbeth lowered his voice. "You've got no idea what I'd *like* to do to you." He rammed the man through the doors into the hallway, then face first into a wall. "I want some answers from you."

"Go fuck yourself." The man sprayed spittle across the wall. "I'll have you arrested. I'll sue your ass."

"Get in line, fuck nuts." Macbeth twisted the guy's arm. "I want to know how those animals got her address."

"What are you talking about?"

"The shitheads that grabbed Lauren, how'd they get her address?"

"I don't know what you're talking about."

"They're from Cabrini," Macbeth said.

"You don't know that."

"Little birdie told me." Macbeth didn't feel it was too much of a stretch. This had to be related to Huggins. It couldn't be a coincidence.

"Lauren couldn't have told you, she's unconscious?"

"Her roommate saw the whole thing, recognized one of the assholes as being with Huggins in Cabrini," Macbeth said.

"How could she?" the man sputtered. "She was never there."

"Don't be so sure." Macbeth watched him.

"Let go of me!" The man struggled against Macbeth's hold.

"Do you know what they were doing with her?" Macbeth let the pressure up and the man turned around. Macbeth kept hold of his arm. He wanted him listening closely.

"How the fuck would I know?"

"I thought maybe Huggins told you when you gave him her address."

"You can't prove that."

"They were taking her to my place to kill her," Macbeth said. "That would make you an accessory to attempted murder, kidnapping, unlawful restraint. And that's just off the top of my head. All we need is a subpoena of your phone records." As he watched, the red in the man's face faded and he paled. Then Macbeth knew. "You did give it to him, didn't you?"

"I don't know what you're—"

"Motherfucker." Macbeth twisted the man's arm again, rotated him once more and slammed his face into the wall. He wanted nothing more than to break the man's arm off, to dislocate his shoulder. To inflict pain. "You motherfucker. You told them. You gave her up to that pack of dogs."

"Ow! Oww!" The man tried in vain to pull away. "Help me. Someone call the police!"

"I *am* the police, asshole." Macbeth ground his teeth and bent close to whisper. "They were going to dump her dead body at my front door. When I can prove you were involved, you're as good as dead."

"You're nuts!"

Macbeth felt hands on his shoulders.

"Relax, man." Zito leaned close and murmured, "Witnesses, dude."

"I'm going to find out." Macbeth let the man go. The man turned. Macbeth poked his chest with an index finger. "And when I do, you're not going to be able to hide." Macbeth drove his finger into the man's sternum. "Remember that."

The man clutched at his chest. His red-rimmed eyes locked on Macbeth. "You can't do that to me."

Macbeth spun the man back around and planted his face against the wall for a third time. "The fuck I can't." He dug into the man's back pocket and extracted his wallet. With one hand holding the man in place, Macbeth fingered the wallet open. The man's driver's license was displayed in a plastic window. "Jay Konrad. Now I got a name to go with your face." Macbeth dropped the wallet and let go.

Konrad left the waiting area, cradling his arm. Macbeth let Zito steer him away. Zito shook his head.

"Dude, what the fuck are you thinking?"

Macbeth couldn't meet his partner's stare. He felt so dirty. He figured that's what being stripped did to you, even when you knew you did nothing wrong. It felt like he was guilty of something. Well, now maybe he was, but it felt so right while he was doing it, delicious even.

"You know this had to be related to Cabrini." Macbeth pointed down the hall. "Those rats were Huggins's people. Don't tell me they weren't. And if they were, where'd they get her address? Huh? You think *she* told them?"

"You want to get fired? Manhandling that puke in front of witnesses, that's not too smart."

"Yeah, well, I'm not feeling particularly smart at the moment."

"Get out of here. Go home or something."

"Fuck that. I'm staying."

They went into the waiting room. Zito got himself a cup of coffee and a diet pop for Macbeth. They settled in to wait, with the clock seeming to stand still. After an hour or so, Ryan arrived and pulled Macbeth into the ambulance bay.

It was empty except for the faint smell of gasoline drifting over from across the street where several news trucks, their aerial towers extended high, idled. Ryan wanted a ride back to his car at the Thai restaurant. Macbeth recognized the request for what it was, a thinly disguised effort on the part of his sergeant to get him the hell out of the hospital and keep him out of trouble.

Ryan said, "By the time we go get my car, maybe have a bite to eat, you can come back and that asshole and any bullshit he tries to stir up should be long gone. Okay?"

Macbeth shook his head. "I can't leave, Ronnie. She's here because of me and I have to see this thing through."

Ryan stared at him, then nodded. "Yeah, I suppose you do, but is being here going to make it better, or worse?"

Macbeth consider this, then shook his head. "I'm staying until I know something."

Chapter 48

Out For A Drive

MONDAY 1745 Hours

Jermaine hated the neighborhood around Midway airport, and they'd been driving around it for a long time already. They were waiting for the sun to go down and had a long time to go.

Tea Bag was driving now and had found the Ford City shopping mall not that far away. They argued about seeing a movie. But Lonnie didn't want to hear anything about it. So, they kept driving, passing the cop's apartment building every half hour or forty-five minutes. No place to hide and not that many carloads of niggers cruising in this neighborhood. They stood out.

Lauren's parents surprised Macbeth. He'd not paid them much attention when they walked in, because they were much older than he would've guessed. He overheard a nurse come out and tell them, Mr. and Mrs. Cahill, a doctor would be out to see them shortly. The father was stoic, while the mother was quietly crying.

Her dad had white hair, wore rimless reading glasses, and seemed quite fit. He wore a lavender Ralph Lauren polo shirt over khaki shorts and well-worn deck shoes that apparently had actually seen the deck of a boat. As her mom cried, he sat there and stared off in a faraway manner. He didn't offer his wife any comfort, but seemed to be wrestling with his own demons.

The woman's hair, colored brown with lighter highlights, was piled haphazardly on top of her head. She had on a summer-weight shift that looked to be covering something, maybe a bathing suit.

A man, dressed from head to toe in blue surgical scrubs, emerged from the ER's inner sanctum. His mask, still fastened behind his neck, dangled over his chest. He had a clipboard clutched under an arm and was holding a steaming Styrofoam cup. He eased the clipboard out and eyed it, then looked around. "Mr. and Mrs. Cahill?"

The couple stood. The husband's hand slid around his wife's back as they approached the doctor. Macbeth rose and stepped over to hear what was about to be reported. The second he took that one step too many, he knew he'd crossed some kind of invisible threshold. The physician looked at him.

"Is he with you?" the doctor asked. Mr. and Mrs. Cahill turned to look at him, too.

Macbeth felt all their eyes on him as if they were a weight on his shoulders. He tried to assess the physician's mood, but the man's face was blank, whether from ambivalence, or years of delivering bad news, or maybe he was just exhausted. Whatever the reason, Macbeth drew a blank on Lauren's condition.

"I'm sorry." Macbeth made eye contact with Mr. and Mrs. Cahill. In the past, he could have just popped his button and had an official reason for being privy to the private information about to be shared. But he didn't currently have his star and couldn't prove he was a member of the department. They continued to stare at him.

"I don't know that Lauren had a chance to mention me to you, but we'd just started dating. I'm—"

"Son," Mr. Cahill said. "I don't think this is the time." He was stopped by his wife's hand on his arm. She looked deep into Macbeth's eyes.

"Are you the cop?"

"Yes, ma'am."

She turned to her husband. "I spoke to her just this morning about this young man. Lauren seems to be quite taken by him. Let him listen, he's a policeman for God's sake." She turned to the surgeon. "How is she?"

The doctor's brow furrowed, but after a moment, he said, "You have one tough daughter." The surgeon looked at the chart. "She's resting comfortably right now but is heavily medicated. She's going to be okay."

He tucked the clipboard back under his arm. "We had to get her right into surgery, she had some swelling on the brain and we had to go in to alleviate the pressure. After we did that, we set some fractures."

Mrs. Cahill brought her hand to her mouth and started to sink. Macbeth helped Mr. Cahill guide her to a chair.

Macbeth's pager vibrated against his thigh. He saw it was almost seven o'clock. The number was Zito's. He and Rachel had gone to get something to eat after dropping Ryan off at his car. Macbeth found a phone.

"Hey, Mike."

"Listen up, I just talked to a buddy of mine who said IAD is headed there to lock you up. Told you about fucking with that guy."

"Damn," Macbeth said.

"We're on the way back, but you need to split," Zito said. "I'll be there in ten, but you gotta go. Like now."

MACBETH FIGURED HE MIGHT AS WELL GET SOME STUFF FROM his locker in the Eighteenth District. He avoided anyone who might question him. He figured he'd have time to thoroughly clean his vest and its cover, so he put them in the Jeep along with his gun belt. He stopped for a beer somewhere no one would know who he was. He ended up having three, but it didn't help.

He wasn't even sure how late it was when he rounded the corner by his apartment, but it was dark. He was surprised to find the parking lot empty but for Camp's rusted Olds Ninety-Eight. He cranked his wheel and rolled to a stop. He shut off the ignition and relaxed, exhaling before he heaved himself out. He reached into the back seat and hefted his vest and gun belt, throwing them awkwardly over his shoulder.

Chapter 49

Out For A Walk

MONDAY 2150 Hours

Jermaine's ass hurt from sitting in the Lincoln. They'd been parked along a tree-lined street near the airport for a couple of hours. He decided it was the most despised place on earth, though he couldn't say why. The trees cast long shadows from the moon and made it look as if the streetlights were out.

They were so close to the airport that planes kept flying low over his head like they were going to fucking crash. Their engines' roar was deafening. Every time one came by, he was startled and wanted to duck. The houses, almost all brick, looked alike. He couldn't tell one from another.

He needed for this shit to be over and done with. He couldn't even think of eating, his stomach burned so bad.

"There he is." Tea Bag pointed through the windshield at a Jeep that rolled past. Jermaine's hand froze on the door handle as Tea Bag sat up.

He couldn't pull it open. Was this what he really wanted to do? Part of him said yes, but there was something holding him back, something gnawing at him, saying he might need to think about it some more.

A hand swatted the back of his head. Huggins spoke, in a coarse whisper. "What you waiting for? Go do that motherfucker."

Jermaine hopped out of the Navigator, more from fear of Huggins than anything else, and jogged across the street. Tea Bag pulled away from the curb, leaving him no recourse. Jermaine slowed as soon as he hit the sidewalk. He wondered again if any black people lived around here. Would he stand out? Would they see him right away? There was a big fat bush of some kind, over six feet tall, at the start of the cement walkway leading between the buildings. Jermaine heard a voice and stopped behind the bush.

THE INSTANT HE ROUNDED THE CORNER, MACBETH KNEW HE should've gone in the back way. There was Camp on his porch smoking a cigarette. *Of all the nights*, he thought. Macbeth felt himself slow as if he carried a thousand pounds. He kept walking, hoping to make it past the old man.

"Little early tonight, ain't it?" Camp blew smoke out of his nose.

"Yeah." Macbeth uncrossed his fingers. "Bad day."

"Had a few of those myself," Camp said. The old cop reached out and tapped the cigarette on the edge of the porch railing. A drink sat on the table next to him. Macbeth figured it for Irish whiskey. "Some days just leave a worse taste in your mouth than others. That's why you gotta wash it out with a little of this." Camp nodded at his drink as he took a drag on the cigarette. "How's your ma doing?" Smoke escaped his nostrils slowly.

"Same, no improvement." Macbeth stopped and looked at the ground. He didn't like talking about his mom or dad. It always brought a lump to his throat.

Camp took another deep drag and shook his head. "That's a goddamned shame. You need to go up there and see them."

Macbeth nodded. He did, but he had to find a way out of this shitstorm first.

"Well," Camp said. "Cheer up. You're off, right? And you got yourself a new pretty little girlfriend, don't you?"

Macbeth said nothing.

Camp blew out a cloud of smoke. "Well, take it from an old pro like me, things could always be worse."

Chapter 50

Final Act

MONDAY 2210 Hours

Jermaine stood behind the bush and listened. He was close enough that he could practically touch them. His feet wouldn't budge, though, like they were stuck in concrete. The pistol hung by his leg. His hand quaked, the bullets rattled in their cylinders. It was so loud. *Move*, he told himself.

The first step was unsure and small. Jermaine tried to take a deep breath, but his breathing was rapid and shallow. Sweat trickled down his spine. Another step forward brought him from behind the bush and onto the walkway. He still couldn't see anyone, but they were so close. He smelled cigarette smoke. The gun was heavy, pulling toward the sidewalk.

In his mind, he saw the boy in the lobby of 500 West Oak, red blotches spreading across his shirt, his brains blown out and oozing down the concrete into a bloody pool on the floor. White Boy's eyes saucer big.

All Jermaine had to do was point and shoot, nothing he hadn't done already. Just point and shoot. This was what he'd been dreaming of for months, ever since Antwan got killed. Why was it suddenly so hard? Shit, what if he missed? What if he couldn't do it?

Then Jermaine thought of his momma, how she looked after sucking Tea Bag's dick. He could hear her saying that she'd done it for him, to get him away from the gang. She'd say that Huggins had been behind Antwan's killing too, that the cop just happened to be there. She hated the gang. Was she all that wrong? She might've been with Tea Bag, but Huggins made her do it.

And Huggins was out there, waiting for him, too. Time was short and got shorter by the second. There'd be no second chance. He saw the grin on Huggins's face as his momma came out of the bathroom. It wasn't much different from the one Huggins had worn that night in the lobby of 500 West Oak. The growing pool of brains, skull, and frothy blood was replaced in his mind by Huggins's leer when he pulled the trigger. That final pull in that dark lobby where the bright flash was swallowed by that boy's ruined mouth, his cheek flapping like an empty balloon.

The gun felt even heavier, but what choice did he have? If he didn't do this, it'd be him with a pistol jammed into his mouth. The memories of Antwan alone weren't enough to make Jermaine's feet move. It was the fear of Huggins and knowing the price of failure. He stepped past the bush. The cop was there, on the sidewalk, looking down. Jermaine couldn't see nobody else, but he didn't care.

He raised the pistol.

The gun shook. The shaking worsened. His eyes teared. His teeth clamped and ground together. He squeezed his eyes shut, trying to force the salty, hot liquid from his vision.

BLAM!

The gun bucked violently. He fought the pistol back down and pointed it at the cop again as he backed away from the black, stinking cloud.

BLAM!

The revolver jerked again, scorching hot fire lit up the night.

From the left, in the shadows, a red spike of searing heat reached out. A sharp punch to his gut forced him to step sideways or fall. Pain exploded in his belly.

Jermaine shifted his aim and fired quickly. The flare of the muzzle blast showed an old guy on the porch. Jermaine fired again as the old man crashed backward, taking down a table and a chair.

Jermaine clutched his side. It burned unlike anything he'd ever felt. His shirt was wet with something thick that could only be his blood. He turned back for the cop. But the cop was gone.

*

Macbeth found himself on the ground looking up at the balconies. He pushed his vest aside. Two hard lumps extended out from the back. His vest had taken the rounds! He'd been holding his gun belt and now it was underneath him. He took a ragged breath. It burned like flames consumed his chest.

He didn't feel any blood when he patted his chest, but pain spiked down hard into his lung. It worsened when he twisted around to get at the holster on his gun belt, only then realizing his weapon was still on his hip. The ringing in his ears battled his reason. The night lit up in one blast after another, colors clotted his vision, and yet the bells rang and roared.

Macbeth's hand closed on his Smith and Wesson's grip and he pulled it free. Agony tore at his shoulder as he sat up. Bile rose and he swallowed against it as he pushed backward until he smacked against the wall of the building. The edge of the balcony provided temporary concealment.

A black kid stepped toward him, pointing a gun. Both their guns discharged. Macbeth was ready for the recoil. Brick splinters raked the side of his face. Searing powder residue blistered down on him. One of his eyes momentarily lost its vision as he fired again.

*

Jermaine staggered backward, his thigh quivering, pumping out blood. *Momma*, he thought. *Momma, you were right.* It all was so suddenly clear. Sure, the cop killed Antwan, but it was Huggins who made it happen. Huggins. Jermaine turned from the cop and stumbled toward the parking lot where he was going to get picked up. He saw the Navigator at the curb and lurched toward it, almost falling.

§

HUGGINS HAD SEEN MACBETH FALL. HE SLID FROM THE FRONT seat of the Lincoln and dashed toward the buildings with the first shot. He heard more shots as he ran and slowed. Then Maine wobbled into view, clutching his belly, stumbling. Blood bubbled through a gaping hole in his pants. Twisted muscle and white bone were exposed to the night. That fucking Macbeth shot him. How'd he done that?

Huggins hollered. The cop's five-shot was in his hand. Maine was done, all but dead on his feet. Huggins ran up and grabbed the younger Cobra, shaking him.

"Did you get him?" he yelled. "You get Macbeth?"

The kid looked at him, his eyes vacant and unfocused. Huggins didn't think Maine even knew who he was. Blood leaked from around Maine's fingers. He'd still serve a purpose, though, just like them motherfucking Arab martyrs did. Huggins smiled at his own cleverness as he brought Macbeth's five-shot up and popped Maine in the back of the head. The kid crumpled to the ground like he'd been pole-axed. Huggins pumped another one into his face, then another.

Huggins looked at the Jeep and raised the gun, aiming carefully. He fired once, twice. The closest rear tire popped and hissed. He quickly wiped the grip and dropped the revolver on the ground, then picked up the gun Maine had been clutching.

Let them motherfuckers figure that shit out, he thought, trotting back to the Lincoln. He could see the headlines now: *Rogue cop kills unarmed black teen—the brother of the boy he killed earlier this year*. This would work. As he climbed into the SUV, he saw White Boy's eyes in the window. They were big as a sack of sliders.

§

MACBETH COULDN'T BELIEVE THE BLACK KID HAD JUST WALKED off. He winced as he rolled to his knees, fumbling with his gun belt. He yanked two magazines from his pouch and stood, shoving the mags into his jeans' back pocket. His weapon was out in low-ready as he crouch-ran to the front of his Jeep. He wiped at his blinded eye the best he could and took a quick peek. The kid, the shooter, lay on the ground. A big black guy was getting into the front seat of a dark colored SUV. Then he saw the man's face. Huggins.

Macbeth lay across the hood of the Jeep and steadied his .45, aiming with just his good eye. He slowed his breathing and squeezed the trigger. The weapon bucked. Glass shattered from the Lincoln's windows.

The scream of tires and an engine roar stole his attention away from Huggins. A silver box Chevy unmarked police car spun around the corner and stopped behind the Navigator. Two white guys were inside, in shirts and ties. They looked too officious to be detectives. Macbeth recognized Agent Kaczynski from IAD.

HUGGINS JUMPED IN THE NAVIGATOR. FROM THE CORNER OF HIS eye, he saw an unmarked police car careen into view. Its brakes locked and its back end spun across the center of the street, exposing the driver, a fat white guy in a shirt and tie. His eyes were nearly as big as White Boy's.

The window on the Lincoln shattered, showering Huggins with glass. He reached into the back seat. "Gimme the gauge."

Munchie's baby dreads stood on end as he handed up the cut-down shotgun. Huggins hopped back out and stepped away from the Lincoln. He held the gun low on his hip, pinned hard against his body, and pulled the trigger. The shotgun jerked hard and roared, belching a cloud of black smoke. The side window on the Impala exploded and holes appeared in the door. The cop disappeared under the dashboard.

The other cop bailed out the passenger side of the car as Huggins jacked another round into the chamber. He stepped further from the safety of the Navigator. The second cop hunched over and tried to run for the trunk as Huggins fired. The side of the windshield flashed as bits of glass peppered off. Pellets ricocheted skyward. The cop went down. Huggins racked the slide again, stepping closer to the car.

The cop on the front seat wasn't moving and was bleeding from several holes in his shirt. The other cop had half dragged himself behind the car. Satisfied that no one was going to shoot at him, Huggins ran back to the truck. Everyone in the SUV was crouched down. Tea Bag pointed behind Huggins as he opened the door and half turned toward the parking lot.

"By that Jeep!" Tea Bag ducked down. "Somebody's shooting!"

A sharp bark and tongue of flame erupted across the Jeep's hood. Huggins thought something flashed by. He lowered the shotgun and fired at the figure. Sparks lit the hood and fender as the shot punched through. It sounded like someone was dropping light bulbs and it took a second for Huggins to realize the back window of the Lincoln was springing holes. The cop behind the police car was shooting too.

Huggins backed into the SUV, wanting to take one more shot at those motherfuckers. "Get the fuck outta here!"

MACBETH TOOK A LAST SHOT AT THE NAVIGATOR AS IT SPED OFF down the street. He stripped his nearly empty magazine from the .45 and stuffed it in his front pocket, then ripped a fresh one from his rear pocket and slammed it home, fully loaded again. He ran to the unmarked squad car, holstering his pistol.

"Police!" Macbeth held his empty hands up so they could be seen. "I'm the police!"

Kaczynski peeked around the trunk. His cheek was streaked with blood. "Where's my partner?"

The cop on the front seat was crawling toward the open passenger door, bleeding in several places. Macbeth shouted. "Here!"

Kaczynski stood; blood trickled from his arm. He ran to the door. "Help me." Macbeth came around and they pulled the wounded cop out onto the street. His breathing was shallow, and his color got paler as Macbeth watched. "I was an EMT on SWAT," Kaczynski said, and started going over the man. Macbeth knelt to lend a hand. Kaczynski stopped, pulled a radio from his belt, and handed it to Macbeth.

"*Ten-one! Officer down! Sixty-Third Place and Austin!*" Macbeth repeated it as radio traffic exploded in response. The dispatcher cleared the air and tried to ask questions, but Macbeth had already tossed the radio on the street.

An explosion of metal made Macbeth duck and Kaczynski cover his partner.

Chapter 51

Running Hot

Huggins watched the street behind them as they roared away from the gunfight. His heart raced. He was sure they were going to get away. Then the Lincoln suddenly swerved and crashed into a parked car. Huggins didn't know if he was thrown to the floor or if the floor came to him. As he pried himself from under the dash, he saw that Tea Bag was slumped over in the driver's seat. He'd been shot.

"Munchie!" Huggins leaned across the wounded gangbanger and opened the driver's-side door. He shoved Tea Bag out. Munchie climbed over the seat and plopped down, his little dreads swinging. He ripped the shifter down and backed up, lurching as they rolled over Tea Bag.

A glance at the back showed Keloid clutching his big nine, watching out what was left of the back window. White Boy whimpered, gripping his hands together tightly across his chest. Huggins looked for blood on the kid, but there wasn't any.

Munchie jammed the SUV into drive and peeled off.

MACBETH SAW THE PLUME OF SMOKE AND DEBRIS RISE FROM THE crash several blocks west. He spun around. "You got this?"

Kaczynski looked up. "Yeah, go."

Macbeth stood, slamming the passenger door closed as he ran to the driver's side of the squad car. He jumped in; the engine was already running. He ripped the column shift down and stomped the pedal to the floor. The Chevy sprang off as he straightened it out, accelerating toward the crash.

The Lincoln's backup lights came on as Macbeth crossed the end of the first block. Two to go. The SUV's tires locked. It stopped, then jerked forward and made the corner fast, leaning heavily away from the turn.

Macbeth was still a full block east when the Navigator went north, so he swung the Chevy in that direction on the next street. He looked through the alley, hoping to catch sight of the Lincoln, but it had already passed the gap. Macbeth stood on the brakes at Sixty-Third Street as the SUV roared by, passing another eastbound car in the oncoming lane.

Macbeth spun the wheel and brought the Impala in behind the SUV, pedal to the floor. That was when he realized he didn't have a radio. A quick peek showed there was none lying around. He reached over to the glove box, but it was empty too. He was on his own.

The Lincoln hooked a wide left onto Central Avenue and raced north alongside the western edge of Midway Airport. The fleeing SUV had a full block on him by the time he was on Central, and it was pulling steadily away. The engine in the Lincoln was out-stripping the older Chevy, particularly in the straightaway. The Lincoln blew through several lights before it screamed through a bold red at Fifty-Fifth Street. It bounced over the tracks, sparks screeching off the chassis frame as it bottomed out but continued northward. They had to be going a hundred or better. Macbeth didn't dare a glance at his speedometer.

Huggins gripped the dashboard with both hands as Munchie steered through the intersection. They hit the tracks. Huggins's head slammed against the roof; somehow Munchie hung on. They'd come this way and Huggins knew an expressway ramp lay ahead. But as his eyes tracked towards where it was, he saw red and blue flashing lights approaching. It had to be a sheriff or suburban cop. "Shit!"

He pointed right as they neared the next signal. "Turn! Turn!" It was an angle street, and wide. Munchie braked and spun the wheel. Huggins leaned against the turn to keep from falling over. Munchie was back on the gas and they accelerated east on Archer Avenue, buildings zipping past. Little traffic and no cops.

"That cop turn?" Huggins looked over his shoulder.

"No," Keloid said. "He kept straight."

"How about that other one?"

"He back there."

Huggins saw a Chevy pull into the oncoming lane several blocks behind them. That had to be one of the cops who'd pulled up. His confidence was building. His breathing loosened. In the back seat, White Boy was curled up, his dirty-milk colored face hidden. Keloid sat next to him. The big Cobra's back was as wide as two men.

Huggins turned to the front and slapped Munchie's shoulder. "Next light, go left!" Munchie nodded, but Huggins noticed his teeth set hard in his face. Munchie was bleeding down the front of his shirt.

"Lonnie," Munchie said. "You think they know we're running for the Greens?"

Huggins pushed Munchie's injury out of mind and looked back. Two people had been shooting at them. Good chance one of them was Macbeth, and he could've recognized Huggins. Where could they go?

"Maybe," he said, more to himself than to Munchie.

The corner of Munchie's mouth rose in what might've been a smile. "I know where to go."

Huggins checked the butt of the nine tucked in his waistband. "Make it happen, captain."

Macbeth leaned into the turn as the unmarked Chevy skidded around the corner behind the Navigator onto Cicero Avenue. The big Lincoln V8 chewed up ground, putting more distance between them. At every light Macbeth hoped they'd eat the back end of a tractor trailer. *Luck isn't with me tonight*, he thought, as the Lincoln continued to pull away. He saw the brake lights flash on the Navigator, but it was far ahead. They had to be running back to Cabrini, not that he had a radio to share that with anyone.

Macbeth kept his foot planted on the gas. He could see the overpass looming above the street a way down. He swung out to allow himself a power turn onto the ramp when a cloud of dust drifted across the street from a stand of trees well before the ramp entrance. He jammed on the brakes and felt the pedal shudder beneath his boot. The brakes spasmed and quaked and the Chevy came to a stop.

Macbeth glanced over his shoulder and saw the Lincoln's brake lights flash for an instant. They were descending to the Sanitary and Ship Canal by the service road. It was just a couple of dirt tracks and as he backed up, he realized this was where they'd been when they'd dumped Lauren. But they'd accessed the road from the other side earlier, the Pulaski side. A grin tightened his face as he extinguished the Chevy's headlights. If they didn't know he was behind them, maybe they'd slow down.

From where he was in the SUV, Huggins couldn't see the road's entrance up the hill. He didn't know if the cop car was back there or not. Munchie had switched off the lights to keep them hidden, but the tracks were rough as hell. He told Munchie to keep going. Fast. But they kept hitting the roof when they hit washed-out parts of the road, so they had to slow down. Once they got to the bottom, the service road smoothed and straightened as it ran along the river. Munchie sped up.

Huggins didn't know where they were, but Munchie did. He said they'd driven out this way after they'd gotten rid of the girl. It was black dark. The moon reflected on the water as they drove along the rough dirt road. There were lights off in the distance, but they appeared and disappeared behind trees and abandoned buildings. Munchie said the lights were to the parking lot and warehouse where they'd hijacked the truck. Huggins didn't like the inky blackness and liked the water even less. He was torn between telling Munchie to hurry up or to slow down. What good was it if they got away but drowned in the process?

Munchie turned away from the river. "Man, I can't see shit. Let me turn these lights on."

Huggins turned to the rear. "He back there?"

"Ain't see 'im," Keloid said.

Huggins patted the dashboard. "Use your parking lights."

"A'ight." Munchie hit the switch, and a faint yellow glow lit the ground in front of them.

"Better," Huggins said.

Munchie's foot dropped, and the SUV took off. The bumps and ruts were worse with the speed. Soon Huggins had a hand on the roof to keep from breaking his neck as the Lincoln shook and vibrated.

"Slow—" The Lincoln's right front tire dropped horribly low. The front end plunged and slammed into the ground. Munchie fought the wheel and yelled. He overcorrected and the Navigator lurched left, bottoming out. The rear tires spun and grabbed. The truck reared up and dove hard. Huggins was thrown into Munchie. Glass broke some-where close by as the SUV flipped onto its side and rolled over.

The tires raced, but since they were suspended in the air they just whistled and rushed nowhere. Huggins tried to sit up and banged his head into the dash. He lay on the roof in the dark. The SUV's engine sounded like it was building to take-off speed. It took him a moment to orient himself inside the Lincoln. He reached up and switched off the ignition. The whining slowed and finally stopped. He heard foot-steps crunch in the dark.

Huggins rolled onto his belly and saw his driver. Munchie had been smashed up against the side window and was out cold, maybe dead.

Huggins crawled along the roof toward the back and bumped into Keloid. The big man was making funny wet noises in the back of his throat. Huggins scooted closer. Keloid was cradling his left arm, his shoulder angled wrong.

There was no sign of White Boy, but Huggins couldn't see the tail end too good. There were cushions and shit spread around, maybe he was under them or maybe he'd pitched all the way out.

"You a'ight?" Huggins felt around in the blackness for his pistol. It had come out of his waistband during the crash.

"Man, I'm fucked up," Keloid said quietly.

"We got to get outta here," Huggins said.

"Let's go, then." Keloid shifted his bulk, grunting in pain, and scooted toward the SUV's side door.

"Where's my nine?"

"Don't know," Keloid said. "The gauge is up against the door by my feet."

"You still got your piece?"

"No."

Huggins kept rummaging through the stuff in the Lincoln. He found his automatic wedged under the dash. He stuck it in his waistband and crawled behind Keloid. The big man leaned over for Huggins to reach around him. Huggins pulled the lever and pushed the door open. It swung away from the SUV. On his way out, Huggins grabbed the sawed-off.

<h1 style="text-align:center">Chapter 52</h1>

<h2 style="text-align:center">Dead End</h2>

MONDAY 2230 Hours

Macbeth slowed the Chevy and lowered all the windows. He'd heard something that sounded like a crash. The question was what, or maybe where? The noise hadn't come from in front of him, but off to the right somewhere. It had been a big noise and metallic. He stopped the car and turned off the ignition. The hot engine ticked under the hood, but still he didn't hear any out-of-place sounds, just crickets and cicadas. The overpowering smell of scorched metal emanated from the brakes.

He sat looking around alongside the Sanitary and Ship Canal, his arms resting across the top of the steering wheel. His injured eye was working now but was unfocused and bloody. His chest ached, and breathing hurt, but at least he hadn't found any other blood. The moonlight was dim, the stars in the sky lost to the orange glow of the city lights. The water emitted a fetid odor, dead fish and industrial runoff.

Then a ghostly cloud of dust drifted down the slope and wafted into his open window. Behind him, more dust lifted above the bank of the canal, white against the black, fusty water. Macbeth scanned the hillside rising from the ship canal toward the industrial park in the distance. It was dark. The crest of the hill was outlined by the warehouses and factories along the ridgeline, maybe a half mile away.

He started the Chevy and shifted into reverse, cursing the bright backup lights. He'd bounced backward less than a block when he spied tire tracks branching off up the incline. A film of fine powder still hung above the ground like the ghost of a vehicle that had passed not long ago. He'd missed it in the dark. The tire tracks climbed at an angle toward a stand of trees that blotted out the lights from the buildings above. Macbeth shifted into drive and followed the tracks.

❧

HUGGINS LEFT KELOID SITTING ON A STUMP BY THE TREES. THE grass all around them was waist high, taller a bit further off the road. Keloid's face was streaked with sweat. Huggins went ahead to find a car or truck to steal, or maybe someplace they could lay low.

Instead, he found a deserted one-room shack without doors or window glass. It had been abandoned long ago if the damp, moldy smell meant anything. Not unlike vacant apartments in the Greens.

He went back down and was careful to whistle quietly to Keloid. The big man looked worried when he'd left, who knew what kind of crazy the dark and the hurt had done to him. But Keloid was sitting on the stump just like he'd left him.

"Dead end," Huggins said.

Keloid looked at the sky. "I ain't feeling so good."

Huggins wanted to know what else was wrong with him besides his arm but didn't ask. It always seemed when you started talking about it, things got worse. They didn't have time for that.

But they weren't hearing any sirens or seeing any searchlights from helicopters circling overhead. Maybe there weren't any police behind them after all. Then a car engine started and silenced the chirping of the crickets and cicadas. The car wasn't far away, it sounded like it was down by the river.

Reverse lights flared down the road, lighting up the night. Huggins and Keloid both hunched over to avoid being seen, even though they were too far away.

"Cops?" Keloid said, his voice a husky whisper tinged with pain.

"Got to be," Huggins said, "but where's their backup?" What if there wasn't any? What if they only had to beat whoever was down the road? If cops weren't hot on their trail, that meant just one thing. Macbeth. That motherfucker was out there by himself. Had to be him, nobody else would take it this far. And if he was with anyone else, they'd have called for backup. They'd have been hearing reinforcements by now.

Huggins didn't think he could push Keloid too much further. The big man couldn't run and would be lucky to make it to the ridge, the shape he was in. And he was only going to get worse. But he could still be of use.

"Got an idea."

MACBETH WATCHED THE WRECK IN HIS HEADLIGHTS AS HIS CAR inched closer. He couldn't see any movement in the overturned Lincoln. It was nose down in a gully. But someone must've shut the engine off. Macbeth stopped and pulled the Chevy's door latch, pushing the door open with his foot. He drew his Smith and Wesson, kept his eyes on the surrounding area. He got out and knelt behind the Chevy's door, listening.

Staying in a crouch, he moved away from the Impala until he was behind the Navigator. He squatted to peer into the upside-down SUV and couldn't see any movement, though he thought he could make out a tennis shoe toward the front. He checked out the far side and couldn't see anyone in the shadow-streaked glow cast by the Chevy's bright lights. How many had there been to begin with?

Macbeth crept to the rear of the SUV and stooped lower. A quick peek revealed nothing. He worked his way to the far side of the truck and knelt at each door to look in, trying not to stare into his own headlights. It wasn't until he reached the front window of the driver's side that he found someone. The door was crumpled, and he couldn't open it. He went around to the passenger side and was bathed in the glaring light.

Macbeth ran back to the Chevy and saw footprints leading further upslope along the ruts. He extinguished the headlights and went back to the Lincoln, holstering his weapon. He opened the passenger door wide before stooping down, then crawled into the SUV and reached out to grab the man's ankles. He pulled. The man was still alive, but pinched tight in the crunched metal of the window. He wasn't going anywhere. Macbeth recognized him from the Sedgwick building because of his baby dreads, but didn't know his name.

Macbeth backed out of the SUV and stood, then turned to follow the footprints.

❧

Huggins pointed at the bend in the rutted dirt. "I'm going to draw him past here to the shack. When you see him right there," Huggins shook his finger for emphasis, "you blast him."

He knew there was at least one more shell in the shotgun, maybe two. He rested the weapon in the crook between the trunk and a branch of the tree Keloid stood behind. He shifted the stock to Keloid. The big Cobra's good hand felt clammy and cold. "You got the gauge, dig. You don't have to hit him square, just close. Let all them pellets do the rest."

Keloid nodded and made a bubbly sound in his throat that Huggins figured was a yes.

"I think you got another shot if you can rack it. But it ain't gonna matter. If you miss, I'm going to be right there. One of us'll cap his dumb ass for sure. Then we got his car and we clean." Huggins was glad Keloid didn't ask what the plan was if this didn't work. If it turned into a gunfight, Huggins's plan was to circle around behind the trees and make for the car by himself. In that case, Keloid was a distraction, and armed with a sawed-off, he made a pretty damned dangerous one.

❧

Macbeth crept down the rutted path as quietly as he could. His night vision had been ruined by the headlights, but he couldn't wait. He had no idea how many assholes there were, or if they were injured. What was certain was that they were armed. And Huggins was one of them. Macbeth was damned if he would let the motherfucker escape tonight.

He contemplated making for the tree line looming up ahead on the left. But he was sure he'd make noise in the grass. So far, on the road, he was practically silent. He just wished he could see more than dark shapes and darker shadows. The trees were easy to figure. The tire tracks were lighter, and the grasses moved and swayed with a breeze that had kicked up. What there was of a draft was hot and stank of sewage and decayed fish. Macbeth stopped and tried to breathe silently. He strained his ears for the slightest noise. All he could think of was getting Huggins. This was it. This had to be it. This was going to end tonight.

He held his .45 in front of him at low-ready. Sweat streamed down his back, neck, chest and across his face. His chest ached but he was getting used to it. His eye hurt, but he could see well enough.

He was rounding the bend when he saw a dark structure looming ahead. It was still a long way off but was pitch black against the sky and hillside. He stopped and sank to one knee. If someone was inside, could they see him? Did they even know he was on their tail? Should he try and go around to the back? He couldn't afford to wait. Every second he did, they got further away.

As he stood to push forward, a voice called out to him.

"Is that you, Macbeth?" He recognized Huggins instantly. "Think I can't see you? I know you're out there, squattin' like a bitch taking a piss."

Macbeth stepped into the grass and crouched. He didn't care about noise, just wanted to find something to hide behind. Grass wouldn't stop a bullet. He aimed his Smith and Wesson, putting his night sights on the middle of the structure. He'd seen two sets of footprints, so someone else was up here, too.

"You won this round," Huggins said. "My leg's broke. I can't go no further."

Never taking his weapon off the structure, Macbeth looked left and right. Huggins couldn't be the only one. They'd never leave him behind.

"C'mon, bitch, come get me. Take my ass to a hospital," Huggins said.

POW! POW! POW! The trees to Macbeth's left erupted with explosions and light. BOOM! POW! A big figure staggered from the shadows of the trees, took a step, then another. Halfway through his third step he crumpled across the rutted tracks and lay still. It had to be Huggins's sidekick, the big asshole. Macbeth couldn't remember his name, but there weren't any other Cobras that large. But who'd shot him?

A roar and a flash emitted from the darkness of the structure. Macbeth snapped off two quick shots in return. He could taste the bitter metallic sting from the gun's discharge. He heard running footsteps, someone crashed through the grass behind the trees.

The car. Huggins was going for the car.

Macbeth spun around and ran back down the tracks, his .45 up and ready. He tried to figure who the third person was, up on the slope. Security? He doubted that. Another Cobra? Could be, but why would he take out the big guy? A mistake?

Macbeth crouched good and low and worked his way toward the car, trying to be as wary as he could. He wasn't too worried about Huggins taking the car, though. Macbeth had the keys. And Huggins would be hard pressed to peel the column with Macbeth shooting at him.

❧

HUGGINS RAN BLINDLY AROUND THE STAND OF TREES, MAKING for where he believed the cop car was. Had Macbeth capped Keloid? No way! Huggins had been looking at the cop when someone lit up Keloid. It hadn't been Macbeth. That was the only thing he knew for sure. Someone else, but who? A security guard? Fuck it. Time to cut and run.

The grass ripped his jeans as he ran downhill. An occasional tall blade snapped at his face like a knife. It felt like he'd been cut. The footing was treacherous, and he fell several times, but he didn't hurt himself or lose his nine.

Huggins ran across the slope, looking for the car. It took a minute, then he saw the washout. The Navigator lay at the top of the gully. The cop car had to be on the other side. He clawed his way up the loose dirt and ran around the SUV. The cop car was there. The driver's door yawned open like an invitation from a whore. He dove inside and slapped the ignition. No keys. He felt the floor, above the visor. Nothing.

BLAM!

The windshield splintered. Glass slivers peppered Huggins's face. He threw himself on the seat and scooted out backwards.

POW!

The glass in front of the steering wheel skittered and spit shards at him. The dashboard blew apart and plastic shrapnel knifed at his face. He covered his head with his arms. He couldn't see where the cop was, so he pointed his nine into the dark and pulled the trigger. POW! POW! POW! Maybe that would slow him down.

BLAM!

The windshield popped again. This time Huggins saw the muzzle flash. Macbeth was down the trail in the grass.

Huggins backed down the ravine and shifted left. He scrambled back up and slowly peeked over the top. He calculated Macbeth's location, then raised his nine and fired. It rose, and he fired again as fast as he could bring the gun back down on target. Huggins scrambled backward down the loose dirt and turned and ran. He had to put distance between himself and Macbeth.

❧

MACBETH JUMPED LEFT AND WAITED FOR ANOTHER SHOT. IT didn't come. He crouched and moved around the washout. He saw someone race downhill through the grass, closer to the canal. It had to be Huggins. The running figure fell.

Macbeth started down after him and fell too. Grass cut his face and deep into his lip. He got up and kept going, trying to be careful and watching the way he'd seen Huggins go down. The footing was horrible, little runoff trenches made the terrain treacherous. It was impossible to see through the grasses and weeds. He dropped to his knees more than once. He was halfway down the incline when Huggins popped up out of the grass and fired.

Macbeth double-tapped two quick rounds at Huggins as the gang-banger fled further downhill. Huggins finally staggered onto the dirt track and turned from Macbeth, running hard. Macbeth took aim at Huggins's back and fired. He brought his pistol back down and aimed carefully at the shimmering silhouette still running along the canal. He squeezed the trigger and shot again. The slide locked back. Macbeth released the magazine and grabbed the remaining mag from his back pocket. He rammed it home and released the slide. He was ready to rock and roll. He tapped the partial magazine in his front pocket just to be sure he still had it, though it couldn't have more than a couple rounds left.

As he scrambled down the slope, Macbeth turned so he could return fire if Huggins appeared. He knew he was horribly exposed, and it seemed to take forever to make it to the track at the bottom of the slope. This road was a hundred times better than the one leading up the ridge. Macbeth brought his Smith and Wesson up to low-ready and started forward. A large pile of rock lay ahead, between the road and the canal. It was the only place offering any cover that Macbeth could see in the waning moonlight.

Chapter 53

Sink Or Swim

MONDAY 2300 Hours

Huggins lay in the grass behind a pile of broken concrete slabs, some half the size of his Lincoln. Many of the pieces bristled with rebar jutting from the jagged ends. He gulped air and willed his heart to slow, with little success. The nine rested on the ground under his chin. He didn't know how many shots he had left, but knew he had to make them count.

Who the fuck shot Keloid? It wasn't Macbeth. Another cop? He didn't think so. It had to be another cop or a security guard. If that was the case, though, Huggins better move before they surrounded him.

He picked up the nine and crawled to the edge of the concrete pile. He lay down and stretched out behind the debris. He didn't see anything. He inched forward on his elbows. Nothing. He crept forward more. Someone was on the road, crouching. Huggins wanted to smile but worried what little moonlight there was might glint off his gold front tooth. He pointed the gun at the figure and pulled the trigger.

MACBETH SPUN AND FELL FORWARD, ROLLING WITH THE FALL. His left arm stung. The pain was jagged hot, like a white-hot poker had been rammed through his forearm. He pulled the arm against his chest and extended his right, still holding the .45. He fired toward the rocks. Once, twice, three times. Gritting his teeth, Macbeth stood and moved farther to the right, away from where the shooter had been.

He heard rocks slide on the far side of the debris pile. What was Huggins doing, climbing? Macbeth stared at one side, then the other, then the top. Nothing. He saw a shadow alongside the pile and fired at it.

HUGGINS JUMPED BACK AND WIPED AT HIS FACE, TRYING TO GET the bits of concrete out of his eyes. That last one had been close. The ricochet next to his face ground slivers of concrete into his flesh. He was sure he'd hit Macbeth, but the fucker was still shooting. Huggins turned and went the other way around the debris pile. Tired of this cat and mouse shit, his new plan was direct. He paused and took a deep breath.

MACBETH WENT TO ONE KNEE TO STEADY HIS AIM. HE DIDN'T dare move one way or the other. He stared at the center of the slab pile, letting his peripheral vision adjust. Any movement on either side would draw his attention.

A shadow broke on the right. Macbeth shifted to fire, but the figure fired at him first. He shot back as Huggins charged. Huggins bowled him over. Both men crashed to the ground, rolling. Huggins clawed at Macbeth's face, his fingernails gouging skin. Macbeth's .45 was somewhere on the ground. He pushed off and staggered to his feet, forcing the pain out of mind.

Huggins rolled up on his knees and stood. His pistol was in his hand, but the slide was locked to the rear. He looked down at the gun and tossed it away.

Macbeth yanked his knife from his pocket and thumbed the blade out. Huggins circled, looking for an opening. Macbeth shifted to keep the gangbanger in front of him. Huggins didn't move like he'd been shot, or even hurt. In the faint moonlight, Macbeth could see the glint off the Cobra's front tooth.

HUGGINS CIRCLED AND WAITED. THIS WAS GOING TO BE SWEET, he thought. After all the shit that had happened tonight, finally something was going his way. All he had to do was break this cop's neck. Then he was free.

The cop's gun was gone, and Huggins didn't have time to look around. Since it wasn't in Macbeth's reach it didn't really matter. Huggins grinned as he squatted into a fighter's crouch. He felt around with his feet for a stone or something to use against the knife. Keeping his eyes locked on the cop's, he grabbed a handful of dirt. You couldn't stab what you couldn't see.

MACBETH KNEW WHAT WAS COMING WHEN HE SAW HUGGINS PAW the earth. He shifted his feet and tried to flex his left hand with some small success, though it came at a cost of radiating pain. Huggins sprang, flinging dirt in his face.

Macbeth covered his eyes with his left forearm and ripped the knife in a wide arc. He felt the steel bite into something. He hacked downward, shifting away from Huggins, not letting the gangbanger get a grip. The men staggered away from each other, Macbeth blinked dirt from his eyes. Huggins brought his hand to his mouth and licked blood from a gash on the heel of his palm. He took a step back, then another. He bent and pulled a piece of rebar from the grass. It was mottled with chunks of concrete still clinging to the metal. Huggins swung it in front of him, a grin spread across his face.

Macbeth faked a charge to draw Huggins into a wild swing. But the gangbanger didn't bite. Huggins backed closer to the slabs, holding the rebar in front of him like a sword. Macbeth stepped forward, pressing the other man further back. He needed Huggins to swing wide enough to let him get through his guard. Anything short of that would get his skull crushed.

℞

HUGGINS GRIPPED THE REBAR. IT FELT GOOD IN HIS HAND. Heavy. Deadly. And as good as any baseball bat.

Even in the dim light from the moon, Huggins could tell Macbeth was bleeding from his arm and had blood smeared across his chest and streaked across his face. Huggins took a deep breath. Time was on his side. He couldn't afford to get too winded. If his reaction slowed, it would give the cop an opening.

Time to take this bitch out. Huggins smiled and readied himself to launch.

℞

MACBETH RECOGNIZED THE FERAL LOOK IN HUGGINS'S EYES. THE gangbanger smelled the blood. Macbeth glanced around for the Smith and Wesson without luck and gripped the knife. He figured Huggins would feint either high or low. Macbeth breathed deeply, taking oxygen into his blood for the burst of energy he was going to need. His plan was simple. Go for the point of attack then lunge for the eyes. But with each passing second, each pump of his heart, he was getting weaker.

Huggins stepped toward Macbeth. His face twisted into a mask of hate as he brought the rebar up over his shoulder. He swung down as Macbeth arched his knife hand up only to have the gangbanger swivel his shoulder and drop the rebar toward his knees quicker than Macbeth could adjust. He swept into Huggins and slashed at his face, ramming Huggins with his shoulder as the makeshift club smashed his knee. Pain exploded up and down his leg.

The steel blade sliced through flesh and sank until it hit bone. Macbeth twisted, yanking the knife clear as he fell to the ground.

Huggins pressed his free hand to his cheek and staggered backward. Macbeth managed to stand up on his good leg. Without the strength to pull Huggins closer, he hopped forward and clawed at Huggins with his bloodied hand.

Huggins swept the rebar around, into Macbeth's shoulder. Macbeth slashed down with the knife, sinking it into the soft tissue of Huggins's hand. Macbeth gritted his teeth against the pain and dug his feet into the ground, carrying Huggins and himself toward the canal.

❧

HUGGINS FELT THE GROUND GIVE WAY. HE GLANCED BEHIND HIM and saw the inky black of the canal shimmer below. Macbeth kept shoving. Huggins dropped the rebar and grabbed the cop's shoulders, trying desperately to twist away. But he was off balance. He felt himself teeter.

Not the water!

"NO!"

❧

MACBETH FELT THE WEIGHTLESSNESS FOR ONLY A SPLIT SECOND as both men plunged down the embankment. He hit the surface. The liquid parted reluctantly and enveloped him in oily blackness. His face stung; his eyes seemed to be melting in their sockets. Macbeth pushed up and broke the surface. Chemical vapors burned his lungs and set his wounds afire. He spat sewage from his mouth and tried to breathe something fresh, but there was only tainted, fetid air. He coughed and retched.

He could feel Huggins nearby, splashing like a man who couldn't swim. Macbeth's knife was gone but he didn't care. He clawed at the embankment and found a vertical mud wall, the top higher than he could reach. A vice gripped his shoulder, an arm wrapped around his neck. Huggins's weight descended on him like a pile driver. Macbeth went under again.

Underwater, he twisted and freed himself from the Cobra's death grip. Huggins struggled like a drowning man. His movements were erratic, but lunatic strong. Macbeth pushed off the mud wall with his good leg and put distance between them.

He broke the surface away from Huggins, who was flailing vainly at the wall. Macbeth swam backward until the back of his head whacked something hard. He looked and found a slab half submerged in the water. The debris pile had spilled into the canal, and the concrete boulders were his ticket back to shore. He twisted around and despite the pain in his limbs began to climb out, using the slabs and rebar for footholds and handholds.

He was clear of the water when Huggins grabbed his pant leg and yanked. Macbeth kicked free with his good leg and kept climbing. He made it to the top and found a chunk of concrete the size of a basket-ball. He saw Huggins below, pulling himself up on the debris pile, and aimed it at him. The chunk missed but splintered and broke, forcing Huggins to stop climbing and crouch. Macbeth cast about and found another hunk of rock, smaller and bristling with rebar. He raised it overhead and flung it down viciously. It hit Huggins with a thunk, and he fell back into the water.

Macbeth launched two more pieces but had no idea if they hit their mark. He stood on the embankment and looked down into the blackness. He couldn't see Huggins. Then he heard a footstep on the gravel behind him.

"Don't move," a quiet voice said. Macbeth didn't have the energy to raise his hands as he stood with lungs burning from whatever compound he'd ingested.

Someone stepped up beside him. The albino teenager from Cabrini. He held a revolver down by his side. He didn't acknowledge Macbeth beyond the order not to move. He peered over the edge.

"Lonnie, you down there?" The kid cocked his head to the side and listened. "It's White Boy."

"That you?" Splashing sounds rose from the canal. A black hand appeared on the lowest slab. Huggins's head came out of the water, his face wet and disfigured. "Shoot that motherfucker."

White Boy glanced at Macbeth before looking back down into the canal. He twirled his gun's barrel in a tight circle. "Come up here and do it yourself. I don't kill cops."

As Huggins struggled onto the lowest slab, he seemed as spent as Macbeth felt, except one shoulder was quite a bit lower than the other. The Cobra enforcer started climbing the slabs one-handed. Very carefully. When he was about halfway, White Boy spoke. "Why you kill Jermaine?"

"Huh?" Huggins paused to look up at the teenager. "Why'd I what?"

"Why you shoot Jermaine? You shot him in the head?"

"Had to," Huggins said. "He was gonna die anyway. That cop killed him. He just didn't know it yet."

"So you put one in his brain to help him along?"

"Something like that." Huggins took another step up. "Only the strong get to survive, little brother. Now gimme that motherfucking gun."

White Boy raised his revolver. "He was my friend. You shouldn'ta done that."

Huggins stopped and stood to his full height. White Boy's arm shook until the revolver's bullets rattled. The gun stayed up for what seemed like a minute. Then it wavered and dropped.

Huggins grinned. "That's right, boy. You can't shoot me." He started up again, reaching for a handhold. "You a Cobra now. Like you always wanted to be." Huggins climbed up another slab. "Maybe you can't shoot that bitch, but I sure the fuck can."

White Boy looked up, tears in his eyes. He held the gun out to Macbeth.

Macbeth took the revolver from him. He aimed it at Huggins and fired.

Huggins's chest absorbed the bullet and most of the muzzle blast. He wobbled. Macbeth pulled the trigger again but heard a click as the hammer struck a spent cartridge. He pulled again. Another click. Huggins staggered forward, grabbing for him, a demonic grin chiseled on his face.

Macbeth backhanded Huggins with the revolver. Huggins reared back. Macbeth shoved him hard. Huggins fell down the concrete slabs and splashed into the canal.

Macbeth grunted in pain and then went quiet, except for the breath easing out of him. For a time, there was silence. Then sirens slowly wailed in the distance, growing louder. White Boy watched Macbeth. "I thought that was Huggins by that tree, Mister. The one time I finally shoot someone, and I get the wrong motherfucker. What you think I'm going to get charged with for shootin' Keloid?"

Macbeth took a deep breath. "Nothing, if you haul ass that way." He pointed up the ridge toward the factories.

The teenager's head cocked. "What you mean?"

"I mean, get the fuck out of here." He threw the revolver into the canal. It hit with a plop.

White Boy turned and faced in the direction Macbeth had pointed, and then he looked back at the cop. "You for real?"

"Yeah, but you'd better get moving. It's a long way back to the Greens."

The teenager took a step.

Macbeth laid a hand on his arm. "You got any money?"

White Boy patted his pants pocket. "Yeah."

"Take a cab, then." Macbeth smiled. "And, thanks, White Boy." Macbeth held his hand out. "You saved my ass."

White Boy took the outstretched hand and looked into Macbeth's eyes. "My name's Ronnell."

The kid left then, vanishing into the darkness. The chemical stench drifting off the canal was overpowering. Macbeth slipped to his knees, dizzy and nauseous, knowing he was going to puke. Huggins's body drifted out away from the embankment, the sewage leeching onto his form. He didn't twitch, just floated, then slowly the body sank beneath the black water.

THE END

Afterword

I began writing CHICAGO JUSTICE shortly after OUT OF CABRINI was finished, but it took a long time to finish—much too long, and even longer to get a publisher. Such as it is, and the fault lies with me.

I have always been blessed by a supportive family; my mom and dad and sister have always been encouraging. I can't begin to express how badly I miss my mom and dad. Luckily, I still have Juli, a fact I will never take for granted. And I can't ever overlook my wonderful kids, Tom, Joe and Emma. And Michael A. Black. And Cathy Siciliano. And Marshae Harvey. Thank you all for your help and inspiration.

It is always such a delight as well to work with my fictional friends, Stacey Macbeth, Mike Zito, Timmy Hagen, Ronnie Ryan, Henry Barnhill, and Amanda Petty. I have so many stories to tell, characters to introduce, cities to visit, locations great and small to describe. I've got a lot planned for these guys.

My career as a cop has been a blessing. I've always liked helping others and locking up bad guys. Being a supervisor and then a commander has been infinitely rewarding in that I've been able to see those for whom I am responsible grow into better police officers and supervisors. While my life as a cop has been rewarding, I also credit my continued passion for painting and writing for enriching my life beyond measure, allowing me the avenues for creative expression. Writing is good for my soul. To me, it is a need as fundamental to my existence as breathing.

Thank you for reading my book. I look forward to sharing more stories about these characters and others with you.

Please visit my website, www.davecasebooks.com. Thank you to Russell A. Schultz (Chicago Police Det. Ret.) and the Police Officers Network (www.PONetwork.com) – powered by RAS Communications (www.rascommunications.com) for their work to promote OUT OF CABRINI and design the website.

Acknowledgments

I'm excited for *Chicago Justice* to see the light of day. It's been a long time coming. I want to thank those who have been there for me and supported my passion, my village, to borrow a phrase, Julianne, Tom, Joe and Emma Case, all deserve a special thank you. Another nod must go out to Cathy Siciliano, thanks for believing. And a very special thank you to Michael A. Black and Marshae Harvey.

I've been blessed.

I would be remiss if I didn't thank John Camp (Sandford) for taking the time to help a beginning writer. Thanks for believing in me early on.

If you're interested in reading more about those Chicago Police Officers who have made the ultimate sacrifice, as Ronnie Ryan did for the St. Paul Police Department in 1994, go to www.CPDmemorial.org.

Take a moment and peruse www.davecasebooks.com, or my Facebook, Instagram and YouTube pages of the same name. Thanks to Russ Schultz and his very talented team at rascommunications.com and the ponetwork.com.

About the Author

Dave served thirty-one years with the Chicago Police Department and is now a commander with the Bridgeview Police Department. He graduated from Northwestern University's graduate program for Creative Writing. He lives on Chicago's southside.